Ghost
Horse

Carol Gimbel

Prepared for publication by www.KrystineKercher.com

Cover design by www.ArtandDesign.KrystineKercher.com

Cover art: DepositPhotos.com

Printed in the United States of America

EPIGRAPH

"And who knows but that you have come to a royal position for such a time as this?"

Book of Esther 4:14 NIV

"Just living is not enough," said the butterfly.
"One must have sunshine, freedom, and a little flower."

Hans Christian Anderson

DEDICATION

Ghost Horse is dedicated to the memory of Steven Hays Holderby who was there when *Ghost Horse* was born in my heart and listened as I wrote and rewrote it. Steve brought me a typewriter and told me to "write or shut up". I wrote.

And to Woody Gimbel. Thanks for the ride, Honey.

And to the memory of my dear friend, Linda Kodad, who loved *Ghost Horse*.

Chapter One

The gunshot terrified my horse. Mariah leaped into the air and executed an airs-above-the-ground maneuver like a Lipizzaner stallion. She took off down the trail as though the devil himself chased her. She neglected to see if I would be coming along.

While she zipped around boulders the size of a Mack truck and flew up canyon trails that would challenge a mountain goat, I struggled to maintain equilibrium. I visualized a broken leg—hers not mine—and my flying over her head and off a cliff. While I fought to slow her down, I tried to convince myself the noise had been fireworks.

The second bullet struck a boulder somewhere near my right ear dislodging a piece of rock which grazed my cheek and removed all doubt. Definitely not fireworks.

Someone wanted me dead. Why? Although I seem to have a talent for irritating people, I arrived only two days ago. Nobody here knows me well enough to have anything against me. Yet.

Mariah repeated her reaction to the first shot. But this time the performance threw me. I landed on my assets with a teeth-jarring jolt, while Mariah, bucking and snorting like she'd been released from Chute Number 3, disappeared into a grove of trees.

I scrambled to my feet. Okay, maybe scramble isn't the best choice of words. I sort of rolled over on one hip and hobbled into the woods. Once inside the cover of trees I felt a bit safer. I turned and peered through the branches. No glint of sunlight on a gun barrel up on the ridge. No sound of someone dislodging rocks. My heart rate didn't slow, but I resumed breathing. I checked for broken bones. Everything seemed to be intact.

Where was the shooter? I had to think. If I thought the shot came from these trees, I wouldn't be sitting here now. It hadn't. The angle was wrong. My figuring angles is a hoot. I learned nothing in geometry class way back then. No, the shooter had been on that ridge. Nothing moved up there. Above me a robin chastised her young. There was no other sound.

I sat on a tree stump feeling like I had wandered into a spaghetti western gone bad. I ran exploratory fingers across my cheek. Salt stung the cut. Hopefully I won't need stitches. Call me crazy but looking as though a centipede ran across my face has never been a dream of mine. I looked around for Mariah who was nowhere in sight and fought terror.

She isn't my horse, by the way. She belongs to Jackson, who I discovered last night was my uncle. To his credit, he warned she could be 'a mite flighty'.

I was in deep kimchee. I couldn't get back to the barn on foot even if my ankle wasn't beginning to resemble an eggplant. Mariah knows the way, but I have no earthly idea where the barn is, where I am, or where she is. Uncle Jackson hadn't lied about the way these canyons twist and turn. I visualized headlines of the next issue of the Cheyenne Falls Times and Free Press. Not that it's free. 'HEIRESS ALEXANDRA FORREST FOUND AFTER 28 YEARS, MISSING AGAIN.' That's a bit wordy. It also sounds like I'm in the habit of losing myself, which I'm not. What would the locals think? Several blond jokes come to mind.

There's one more thing I'm sure of. I do not want to be in this canyon alone after dark. Jackson said mountain lion screams echo down here. Also, a madman, armed with a hunting rifle and scope, may still be lurking. Which brings me back to who shot at me. Jackson knows I went for a ride. Nobody else even knows me.

Because of reasons mentioned I need to find that horse. I stood up and eased some weight onto my injured ankle. Pain shot through it, but I don't think it's broken.

A sort of trail meandered through the trees. Not really a path, but the grass was worn in enough places for an occasional hoof print to show in the dirt. A horse would eventually stop to graze. I figured I'd follow the tracks until they ended where a calmer Mariah nibbled clover somewhere. See how that plan came together? I'm good like that.

I had no trouble following the tracks—at first. But then the ground sloped downward and became dry and rocky. Clues came farther between. The trail stopped directly in front of a sandstone wall which rose a good 40 feet. There's no way out of this canyon, also no horse. Like a ghost, she'd simply vanished. I looked back through my life trying to recall other instances when a situation seemed impossible at first but became hysterically funny when the simple solution presented itself. I came up short. I'm trapped in a remote box canyon, possibly with a crazed killer. I am not having a good time.

A hawk's shriek broke the silence. I looked up. A hawk watched me from the top of a giant cottonwood. I knew from a college horticulture class that cottonwoods grow near water. Maybe this tree had at one time. In this rocky canyon water would be a distant memory. I'm no expert but from its size I'm guessing the cottonwood had been there well over a hundred years—maybe several hundred. The trunk was enormous. Scrub oaks and anemic cedars grew around it like sentinels guarding their monarch.

The hawk shrieked again. It seemed to want something from me. That not-knowing-what's-wanted-of-me thing happens a lot, but not usually from a hawk. I limped closer to get a better look. It cocked its head and looked back.

Ahead, silvery strands of Mariah's mane tangled in a cedar. Hoofprints circled the tree. I ducked in a vain attempt to avoid branch attacks and followed. I shimmied between the cottonwood and a cedar. I wondered what would possess a horse to go through there. Behind the cottonwood's massive trunk gaped an opening in the stone wall.

I peered in. No hibernating bears. A bear wouldn't hibernate in August. I also didn't see any sign of the afore-mentioned mountain lion. The cave appeared to be a short tunnel. Sunlight slanted through a waterfall which cascaded over a rear exit. Hoofprints in the damp sandy floor led through the cave and into the falls. I followed them.

The cave temperature dropped 20 degrees. The air felt not only cool, but alive with intense energy. It crackled around me. I stared at my arms in fascination. The hair on them stood straight up. In a blinding flash, light illuminated the entire cavern. Thunder rumbled from all directions at once, echoing off rock walls. Shock waves knocked me to my knees. I staggered to my feet, lurched to the exit, and fell through the waterfall landing in a shallow rock-lined pool. Too dazed to be frightened, I shook my head. What happened?

Chapter Two

Rocks were still damp where Mariah had left the pool. I followed her lead. Still baffled, I looked around. I found myself in another canyon, narrower than the one at the entrance of the tunnel. A path, essentially a rock ledge, hugged the wall along the pool. If finding a hoofprint hadn't become a challenge, I might've missed the copper coin on the path blinking in the sunlight. I bent to pick it up. It lay, bright and shiny, in my palm. I flipped it over. 'One Cent' was stamped on one side, an Indian head with the date 1889 on the other.

"No way," I whispered. "This must be worth some money." I pocketed it. I'd celebrate when I'm not desperate to find a horse.

Farther down the path I discovered an arrowhead in perfect condition. While I examined its chiseled edges, the certainty of being watched shivered down my spine. I peeked behind me. Nothing. I looked around. Nothing. Shading my eyes with one hand I looked up and swallowed my tonsils.

Twenty or thirty pairs of eyes stared down at me in somber silence from the rim of the canyon. Beneath garish war paint the warrior's expressions were grimly stoic. Pictures of Indian war parties I'd seen in movies and history books weren't nearly as terrifying as these dudes. The horses stood like statues. Only feathers hanging from bows and spears floated on the breeze. My heart began a drum beat against my rib cage. I forgot to breathe. I stepped back. I imagined a wagon train rounding a corner and coming face to face with this crew—death staring from the back of a paint pony.

I froze, too scared to move. Time stood still. They stared at me. I stared back. I had an idea. Maybe in all my twists and turns I wasn't far from the backside of Tribes, the Indian tourist attraction my uncle owns. In that case, a war party might very well be part of an act. The thought brought a rush of relief.

I plastered a campaign grin on my face. "Hey, guys." I yelled. "Have you seen a gray Arabian mare? I seem to have lost my horse." I should have been an actress. I'm wasting all this talent.

The pool of water hadn't been as chilling as the silence of their intense stare. I felt like a beetle on a pin in some biology class—running in circles under the impassive gazes of its tormentors.

They began talking loudly in a language I couldn't understand with adamant grunts and broad gestures, mostly in my direction. Their argument concerned me. Hope, like the dance of a flame, flared, flickered, and died. Panic slammed into me again.

Swallowing it, I yelled, "Hey. I'm Jackson Dale's niece."

Less than impressed, they continued to argue.

"Jackson Dale. Your boss," I yelled. Although I'm quickly becoming aware they don't speak English, I'm too stubborn to give it up. "Hello, I'm his niece." I planted my hands on my hips for emphasis.

Their voices grew louder.

"Have you seen my horse?" I stomped my foot, the one without the swollen ankle.

Totally ignoring me, in one accord, they reined their ponies around and rode away.

"Hey." I yelled.

They kept going.

I continued walking. Actually, I limped and shuffled. Hot, exhausted, thirsty, scared, and hurting in places I didn't know I had, I couldn't hold back tears.

A hawk shrieked. Could it be the same one? I supposed so, but why would it have followed me? As I turned around to look for it, I glimpsed Mariah through a break in the trees. If the hawk hadn't stopped me, I would have missed her.

"Well, thanks," I said. I'm pretty sure the hawk winked.

Weak-kneed with relief, I made my way to a clearing beside a small lake. Mariah cantered in large lazy circles. Her tail, held high, waved like a banner behind her. A young woman wearing a rapturous expression along with a faded yellow dress was on her back. Totally oblivious to anything except the joy of the moment, the girl raised her face and arms to the sun, laughing with delight. Horse and rider moved as one through an explosion of wildflowers sending up clouds of butterflies. They circled the clearing then made their way toward the edge of the trees where I stood. The girl slid to the ground and threw her arms around the mare's neck. Mariah rested her head on the girl's shoulder, saw me approaching and nickered a greeting.

The girl turned; her face beamed a surprised welcome. She looked as though she'd found a long-lost friend.

She wasn't the only one surprised. I blinked and shook my head. She was still there. Everything about her looked exactly like me. Okay, maybe not the pantaloons. Good grief. Could this day be more bizarre?

Chapter Three

Well, lawsy me," the girl exclaimed. "Where did you come from?"

She scampered toward me. Like a puppy. Seriously. It was like hop, skip, and run, hop, skip and run. She pulled me into a bear hug. I'm not used to being hugged. She released me and I stepped back. Her eyes devoured me. I've been looked at like that before, but it scared me. I took another step back.

"Well, I..." Actually, I didn't know. To cover that gap in my knowledge I thought about reminding her not to end a sentence with a preposition but decided that might not be the best way to begin a relationship.

"If you aren't a sight for sore eyes." Excitement blazed in her eyes.

She thinks I'm someone else, probably a relative because of our resemblance. She hugged me again. "I haven't seen the likes of you since…" She eyed me speculatively from top to bottom. "…ever," she finished.

"Well. Thank you." I backed away. I considered asking what she thought the 'likes of me' were, but do I really want to know?

"Where'd you say you're from? There are no women my age around here for miles. I get lonesome for a friend." Her whole face smiled. "I am so glad to see you."

That was apparent. I backed up in case she tried to hug me again. That thing she said about 'no women her age around for miles' sounded like heaven to me. It's not that I have a debilitating aversion to other humans. It's just that having to relate to them is exhausting. Which is why I have so few friends. Well, that and other reasons. "I came from Cheyenne Falls," I said. "Although, I arrived yesterday. I can't say I live there yet."

"I don't know where that is," she said.

"That's a problem. Neither do I." We chatted for a while. The conversation had been normal. But then I showed her the penny.

She flipped it over. "Where did you find it?"

"By the waterfall."

"Peculiar. Why would a shiny new penny be by the waterfall?" Her brow wrinkled.

"You said it's 'new'," I said.

She lifted her eyes to meet mine. "It's two years old. Did you not see the date?"

"Yeah. 1889," I said. "Wait, what? If it's two years old this year would have to be 1891. This is not 1891."

"Yes," she said slowly, as if speaking to an unbalanced child, "it is." This demented woman thought I'm the crazy one. I wanted to slap some sense into her. I just wanted to slap her. I'm not normally violent but I've never been this scared.

At some point in the conversation, the rapturous expression she'd worn earlier had been replaced. Worry puckered her brows. I recognized the look. My face wears it a lot. Looking at her was like looking into a mirror. We had the same oval face. Only my face looked better on her. Her eyes were bluer, but similar to mine in size and shape. Our noses and mouths were similar. She even had the chin that makes me look like Jessica Simpson—not the body—only the chin. Really. People tell me that. I don't have the girl's smattering of freckles or sun-kissed cheeks which glowed with good health. Makeup would have only diminished her natural beauty.

Her hair frantically tried to escape from the rag thing tying it back. And after being shot at twice, chasing a run-away horse, nearly struck by lightning in a tunnel, running through a waterfall, slogging through steam-bath humidity on an ankle which should be packed in ice right now, and staring down a war party, I'm sure my hair looks worse, only in better condition. Her highlights are a gift from the sun. I paid a small fortune for mine.

Okay. If I'm really in 1891—boy did I make a wrong turn somewhere—this would explain the Indian-head penny and arrowhead in my pocket. And the Indians. Yikes. They were real? Come to think of it, I haven't seen utility poles for miles.

"What year did you think it was? She asked.

"When I left the barn this morning it was significantly later."

"How much later?"

"Over a hundred years."

"That's quite a walk. No wonder you're so tired."

"I rode a horse part of the way," I said, as though that made perfect sense. I watched dubious expressions flit across her face. She should never play poker.

"How old are you," she asked.

"I'll be thirty in three weeks," I said. "How old are you?"

"Thirty," she said.

"Nice. Someday we'll get group rates at the home."

"Home?" Her brows knitted in confusion.

"Never mind," I snapped.

"If you are from the next century, prove it," she said, finally. She seemed ready to believe me but needed something to nail her trust to.

"Of course," I said, wondering how. "My ID has dates, but I left it in the car back at the barn. Didn't think I'd need a driver's license for a horseback ride in a canyon. Silly me."

She gave me a blank stare. I thought fast. My cell phone. I pulled it from my pocket and snapped a picture of her and the small boy I finally noticed, playing in the shade of a tree. I also took a picture of Mariah and handed her the phone.

"What is this?" she asked. She turned it over several times and tried to open it to look inside. The screen went blank. She shrugged and handed it back. I retrieved the pictures and showed her.

Her eyes widened. "How did you do that?"

"This is my phone, but I haven't had service since I left the barn this morning so I can't call anyone..." My voice trailed off as I realized she didn't know what I was talking about.

"What's a phone?" she asked. Her head tilted.

Oh. She wouldn't have a phone of any kind. Not even one of those wall-crank things that I'd seen in Green Acres reruns. She'd stopped looking at me as though I'm some crazy wild woman who

10

wandered out of the woods. Although that's pretty much what happened.

"Telephone," I explained. "It takes pictures, but I can also talk to people on it."

"You can? Show me."

"There's no service," I said again. "But look, you can see how much we look alike."

"We do?"

"Well, of course we do. Good grief." I pointed to the picture of her. "This is you."

I didn't mean to snap at her, but I get grumpy when fighting panic. I have no idea how I got here. I could be trapped. Forever. Where would I sleep? What would I eat? Who would do my nails?

"I don't know how I look," she said as though not knowing was perfectly normal.

"You—what? You don't have a mirror?"

"We used to. It got broke on the way out here."

"How did you get here? Covered wagon?" Oh, wait. She probably did.

"Yes. Before my little brother Johnny was born." She jutted her chin in the direction of the little boy building an elaborate dirt something under a tree. Hearing his name, he looked up.

"Ma'am says ladies don't wear men's trousers," he informed me. He eyed the tatters in my expensive jeans. "Ma'am can mend them."

"Good to know." I turned to his sister. "You haven't replaced your mirror?"

"Ma'am says mirrors are tools of the devil. Looking into a mirror is a prideful thing. Pride goeth before a fall," she said rather smugly.

"I think it's 'pride goes before destruction.'" I made a mental note to look it up in the Gideon Bible back at the motel. If I get back. I fail to see how checking to see if I have spinach in my teeth before going out the door is a 'prideful' thing. But I'm not here to judge. "Who is this Ma'am person?"

"My mother." She rolled her eyes.

"Bless your heart." I've been trying to remember to say that instead of 'your life is really screwed up.'

"You have no idea," she said.

"Come here." I snapped a selfie of us and showed it to her.

She studied the picture, looked at me and handed it back.

"Well, you can see we look alike."

"We do. What's your name?"

"Ali," I said. "I used to think my name was Alison Taft. Now I know Ali is short for Alexandra." I don't know why I added that. I chatter when I'm nervous. I didn't throw in the thing about my kidnapper not knowing my real name.

"My name is Lexy," she said. "It's short for Alexandra."

I stared at her. We have the same name which isn't something simple like Anne or Cindy. I needed to sit down. "What's your whole name?"

"Alexandra Jeanette Dale. What's yours?"

"Alexandra Dale Forrest. Dale is a family name. My mother's name was Dale before she married my father. Now it's Forrest. We have to be related…" I realized I was rambling and shut up.

"Yes. There's a strong probability you're related to your mother."

I wanted to slap her again.

She grinned.

"You and me," I grumbled, too frustrated to acknowledge her joke.

She chewed her bottom lip. I do that too when I'm thinking. "You're right. Maybe I'm your grandmother and you were named after me."

I did a quick calculation. I'm not great at math, but I can see she would be more like a great-grandmother or great-great grandmother.

"Look," I said, "I don't want to be rude, but I'm on the verge of hysteria here. I'm not in the habit of dropping into the wrong century. I can't hold it together much longer." My voice shook. Tears of frustration blurred my vision. "I think I'm doing quite well under the circumstances. But I don't have anything to compare this to. I want to go home."

It occurred to me I don't know where home is. I've lived in the same shabby neighborhood of Dallas most of my life. Two days ago, I arrived in Cheyenne Falls. I can't really call it home. Yet. If I never see Dallas again it would be too soon. She doesn't need to know all that.

"There has to be an explanation for how you got here," Lexy said. "We can figure this out."

I was impressed by her calm-let's-get-this-done attitude. But she isn't the one trapped in the wrong century. She pulled her bloomers above her knees, sat down cross legged, and smiled.

I sat down facing her. Her confidence stalled my rising panic.

"Now," she said, "start from when you got up this morning. Tell me everything."

I quickly ran through it.

She leaned in, intent on my every word. I liked that. People who listen are rare.

"Wait." Lexy raised a hand. "You heard thunder in what tunnel?"

"The cave behind the waterfall."

"There's a cave behind the waterfall?" She looked at me like my nose just fell off.

"Yes. It's completely hidden."

"Your horse is always wet when she comes. I wondered why." She frowned. "You heard thunder?"

I nodded. "In the cave. It vibrated all around me. No rain, only a loud boom."

"It happened then. You broke through something. A wall you couldn't see."

"You're right. Like a sound barrier." I didn't try to explain. "A time barrier."

"If you go back exactly the way you came you can get home."

"I don't know the way back."

"Your horse does. She comes," Lexy waved a hand, "She goes. Our friends the Kiowas call her the Ghost Horse because she appears and disappears often."

Back at the barn before I left, Jackson had also said 'she comes and goes' but without Lexy's hand waving thing.

Well, okay. Feeling better.

Mariah lifted her head and munched on the buffalo grass hanging from her mouth as she watched us approach. She nickered a soft greeting so sweet I almost forgave her for throwing me and running away. But not quite.

"Wonder why she comes here?" I asked, thinking out loud.

"To see me. And she loves this grass. It's lush and green because of the lake. And we've had a lot of rain. For which we are thankful," she added quickly in case God was listening and displeased by a lack of gratitude. "Your horse and I have become good friends. What is her name?"

"Mariah," I said.

Lexy nodded. "Like the wind."

I gathered the reins, swung into the saddle, and groaned as I settled onto my left hip.

"Promise to return," Lexy pleaded. Her eyes did me in. "You are the only female near my age I've seen in years. Please come back in three days. I'll wait by the lake."

"I'll try," I said. I'm sure Ma'am would say I'm going straight to hell for lying, but if I get back to Cheyenne Falls, I'm never leaving.

"Wait." Lexy lifted a hand like a traffic cop. I stopped.

She ran into the trees and came back with a basket of droopy flowers. "Hollyhocks. Take them with you," she said shoving them into my hand. "Plant them. I'm planting some today. If yours grow, we'll have the same flowers growing in different centuries. Wouldn't that be exciting?"

After the day I've had, puny posies in any century are not exciting.

"Astonishing," I said, as though planting her flowers had elbowed getting home from the top of my priority list.

Waving what I hoped looked like a cheery goodbye, Mariah and I jogged off. Not exactly into the sunset, thank goodness. We had a chance of getting back to the barn before dark. If we hurried.

There should've been the kind of background music which swells at the end of westerns when our hero rides away. The sun sinks low, and a kid goes running after him yelling for him to come back as the credits roll across the screen. The kind of music that needs a good harmonica. Or two.

Chapter Four

I flattened myself on Mariah's back. She wasted no time in the cave and didn't slow down after we exited. We were beyond the cottonwood before the thunder ceased rumbling. That mare can run.

The trip back was uneventful. Nobody shot at me with guns, arrows or otherwise. Which is always a plus. The three-hour ride to the barn might have become boring except for being on high alert for the shooter. And the pain in my left hip. I landed on it with my foot under me when Mariah threw me. The experience wasn't good for my foot or my hip.

But thank goodness I didn't have to hobble back to town. Not that I would have known where town was without Mariah.

My surroundings looked like a picture postcard. Sienna cliffs rose to meet an azure sky. Cedars grew out of solid rock. And there was the hawk. Always the hawk.

At first, I thought the area had a hawk problem. But this hawk flew ahead of me and waited until I caught up before flying ahead of me again. Weird as it sounds, I enjoyed its company. It seemed to be guiding me, which gave me a sense of peace. I began to relax and think about the events which changed my life and brought me here.

***

Here's where my crazy story began, in Dallas. After the death of Margaret Taft, the woman believed to be my mother, I had gone to clean her apartment. I removed her things and took them to the Salvation Army. I would rather pass a kidney stone. But as 'the next of kin' the responsibility dropped in my lap.

I'd worked at the corner diner after school and weekends through my high school years. By my senior year I'd hoarded enough money to get an apartment as far away from Margaret as I could afford. A fact which probably made her as happy as it made me. She didn't attend my graduation. Because I had no life and spent my spare time in the library, I got a full ride to UT. A professor there steered me toward law and got me a job in an attorney's office after graduation. I can count on one hand the times I've used the key to this apartment since I moved out. I hadn't heard Margaret's voice on the phone in over five years. I'd almost convinced myself she didn't exist.

She'd been cremated before the doctor notified me of her death. Her wishes. No funeral. No memorial service. She'd been hit by a bus crossing the street in front of her building. That information is too new to sort through.

I climbed three flights of stairs, closed my eyes, leaned against the door, and took a deep breath. She wasn't there. Still, my hands shook as I unlocked the door. I genuflected before stepping across the threshold, which is a little weird. I've never been Catholic.

It wasn't the chamber of horrors I remembered. Sparsely furnished, it looked like the dwelling place of a sad old lady. No pictures or decorations of any kind to indicate the occupant had a personality or family. Like she'd dropped in from another planet.

Going through her meager possessions now felt like committing the unpardonable sin. Not that I know what it is. I reverted back to a five-year-old child terrified I'd be locked in the closet for touching her stuff. Although that particular abuse stopped when I got old enough to outrun her.

What an idiot I've been for ever believing I was this woman's daughter. Margaret had been tall. Large boned but thin. She had dark hair, complexion, and eyes. She also had a large hook nose. Picture the Wicked Witch of the West. Margaret didn't have the green face. But if you put the witch and Popeye's Olive Oyl together you have Margaret. As a child I ended my nighttime prayers with 'Thank you, Lord for not giving me that nose.'

I, on the other hand, am short, blond, and gain five pounds if I look at a bag of chips. Trust me. We looked nothing alike.

While emptying a drawer, I found a newspaper clipping, brittle with age. The clipping was about a wreck in Oklahoma City in which a two-year-old child disappeared. I puzzled over it. Margaret was not sentimental. Unlike most mothers, she had never kept a scrap of my schoolwork or pictures I'd colored. We lived in Dallas. The wreck happened in Oklahoma involving people we didn't know. Why had she kept it?

From the clipping I learned the accident had claimed the life of the child's grandmother and injured her mother. Because of the severity of the injuries of the occupants of the front seat, the occupant of the child seat in the back had been overlooked. In the confusion, she had simply disappeared and wasn't missed for hours. One picture showed a mangled car, another the missing child. She had a halo of blond curls and huge blue eyes. As I scrutinized the picture, I became convinced the round eyes staring back at me were mine. I sat down.

The Dales, a prominent family who lived in a small town in southwest Oklahoma, had offered a substantial reward for the return of the child—very substantial. Margaret could have lived on it for the rest of her life. If I'm the child, why had she not returned me and collected the reward? If I'm that child, I have a family in Oklahoma— possibly a normal family. A wave of hope crashed over me. I jumped up and danced around the room singing and shouting until neighbors pounded on the wall and told me to shut up.

Chapter Five

My fiancé, David Bentley Phipps III, didn't buy it. David is the youngest partner in a prestigious Dallas law firm because of strings pulled and people walked on. He comes from a very powerful family. He didn't do the pulling and walking. He believes he rose to the top with record-breaking speed because he's brilliant. My LSAT scores are higher than his. He doesn't know I know that.

David is movie star handsome. But I sometimes get the feeling he wishes he wasn't. He thinks it gets in the way of his projected image of being a force to be reckoned with. I get that. What I don't get is why it was my finger he chose to slip his engagement ring on. He had his pick of dozens of girls who dreamed of being Mrs. David Bentley Phipps III.

I showed him Margaret's clipping. He played devil's advocate because that's what David does. Along with the fact he believes I'm barely capable of an original thought of my own. He has this supercilious attitude he's honed to perfection. He uses it in court on opposing attorneys with great success. Unfortunately, he can't seem to turn it off. He gave the clipping a dismissive shake and handed it back.

"Cute kid," he said, giving me his 'so what' expression.

"Can't you see this could be my baby picture?" I insisted, looking down at the blond curls. "I have no baby pictures to compare this to. There is not one baby picture of me anywhere. That's weird." I jabbed the clipping for emphasis. "David, this baby is me."

"Come on, Ali, it could be anyone's baby picture. Babies all look alike."

"That's like saying all puppies look alike—Chihuahuas, Great Danes, Shi Tzus...."

"There are no pictures of you after two either. She didn't have a camera."

"That's another thing, David. Mothers take pictures of their kids. It's what they live for. Why did she keep this? She was not a sentimental woman."

"And had no maternal instincts," David said. "Why would she steal a kid?"

"That has me stumped, too. I think she wanted to take me back and collect the reward but was scared. Why?"

"Drop it, Ali." When he used that tone, he expected obedience. I usually complied.

"I can't. What if I have a mother who never stopped looking for me? Who took pictures of me?" I swiped at a tear with the back of my hand. I had so hoped he would understand. "You've been adored since you pushed your way through the birth canal. You can't relate."

David raked his fingers through his hair, a sure sign of growing irritation. "What do you want me to do?"

"Nothing." I lifted my chin. "I'm going to Cheyenne Falls."

He began pacing. Okay, he would've paced if my apartment had been bigger. He banged his knee with every step. My apartment shrinks with David in it.

"Look, Ali," he dropped the attacking attorney pose and adopted his consoling-a-small-child tone, "you could do this online and save a trip." He stopped pacing and rubbed his knee. His face had relaxed.

"I'm going, David. Tomorrow." I held my breath and waited for the tirade that didn't happen.

"You've made arrangements to be away from your job?"

"Yes."

"And law school?"

"Of course. I have this, David." He must think I'm a total ditz.

"You're leaving in the morning?" David sighed. His sighs can mean any number of things. Usually it means, 'your stupidity is killing me.'

"Yes."

"What about Cricket?"

19

"Your mother took her to the farm."

Evidently, he hadn't missed my black cocker spaniel. He looked around. I hate when he does that. He verifies everything I say like I can't possibly know what I'm talking about.

He exhaled an exasperated breath. "Okay. Call me when you get there." He gave me a peck on the cheek as he moved past me to the door. "I love you."

"Love you too," I replied automatically, still staring at the clipping.

Normally I would have followed him to the door and watched until his taillights disappeared. Instead, I went to the bedroom and began tossing things into a suitcase.

Chapter Six

The next morning, long before the sun peeked over Reunion Tower, I crossed the Red River into Oklahoma. I'd left early—really early—to avoid traffic. I hate traffic. To be honest, I hate Dallas. But now Dallas is only a tangle of lines on a map which blew out of the back seat as soon as I put down the top of my Mustang. I felt liberated.

A hawk watched from the billboard which announced my arrival to Cheyenne Falls as I breezed by. I drove through town to the small airport outside the west edge, turned around and backtracked to what seemed to be the only motel. A white sign sporting a black silhouette of a horse-drawn buggy welcomed me to the Buggy Creek Inn. I saw no evidence of a buggy or a creek. I went inside and registered.

The motel might have once been appealing. Exterior room doors opened into the parking lot. My room, 101, was actually just 1. Being the first room past the lobby exit gave me quick access to the restaurant and a feeling of safety. The vending machines right inside that door were a plus. I get hungry at night.

The room wasn't old enough to be quaintly charming, but it looked clean and comfy. If shabby chic is still in, we're good. I unpacked, took a quick shower, and changed into clean shorts and t-shirt.

I headed back to town and drove around until I found the courthouse, a large tan stucco building with Indian designs in turquoise tile around the door. I parked and went inside.

I spend a lot of time in courthouses. The first thing I noticed was the odor. Courthouses all smell the same. Pine Sol and Murphy Oil soap can't wipe away body odors. Sweat smells differently with the stress of lives about to be changed.

The place was eerily quiet. Hallways lined with closed doors led away from the lobby in both directions. Across the lobby ahead of me, glass doors opened to the rear parking lot. A monstrosity of a dog stared at me through the glass. I smiled and his plume tail flopped on the ground raising a small cloud of dust.

"Where is everyone?" I asked him.

He raised a paw and scratched at the glass.

The clock on the stair landing informed me it was 12:20 PM. So, I used my clever deductive skills and concluded everyone had gone to lunch.

The scuff of a boot and a smothered cough coming from down the hall caught my attention. A man leaned against the wall obscured by shadows.

I walked toward him and hesitated.

He lounged with one leg bent at the knee and the sole of a worn boot pressed against the marble wall behind him. His head drooped forward. A straw cowboy hat, once possibly white, hid most of his face. Dark stubble covered the part I could see. Every line of his lean frame sagged. I'd seen men stand like that in old westerns.

I sniffed. There was no sour scent of alcohol. I've seen my share of drunks hanging out in courthouses. Maybe this guy wasn't the town drunk. But, at this point, I wasn't ready to place a bet.

I tapped his arm and stepped back. Beneath the sleeve of his faded chambray work shirt his arm twitched as though shaking off a pesky fly. He made no other movement.

"Excuse me," I said.

"You're 'scused," he growled.

"Look, I'm truly sorry to bother you, but could you tell me where the Department of Public Records is? Sir." I added that last part as a sign of respect; to give him a good reputation to live up to in case he turned out to be a murderer. Dale Carnegie would've been proud I remembered that from his course.

Without looking up, the guy mumbled. At first, I thought he was delirious. Poised to run, I listened and began to understand snatches of his commentary.

"Zat correct English? 'Records is'? Should be records are. No, department is singular. 'Of public records' modifies department. Yeah, that's right. I guess. 'Can you direct me to the Department of Public Records?' might have sounded better."

"What?" I pulled myself up to my full height, not believing this guy had the audacity to question my grammar. "Now, see here …"

"See where?" He thumbed up his hat and gazed at me from beneath the brim. His head was bent so he started at my feet and worked his way up. When his eyes met mine, I gasped. They were so mesmerizing I didn't catch what he'd said. It took a minute to realize he was still speaking.

"Is there no directory around here?" he asked.

"Now, see here …"

"You've already said that. You're starting to repeat yourself and I haven't known you all that long."

"You," I huffed, "don't know me at all. I've only been here five minutes."

"Zat all. Feels like hours."

I gulped. Under the beard was the face I had fantasized about since puberty when I fell in love with the Marlboro Man mustache and all.

I'd been in the seventh grade. The Marlboro Man inhabited the billboard above the bus stop. And my dreams. He sat his big chestnut horse like he was born there, protecting his lit cigarette from the rain that glistened on his yellow slicker and dripped from his Stetson. Over his cupped hands he stared down at me. Nobody had ever looked at me like the Marlboro Man. I could tell he wanted nothing more than to ride down off that billboard, sweep me up, and rescue me from my miserable life. Maybe it was hormones. Maybe it was a lack of friends. Maybe I spent too much time shivering in the cold waiting for an unfailingly late bus, but I never outgrew my Marlboro Man crush.

And now he stood right in front of me *sans* the yellow slicker. And chestnut horse. His expression softened. He didn't smile, exactly. But the dimple in his cheek moved and his mustache twitched which could be a good sign.

On-the-job training taught me not many people have qualms about altering the truth. As I take notes of witness testimonies, I've realized I have a talent for reading people's eyes. I know when they are lying. I can do it with juries, too. I know what verdict they will bring in. I relaxed a bit now that I've seen his face, especially those amazing eyes. Not quite green, not quite blue, they were the color of the shallows of Bocas del Toro. Eyes a girl could drown in. But most importantly, they were honest eyes. This man had a good heart.

I stared.

"Well, it's a pretty sad state of affairs when a man has been up for three days and can't doze for a few minutes."

"Only three days? You look as though it could have been months."

He chuckled. I think. It might have been a cough. "The point is …"

He was interrupted by a crash on the other side of the wall. A woman screamed.

I yelped and jumped like a puppy narrowly missed by a Peterbilt. The scream was followed by a man bellowing obscenities, another crash, and more screams. One of them might have been mine. Don't judge me. I'm not good in critical third-down situations.

Marlboro Man muttered something I couldn't understand as he pushed himself away from the wall. "Maybe it's me, but I'm beginning to think nobody around here cares if I get any sleep." He looked more annoyed than concerned. "I feel like I've been hit by a train."

"I wouldn't rule that out," I said.

His mouth widened into a slow-motion smile that transformed his face. I couldn't have looked away if my life depended on it.

"Hey, Sunflower, run down the hall and get the sheriff, okay?"

I gulped. "Where?"

"In his office," he indicated the direction with a jerk of his head. "I hope." He turned toward the door. "I'll see what's going on in there."

"Wait," I practically yelled. You can't go in there. Are you crazy?"

He stopped and glanced back. "No, but this isn't the first time I've been asked."

Just my luck. I finally find the Marlboro Man and he's suicidal. I mentally ran through ways to stop him. I ruled out tackling him, but it was my first thought.

"What kind of flowers should I send to your funeral?"

"Sunflowers I guess." He winked. "I like sunflowers."

Chapter Seven

I slid to a stop beside a birth-defect poster depicting a baby with what looked like a giant toe growing out of its cheek. It informed pregnant mothers of the dangers of taking drugs. Normally I would have been grossed out. Today I didn't have time. Next to the poster was a closed door with the words *County Sheriff* stenciled on the window in gold leaf. I started to knock but decided this was no time to stand on ceremony. I flung the door open. It banged against the wall with so much force an oil painting of a lone wolf in a massive frame bucked and shimmied on the wall in serious danger of falling. I watched in stunned fascination. The painting hung in there so my attention turned to the two men staring at me.

A rather large man sat at the desk nearest me. I guessed the other one to be the sheriff. The *Sheriff Anthony Checotah* name plate on his desk was a clue.

"There's an emergency down the hall." I shouted.

"What?"

"An emergency." I pointed. "Down the hall."

"Emergency? What kind of emergency?" the deputy asked.

"People are being killed," I yelled. "Good grief, get up." I wanted to say, 'get off your fat ass,' but I'm new in town and didn't want to make a major *faux pas* this early.

The men looked at each other. The sheriff stood. The deputy lumbered to his feet.

They both followed me down the hall. I ran ahead, stopped at the door, and stepped aside so they could go in. I pressed myself against the wall in case of shooting, which I learned from watching *Blue Bloods*.

I heard nothing. The deputy stood in the doorway. Curious, I peeked around his bulk.

The room looked as though a tornado had roared through. Papers, riding drafts of air from the ceiling fan, drifted lazily. I quickly determined the floor was clear of bodies, bloody or otherwise. Three women, apparently the screamers, appeared shaken but seemed okay. In the corner Marlboro Man pulled an even scruffier guy to his feet.

A young woman had another man's arm twisted behind his back. He tried to jerk free, but stopped short, howling in pain. She spoke to him in a conversational tone as though asking if he would like one or two lumps of sugar in his tea. I inched forward.

"Your manners could use some maintenance. You scared these poor ladies. Not nice." She made a tsking sound. "Look at this mess."

"They wouldn't renew my unemployment," the man snarled. "I got kids to feed."

"Poor, lamb," she purred. "I understand how difficult life must be with you having no skill, Mister—uh, you know, I don't think we've been introduced," she glanced at the sheriff.

"Rafferty," he supplied. "Melvin Rafferty."

"Marvin," she finished.

Rafferty tried to pull away again. This time he screamed and fell to his knees.

"Now, Mervyn, may I call you Mervyn?" she asked sweetly.

"Melvin," he growled. He staggered to his feet.

"Sorry, Marvin. You're going to have to be still. I'm supposed to be able to do this hold without breaking bones, silly me." She shrugged. "I've never got the hang of it." She looked over her shoulder at the sheriff. "Hey, Tony, did they find that guy's arm?"

"The one you broke off?" The sheriff chuckled. "Not as far as I know, Stormy. You really need to be more careful about where you leave body parts. Picking up after you is a chore." He leaned against a desk cleaning his nails while observing the situation from under the brim of his hat. He caught me watching him and winked.

Does everyone in this town wear a cowboy hat?

"You want to take over here, Tony?" Stormy asked.

"You seem to have it under control." He tossed her a pair of cuffs which she caught with one hand and deftly clicked onto Rafferty's wrists.

She pushed Rafferty toward the deputy and turned her attention to Marlboro Man. "Hey, Lanigan, are you asleep over there?"

"I wish," he said. He cuffed the other guy and shoved him toward the deputy, who ogled Stormy.

"I need help getting these guys into a cell, boss," the deputy said. "Can I borrow her?" He drooled as he watched Stormy.

The sheriff laughed. "Watch it, Danny. You saw what she did to Rafferty. You're wanting to bite off more than you can chew there, Son."

Ignoring them, Stormy surveyed the damaged room. Her eyes, large and elongated, dominated her face, and gave her an exotic appearance. Auburn hair, cropped short, curled slightly around her ears. She reminded me of Audrey Hepburn in *Love in the Afternoon*. My all-time favorite movie. With that incredible face and height Stormy could've been a model, but the skin-tight black spandex she wore suggested she was most likely a pole dancer who rode in on a Harley. With the grace of a ballerina, she glided across the room and bent to retrieve Lanigan's hat from the floor. As she straightened, her eyes locked on me. Her gaze raked over me assessing, measuring, and dismissing. I'm used to being looked down on by David's snooty friends. But being blown off by someone so sleazily dressed ouched. The class of people who find me lacking lowers all the time.

Stormy plopped the hat on Lanigan's head. "Hey, Lane, what have I told you about leaving your stuff lying around?"

"You okay?" He looked her over to make sure she was. Not the way the deputy had.

"Yeah," she said. "Are you?"

"He looks like death warmed over," The sheriff said. "I thought you left, Renegade."

"Hey, I tried, Chief," Lanigan said. He scooped a pair of sunglasses off the floor and jammed them into his shirt pocket. "Stormy had to pee. Her bladder must be the size…."

"Shut up, Lane." Stormy punched his arm. "Leave my bladder out of this. When a girl has to go, she's gotta go."

"Very profound," Lane said.

"Speaking of going, you two git before you're seen," Sheriff Checotah ordered. He glanced at me as he realized it was too late. "Stormy, find him a bed before he drops in his tracks."

"Gotcha," Stormy said. "This place doesn't need one more thing on the floor and stepping over him would be inconvenient." She looked around. "Although he does match the décor. You could decorate around him. Maybe make him the focal point." As she walked past Lane, she swiped his hat off his head and hit him with it. "Come on Lanigan, let's get you out of here while you can still move."

He snatched his hat back and meticulously replaced it as he moved toward the door. He walked by me and winked. "Thanks for rounding up the troops, Sunflower."

"Uh, you're welcome," I mumbled to his back.

They'd had the situation in hand before the sheriff and deputy arrived. Who were these people? They knew the sheriff. Quite well. There had been an easy camaraderie among the three of them, the kind that takes years to build. The sheriff called him 'Renegade', and he'd called the sheriff 'Chief', probably nicknames that go way back. I liked his name—Lane Lanigan. School girls had probably scribbled 'Mrs. Lanigan' in the margin of their notebooks, surrounded by hearts and flowers. I wouldn't have, of course. Right.

I followed the pair down the hall, trailing well behind. They strolled, in no particular hurry, toward the rear exit. Laughing, Stormy grabbed at his hat.

"Dang it, Stormy," Lane said, "keep your hands off my hat. I've told you about that. Touch the hat again and you have to die."

"Yeah? Then who would save your scrawny posterior?"

"I have to admit you came in handy once and I'm not saying I wouldn't miss you. But you don't mess with a man's hat."

Stormy's undignified snort echoed through the hall. "Yours is such a prize. It looks like it was dropped under a combine."

"Not the point."

"Yeah, yeah, I know. You were wearing that hat when you snorkeled into Guadalajara with the terms for the peace treaty."

I stopped well behind them and watched Lane open the door. As Stormy walked out, he looked back at me. Dang it. He knew I'd be there. He grinned, gave me a small salute, and followed Stormy though the rear exit.

Mortified, I felt my face flush and prayed for the floor to swallow me. How stupid could I be? That's a rhetorical question. As it turns out, my stupidity has no bounds.

The dog I'd noticed earlier stood and stretched, his tail waving a greeting. Stormy bent and placed her hands on each side of his face.

"Hey, Austin, did you think we weren't coming?" I heard her ask before the door closed. She straightened and hurried after Lane, the dog running in circles around them.

Then they were gone, leaving me feeling empty.

Chapter Eight

The clerk at the Department of Records had a face that looked as if it might shatter if forced to smile. Evidently, she wasn't one to take chances. Since I didn't know what to ask for, she wasn't much help. She sent me to the local newspaper office thinking the Cheyenne Falls paper would have more details of the accident than Margaret's clipping.

They pulled their papers from the time of the wreck. I hit a goldmine with the obituary of the woman who died in the wreck. If I'm right, she would be my grandmother. I held my breath as I read. She'd been 'survived by' three children. Two daughters, Sharon Dale Morris, and Abigail Dale Forrest, and one son, Jackson Dale. Their addresses were all listed as Cheyne Falls, Oklahoma. She had also 'left behind' three grandchildren, April Dale, Alexandra Forrest, and Fredrick Morris. They were all listed as Cheyenne Falls residents.

April Dale would be Jackson's daughter. Fredrick Morris would be Sharon's son. So, Alexandra would be the daughter of Abigail. See what I did there, pairing the last names of the grandchildren with their parents? I'm clever like that. If I'm Alexandra Forrest, my mother's name is Abigail. Abigail had been driving the car when the accident occurred, further evidence that she would be my mother. My heart skipped a beat and began racing. I know my Mother's name. I know *my* name. I whispered it several times, trying it on for size. I choked on dust stirred up by my happy dance.

The thought of being this close to my parents filled me with excitement and a desperate need to find them. I'm used to things not working out but finding a place where I belong goes way beyond anything I've ever dreamed of.

I went back to my motel room, spread copies of newspaper clippings on the bed, and thumbed through the local phone book to the 'F' page. There were no Forrests listed. There was also no Sharon Morris or Jackson Dale. I fought rising panic. The newspapers had been twenty-eight years old. Plenty of time for them to have all moved on.

If I found an address, what would I do? Just show up? And say what exactly? "Hi, I'm your daughter. I've been away for twenty-eight years. Miss me?"

The jig-saw puzzle piece that I take with me wherever I go lay on the nightstand beside my keys and sunglasses. I picked it up and tossed it in my hand as I thought.

Margaret hadn't believed in lavish Christmas presents. Her gifts were usually socks or underwear, always urgently needed and deeply appreciated, wrapped in brown paper. But one year the church gave me a box so beautifully wrapped I hated to tear the paper. It contained a thousand-piece jig-saw puzzle. I was beyond ecstatic. At home I dragged the scuffed card table with the wobbly leg from the closet and began sorting pieces according to color. The picture on the box was a glorious snow scene. Welcoming light spilled from church windows and puddled on the snow. Families laughed and called to friends as they trooped up the stairs and into church. I'd never been to a church like that. I'd traced their path with a forefinger and wondered what they were saying and what that kind of joy and camaraderie would feel like.

One day I found a dust covered puzzle piece under the sofa while looking for my run-away Jacks ball. I tried to fit it into my puzzle but no matter how many places I tried, how many ways I turned it, how hard I shoved, it didn't fit. It's a symbol of who I am. I don't know where I came from, and never fit into my own life.

I returned to my clippings and found the picture of Jackson Dale accepting an award for a place called Tribes. The award had been bestowed by the Cheyenne Falls Chamber of Commerce for Tribes bringing tourists to town. I studied the picture, willing myself to recognize him. Tall and lean, he wasn't movie star good looking, but handsome. Nice eyes. They smiled when his face didn't. He had no hair, as in completely bald, but an unwrinkled face. I guessed him to be fiftyish but his age could have been anywhere from forty to seventy. I look nothing like him. I selected another clipping which featured him receiving the Chamber of Commerce 'Man of the Year' award. In this picture he wore a cowboy hat and boots with a suit and tie. I hadn't realized that I like cowboy hats until today.

Tribes, a tourist attraction, represented a number of Indian nations. Located three miles south of town in a natural setting, Tribes sounded interesting. Tourists wandered from camp to camp to experience the lifestyle of each tribe. Campsites were staffed by tribal representatives, dressed in cultural costumes. They cooked, tanned hides, wove blankets, made jewelry, beaded moccasins, or whatever their ancestors might have been doing. Tourists could try authentic meals and snacks and samples of their work at the lodge. I learned all that from the same clipping. I was intrigued.

Chapter Nine

Twenty minutes and three miles later I drove between massive cedar posts holding a sign which announced *You Are Now Entering Tribes*. The road wound around the hill past pens of buffalo, deer and a sign that proclaimed *These are the Cheyenne Hills. You are about to turn back the pages of history.* Boy was that an understatement.

The lodge perched on the edge of a cliff. Fashioned from canyon rock and giant cedars, it rose from the earth, not looking man made. Its large expanses of glass reflected the afternoon sun and offered breathtaking views in all directions. I hurried between the menacing totem poles guarding the entrance and went in.

A bin of Indian art caught my attention. I leaned in for closer examination. Artists had used mystical techniques with spiritual qualities. Concealed in clouds, eagles, hawks, and wolves spied on mere mortals below. I selected a print and carried it to the counter.

A lady looked up as I approached, her face forming a question. "May I help you?"

"I'm looking for Jackson Dale."

"He's working buffalo."

Working buffalo? What does that even mean? I started to ask, but do I really want to know? "Okay. Will he be back this afternoon?"

"I never know. He comes. He goes." She waved expansively.

"Right. Well. Can I leave this with you?" I asked, handing her the print. "I've never been here. I'd like to look around."

"Sure," she said. "Look around as much as you like. There's a tour in thirty minutes. You'll want to do that. I have the tickets." Assuming the sale. Good technique.

"I'd like to look around right now."

"Okay," she said. "But they go fast." She was good.

Only a handful of tourists nosed around. I probably didn't need to worry about a spot on the tour.

"A bus could unload any minute," she said.

"I'll take my chances." I smiled.

"Suit yourself."

I walked outside. The plateau dropped away sharply on three sides, providing a view of canyons and valleys more spectacular than the view in front. I sat on a bench in the shade of a gnarled Russian olive tree and watched a hawk glide over the canyon.

The sights and sounds enveloped me in a cocoon of tranquility. Gossamer memories floated beyond my consciousness. I couldn't pull them into substance, but I've been here before. I closed my eyes and listened to the constant Oklahoma wind rustling the leaves above me, the piercing cry of the hawk, and the music. The unobtrusive flute melody rode the breeze like the hawk. At first, I thought I'd imagined the pure tones.

I stood up but couldn't find the music's source. I stepped up on the bench and peered over the edge of the cliff clinging to the olive branch for balance.

And there he was. A young man sat cross legged on a shelf of sandstone about twenty feet below. His bronze skin blended with the cliff walls and the ledge that held him. He looked as though he belonged to and yet owned the earth. The wooden flute might have been an extension of his body. The melody, birthed in his heart, was released by his breath through an instrument made by his hands. Each golden note hovered, exquisitely haunting, waiting to be joined by the next.

I sat back down. The music, which filled me with sadness too deep to verbalize, demanded total emotional involvement. Threading its way through time, it bound the past, present, and future. It gave me a feeling of expansiveness and insignificance at the same time. Total peace.

Lost in the music, I didn't notice the man sitting on the bench beside me until he handed me a handkerchief. I swiped at the tears coursing down my face, wondering how long he'd been sitting there. I stole a glance at his profile.

"Beautiful, isn't it?" he said gazing into the distance.

I didn't know if he meant the music or the scenery, but since it was impossible to separate the two, I sniffed and nodded.

"When I get bogged down in there," he jerked his head in the direction of the lodge, "I slip out here."

I'd been right. His eyes smiled even when he didn't.

"You're Jackson Dale," I said.

His face lit up. "Guilty as charged."

I glanced down at his handkerchief. The dust on my face laced with my tears had left steaks on the cloth. Embarrassed, I didn't know what to do. My default mode.

He noticed. "Keep it," he said. "You haven't told me who you are, but I'm guessing you're my niece."

My heart hammered in my ears. I pressed my fingers to my lips to keep them from trembling.

Laugh lines crinkled around his eyes. "Aren't you?"

"I think so. That's why I'm here." But then I didn't know what to say. I swallowed hoping he would ask questions. But he didn't. He sat there waiting for me to say more. And after a few false starts, I did. The flood gates opened, and the words poured out faster than I could think. Which isn't a new experience. I need a speed bump between my mouth and my brain. I explained about finding the clipping and my nagging doubts about Margaret. I ended with, "I couldn't shake the feeling that the child in this clipping might be me. So, I came to see." I showed him the yellowed picture.

He nodded. "Looks like you might be."

My mouth was dry. I swallowed. "Why do you think so?" I held my breath.

"Molly said you had asked for me. I watched you for a minute before I came out. You're a Dale. Dale women have strong genes."

"Seriously?" I so need a speech writer.

"You look like your aunt Sharon."

"And my mother?" I sounded calm. I wasn't.

"More like Sharon. May I?" he asked reaching for my left wrist. My heart jumped into my throat. I knew what he was looking for. He turned my wrist over, exposing the heart shaped birthmark below my thumb. David teased me about wearing my heart on my sleeve. More accurately, it's under it.

"Well, that pretty much settles it I reckon," Jackson said with a smile. "The birthmark wasn't mentioned in any of the missing-person flyers. The other girls who've showed up claiming to be you didn't know about it."

I felt dizzy and realized I hadn't eaten. All day. Food hadn't crossed my mind, proof of how weirded out I am. I rode through this day on a wave of adrenaline. I took a deep breath and asked the question that's dominated my every waking moment since finding the clipping. "Where are my parents?"

"Dang if I know," Jackson said.

"W-What?" My lip trembled. Tears threatened. "I want to see them. Where…?"

"Abby sent a Christmas card from Naples."

"Christmas? Eight months ago. Naples, Florida?"

"Italy."

"Italy?" My heart sank. "Can we call them? Please? I have to find them." My voice rose three octaves. To be this close and yet so far was torture.

"Settle down. We'll find them."

"Why are they in Italy?"

"Your father is a senior systems analyst for a global corporation. They send him all over the world. Abby recently started traveling with him. She and Russ were in Japan. From Japan they went to Italy. I'm not sure they're still there. Ron Lang keeps up with them. He'll know."

"So maybe I could talk to them tomorrow?"

Jackson dropped an arm around my shoulder and gave me a squeeze. "Now, hold on, Sugar. We'll find them. This will be priceless." He shook his head. "Birthday and Christmas all rolled into one."

"I have to find them," I said again. I could barely breathe.

"Yeah, that's pretty obvious." He grinned.

"I've dreamed about this all my life, but never really believed this moment would happen—I still don't."

"You're coming to dinner tonight. We'll talk then," Jackson said.

"Dinner? Where?"

"My house."

"Oh, no." Small talk isn't one of my greater skills. "That's too much trouble."

"Penny will throw another tater in the pot. No big deal. She does it all the time. You'll want to see family pictures I'll bet."

"Pictures? Yeah. Well. If you're sure."

"Where are you staying?"

"Buggy Creek Inn."

"Go pack up your things. You're moving in with us." He pulled a receipt from his pocket and scribbled on it. "Here's my cell number. Give me yours and your room number."

"Okay," I said. I fished a business card from my purse and wrote my room number. David had insisted I have those pretentious cards made. It's not like anyone had ever asked for one before. But David said anyone who is anyone has business cards. David. Woops. I'd forgotten to call him.

"Uh, that's really kind of you. But you don't know me yet. I think I'd like to stay where I am if you don't mind. Until..." My voice trailed off. Until what? I didn't know where to go from there. I didn't want to hurt his feelings, but I'm very private. I handed him the card.

Jackson glanced at it and tucked it in his wallet. "We'll talk about that later." He gave me a hug. I am so not a hugger. "I'll pick you up at five thirty."

I have an uncle. He'll be picking me up for dinner. Normal everyday words. But to me whose only family has been Cruella De Ville, they sounded like an ode to joy. I burst into tears. Good grief.

Chapter Ten

Driving with his knees, Jackson eyed me over hands cupped around the cigarette he'd just lit. Like the Marlboro Man. Sort of. White cowboy hat and lit cigarette. What if my Marlboro Man obsession had been triggered by forgotten memories of a chain-smoking uncle?

"Not a fence built that can hold that mare," he said, gesturing toward a light grey horse grazing in the box canyon as we passed by. "Lately, she's been a ghost. She disappears." He did a one-shoulder shrug.

"What do you mean?"

"I have no idea where she goes, but she always comes back."

"Can I ride her."

"I don't know. She's a handful." He blew smoke out the open window.

"I love horses."

He nodded. "So does your mama."

"Tomorrow?"

"Maybe. Ron Lang wants you to drop by his office in the morning about nine. He's set up a DNA test. It's a formality as far as I'm concerned. You're a Dale. He'll know when he sees you."

"You've mentioned him earlier. Who is he?"

"Family attorney. He's also a family friend. For a while I thought my oldest daughter, April, would marry him, but she met a guy at college."

"You've already talked to Ron Lang?" I pulled my gaze away from the horse. "Does he know where my parents are?" I waited, holding my breath.

"No. I told him to get you into the account Abby set up. In case you needed cash and she wasn't here when you were found." He jerked the steering wheel to dodge a rut. "She knew you were still alive. Said she'd know if you weren't. She never gave up."

I fought back tears. For both of us.

"Ron can give you more details," Jackson went on. "A hearing was scheduled for your thirtieth birthday, the twenty first of August. Did you know that's your birthday?" From the corner of his eye he checked my reaction.

I shook my head. "No. Margaret came up with a fake birth certificate. That wasn't the birth date on it. She wasn't much into birthdays. What kind of hearing?"

"Declaration of Death. You've been missing for twenty-eight years. Your grandmother left you land and money in her will. You would have inherited it on your twenty first birthday. Since you weren't here, the date was changed to your thirtieth birthday and if you hadn't been found by then, the court would declare you deceased. The land would go back into the estate to be redistributed."

"I see," I said. Although I didn't.

"I'm glad we're getting this cleared up before Abby knows you're here. Not that she'd be hurt this time." Jackson exhaled and flicked his cigarette into an overflowing ashtray. Ashes rained down on a work glove that didn't seem to have a mate.

"This time?"

"Yep. It broke her heart. Girls claiming to be you."

The thought of someone deliberately hurting a mother I have yet to meet made me angry. "You mentioned it before. I work for a law firm. I'm no longer surprised how casually people cheat and lie."

Jackson exhaled a stream of smoke through the window. "We all hide behind masks of some kind. Even from the people who know us best."

I studied his profile. "You think so?"

"Know so." He blew smoke out the window.

"Why would anyone claim to be me?" I asked.

"The estate. I'm sure the money has earned a good bit of interest. The land has appreciated too." Jackson glanced at me, judging my reaction. "Fred's been farming your half-section adjoining his for years.

Your full section by Tribes is idle. And you own a leased quarter section a farmer is running cattle on."

I had no idea how much land was worth, or how many acres are in a section. I'm guessing it's a lot more than I have now. I think Jackson waited for me to ask, but I didn't.

"Fred is my cousin, right?" I asked instead.

"Yep. Your aunt Sharon's boy." The road began a steep incline, and Jackson kept his eyes glued to it. "Glad you finally got home." He seemed to genuinely mean it.

"Me, too," I said. He had no idea.

"That's my place," Jackson pointed out as the pickup started down into a valley.

In the light of late afternoon sun, Jackson's home was about as picturesque as anything I had ever seen. Across the valley the log house was set on a rise below the crest of the hill overlooking a small lake. A stream wound its way down from the lake through a valley dotted with grazing Angus.

"It's spring fed." Jackson said, following my gaze to the lake. "It's pretty, but so cold only a masochist would try to swim in it. My twins do, but not for long." The pickup eased between the gate posts of a rail fence and rattled over a cattle guard.

"It's gorgeous out here," I said.

Jackson nodded. "It's a hassle getting to town when the weather's bad," he said as he dodged a hole big enough to swallow Cleveland. "But it's worth it."

I laughed. "It's no picnic on a good day. Your twins are lucky to grow up here. I spent my childhood dodging stray dogs and drunks."

"Well, we're here." Jackson climbed out of the pickup. I didn't move. He opened my door and waited. Realizing I had no choice, I slid out. With his hand in the small of my back, he propelled me toward the welcoming committee gathered on the porch.

Jackson's wife wore an apron-covered summer dress. The dish towel dangling from her fingers suggested she'd dropped everything to rush out to greet me. Her face was creased in a smile. Identical blonde heads peeked from behind her.

Jackson made the introductions. "This is my wife, Penny. The twins, Jill and Jacy."

"Jacy rhymes with lacey," one of the twins informed me.

"Do you tell teachers that?" I asked. "Are you Jacy?"

She nodded. Both girls giggled, knowing I had no hope of telling them apart. I was instantly captivated by their mischievous elfin faces.

Penny laughed. "Trying to tell them apart gives everyone fits." She pulled me into a hug. My shyness melted in its warmth. "Come on in, Hon, dinner is ready." She led me along a wide veranda which skirted the house and offered a view of the lake. She opened the door and waited for me to enter.

Wonderful kitchen aromas filled the air. I walked past Penny into the great room and surveyed my surroundings. Cedar walls led the eyes upward to clerestory windows. The setting sunbathed the room in an orange glow. High ceilings made it look even more spacious. An enormous stone fireplace dominated one end. Beside it, an oversized recliner dwarfed the old man sitting in it. His leathery face, darkly tanned from years in the sun, split in a wide toothless grin when he saw me. He fairly bounced up and down in his seat.

"I forgot to tell you I picked up Papa Jay this afternoon," Penny told Jackson. She included me in the conversation by explaining, "Papa Jay lives at the nursing home in town, but also has a room here. We bring him out often. He enjoys being here and the girls adore him, but they wear him out."

The twins had made a bee line for the elderly gentleman's chair as soon as they came back into the house. I joined them.

The old man's watery eyes peered at me through thick glasses.

"Papa Jay, this is Abby's daughter, Alexandra. She's been lost," Jackson said, joining the group. He bent to adjust the Pendleton blanket draped across the old man's boney knees. "We're happy she's home."

"Ali's home?" Papa Jay acted as though this bit of news was too good to be true. He glanced behind me toward the door I'd come through. "Where's Lexy?"

"Who's Lexy?" I asked.

"Beats me," Jackson said.

Myopic eyes tried to focus on my face. "You know Lexy," Papa Jay insisted.

"His mind wanders. He often thinks I'm his brother," Jackson said quietly.

Papa Jay would not be put off. "You know her. Had that guitar and a real purty voice. You used to sing with her. You don't sing too good."

"You got that right," I agreed. "I'll never be famous for my singing."

"She left with that guy." Papa Jay's imploring eyes focused on my face. "But you know where she is," he accused.

"Who does he think I am?"

"Know who you are," he muttered, but confidence faded from his eyes.

"Are you hungry, Papa Jay?" Jackson asked. "We'll bring you a plate when we get the food together." He draped an arm over my shoulders and steered me to the kitchen.

As we came in, Penny looked up and handed me the silverware. "Would you mind setting these on the table, Hon?"

"Sure," I said.

"My goodness, you sure favor your aunt Sharon," she said, picking up a pitcher of lemonade, and following me to a table large enough to feed a harvest crew. "Jackson said you did. The twins and I have been talking about you ever since he told us you were coming for dinner," Penny looked up at me. Her smile was as warm as her hug. "We're pretty excited." She filled a plate for Papa Jay from the bowls on the table. One of the twins took it to him on a tray.

Before I had a chance to take a bite of anything, the questions started. They wanted me to tell them in one evening what I had been doing for twenty-eight years. Hitting the high points, I told them about my education, meeting and becoming engaged to David, and going on the horse-show circuit with David's mother. I sidestepped my childhood.

Desperate to know about my parents, I asked questions about the family. While they talked, I finally had a chance to eat. Then we settled into silence, broken only by the requests of hearty eaters: "Please pass the fried chicken." "I'll have more tater salad if you don't mind." "Can you send the iced tea down this way?"

I'm not used to being the center of attention. I thought I would feel too self-conscious to eat. The first taste of Penny's fried chicken proved me wrong.

After dessert Penny said, "Why don't you and Jacks go into the living room while I tidy up?"

"I'll help," I offered, and grabbed a plate.

"You certainly will not," Penny said, taking it from me. "Scoot."

Jackson laughed. "Better take advantage of it while you can. Next time you're here she'll have you elbow deep in dishwater."

"That's okay. I know how to wash dishes," I said.

We walked into the living room. He settled on the sofa, patted the cushion beside him in invitation, and reached inside a box. "The pictures in here might interest you."

Might interest me? Are you *kidding* me? As long as I can remember, the empty places inside me cried out for the family I'd imagined. And here they were in a battered shoe box. I dove in beside him.

Chapter Eleven

Jackson began handing me old photos, explaining as he did what was happening and who the people were. Many were early pictures of him, his mother, and his sisters during various stages of their childhood. Since my grandmother died in the auto accident and I would never have a chance to meet her, I carefully studied her image. She was a tiny woman with dark eyes. I could feel her energy through the pictures.

"This has to be my mother," I said, pulling a picture from the stack. A girl of about twelve was poised to dive off the dock behind Jackson's house. She wore a bright red bikini and a brighter smile. Her blond hair, cut short, was plastered to her head in wet wispy curls.

Jackson glanced at it, "Nope, that's Sharon, Fred's mother. Your aunt."

I stared at the dog-eared print. "Good grief. Penny was right. That could be me." Except for the smile. I've never smiled like that.

"Told ya. Here's your mama," Jackson said. He spoke the words casually; totally unaware how momentous this was for me. Handing me a picture of his sister was an ordinary occurrence for him. No big deal. It's only his sister.

Until a few days ago, I hadn't dared to believe she existed. I've kept the hazy images of my imagined mother carefully tucked away in my heart. So exquisite was the anticipation of actually seeing a picture, I hated to break it. But curiosity took over. I nearly ripped the snapshot from his hand. Words can't express the thrill.

My eyes devoured her image. My mother wore a one-piece bathing suit, much more conservative than that of her sister. Her long blond hair curled slightly at the ends. She looked to be about fourteen. Even at that age she was lovely. Not snobby beautiful. Sweet. Classy, like a young Elizabeth Smart.

Jackson handed me a photo of the two girls together. Even with their resemblance, the difference in their personalities was apparent. While my mother looked serene, Sharon looked ready to throw herself into the next big adventure. I looked amazingly like her. No wonder Jackson recognized me.

"Where's Aunt Sharon?" I asked.

"Who knows? She takes off with some guy. She's gone awhile then turns up again when she's had her fill." He scratched his head. "She was here for Thanksgiving and Christmas. Come to think of it, we haven't heard from her since 4th of July."

"Does her son know how to get in touch with her? I'd like to meet her."

"I doubt it. Sharon and Fred had a falling out before she left."

"Well, that's sad. You should treasure family."

"Here's one you need to see," Jackson grinned. "I think it was taken the day they brought you home."

I studied it intently. Aunt Sharon held a blanket-clad me. She stood between my mother and grandmother. Everyone beamed at the new baby. Except one.

"Who's this little boy?" I asked, aching for him. I recognized that lost expression. It hurts to be invisible.

He stood apart from the rest of the group. He looked to be about three or four. He had unruly red hair, freckles and ears that stuck out. Not a pretty child, he wore overalls with holes in the knees.

"That's Fred. Sharon's son." Jackson said, glancing at the picture. "It was too easy to dislike that kid."

"He looks so sad," I said.

"He was a bit of a bully. Thank God he finally outgrew it. Like Sharon he isn't much into family. But he has a pretty little wife and cute kids."

"Are there any pictures of my father?"

Jackson dug back into the box, discarding pictures as he went. "Here we go." He handed me my parents' wedding picture. "I know there's more." He reached further into the box and pulled out several. I examined them carefully, deciding I look nothing like my father.

Russell Forrest had a close-cropped moustache, dark hair, and a cleft chin. He resembled Rhett Butler in 'Gone with the Wind'. Only better looking. In the wedding picture my father smiled into the camera. In another he and Abby danced in formal attire. They looked happy—totally wrapped up in each other. I hoped they still were.

"Abby wore the same necklace in every picture." I wanted to call her Mom. But I thought Jackson might think me presumptuous. I was captivated by the gold necklace. A vine wrapped in the shape of a heart occupied the center of a cross which hung from a dainty chain.

"Uh huh," Jackson said, clearly disinterested. He handed me a picture of a man carrying a tiny blond girl on his shoulders. A white Stetson hat shadowed his face. The child laughed in delight. He watched me as I studied the picture.

I looked up at him. "This is me?"

He nodded.

"And you?"

"Yeah. Do you remember what you called me?"

I frowned and shook my head. Then suddenly I knew. "Yes. I called you Unca Dax. Wow, that's my first real memory." I liked that my first memory was Jackson. I could tell that he did, too.

He grinned. "Yep. Your mom calls me 'Jacks'. You couldn't say it. Great. Let's see what else you might remember." He found a picture of two girls, who looked to be about twelve and two, sitting on a piano bench. Sunlight streaming through lace curtains backlit their blond heads, giving their curls a halo effect.

"Pretty angelic, huh? Ring any bells?"

"No. Who are they?"

"The little one is you. Thought you might remember my daughter, April."

"The daughter who dated Ron?"

"Yeah. April was crazy about you." Jackson paused to light another cigarette. "April's mother and I lived next door to Abby and Russell. April seemed to think Abby had you so she could have a real live doll to play with. She changed more of your diapers than Abby. They had a path between our houses." Jackson laughed then turned serious. "My first wife, April's mother, died of cancer. April lost her mother right before the accident. So, she lost her mother, grandmother, and you within a three-month period. She went through a rough spell. I was too wrapped up in my own grief to notice. Good thing April and Abby had each other. Abby lost her mother and daughter at the same time." He exhaled a long stream of smoke and jabbed the cigarette out in the oversized horseshoe-shaped ashtray on the table. "April's going to be thrilled to find out you're here. In fact, she might know where your mama is. Abby stays in better touch with April."

My heart raced. "Let's call her and see. Now."

"I tried this afternoon but kept getting that dang answering machine."

"You lost your wife and mother close together. I'm so sorry."

"Within months," he said brusquely, clearly not wanting sympathy.

Penny walked in from the kitchen, drying damp hands on her apron. "I think April is speaking at a women's conference in Richmond, Virginia this weekend," she said, sinking into the couch on the other side of me. She draped an arm across my shoulder and added, "Poor dear. You must be exhausted." She smelled of soap suds, freshly baked bread, and White Diamonds.

I covered a yawn. "My day started at 3:00 this morning."

"Good grief. Jackson, take her back now. I found more pictures. Thought you might like to browse through these at your leisure. Make copies and bring them back whenever." She handed me the envelope of pictures and a plastic-wrapped heaping plate of leftovers.

"Thank you so much." I couldn't wait to get alone with those pictures. I was pretty stoked about the food, too. Penny is a great cook.

She followed us to the door. I allowed myself to be hugged again. This time I returned the hug. "Come back soon," she said.

As Jackson's pickup bucked along the road to town, I clutched the pictures to my chest. Leaning against the seat, I smiled through a yawn. I have family.

Chapter Twelve

Jackson dropped me off at my room with promises to contact Ron Lang and get back to me in the morning. On my way to the bathroom, I laid my watch, room key, and puzzle piece on the nightstand. I toed off my sandals, wriggled out of my clothes, and slipped on my robe, tying it tightly around me. The robe, a luscious shade of pink, is pretty much my security blanket. I would never have bought a robe, or anything else, so luxurious for myself. It was a Christmas gift from David's mother, Daydreon, the first Christmas I spent with David's family.

Being David's fiancé opened a whole new world. Extravagantly wealthy people existed, but I never thought I'd know any of them. North Haven, the Phipps' family palatial home, had left me speechless. The grounds looked like a movie set. But when I saw the immaculate horse barns, whitewashed paddocks, and beautiful horses, I bypassed dying and went straight to heaven.

Actually, I went straight to the barn. David went to the house. His mother found me an hour later in a stall with a bay gelding.

She saw the look in my eyes. "You love horses, don't you?"

I nodded. "I'm sorry you left your guests to come find me."

"I'm exhausted from the stress of planning holidays. By the time they get here, I'm too tired to enjoy my guests. Coming to the barn was the escape I needed."

"The mass of men lead lives of quiet desperation," I said brushing a strand of black forelock from the gelding's large liquid eye.

She beamed a smile at me. "You quote Thoreau and love horses. We are going to get along just fine." She draped an arm around my shoulder and ushered me to the house. I began spending more time at

North Haven than David did. Daydreon trained me, said I was 'a natural', and had me on the show circuit with her. I loved it. Her confidence in me, along with the ribbons I won, began to change the way I see myself.

A hot bubble bath called my name. While the tub filled, I worked conditioner into my hair and pulled the soggy mass into a shower cap and let the conditioner work its magic. I slathered a mask on my face and laughed at my reflection. Green face, orange and purple shower cap, and pink robe. I looked like Walt Disney threw up on me. I also resembled a zombie, not that I've known many personally. The clock on the nightstand informed me it was 2:00 AM. I have been up 23 hours.

I turned off the bath water and tested the temp with a toe. Scalding. As it cooled, I wandered out of the bathroom, dumped the pictures onto the bed, and began sorting through them. A snapshot of my mother and Aunt Sharon caught my attention. It had been taken the same day as the ones I had seen at Jackson's. The girls huddled on the dock, sharing a blanket, backlit by the setting sun. They faced away from the camera looking out over the water.

When I was about ten, I found a *Winnie the Pooh* book. Once the faded illustrations had been beautiful. I loved the picture of Pooh and Piglet sitting on a hill looking into the distance much like the sisters in the snapshot.

"Pooh," said Piglet.

"Yes, Piglet," said Pooh.

"Nothing," said, Piglet. "I just wanted to be sure of you."

Though Pooh sat next to him, Piglet needed reassurance. I had longed for someone, anyone, to be sure of—or to sit beside me enjoying the companionship. David hadn't filled that need, which seems strange now that I think about it.

Thumbing through Dale family memories left me feeling numb. I fought the self-pity I so easily sink into. I should have been in more of those photos. They should have been my memories too. I studied the snapshots of a two-year-old me with my mother. Because I'd never seen pictures of me as a young child, both people were strangers. My mother looked nice. The photos must have been taken shortly before

Margaret lifted me out of a car and changed my history. Before the world spun off its axis.

All my life I'd imagined a mother, perhaps a bit forgetful, out there in the great beyond who hadn't yet noticed she'd misplaced me. I'd never for a moment believed that God in a whimsical mood had dropped me into Margaret's uterus. It didn't make sense.

I hadn't hated Margaret because of the abuse. She'd convinced me that I'd brought the brutality on myself by being such a terrible child. But…

I had to stop. Ultimately that line of thinking wasn't productive and definitely not conducive to sleep. It made me thirsty. I craved a can of orange pop, my go-to drink of choice. I remembered seeing a soft drink machine right inside the rear door of the motel lobby not twenty feet from my door. Surely at this hour I could slip in and out without being seen. I grabbed quarters and my room key. I couldn't find the shoes I'd worn home from Jackson's. They'd cleverly hidden themselves under the bed and out of sight, so I dug my sexy red strappy sandals from the suitcase. I have no idea why I brought them. I've never worn them. They had four-inch pencil-thin heels, matched nothing I brought, and I look like a buzzed stork trying to walk in high heels. Further proof I hadn't been in my right mind when I packed.

I peered outside. A mercury vapor lamp lit the parking lot. Otherwise, the night was extremely black. A glow from the neon vacancy sign in front of the motel might have been inviting if one of the hissing tubes would only die a quiet death.

I stepped out. A June bug veered off his flight pattern around the yellow lightbulb beside my door and crashed into my shower cap with the force of a B52. It spiraled to the sidewalk where it landed on its back, noisily spinning in circles beside my toes.

"Are you crazy?" my inner voice demanded. "What are you doing out here in the dark?" I wobbled to the lobby door and yanked it open.

"People will hear me if I scream," I said out loud, as I hesitated on the threshold.

"Will they, now?" The inner voice argued. "And if they did, would they get out of their comfortable beds to help? Ali, sometimes you can be so stupid." That last part sounded more like David than my inner voice, but it's getting increasingly difficult to separate the two.

Worrisome thought. The door slammed shut behind me, knocking me into the lobby where I teetered on my heels.

I heard a male voice coming from one of the three payphones beyond the row of vending machines around the corner.

"Yeah, I'm in the lobby at Buggy Creek Inn," I heard him say. "My phone died." Long silence, then he added, "I just woke up." The voice sounded sleepy. I'd heard it before.

At the soft drink machine, I made my selection after dropping quarters into the slot. The last quarter had clanked in when I remembered the voice—the guy at the courthouse. Lane Lanigan.

What are the chances of running into him at 2:00 AM? None, if I can help it. As soon as the can rolled into the bin I grabbed it and backed toward the exit. As I wheeled around to make my getaway, my heel caught in the jamb, sending me crashing to the sidewalk. I made a three-point landing.

The pop can sailed out of my hand, ricocheted off a planter and rolled across the cement. Sprawled in an ungraceful heap, I watched it plunk off the curb and come to rest under a Jeep.

Carefully, I raised myself to my hands and knees and looked for the room key. It hadn't fallen anywhere near me. I crawled to the curb. The key lay beside the can of pop in a pool of oil, barely out of reach under the Jeep. I could possibly survive without the pop but couldn't get back in my room without that key.

Cement ridges and gravel bit into my knees as I slithered under the Jeep's front bumper and inched forward. My fingertips slid through gooey oil. I could feel the key but couldn't quite get my fingers around it. I stretched a bit more.

"We have to stop meeting like this," someone whispered. Lane Lanigan. How did he get under here without my seeing him?

My head jerked up, bumping soundly on the undercarriage of the jeep. "Ow. You scared me."

"I scared you? Have you looked in a mirror lately? There's enough oil smeared across your left cheek to service a fleet of trucks. What's that green goo on your face?" He reached out to wipe at it.

"Keep your hands off me," I snapped, jerking my head away from him, and bumping it again. Giving him my fiercest scowl, I began crawling backwards.

He grinned.

"What?"

When he said nothing, I glanced down. Horrified, I realized my robe had come untied. Not only that the robe's bottom had bunched up around my knees, and the more I moved, the more thigh was exposed.

He grinned and said nothing.

Infuriated, I grabbed at the top of the robe and tried to push down the bottom, leaving oil smears in several places.

Lane was enjoying the situation and made no attempt to hide his amusement.

"Go away," I said.

"Can't," he said, still grinning. "You're under my Jeep. And I'd appreciate it if you'd stop trying to destroy my oil pan with your head."

I glared at him.

"Look," he said, "I'll get out and turn my back while you crawl out. I won't watch."

"Like that's going to happen."

"Where I come from, a man keeps his word," he said. He'd managed to wipe the grin from his face, but not from his voice. "If you don't trust me, keep doing what you're doing. It's up to you."

"Oh, all right," I said finally, "Go." I watched him back out, wondering how on earth he had gotten under there without my hearing him.

"Okay," he said when he was on his feet.

He stood beside the jeep. I could see by the position of his feet that his back was turned. I didn't trust him, but I had no choice. I crawled out, which wasn't as easy as it sounds.

Lane gave me enough time to scramble to my feet and straighten and re-tie my filthy robe, before he turned around.

"See," he said with a boyish grin, "I'm true to my word."

"Obviously, a boy scout," I said.

He offered me the now-dented pop can. As I stepped forward, the heel I'd caught in the door snapped off sending me crashing into him. He dropped the pop but managed to catch me and keep us both from falling. He seemed to be in no hurry to let me go.

"Hey, Sunflower," he murmured, "Didn't your mother teach you not to throw yourself at men?" His breath smelled like cinnamon gum. "It's unattractive."

I should've said she hadn't taught me much of anything. But his face was inches from mine. I would be breathing into his chin. If I could breathe. "You have beautiful eyes," I said. It came out in a rush.

Okay, you know those things that keep people from blurting the first thing that comes to mind? I don't seem to have one. I'm not a hormonal twelve-year-old. I'm almost thirty, and quite bright, but when this guy is around my brain malfunctions. It's not like I've never been around men. But none of them had those eyes. Margaret once told me that saying anything was better than saying nothing at all. This was not the first time I'd questioned her wisdom.

Mortified, I jerked away from him and tottered on one high heel while I removed the broken one. Lane held my arm to steady me. Amusement danced in his eyes.

"Well," said a voice behind me. "You have to walk before you run they say. Looks like you're making progress."

Startled, we both jumped. Stormy stood outside the restaurant door, holding two steaming Styrofoam cups. She scowled at me with contempt but directed her next comment to Lane. "I see you have matters firmly in hand, Lanigan."

Lane dropped his hand but ignored her. He scooped up the pop can, handed it to me, but kept the key. "Which one," he asked.

"Which one what?"

"Good grief," Stormy exploded.

"Which room is yours?" Lane asked.

I pointed.

He walked me to the door.

"How imaginative. I would never have thought to put those colors together," Stormy said, cocking her head as I limped past. "Now this little number is a totally new look for summer," she intoned, as though moderating a style show. "Very innovative. Orange and purple flowers in exciting plastic headwear paired with a hot-pink robe."

I gritted my teeth and kept walking.

"Not everyone, of course, can wear it. Extremely bold, obnoxiously loud..." Stormy broke off as she looked down at my feet. "You're only wearing one shoe."

"I am? Thank goodness. I thought I was crippled."

Lane grinned, glanced at the key, wiped the oil on his jeans, opened the door and stood aside to let me in. "Ignore her," he said, handing me the key. "She lacks social skills. She was dropped on her head as a child."

"Shut up, Lanigan," Stormy said. "I hear you."

"Numerous times," he added.

I practically fell into the room. The door closed behind me. I leaned against it hardly feeling the knob jammed into my back as I listened to Lane's retreating footsteps.

"Was that the girl from the courthouse?" Stormy demanded. "Who is she?"

I would've loved to have heard his reply, but an engine roared to life. The Jeep backed out and drove away. The sounds faded into nothing.

I caught sight of my reflection in the mirror across the room and screamed.

Chapter Thirteen

The morning fog that blanketed the county had dissipated, except for the canyon where it still hung heavy and low. I drove down through it to the box-canyon corral where Jackson kept his horse and parked beside a small barn.

A meandering path followed a crudely cut fence. It led to the gate. Resting my elbows on the top rail, I scanned the canyon. Jackson had referred to his horse as a mare when he called this morning to say he could meet me out here. I thought she'd jumped the fence and taken off when I finally saw her drifting in and out of clouds of mist at the far end of the canyon. Her grey coat, nearly white, blended into the fog.

"You look like a phantom," I said, "like a ghost."

She turned a finely chiseled head toward me. For a full minute we stared at each other. Only a ranting blue jay broke the silence until a whinny rang through the air. The horse exploded into motion. Hurling herself toward the fence she slid to a stop inches from where I stood and studied me with what I would have sworn was confusion.

"Who were you expecting?"

The mare blew softly through her nose and tossed her head, as though answering the question. I laughed.

"I'm not who you thought, but maybe I'll do." I stepped back. "Aren't you pretty?" I said, moving silvery strands of forelock away from the eyes that considered me. I reached into my pocket for the peppermint candy I'd picked up at the restaurant. "This probably isn't what you want, but the horses at North Haven like them."

The offering was taken with velvety lips that skimmed my palm. When it was gone, the mare nibbled at my hair. She rested her head on

55

my shoulder. I wrapped my arms around her neck. This horse and I have a bond that defies words. I loved her instantly.

"Well, you seem to have bewitched Mariah." Jackson's voice startled me. "How did you catch her?"

"She caught me." I smiled. "Her name is Mariah? Like Mariah Carey?"

"Who? No. Mariah. Like the wind in that Frankie Laine song. *They Call the Wind Mariah*. She can run like the wind. Glad to see she graced us with her presence. When she gets the urge, she's gone. Blows right over this fence. Like the wind, she goes where her fancy takes her."

"She's an Arabian, right?"

"Yep. Completely worthless," Jackson said, the affection in his voice belying his words. "She eats me into the poorhouse and when I need her, she's gone. Never should've bought her. Too small to herd buffalo. I saw her in that sale ring, and she looked right at me like she was telling me to bid. And dang if I didn't." He shook his head as though he still couldn't believe it. "But she has heart. Gotta give her that. Gets in there like a boss."

"She has a beautiful head," I said.

"It's that Arabian dish face," Jackson agreed. "She's a pretty thing. I like having her around just to look at."

If I hadn't already liked Jackson, that statement would have won me over.

"She sure likes you," he added.

"She thought I was someone else. Who rides her?" Mariah pushed her head against my chest. I gave her another peppermint.

"Nobody lately. That's why she's so spoiled. Keep her on a tight rein for the first few miles. She likes to run. She's a good trail horse. She'll go for miles when other horses are dropping out. She's like a mountain goat. You'll see." He unlatched the gate and held it open for me. A bucket hung upside down over a post. Jackson handed it to me. "Want to get some oats?"

"Sure," I said, scurrying off to the barn.

I paused at the door and inhaled deeply savoring the smells of hay, leather, and sweet feed while my eyes adjusted to the dim light. This wasn't the first time I'd realized barns were where I felt most at home. I found the feed bin and gingerly reached in sighing with relief when my fingers closed over the cool handle of a metal scoop instead of a mouse, dead or otherwise. You never know—even in the best of barns—and this wasn't the best of barns. I threw in an extra scoop and grabbed a brush and curry comb on the way out. The brush was flying over Mariah in long sweeping strokes when Jackson came out with the saddle and bridle.

"I stopped on the way out and had this made for you this morning," he said, handing me a key. "It's to that gate over there."

"Thanks," I said around the lump in my throat. I pocketed the key and fought back tears. It sounds like a small thing, but not to me. Without words it said, 'I took the time. I thought of you.' It also said, 'you are family. You have my faith and trust.' Yeah, it said all that. And more. Besides that, the barn is between his house and town. He hadn't 'stopped on his way'. He'd made a special trip to town to have the key made.

"Don't have time to be running out here ever whipstitch to unlock this gate when you want to ride," Jackson grumbled. "Got better things to do."

I grinned and resisted the urge to hug him.

He checked the blanket for burrs and thorns before swinging it across the mare's back. "The same key unlocks both the barn and the gate." He swung the saddle into place, tightened the cinch and tested it to make sure it was snug. He reached for the bridle to stop Mariah's sideways dance. "Okay, get your fanny up there, girl."

I gathered up the reins and swung into the saddle. When I was firmly seated, Jackson stepped back to regard me. "Where'd you learn to ride? Not many horses in the city I'm guessing."

I smiled and rocked in the saddle to test the tightness of the girth. "My fiancé's mother taught me. She breeds and trains horses. They have a large farm outside Dallas not far from South Fork where that TV series was filmed."

"You sit a horse like your Mama. Nobody can teach you that," Jackson observed. "By the way, I talked to Ron this morning. The DNA test shows you're who we've been lookin' for." He glanced up from beneath his hat brim and grinned. "Knew it would."

"Huh uh. You can't get a DNA test back that soon. I work in law. I know." A wave of emotions—surprise, relief, elation—swept over me all at the same time.

"You can if you know the right people. It's what you know about who you know that gets the job done." He winked.

While dubious, I didn't argue with what I most wanted to hear.

"These canyons are like a maze." Jackson adjusted a stirrup then came around to fix the other one. "It'd be easy to get lost, so be careful."

"There I was without breadcrumbs to drop," I joked.

He dropped the stirrup. "Howzat?"

I leaned into it. "Fine. Thanks."

"If you do get lost, give Mariah her head. She knows the way home."

"Good to know." My eyes followed the rise of the canyon. "It's beautiful out here."

"Yep. Four generations of Dales have poured their blood into this land. Hearts and souls were planted here and watered with sweat and tears."

"I already love it." I tightened my hold on the reins. Mariah pushed her head forward trying to pull them from my hand.

Jackson grinned. "I can see that you do. God only made so much earth. He got out of that business a long time ago. When you're blessed by living on land that belongs to you, well there ain't nothing like it." Jackson took off his hat and scratched his head. "Of course, nobody ever really owns it. If we're lucky, we get to be stewards while we're here. It comes with a responsibility to take care of it, though."

"I believe that, too," I said.

"Course you do." He grinned. "You're a Dale."

Mariah pawed impatiently. In a fair imitation of John Wayne, Jackson said, "Well little lady, it looks like you better get going, before your horse leaves without you." He wasn't kidding. I loosened the reins and Mariah moved out at a mile-eating jog.

I relaxed and absorbed the beauty of the land. My mind returned to Jackson.

My uncle. Who likes me. I'm pretty pathetic that it takes so little to make me ridiculously happy. But you have to remember feeling loved isn't normal for me.

The trail through the trees emerged into a clearing and rose steeply. I had no time to think about anything but staying aboard as Mariah began the climb. I didn't really care where we went, which was a good thing. She had a destination in mind. It was easier to let her choose the route than to constantly fight with her over where we were going.

My senses feasted on my surroundings. I savored the scents of the horse beneath me, the earth, cedar, and clean air. My eyes devoured the sights, a profusion of extravagantly colored wildflowers dancing in the distant field and the clear cerulean sky. Trees were a mosaic of greens in the distance. The only sounds were a mockingbird going through his repertoire and the jingle of the bridle as Mariah mouthed the bit. The serenity of this place was a far cry from the Dallas slum where I'd worked two jobs through college to escape. Through it all, my soul had cried out to be where I could breathe. Had it remembered this place?

I belong with these people on this land. And after a lifetime of feeling I never fit anywhere, the knowledge was intoxicating.

I bent to slap a fly on Mariah's neck. If I hadn't the bullet would have plowed into my brain instead of whizzing past my head. Mariah threw me and bolted. I tracked her into 1891 where I met Lexy.

You already know about that, so now you're up to date. Let's pick up when I got back to the barn.

Chapter Fourteen

I burst into tears of joy and relief when I saw the barn. I have been to 1891 and *back*. Now that I think about it, I'm blown away. Or totally tired and delirious. My cell phone worked fine now, complete with 1891 pictures. I tried to wrap my mind around that and gave up.

Jackson wasn't there. I put Mariah back in her pen, brushed and fed her, locked the gate, and drove back to the motel. A long hot bath eased my aching muscles a bit and sore hip. I needed ice for my ankle, but I was too exhausted to get out of the tub and crawl into the restaurant to get some. I fell asleep before my head hit the pillow and didn't move until my phone rang the next morning.

I groped for the phone, knocking it to the floor. I found it and answered before it stopped ringing.

"Hello?" I croaked.

"Ali? Is that you?" David asked.

"Hmm."

"You sound groggy."

"What time is it?" I opened one eye and was blinded by a shaft of light slicing between the drapes.

"Nine thirty. Are you sick?"

"No, I had a long day yesterday, and had an exhausting dream about Indians and time tunnels." I sat up in bed, fully awake and reached for my discarded jeans. Every muscle in my body screamed in protest, reminding me that I had been in no shape for yesterday's epic ride. I reached into the pocket, pulled out the arrowhead, then the penny and stared at them in disbelief. The tunnel hadn't been a dream.

I've been to 1891. The proof in my hand winked in the errant beam of sunlight.

"Ali, did you hear me? I didn't call to listen to you prattle about…"

"I heard you. So, what did you call to hear me prattle about?"

"Have you had time to take care of the insurance papers?"

"Take care of—as in…?"

David's sigh carried his exasperation through the wires. "Ali, I filled them out for you except for that one section." I could imagine his expression. "You said you'd supply the information I don't have and drop the papers in the mail."

Woops. I do remember that. Sort of.

"You do have them with you. Right?"

"Well, of course I do." I think.

"Randall needs to have those papers in hand by the end of this week."

"Okay." I felt I should apologize but bit my tongue. David continually made me feel like a dense child. Margaret had made me feel evil. Between them I've apologized my whole life. That is going to stop. Now.

"When can I expect you home?" he asked, after a long pause.

"I don't know."

"I would like to know when to expect you." David enunciated each word, a sign of growing irritation. "I feel that is not too much to ask."

"Ask away. But I still don't know," I said. "Ron Lang, the family attorney, is trying to locate my parents."

David let out his breath in a rush of air. "So, you aren't returning anytime soon."

I bit at a hangnail. "I'm not leaving without seeing my parents."

"It could take a while to find them. Come home. Go back when they're located." A pencil tapped against the receiver, a sign David was bored, impatient, or both. Finally, he said, "Your parents haven't been located?"

"I just told you that, David. No. Ron Lang discovered they've been in Italy. They aren't there now, but nobody seems concerned."

"Who's Ron Lang?"

"The family attorney. You don't listen."

"I'm due in court in ten minutes. We'll talk more about this later, okay? Gotta run. Sorry you think I don't listen. Love you."

"Love you too," I said automatically. "Bye."

I ended the call trying to remember David ever saying he was sorry. I came up empty. Now that I think about it, he hadn't actually apologized today either. He didn't say he's sorry for not listening. He said he was sorry I *thought* he didn't listen, tossing the fault back in my court. Dang, he's good.

Chapter Fifteen

The phone rang as I finished dressing which took twice as long as normal. My muscles resisted every movement.

It was Jackson. He asked about yesterday's ride, then said, "I need to move buffalo today and wondered if you were planning on riding again."

"No, I can barely move this morning."

Jackson laughed. "Been awhile since you've been the saddle, huh?"

Should I tell him about stumbling into 1891? Intuition told me not to. I need to think about it.

"Yeah. On top of that Mariah threw me."

"I was afraid of that. Are you okay?"

"The gunshot scared her. Someone shot at me," I said.

"Shot at you? What? Where?"

"In a canyon. I'm not sure which one."

"Nobody would shoot at you. It must have been a hunter."

"Pretty sure it wasn't. He shot at me twice."

"He? You saw him?"

"No. I assumed a woman wouldn't be out in a deserted canyon."

"Probably not. But you were."

"Well, there's that. She must have had a scope. She missed my head by inches."

Jackson exhaled forcefully. I didn't have to see the cigarette to know he was smoking.

"You smoke too much," I said.

"Wondered when you'd jump on that train, too."

"You do."

"Who would want to shoot you? Nobody knows you're here."

I didn't say 'except you'. I didn't have to. It hung in the air between us.

"Ron Lang knows. He might have mentioned it" Jackson said. "If you ride again, stay closer to home."

"I'm in no hurry to go out there again." But as I said it, I thought about how disappointed Lexy would be if I never go back. And I couldn't deny the intrigue of getting to know someone who looked so much like me.

"By the way, Penny is planning a get together Friday evening so family can meet the prodigal."

"I can't come."

"Got a big social to-do lined up already, have you? Of course, you'll come. Your family is dying to meet you, girl."

"No." I gulped.

"It won't be bad."

"Yes, it will. I hate large groups."

"It's a few people."

I chewed a nail. "How few?"

"I don't know. I'll protect you. By the way, Penny got in touch with April."

"Does she know where my parents are?" I held my breath.

"No. She hasn't heard from Abby since Christmas either. She's anxious to see you."

Disappointment blindsided me. I'd so hoped April would know.

"Would Penny mind if I plant flowers at your place?"

"Flowers?" Jackson sounded a bit surprised.

Well of course he did. Why would I be planting flowers?

"I'm sure she'd be delighted. You'll get more help than you need from the twins." He paused and exhaled. "Be careful on that road. Your Mustang has a low carriage. Well, I'd better git before the day gets any hotter."

"Okay, thanks." Conversations with Jackson leave me feeling—what? Protected? Valued? Maybe both. I smiled.

***

I zipped by the post office to mail the insurance forms that got David's panties in a wad. I should be grateful he's providing insurance I can't afford instead of being so irritated by his attitude.

I skipped up the post office steps happier than I remember being in a long time. As I reached for the door Lane pushed his way out. His impassive face gave no indication he recognized me. Mirrored sunglasses hid his eyes but I'm pretty sure he didn't glance my way.

"'Scuse me," he grumbled, as he shoved past.

"Hey. You nearly knocked me down. No 'I'm sorry'?" I turned to stare after him as he jay-walked across the street to his Jeep. Without glancing my way, he pulled away from the curb and drove off.

Well. That felt weird. Bad weird, not good weird—like I'd been slapped. I shouldn't be surprised considering how I looked the last time he saw me. The behavior seemed out of character and the snub still stung when I arrived at Jackson's.

An hour later after digging in the hard-packed Oklahoma soil, I'd forgotten about it. Not completely. But embarrassment and hurt feelings were no match for the mischievous humor of the twins.

Jackson had been right. I'd hardly been able to take a step without tripping over one of them. I could have planted the hollyhocks in half the time without their help but they're so stinkin' cute.

The fact that the hollyhocks had survived the ride out of the canyon in yesterday's heat was a miracle. Flowers, grown from the same seed, blooming in 1891 and over a hundred years later at the same time would be pretty cool. I watered them again.

Back at the motel I showered, changed clothes, and went off in search of the local library and a museum.

Time flew as I lost myself in the lives of early Cheyenne Falls settlers. I'd hated history in school but now I inhaled anything I could find on life in Oklahoma Territory around 1891. In fact, I couldn't believe how much of the day was spent when I closed the last book. Maybe it was the by-gone era I'd encountered, but I felt a need to be in touch with these people whose blood flowed through my veins, as well as Lexy's. The cemetery drew me.

Chapter Sixteen

I drove south on Cemetery Road contemplating the pictures I'd seen in the library. I'd been especially fascinated by the crude homes of the squatters. Which would be Lexy's family since land runs didn't occur until 1891 and anyone possessing land before then would be doing so illegally. Squatters. Not a nice word now that I think about it.

The women in the pictures wore discouragement and clothes similar to Lexy's. Even the children looked old. In contrast Lexy seemed so.... I searched for words. Spirited? Vivacious? Out of place.

A cattle guard stretched in front of a black wrought-iron cemetery gate. How quaint. I drove across it and along the main road. A large marble monument inscribed 'DALE' came into view. I parked and got out. Wandering through people's final resting places felt weird. People who had laughed, cried, dreamed, and suffered loss were now only names.

I found the tombstone of my grandparents, laid the flowers I'd brought in front of it, and sat down beside it. With a forefinger I traced the date of my grandmother's death. The date of my abduction. I'd seen photos of her at Jackson's. She'd been holding an infant, then later a small child. Me. She would've been only seventy.

A hawk swooped down to land on the branch above my head and watched me.

I stared back. I'm no longer surprised it appears everywhere I go. I added picking up a bird book to my mental to-do list.

"Don't you have anything better to do?" I asked, "besides watching me like a hawk?" I crack myself up.

The hawk cocked its head as though listening.

I stood up, brushing weeds and twigs from my shorts, and walked back to the car. Instead of leaving, I drove farther into the cemetery and stopped at the top of the hill. This much-older section only rated a sagging strand of rusty barbed wire to separate it from the white-faced Herford who chewed her cud in the shade of an elm. She watched me with bored indifference.

I found a 'DALE' marker which was nothing more than a pock-marked cement post. Tombstones were only names and dates crudely stamped into cement. Lexy had mentioned that her family came in a covered wagon, so I assumed they would be the first family of Dales here. I looked for death dates within the range of 80 years of 1891. Before Lexy dropped the bombshell of what century I'd wandered into, conversation about her family had been relatively normal. She'd mentioned brothers Ethan, Josiah, Seth, and Paul. I found markers for each of them. Graves of others within that time were probably wives and children. I found tombstones for Aunt Mattie, Uncle Les, and Lexy's father, Alexander John Dale. Lexy had been named after him instead of any of his sons, but then she was the oldest. Her mother's grave was next to his. Ma'am had a name—Hannah Jeanette.

I had also brought flowers for Lexy's grave, but after a thorough search I came up empty. She hadn't been buried here. Neither had her little brother, Johnny.

"Strange," I said to the hawk, not at all surprised it had followed me back here. "Maybe Lexy moved away." That seemed rather unlikely. The graves of Lexy's family proved these people once existed. And further, that I hadn't totally lost my mind. I had visited 1891—and managed to get back. Knowing this felt reassuring and weird at the same time.

Would anyone believe me? Of course not. I barely believed it myself. The event seemed to take on a life of its own, a secret too enormous to keep. Who would I tell? David? Not a chance. He's already on the verge of having me committed.

I had wanted to tell Jackson immediately. Instinct told me not to. I couldn't shake the feeling that the cave had been carefully guarded, waiting for me. I needed to protect it until I figure out what I'm supposed to do. That sounded presumptuous. Like I think I'm special.

I don't. I feel like I fell into a maze, not knowing what to do with what I know.

I wandered back to the Mustang too deep in thought to notice the guy leaning against my fender, until I was practically on top of him. I stopped short.

"You scared me," I said.

"That's the second time you've said that. What happened to your cheek?" Backlit by the glow of the setting sun, Lane seemed perfectly at ease, but I heard tightness in his voice. He wore the same clothes I'd seen him in earlier at the post office. Long legs stretched in front of him, he half-sat against the car.

"Old war injury," I said. I don't know anything about this man. Only that I turn into a blithering idiot anytime he appears. My stomach tied itself in a knot. I forgot to breathe. Nobody in my entire life has ever had the effect on me that Lane Lanigan does. I'm in a remote cemetery, alone with a man. For all I know, he's on the FBI's ten-most-wanted list, and my heart stopped beating the instant I saw him.

"It's not that old," he said.

"Go away," I demanded. I was closer although I don't remember moving.

"Well, I have a bit of a problem with that." He wiped sweaty palms on his Levi's.

I looked around. "Where's your Jeep?"

"Ah, you've picked up on the problem." He glanced at his watch. "Yeah?"

"Look, there is no reason for you to trust me. And come to think of it, I really wish you wouldn't. But I'm in a bit of a pickle here. If I could get back to town without involving you, I would. You seem to be my only way out of this mess."

I stared at him. "You blew me off at the post office this morning."

His breath came out in an irritated huff. "Yeah, I know."

"You should be nicer to people you might need a favor from."

"Sunflower, we're wasting time chatting. I gotta get out of here." He grinned lazily, although Gene Kelly could tap dance on the tension in his voice. I couldn't read his eyes. The only thing reflected in his mirrored sunglasses was my worried face. I thought fast. I avoid danger like smallpox and have no patience with stupid people who don't. With the ten o'clock news vomiting its version of the day's horrors, a girl can't be too careful. Details are always delivered by a newscaster in a dispassionate voice. "The body of the woman abducted in the Wal-Mart parking lot has been discovered in a ditch along Highway 9. Half clad. Missing shoe. Partially decomposed."

I'm more than capable of filling in the gaps, imagining me in her place feeling every bit of the terror and hopelessness of her last moments. I know I will die. I just refuse to be the body in the ditch along Highway 9. Why, in this day and time, any woman who let a strange man in her car would have to be a total idiot.

"Get in," I said.

He'd opened the door and slid in before I could walk around to the other side.

My shaking hand couldn't get the key into the ignition. He has that effect on me. Lane took the key, inserted it, and turned it.

"Don't switch on the headlights," he said. "I'd rather nobody see us."

"Nobody who?"

He pointed to the far side of the cemetery where several bobbing flashlight beams crisscrossed.

"What are they looking for?"

"Guess."

I put the car in gear, letting it coast down the incline to the front gate, praying I wasn't driving across graves. I barely missed a lane sign that read "Tranquility." The irony wasn't lost on me.

We coasted through the gate, turned the corner, and were out of sight.

"Okay, Sunflower, hit the lights and go." He didn't say where.

I didn't care. Where Lane Lanigan is concerned, my usual good judgment doesn't seem to be worth a plugged nickel.

Chapter Seventeen

There's this illusory quality to my memory of what happened last night. I replayed the scene in my mind until 3:00 AM when I finally drifted off to sleep. The events were even more disjointed and weird in my dreams, some of which should be major red flags. I tossed around until my bed looked like a mine field. I kept feeling the warmth of Lane's hands on my face and that impetuous kiss on my nose. This morning I've tried to sort things out and put them in order. A significant piece of information was AWOL. It felt like attempting to hammer a nail into a wall with a pair of tweezers. Not that I've ever done that. But you get the idea. Here's what happened:

Town isn't that far from the cemetery and it was still dusk when we left. I drove at speeds way above my comfort zone. Yet by the time Lane directed me to a house in a rundown neighborhood, the night had pulled in around us thick and black. I stopped at the curb where he indicated. He hopped out as the car coasted to a stop. Not quite a tuck-and-roll thing. He came around to the driver's side and squatted between the car and a row of pathetic Crepe Myrtles. He leaned over and took my face between his hands.

"Thanks for the ride," he said, his voice tense.

"You live here?" I asked, appalled. I peered through the dark at the shack.

"No. I work here."

"Doing what? Cooking meth?" I was joking but realized it could be true.

"I can't explain now. You have to leave. Don't stop for anything until you're back at the motel." He glanced around quickly to make sure no one watched us. He missed the small child staring at us from a porch across the street.

The strong south wind had settled into a gentle breeze and carried the scent of beans cooking. A dog barked nearby. In the house next door, a baby cried. I looked up into a purple sky. Venus was visible above the roof. "Okay. But Lane…"

"If you see me in town, you don't know me. Got it?"

I nodded. "No."

He chuckled. "Yeah. You gotta be confused. I'm trying to keep you out of this mess, but you keep showing up."

"Look, I had as much right to be in that cemetery as you did. I went…"

"Later, Sunflower." He kissed the tip of my nose and disappeared between the bushes. "Go." he ordered from the other side.

I went.

This is crazy. I'm not a child with no common sense. Okay, I proved that last part wrong. But aside from the cloak and dagger stuff surrounding Lane, I'm engaged to David, who loves me. I think. And, by the way, who is Stormy?

The next morning on my way out to the barn I thought about all that along with the decision I need to make. This is the morning Lexy wanted me to return to 1891. When I'd left her, I had no intention of ever going back. However, after spending the afternoon yesterday in the library pouring over history books, I'm interested in learning more about her life. I could think a multitude of reasons for not going— being shot in the canyon loomed first and foremost—but in the end my desire to know Lexy outweighed them all. I'm more than a little curious. Do we have more in common than looks? Strange as it sounds, I think we could be good friends.

As I drove through Cheyenne Falls, Lane's Jeep pulled up beside me at the town's only stoplight. The Jeep's radio blared "Honky Tonk Heroes". Stormy, in a pair of cut-offs, sat in the passenger seat with her bare feet propped up on the dash. She and Lane were both laughing. Neither glanced my way. This time I wasn't surprised. There is no reason for my heart to flop around like a fish out of water every time I see Lane. Unfortunately, it does. He might've looked even scruffier than he had yesterday. I'm not sure because I'm better at ignoring him. I wish I was better at ignoring my jealously.

I drove through Sonic on my way out of town and grabbed breakfast. I washed down the last bite of my egg burrito with a swig of coffee almost too hot to drink. I turned onto the lane that led to the barn and made a mental note to never again drive over a bumpy road with scalding coffee.

Mariah paced back and forth along the fence, following me as I walked in and out of the barn with the saddle, bridle, blanket, and a bucket of feed. While she ate, I quickly ran a brush over her enjoying her warmth, her scent—only a horse lover would get that—and the automatic motions of the task. I soon had her saddled and we were on the way. Knowing Mariah does this often lessened my fear.

From the top branch of a dead tree a red-tailed hawk watched me. I shaded my eyes with one hand and looked up as I passed. It stared back. Abruptly a shriek split the air. Diving from its lofty roost, the hawk swooped past close to my right ear then flew ahead of me down the trail.

I rode along the ridge until we reached the place where the trail began its steep descent into the last canyon. Probably the place the shooter had waited for me. In spite of what Jackson thinks, that shot was not a hunting accident. It was an ambush.

I tightened the reins and Mariah stopped. There wasn't a sound except for the squeak of the saddle as she shifted her weight. A far cry from Dallas. No traffic noises, no screams, no cursing, no objects crashing behind closed doors. Only sweet silence. It draped over me like a warm blanket on a frosty night, forming a layer of protection from the rest of the world. I settled into it.

Chapter Eighteen

When I arrived at the tunnel, instead of going through, I dismounted and tied Mariah to a scrub oak. Looking around, I made notes in a small notebook I'd jammed in my back pocket. A giant cottonwood hid the cave entrance at this end. In 1891 a waterfall hid the opening at the other end. I'd been curious about what it would look like today—in this century. In order to find out, I needed to scale this wall.

The hawk watched from the top of the cottonwood. After leading the way all along the trail, it seemed content to wait and observe.

"I'll only be a minute," I said. "Sorry to hold you up, but I'm really curious about what the tunnel exit looks like in this century." The hawk had become such a constant companion, talking to it seemed natural. I'm glad there's nobody around to hear. "I'm doing a scientific study, so to speak," I explained. "You have to admit a tunnel taking you from one century to another is most unusual."

The hawk admitted nothing.

I began to climb. Ten minutes later I stood triumphant and rather breathless at the top. Okay, a lot breathless. The height and proximity to the edge of the cliff made me dizzy. I sat on a boulder to take more notes.

A waterfall should cascade over these boulders hiding the tunnel opening. But it didn't. There was no water up here, cascading or otherwise. Weird. I leaned out a bit farther to see the tunnel exit. Not only was there no water to hide it there was no exit. As in none. The tunnel didn't exit into this century. It only emerged into 1891. Why that particular year? Below was a wall of solid rock. This quest had only created more questions.

I'd turned around and begun my descent down the cliff, fighting my way through a cloud of buffalo gnats. When I heard the rattle, I froze. Tilting my head slightly to the left I could see the diamondback from the corner of my eye. I'd only seen pictures of rattlesnakes. Seeing one up close and personal was not on my bucket list.

The snake, coiled on a rock shelf beside my head, had me in its crosshairs. It must have been sunning and resented the heck out of being disturbed.

I grew up in a city stepping over drunks on the sidewalk, avoiding street-roaming gangs, and ducking drive-by shootings. Encountering rattlesnakes had never been an issue. The depth of my snake experience doesn't run deep. But I did know not to move.

None of the fragmented ideas whizzing through my head stopped long enough to form a plan, or a complete thought. I couldn't catch my breath. My heart slammed against my ribs at an alarming rate. I had to pee.

That 'having to pee thing' had me concerned. Do I stand here until the snake decides I no longer present a threat and slithers away? What if it doesn't slither? What if it likes that rock and stays there forever, rattling every time I move? My brain shouted run. That would be suicide. And impossible. I'm standing on a rock on the side of a cliff.

I'm a two-hour horse-back ride from the nearest hospital. I have no idea how long it takes snake venom to kill a person but being alone this far from help can't be good. I thought about poking it with a stick, like maybe it would go away if irritated. But it already seems rather irritated. And I'm stick-less.

Suddenly the matter was taken out of my hands. With a shriek ninja hawk dove from the top of the tree, flew past my head, and, in an amazing maneuver, snatched the snake and swooped back into the sky. The snake's tail, still rattling, turned and twisted.

Shocked, I stood rooted to the spot watching until the hawk with its writhing cargo disappeared into the distance.

How I got back to the ground I have no clue. But when I did, my knees were too weak to hold me. I sat down and waited for my pulse to return to normal. Even then my hands shook too violently to untie Mariah. I don't remember how I pulled myself into the saddle.

I rode Mariah through the cave. I couldn't have walked if my life depended on it, and I wanted to see how she managed it on her own. I loosened the reins, flattened myself on her back and held on tight. She flew through the tunnel and leaped through the falls. We landed in the middle of the pool on the other side near the place she exited last time.

How had she found this tunnel? What would possess a horse to go through it? This goes against their nature. Why hadn't she been too scared of the thunder and lightning to go back home? I'll never know.

The first time I rode her, Mariah had been in a big hurry to get me to 1891. This ride had been different. Except for the race through the tunnel, she'd been willing to settle into a slower pace. I know I'm attributing human rationale to a horse, but on the first ride Mariah seemed eager to get me to Lexy. Maybe *she* wanted to get to Lexy. After all, she hadn't shown much remorse about throwing me off and running away. If I hadn't been a master tracker, I would never have found her. I'm kidding, right?

I found Lexy by the lake where she'd said she'd be, wearing the same faded dress. Probably the only one she had. She read while she waited, sitting on a dozing work mule. She looked up, saw me, slipped the book in her pocket and waved an enthusiastic greeting.

"This is Jeremiah," she said, indicating the huge animal. "Aunt Mattie went on a trip. I'm supposed to be at her place feeding her chickens and checking on livestock. She has two cows and a calf. If she wants to call them her livestock, who am I to argue?" As she talked, she leaned down to rub behind Mariah's ears. "Come with me? We can visit on the way."

Mariah and Jeremiah seemed to know each other. There was none of that squealing, stomping, snorting stuff horses do when getting acquainted.

"Uh, how far is it," I asked.

"Not far at all," she promised.

Famous last words. Why do I ever believe her? We'd already gone about three miles when Lexy said, "We're approaching the Kiowa camp." She wiggled her fingers in the direction of teepees scattered along a stream.

The village buzzed with activity. As we rode in, we were enveloped by vibrant colors and a cacophony of life. Copper-skinned children screamed as they chased each other around tents and through the trees. Dogs of assorted shapes and sizes stopped barking at their heels to bark at our horses. Women carrying pots of water from the stream called to others weeding a cornfield, their conversations dotted with bursts of laughter as they worked.

In stark contrast, the men of the tribe seemed to be conducting somber business. They sat in a circle under a giant oak, their voices low. Yesterday the pictures I'd seen of a Kiowa camp in a history book were black and white, and slightly out of focus. Quite a contrast to this sharp, colorful, and noisy panorama.

I heard haunting strains of a flute. When I'd first heard the flute at Tribes, the magical notes transported my mind back through time. Now I'm physically here. The melody had a life of its own. I wondered if it echoed through trees playing hide and seek in the forest like the Indian children when no one was around.

"The Kiowa people treasure the flute as a gift from the Great Spirit," Lexy explained. "His breath gives us life. Their breath gives life to the flute. They give thanks to the tree that gave the wood," Lexy went on, pushing a wisp of windblown hair from her eyes. "The talent to create a flute that can produce tones that pure is rare."

Their relationship with the "Great Spirit" must be better than mine. I had a flash back to a Sunday morning sitting on a hard church pew while Margaret pounded out *Bringing in the Sheaves* on the piano. A lady behind me sang, "We will come rejoicing—" in a thin reedy voice missing notes she should've never tried to hit. I remember not being able to get comfortable because of the bruises on the backs of my legs and cramps from being locked in a small space all night. Was the Kiowa's Great Spirit the same God who allowed little girls to be locked in dark scary places? The God I'd begged for protection?

"Lexy." a voice called. A young woman emerged from the group working in the garden and ran toward us.

Lexy greeted her in a language I didn't understand, and they chatted. Then Lexy said in English, "This is my friend, Moonflower."

"Moonflower. What a lovely name." I smiled.

"It's what Lexy calls me," Moonflower said in English. "The Kiowa word is much longer. It means 'flower that blooms beneath the little sun.'"

"This is my friend, Ali," Lexy said. "She's uh—not from around here."

"That's a bit of an understatement," I muttered.

"We're on our way to check on Aunt Mattie's animals," Lexy said.

Mariah stomped her impatience at the delay.

"Be watchful for the warring Apaches roaming this area," Moonflower warned. "They're angry at the horse soldiers and they're massacring everyone in their path. They recently attacked a Kiowa camp upriver. No one survived. The council decides what to do." Moonflower did a Vanna White gesture toward the group of men. "James White Eagle is here." She uttered his name with reverence. It was as if she'd murmured, 'POTUS is among us'. "You should be safe," she added. "You are with the Ghost Horse and Ghost Woman."

"Ghost Woman?" Lexy looked confused.

Moonflower nodded toward me.

"What?" I said.

"Apaches were on their way to attack our camp. When they saw Ghost Woman and Ghost Horse walk through the rock wall, they were frightened. Powerful magic. An omen. They did not attack."

"So, they did see my horse," I fought a ridiculous urge to be irritated.

"They were afraid? Of Ali? Why?" Lexy's incredulous tone was rather rude and totally uncalled for.

"She showed no fear," Moonflower explained. "She became angry. She waved them away with loud words."

"They didn't look frightened. I was looking for my horse." Neither Lexy nor I mentioned the tunnel behind the waterfall. I remembered stomping my foot. Nice touch.

"Goodness, Ali. You saved Johnny and me, too." Lexy exclaimed with new respect. "I'd been between the Apaches and the Kiowa camp."

Moonflower edged closer. She hesitantly patted Mariah's shoulder and my knee. "You are both real," she whispered. "How do you get through the rock?"

I smiled my mysterious Mona Lisa smile. Seriously, it's very mysterious. I've practiced it in front of a mirror.

Moonflower seemed unimpressed. "Our warriors had not been ready for an attack," she said. "The Apaches would have killed us all. We did not know of danger. The Great Spirit often protects the unaware pure of heart from peril. The Great Spirit sent Ali."

"Interesting," I said. This is a bigger deal than I thought.

"Since we speak of danger," Moonflower added, "do not go to Aunt Mattie's today. A devil storm comes this way. James White Eagle says so."

"We'll be okay," Lexy said, looking up into a cloudless sky.

"He's never wrong," Moonflower said. There was that quality of reverence in her voice again. It piqued my curiosity. I've never been in the presence of greatness.

"Who is this White Eagle guy?" I asked.

Moonflower looked as though I'd blasphemed. "Leader, father, advisor of the Kiowa nation. He has no wife or children. He lives in the wind, goes where he pleases, appears when needed."

"Why is he here now?" Lexy asked.

Moonflower shifted the basket she carried from one hip to the other. "The warring Apaches bring us great concern. If they attack white settlements, they bring trouble to all tribes. White people do not know one tribe from another."

"You're saying your tribe could suffer for what another tribe does?" I asked.

"Yes," Moonflower said. "We could be punished for harm caused by another tribe. The horse soldiers do not care. They kill everyone. The orders come from powerful white men who live far away. They know nothing of our people."

Government hasn't changed much in a hundred years, I realized.

A man who had been sitting with the tribal council rose in one fluid motion. He moved toward us like a panther. Not stalking, a muscular loose easy stride. His copper face, smooth and unlined, glowed with good health. His hair, worn in a single braid, was snow white.

"Speaking of James White Eagle, he comes this way." Moonflower looked as though she might faint. As he neared, I felt I might also. Like the ever-present hawk, his eyes found their target and bored a hole through me.

Chapter Nineteen

You are Ghost Woman. Apaches fear you," James White Eagle said, cutting to the chase. He wasn't handsome, exactly, but I couldn't have pulled my eyes from his face if my life depended on it. I swallowed hard. It wasn't a question. I didn't know how to respond. Oh, who am I kidding? I couldn't respond.

He needed no affirmation. "You have come to this time and place from a distant land." He spoke deliberately in perfect English.

"Yes," I said, not even wondering how he knew both were true.

"You have saved many lives. Not only this camp but other camps the Apaches intended to destroy, and white settlements, too."

I gulped.

"You have been chosen. Much responsibility is on your shoulders. Evil forces oppose you. The Great Spirit protects you. Still, you must be wise. Do not miss the guides he sends." White Eagle's gaze was steady, his eyes clear.

I felt as though he looked deep into my soul. Like back in 7th grade Lit class when Mr. Harman could reduce me to tears with a look.

"Do you understand?" he asked.

"No."

"Always follow the hawk. There are other guides. The Sister of Your Heart." He indicated Lexy. "The two of you will learn much from each other. She will teach you. You will teach her."

"Will I find my mother?"

"A smiling woman waits for you. You will go to her in a long white dress."

Don't know what that means, but it sounds nice.

"An evil man attempted to kill you."

"Yes," I whispered.

"He will again. But you will find strength to fight. Your past has prepared you."

"I don't want to find strength to fight. I am not good at fighting. I need a massage."

Moonflower, shocked that I had the audacity to speak to White Eagle, stepped away from me like I was in danger of being struck by lightning.

"You have power you know not of," White Eagle continued as though I hadn't interrupted. "You will show greatness. You were born for this time."

"Which time?" I asked. Come on, it was a reasonable question. I wouldn't be born for over a hundred years.

Moonflower looked as though she'd passed a kidney stone. She turned green.

"Time. And time again. You were led to the portal to change history for your family—her family." His chin jutted toward Lexy. He waved two fingers between us. "Many will suffer if you fail. But you will not." He turned and was gone.

"Wait. What? I have questions." I yelled after him.

He never looked back.

"He spoke to you." Moonflower's eyes were round with shock. "He never speaks to women," she whispered. "Ever."

"Well, that explains why he has no children," Lexy said.

"'Time and time again'? What does that mean?" I asked. "That freaked me out."

I don't do well with responsibility. I'm a follower. I don't want to find strength to fight. Someone else can fight evil. Someone better equipped. Someone with a Wonder Woman bracelet. My voice raised three octaves. "I was born for this time? What?"

"Like Queen Esther," Lexy said. "For such a time as this."

"So, he's Mordecai? From the Bible?" I asked. "I'm going to save the Jewish nation?"

"Probably not," Lexy said. "We need to get going." She urged a reluctant Jeremiah out of his slack-hipped stance. It involved a lot of kicking and arm waving. She waved goodbye to Moonflower over her shoulder.

My stomach tied itself in knots. James White Eagle's words terrified me. If they proved to be true, I would *not* show signs of greatness. I know me better than that. The "Great Spirit" chose the wrong girl. Lexy should tell him that. Why am I out here fighting rattlesnakes, and dodging renegade Indians? I need safety. Security. Convenience. A recliner. A pedicure.

"Lexy, turn around." I ordered. "I changed my mind. I'm not going to Aunt Mattie's."

"You will be fine," Lexy said. "You have been chosen for greatness."

Sarcasm. She's miffed. "I want to go back. A storm is coming."

"We don't know that."

"Yes, we do. James White Eagle said so. He's never wrong."

"Ali, if I worried about everything that could happen, I'd never get out of bed. I'm too busy dodging the things that are happening."

"Yeah, but…."

"When the time comes to worry, I'll let you know."

Well, that was presumptuous. "Yeah, but…."

"For pity sake. Think about something else."

"I don't like you," I huffed.

She ignored me. I could have gone back by myself, but I didn't because I was afraid of—what? Apaches? Irritating Lexy?

The trail narrowed. Lexy, riding Jeremiah, dropped in behind me, which was a good thing. I was too frazzled to talk. Frazzled is a good word to describe how I felt. It's a cross between fright and frustration. I think.

That's good. Ursula, my counselor, would like for me to be aware of how I'm feeling 'in the moment'. I forget to do that. I usually don't know how I feel. If Ursula was here right now, she'd ask why I'm upset. So, I thought about that. I'm frustrated Lexy doesn't care I'm afraid of weather and Apaches and want to go back. Maybe I'm angry with myself because I'm not standing up for what I want. As usual. Okay, I'm getting somewhere. See how well I worked through that? Ursula would be proud.

Ursula says my actions are mostly fear driven. She's right. I've been working on that. She says I stay in situations that 'aren't productive' because I'm afraid of change or I'm afraid people won't like me if I make waves. I think she sees my relationship with David as a more benign version of my relationship with Margaret, but she hasn't said so. She's waiting for me to figure it out.

Ursula is European, probably German. She speaks with an accent that I find charming. But then, I'm from Dallas. Anyone without a Texas accent sounds foreign. She has faded graying-blond hair, which she wears in an elaborate braid thing on top of her head. She's probably sixtyish, and rather matronly. She's also probably the sole reason I'm sane. Her office is the only place I've ever felt truly safe.

Ursula uses a lot of 'feel' words. When she asked me to choose a word that I felt best described me, after considerable thought, I came up with 'insignificant'. I got Mr. Webster's opinion of the word. He says it means 'without importance'. Another dictionary said, 'that which is without meaning'. Yep, that pretty much sums me up.

That's why James White Eagle's words scared me. He predicted that I will be a heroine in a story I don't want to be in. That would involve me stepping up and stepping out. I'm better at blending in. If people don't notice me, they don't have to decide if they like me—especially people like Stormy who instantly decided she didn't. But come to think of it, I don't like me much either.

Chapter Twenty

The trail widened. Lexy rode up beside me again.

"Moonflower speaks English well," I said, in an attempt to prove I'm more mature than I've acted. Too late.

"She was one of Aunt Mattie's first students," Lexy said. "She learned quickly. I wish I'd picked Kiowa up as fast. It's a difficult language. Full of consonants most of us can't distinguish or pronounce."

"You spoke it quite well to Moonflower," I said.

"Thanks. The Kiowa people tease me but welcome me into their village. I've learned so much from them."

"Like what?" I asked preoccupied with James White Eagle's warning.

"Life. Kiowas believe the Great Spirit inhabits all the earth. Dirt, rocks, sky, water, trees, animals, and people. There's a—" she searched for a word.

"Continuity?" I suggested.

"Yes."

"What else have you learned?"

"Moonflower told me about escaping enemies by erasing tracks as her people fled."

"How?" I glanced at the sky but pretended to be interested.

"She said she cut cedar branches and followed behind them sweeping footprints away so her people couldn't be tracked. They escaped. But when they returned to the village, they found everything destroyed."

"Wouldn't the enemies see brush marks from the branches?" I asked.

"In this wind? In case you haven't noticed it blows all the time in Oklahoma."

"I'm sure that information will come in handy," I muttered sarcastically.

"You never know when knowledge will be useful," Lexy admonished.

We're the same age. Why does she seem like a wiser big sister?

"Many tribes believe the spirits of ancestors inhabit animals," Lexy continued, "giving them wisdom, protection, and guidance. Hawks, for example, are a symbol of life. They believe we move to another plane after death. We can still see what is happening on earth possibly as a wolf, eagle or hawk."

That caught my attention. "Do you believe it?"

"Have you ever looked into the eyes of a wolf?"

"No. When would I have looked into the eyes of a wolf?"

"Oh. Well, I haven't either," she admitted.

"Hmmm." I thought about that. "Wonder whose spirit inhabits the hawk that constantly follows me." I'd already told her about the rattlesnake thing.

"Maybe mine," Lexy said.

"That can't be. You haven't died."

"Well, I'm not going to live for a hundred years," Lexy pointed out. "So, maybe."

Her words reminded me I hadn't found her grave yesterday. But I didn't want to get into that now. In fact, I don't want to contemplate Lexy's death at all.

"Do you have an ancestor who died recently?" she asked.

"My grandmother. She died the day I disappeared 28 years ago. This is crazy and I don't believe it for a minute, but I've seen pictures of her with me and she looked quite protective. She was a little thing but...."

"Though she be but little, she be fierce," Lexy said.

"How do you know Shakespeare?" I asked.

"Aunt Mattie has *A Midsummer Night's Dream.*" She taught me to read with it."

"You grew up reading Shakespeare?" She speaks Kiowa and quotes Shakespeare. She's full of surprises. I wondered if this is how Daydreon saw me.

I glanced at the sky again behind us. I was stunned to see a bank of dark clouds building in the southwest. "Lexy, can we please go back?"

"We're almost there." She urged a balky Jeremiah to walk faster but kept an eye on the sky. "Look, there's your hawk."

I looked where she pointed. A red-tailed hawk hung in the sky over the valley as though suspended from the billowing clouds. Strange. There wasn't a whisper of wind. The only sounds that broke the silence were the shriek of the hawk and hooves on the rocky path.

"I don't suppose it's the same one," I said. "How would he have gotten through the tunnel."

"If that is your hawk, he's a she."

"Really? How can you tell?"

"Female hawks are larger than males," Lexy said. "They're often mistaken for eagles. That's a big hawk."

I made a mental note to Google hawks when I get back to my room. *If* I get back. The sky suddenly looked fierce. The cloud base had lowered and turned black. Ragged tails hung from it in several places. I no longer tried to keep the alarm from my voice.

"Lexy, look." I screamed over my shoulder.

"Okay, time to worry. Go," she shouted to be heard above the wind, "Jeremiah isn't as fast as Mariah. We'll catch up. It's down there." She pointed to a little house and barn in the valley.

I loosened the reins. Mariah needed no urging. She raced over the rocky terrain.

Lightning snaked sideways across the sky ripping it open. Rain gushed out at an alarming rate. Thunder exploded in stereo. Mariah slid down the steep trail. I gritted my teeth and braced against the saddle. In a matter of minutes rain had turned the clay trail into a slick mass.

Not quite a mile behind us the cloud dropped a funnel. Like a runaway freight train, it swirled up debris as it roared down upon us. Chunks of ice splattered with the force of bullets, stinging exposed skin.

Mariah slid down the trail practically on her nose. She tripped, throwing me forward. I grabbed the saddle horn. Amazingly, the game little mare recovered and landed on level ground at a full run.

When we reached the house, I pulled on the reins. Mariah slid to a stop; rear legs tucked beneath her. I slid down her rump and landed hard on the ground, jarring my teeth, and biting my tongue. This is the second time in a week I sat on the ground and watched that mare run into the woods. The first time I'd merely been shot at. This time rain and debris made seeing her virtually impossible. The ground vibrated beneath me from the force of the tornado which had marked me for death.

Jeremiah plodded to a stop beside me. Lexy slid off, grabbed my arm, and yanked me to my feet. I staggered toward the house. "No." she screamed above the wail of the wind, "This way."

She ran in the opposite direction. I tasted blood as I trudged along behind her, my legs heavy as lead. It was like wading through quicksand. Not that I've ever done that. But then, I've never been in a tornado either. My feet slipped on the slick clay and I went down hard, landing on a jagged rock. With detached fascination, I watched blood from my knee mix with rain and stream down my leg in crimson rivulets.

Lexy jerked me to my feet again. "Get up."

I stared at her. "Who are you? Simon Legree?"

She grabbed both shoulders and shook me. "I can't move this boulder by myself. You have to help." The wind blew the words away, but I read her lips. She leaned into a chunk of sandstone the size of a recliner.

"Are you crazy? We can't move that."

"Yes, we can. Aunt Mattie does it by herself."

My legs wouldn't hold me. I collapsed in a heap.

"You've got to help." She jerked me to my feet and slapped me. Hard.

I wanted to rip her head off. Instead, I shook off the fog, leaned my shoulder into the boulder and pushed.

Behind us limbs and small trees crashed to the ground which trembled with the fury of the storm. Debris swirled in the air. Rocks and sticks pummeled us from all directions as the freight train rumbled ever closer.

I'm going to die. The thought settled into my brain. The irony of my death happening over a hundred years before my birth wasn't lost on me. Leave it to me to set that kind of record. I'd be in the Guinness Book of World Records except my body would never be found so nobody would know. Again. I would simply disappear from my family. Without a trace. Like Jimmy Hoffa. I laughed, proving I'm way beyond hysterical.

"Ali," Lexy screamed. "Stop lolly-gaggin'."

"Sorry," I mumbled.

"It rolls. We have to get it started."

Yeah, right. I nodded, too weak to argue.

A surge of air lifted me then set me back down. My mouth flew open, but the wind blew my scream, along with what felt like a pigeon, back down my throat. I lunged against the rock and fought for footing.

The boulder moved. Ever so slightly at first. But Lexy was right. Once it gave, rolling it away from the opening was easier.

I heard a crack and a loud crash. Blinded by rain, I could see nothing. Lexy grabbed my arm and yanked me into the root cellar. I fell into the hole. A limb the size of Shaquille O'Neal crashed to the ground where I'd stood only seconds before.

Chapter Twenty-One

I landed on top of Lexy and froze, a paralyzed bunny, unable to breathe. The storm roared over us like a giant Hoover sucking up everything in its path. I expected any second for both of us to be pulled up out of that hole. The wind howled outside our make-shift storm cave for what seemed like an eternity. It finally dawned on me that we were safe. We didn't die. My heart rate returned to normal. Lexy shoved me off her lap rather rudely and began shaking violently. Must be delayed shock. Bless her heart.

"Lexy, honey, we are okay."

The shaking increased.

I turned around to comfort her. She wasn't crying. She was laughing.

Seeing my shocked expression, she laughed harder.

"We almost died. What is so dang funny?" I demanded.

"We…we…" She was laughing too hard to talk. "We almost died," she finally choked out. She grabbed her sides and doubled over. "That was close."

Her laughter made me angrier than I'd been when she slapped me, which seemed like a weird reaction even to me. I'll have to ask Ursula about that. I'm savvy. I know ROFL means 'rolling on the floor laughing'. I've never seen anyone do it. Until now.

I was still mad at not being let in on the big joke, but in spite of myself I started laughing too. Laughter really is contagious. Before long we were both laughing uproariously. It felt good. Cleansing.

After a while we realized the roar above us had subsided. Lexy regained control and wiped her eyes. We looked at each other and started laughing again. When we finally stopped, I looked around at my surroundings. The root cellar was nothing more than a large hole dug into the side of a hill with wooden shelves containing jars of canned goods jammed into one side. Roots from the oak had pushed through the walls.

Finally, Lexy stood. "That was fun."

"Fun?" I gasped. "Fun? You are seriously demented. We almost died."

"Hush." she said. "We didn't. Let's go outside and see if anything is left."

"No, seriously, there is something wrong with you," I said. "When God made you, He lost a part."

She balanced precariously on one leg then hobbled toward the exit.

"My leg went to sleep. Probably from you sitting on it," she said.

"Once we landed, I was too scared to move. Sorry." I got up and followed her.

The limb blocking the exit kicked my claustrophobia into overdrive. We managed to push enough branches aside to slither through and escape before I made a spectacle of myself. We emerged from the root cellar into a shaft of sunlight. I looked up into an incredibly blue sky.

"Quite a change in the weather," I said. Al Roker would have been proud of my astute observation.

A bird chirped tentatively as though afraid his nervous twittering might bring back the storm. His cautious song was joined by another voice, then another, and suddenly, the air was filled with a joyous chorus of celebration.

"How do we find Mariah?" I asked.

Finding her was the foremost thing on my mind. Lexy stuck two fingers in her mouth and whistled. The mare, wild eyed and snorting, galloped out of the woods, with Jeremiah lumbering after her. Although Lexy and I ran our hands over them several times, we found no injuries. Even the saddle wasn't scratched. Except for being skittish, Mariah seemed fine. I breathed a sigh of relief and flung my arms around her neck. I'm crazy about that mare. I removed her saddle and bridle knowing she would stay close.

"Let's find out what's left of the house." Lexy ran backwards up the hill watching to see if I was coming.

The little sod house stood intact. The yard, looking like a war zone, was littered with debris, branches, Aunt Mattie's tools, and a dead chicken. We spent the next few of hours salvaging what we could, rounding up the cows and calf, and retrieving the surviving chickens.

I ran my hand over the thick, rough sod wall of Aunt Mattie's house. History had not been my favorite subject but seeing it up close was fun. Well, part of it, anyway. Do history book authors compete, I wondered, to see who could make facts, figures, and dates the most boring? It's such a gift to have a teacher who can make a dull subject like history come alive for her students—get them involved. I never had one of those.

Aunt Mattie's house was larger and more substantial than I'd expected. The fuzzy photos at the library didn't do this house justice. Sod rectangles formed the outside walls. They'd be capable of keeping out the most wicked north wind. Flowered wallpaper covered plasterboard on interior walls. Gingham curtains framed the windows, which to my surprise, were actually glass and unbroken. The earthen floor, hard as tile, had been treated.

"What are these fibers in the bricks?" I asked, as Lexy walked up.

"Buffalo grass roots. Uncle Les brought a sod plow with him," Lexy began. Her answers are usually short stories. This one wouldn't end quickly.

"I would think most men would," I said.

"Covered wagons don't hold much," Lexy explained. "Our wagon was full of kids. We brought bedding and food for the journey, the plow, and little else."

Lexy gathered up trash as she talked. "When other settlers saw this house, they wanted one like it. The secret is the buffalo grass. The roots, dense and compact, hold the soil together. They go down six feet. Only Uncle Les had a sod plow."

Lexy handed me trash and I followed her to the pile she'd been making.

"This house is similar to ours," Lexy continued, "Uncle Les plowed up the sod for the bricks and when they dried, he helped Pa build it. The bricks had to be baked by the sun."

"What happened when they ran out buffalo grass?" I asked.

"The Kiowas showed Uncle Les where to find more. It was a good trade. Along with beads and sewing supplies, Aunt Mattie brought seeds. She taught the women how to sew, and plant and cultivate a garden. She was an instant hit. They taught her how to find medicinal herbs and showed her where to find edible berries. When there was plenty, the men brought fresh meat. Uncle Les repaid them for the meat and for helping him find buffalo grass by buying them needed supplies at the trading post—garden tools, etc. Friendship with the Kiowas brought us protection from other tribes. But now with the Apaches having their bloomers in a tangle…"

I smiled at the image.

Lexy struck a match and tossed it into the pile of trash we'd gathered. "Are you getting hungry?" Not waiting for an answer, she picked up the dead chicken. In no time, she had it gutted, plucked, and cleaned.

"We're going to eat that?" I asked.

"Of course," Lexy said, "you do eat chicken, don't you?"

"But it's dead."

"They don't like it much when you eat them alive." She glanced up and grinned.

"Mine comes from the supermarket."

Lexy washed the chicken, patted salt into the skin, stuffed the cavity with herbs, poked a sapling through it and placed it over the pile of burning branches.

"Well, Your Royal Highness, there was a loaf of bread and butter in the pantry," she said. "Would Her Nibs mind grabbing a jar of sand plum jelly from the root cellar while I finish this?"

I minded, but I went.

Lexy pulled green onions from the garden and picked cucumbers and tomatoes. She washed and sliced them while I found a crusty loaf of bread in the house to go with the sand plum jelly. She poured buttermilk, which she'd retrieved from the cistern with the churned butter. I'd convinced myself I wouldn't like buttermilk, but I was wrong.

Lunch was delicious. My brush with death had heightened my senses. Or maybe I was starving. It had been a long time since I'd scarfed down the egg and sausage breakfast burrito I'd picked up at Sonic.

"Do you want to talk about why the root cellar scares you?" Lexy asked.

"Not really," I said. I'd told her a little about my childhood before we got to the Kiowa camp, but I've never talked to anyone, except Ursula about the aftershock of Margaret's abuse—the claustrophobia, fear of dark places, nightmares, and inability to trust anyone enough to let them get close to me.

"I would like to know more about you. We are becoming friends," Lexy said.

I looked into her honest blue eyes. She could be trusted.

Lexy leaned toward me, her eyes glued to my face. She listened with the rapt attention of one hearing the first news reports of 9/11.

"Land sakes," Lexy exclaimed when I finished, "How awful."

"I couldn't think about anything but the tornado when we jumped into the root cellar. But then the limb fell over the opening."

She nodded. She understood. Which goes a long way to make up for how irritating she can be. How pathetic that I'm desperate to be listened to. In my defense, I've never had that. Lexy not only listened, but she also understood.

We gathered up tools the storm had scattered and took them to what was left of the barn. I carried a hammer and screwdriver as I followed Lexy back to the root cellar. The tornado had taken out the top of the tree, but most of it remained intact. Lexy pointed to a heart carved below the first fork.

"Thank goodness this is okay. We'd have to bury Aunt Mattie if it wasn't."

"Love will guide us," I read. The inscription had been carved into the tree inside a large heart. I traced the outline with my finger. "There's gotta be a story behind this. I don't suppose I'm in danger of you not telling me."

"Only if you insist." Lexy gazed up at the carving for inspiration. "Uncle Les and Aunt Mattie had recently moved out here. It was their anniversary," Lexy began in a dramatic voice. What makes Lexy's stories appealing is she tells them with such relish, believes them so strongly and dares me not to be carried away by them. Of course, I always am.

Lexy sat down cross-legged in the grass under the tree and pulled her bloomers above her knees. Visible tan lines were evidence that this was not a rare occurrence. I sank into the grass beside her, picked up the hammer and screwdriver and began chiseling my initials into the boulder beside the root cellar. Not the initials of the old me scaredy-cat Allison Taft. The new me—Alexandra Dale Forrest—woman who stares down rattle snakes, out runs tornados, and, with a little help from Lexy, dominated this boulder.

"They were young and homesick," Lexy explained. "If they hadn't sold the wagon, they probably would have turned around and gone back East. We hadn't come out yet, so they were lonely, exhausted, and depressed. Aunt Mattie felt trapped. This was Uncle Les' gift to her. He spent the whole afternoon carving it. You would have thought he'd given her a gold mine. Nobody visits without being drug out here to see this tree and hear the story."

"It's a nice story," I said. "Sort of sad, though."

"I worry about what will happen when these lands are opened in the run. Aunt Mattie won't have a chance of getting this piece of land. A young whippersnapper on a fast horse will snap it up." Lexy swiped angrily at a tear and left a smudge on her cheek.

"That's not going to happen, Lexy. I read a history book yesterday in the library. This area of Oklahoma Territory was distributed in lotteries, not a land run. People registered at a fort."

"Ft Sill or Ft. Reno?" Lexy asked. "How did they register?"

"I don't know. I should have paid more attention. They provided ID I guess."

"What's that?"

"You know—drivers licenses." Okay, I realized how stupid that was. "Verification that they're who they say they are."

"If that's true, Elmer might not stop us from getting land. We only have Jeremiah. Pa wouldn't have gotten any worthwhile land riding an old mule in a land run."

"Probably not," I agreed. My initials finished, I started the date—8.16.1891—the day we cheated death. "This boulder will be a monument to our triumph for years to come." A woman on a mission, I carved with renewed strength.

"We'll never have anything if we can't get land." Lexy said. She slapped a mosquito on her knee. "Pa and the boys would always have to work for others."

"Does your pa know what land he wants?"

"Sure. The land around the swimming hole. The canyon walls make a natural fence, as well as a wind break. There's lots of water. Good water, because of the lake, and the soil is so rich you could eat it with a spoon. Elmer has it now, but he didn't possess it legally. If Pa can get that land, maybe I won't have to marry Elmer."

"You're getting married? Who is Elmer?"

"A toad. Elmer Perdue. The rancher Pa works for. He brought a herd of cattle from Texas. He's claimed most of the good land already." Misery clouded her eyes. "Ma'am thinks if I marry him, he'll let us live on his land, since we'd be family and all."

"Why did you say he's a toad?"

"He looks like a toad. He's squatty like a toad—square with no neck. The Hispanic men who work for him call him Cerro Sappo which means toad mountain. He's enormous. I feel sorry for his horse."

"Who wouldn't want to marry that? Surely your mother won't make you marry a man you don't love."

"Ma'am don't put much stock in love. She says it's my duty to keep my family safe. Like me marrying Elmer would be a guarantee. I'd always be making him mad."

"Does he want to marry you?" I asked, thinking a mother who would coerce her daughter to marry an amphibian is no better than one who locked her daughter in a closet.

"I don't know. He wants what he wants now. He's getting more brazen about it. If he ever catches me alone, I'll be in trouble."

"Is there no law out here?" I asked.

"He who has the power is the law. That would be Elmer. That's why he gets by with taking whatever he wants. He'd steal a dead man's pine box. His men are as bad, or worse."

"No scruples, huh?"

"If the Rafferty's have 'em, they stole 'em." Lexy said.

"Are you saying there would be no repercussions if he raped you?"

"If I told. Pa and my brothers would go after him. But they wouldn't have a chance against Elmer's men. They'd be beaten. Or killed."

I stopped working and stared at her. She angrily swiped at the tears in her eyes with the back of her hand. She hurriedly changed the subject by examining my work.

"Beautiful," she decreed.

Mount Rushmore, it isn't, but I'm proud.

Lexy leaned forward to pick a wildflower. That's when I saw the necklace, hanging from a black velvet ribbon around her neck, hidden inside her dress.

"Your necklace," I breathed. "My mother's worn it in every picture. Where did you get it?"

"Grandpa gave it to grandma. He got it from his mother who lived in Europe. Granny left it to Aunt Mattie, who doesn't have a daughter. She gave it to me." Lexy grinned. "She may have done it for spite. If she set out to irritate Ma'am, she did just fine."

"Your mother isn't happy for you?" I'm beginning to pick up on the fact that Lexy's relationship with her mother is as bad as mine was with Margaret. In life's poker hand, Lexy and I both drew uncaring maternal figures. We have more in common than I realized.

"Ma'am was not so happy. She didn't want it but was mad I got it." Lexy smiled. "I like the idea that you'll wear it, too."

"I'm glad you have it now." I stood. My back hurt from sitting in a cramped position. I bent and stretched. "I have to be going. I want to get back before dark."

"I'm coming with you," Lexy announced.

"Where?"

"To your time. Nobody expects me home tonight. You can bring me back tomorrow. I want to see how you live."

"No. Absolutely not."

Excitement sparkled in Lexy's eyes. "It will be so much fun. What could go wrong?"

I thought of about forty things.

Chapter Twenty-Two

I'd tried to prepare Lexy for how different things would be here. Impossible, right? But when we emerged from the tunnel into the present century, nothing appeared different. The canyons looked pretty much the same on both sides of the tunnel—deserted and remote. Even Jackson's barn and make-shift horse corral could have been in 1891.

But things changed fast starting with my car.

"What is this?" Lexy slipped into the passenger seat.

"My car," I said. "It's how I get around."

"Around what?"

"It takes me where I need to go. You'll see." I fastened her seat belt.

"What makes it go?"

"Combustion," I said, like that explained everything. I think that's right, but what the heck does it mean?

"What's combustion?" she asked.

"I turn this key and that makes the spark plugs fire, and I'm lost from there."

"Does it go fast?"

"You'll think it's pretty fast." But if I'd worried about speed scaring Lexy, I shouldn't have. She loved everything from the wind in her hair to the country music blaring from the radio. She asked thousands of questions.

As we passed poles and highline wires I tried to explain electricity, but at Lexy's blank stare, I gave up. "You'll see when we get to my room," I said.

She stood behind me looking around as I unlocked the door.

"Ta da," I said, flipping on the light switch and stepping aside.

"How did you do that?" Lexy demanded, walking past me into the room. She marveled at its cool temperature and wanted to see everything at once. She considered the bathroom a miracle. She was astounded that a toilet, in the house, no less, could be used and running water carried waste out of sight.

I'd left the room in a mess. While I made the bed and straightened up, Lexy poked around looking at everything. She found a paperback and began reading while I took a shower and did my hair and make-up.

"Make me look like that," she requested, looking up from the book. She popped a handful of roasted peanuts in her mouth and chewed like she was starving. "I love these things." She often speaks in exclamation points. Her enthusiasm knows no bounds.

I lifted Lexy's hair, letting it run through my fingers. "Let's start here. That hot sun you live in is murder. We'll trim the dry ends and do a deep conditioning. I'm going to layer it a bit like mine. It will give you more volume."

"How is cutting my hair going to make it louder?"

"Fuller." I laughed out loud. I've laughed more with Lexy than I have in my entire life. I've never known anyone like her. I'm even getting used to spontaneous hugs.

After the conditioner had time to do its magic I said, "Let's get you in the shower and get that washed out." I adjusted the water temperature, pointing out the soap, shampoo, and washcloth. I closed the glass shower door. Lexy was stomping, squealing and splashing like a delighted child. For someone who lives with no running water, a warm shower must be heaven.

Lexy sang an Irish folk song. It's upbeat lilting melody belied the fact the song was about a man slowly dying in a dungeon for killing his unfaithful sweetheart. It went on and on until she finally emerged dripping from the shower wrapped in a towel. She raved about its softness and absorbency, sounding like a Downy commercial. I take a lot for granted.

I blow dried Lexy's hair, plugged in the curling iron and started on her makeup while it heated. When I finished, we stood side by side looking at our reflection.

"Our resemblance really is amazing, isn't it?" Lexy said. "We could be twins." She screamed. Her hand clutched her throat.

I jumped away. "What's wrong?"

"My necklace is gone."

"Calm down."

"If it came off in one of those canyons, I'll never find ..."

"Stop. Let me think."

"Or when we came through that tunnel ..." She was on the verge of screaming again.

"That's it." I clapped my hand over her mouth.

"What's it?" she mumbled between my fingers.

"It happened when we came through the tunnel. It isn't lost. It's here. The necklace is in my mother's safety deposit box. It can't be in two different places on the same side of the tunnel."

"Are you sure?"

"Yes." I showed her a picture of my mother wearing it. "See, it's here."

"This is so strange," Lexy muttered.

"It gets stranger all the time," I agreed.

Lexy was fascinated by my television and promptly began calling it 'the picture'.

"Those girls on your picture were wearing trousers like you do. Can I?"

"Mine might fit you. But I'll have to wash them. I only brought two pairs."

"Washing clothes will take all day," Lexy complained.

"No, it won't," I said. "I'll go toss them in the washer and be right back."

"I'm coming with you. I want to see. Ma'am and I carry water from the river."

I threw her a pair of shorts and a t-shirt and waited by the door for her to put them on. "Bring your dress and bloomers. We'll wash them, too."

She gathered them up and followed me. At the door she stopped and pointed to the flat screen on the wall. "Hey, look at the people on your picture. What are they doing?"

I glanced at the TV. "A line dance."

"Let's go where they are and do that too, Ali."

"No."

"Why?"

"It could be dangerous for women alone at night."

She laughed. "You're serious?"

"I never go anywhere at night by myself."

"Why? Do Indians attack?"

"No. Well, maybe not. But all kinds of terrible things might happen."

"Nothing will happen. If it does, we will take care of it."

Lexy's rather superior tone ticked me off. "You've been in this century less than two hours and you're an expert? Do you know how to change a flat tire?" I shot back.

"What's a flat tire?"

"I rest my case."

"Nothing will happen. You have to stay alive to save your people." She flashed a mischievous grin. "Look, Ali, life is dangerous. Lawsy me, none of us are going to get out alive. So, while we're here, shouldn't we enjoy it?"

Lexy may be right, but I'm conceding nothing.

"I could get kidnapped," Lexy continued, "by drifters making their way home from the Civil War. I could get killed by a renegade band of Apaches any time I go to the river to do laundry. Rattlesnakes are everywhere. Elmer and his men are waiting to catch me alone. Then there's the plague. I live with danger. The things you are frightful of are in your head."

"The tornado wasn't in my head. Why should I listen to you?" Good point, why was I listening to her?

We could go to a movie. Do something sedate. Something safe. She would like that. She's not used to much. I seriously did not want to go bar hopping. David and I'd gone to Gilley's once and a friend of his had been injured. Why a fifty-year-old attorney who'd never been on a horse thought he could ride a bull—mechanical or otherwise—is beyond me. Maybe it was the four bottles of Tecate he'd downed, or he was impressing his buxom date. In any case, it had not gone well. We spent most of the night in E.R.

"Ali, you need more excitement in your life. We battled a tornado and won," Lexy said, dramatically. "It's exhilarating when you run the race and win. Paul said that in the Bible. We did that. And now you have at least one great story to tell your grandchildren. You don't want them to think you spent your life in a rocking chair."

"If I listen to you, I won't live long enough to have grandchildren."

"I want to get out of here and see how you live."

"I don't live at a dance club," I said. "There could be fights. Shootings."

"We'll duck."

"Well …" It was that look in her eyes. I couldn't say no.

"Woo hoo." She gave me a giant hug. "You won't regret this, Ali."

"I already do."

I went to get the jeans from the dryer and handed them to her. My clothes fit Lexy perfectly. We looked presentable. In fact, we looked pretty darn good.

If we're going to do this, let's get this party started," I said. I kind of liked the way that made me sound. Like a normal person who knew what it meant.

Lexy caught our reflection as we walked out the door. "Hey, we look like the people on your picture. We are going to have so much fun."

"Yeah, right," I said. "The best I can hope for is not to do jail time."

Chapter Twenty-Three

While the Blue Sage was not the Taj Mahal, it also wasn't the total dump I'd pictured. Located five miles outside of El Reno, it featured a live country band, a good-sized dancefloor, and thank goodness, no mechanical bulls.

Lexy and I elbowed our way through the crowd and found an unoccupied table. I went to get two beers and when I returned, she had already joined a line dance. When the song ended, she flopped into the chair across from me laughing and breathless.

"What are you drinking?" she asked.

"Beer," I said. "I didn't ask you what you wanted. You probably don't drink beer."

"I've never tasted it," she said. She sipped and wrinkled her nose. "I have to go to the lady's room. Weird name for an outhouse. I'll be right back." She two stepped her way across the floor.

While she was gone, I idly watched people dance. Most of them didn't know their right foot from their left. Others were quite good. On the far side of the dance floor, people had stopped dancing to watch a couple. The guy wore a melon-colored shirt. The gal wore jean shorts, an off-the-shoulder peasant blouse, and cowboy boots. They were doing a two step with a lot of intricate moves. He twirled her out and she spun back to him, ducking under his arm. He followed her and they did some fancy footwork in sync. The people in front of me moved aside and I gasped. I knew them. Lane and Stormy. When the music ended, they walked off the floor laughing, accepting compliments on the way.

I don't know why I'm shocked. Okay, I do know why I'm shocked. That dance could only be done by two people who dance together often or have practiced for hours. Either way, those two people have spent time together. A lot of time. I keep trying to convince myself they aren't a couple when they are. Why am I so crushed by that realization? I want to go home. I'm going to tell Lexy we have to leave. If she ever comes back.

Lexy returned to the table laughing with a bottle of water. When I asked who bought it for her, she shrugged, flashed a huge smile and downed half of it.

"Thanks." she shouted to be heard above the noise.

"For what?" I asked.

"Everything." She flung her arms out wide and turned in a circle. "I've never done anything like this. I am having such a good time."

Well. Great. I watched her with more than a hint of envy. Lexy throws herself into everything she does. With the lost necklace she wasn't merely upset, she was devastated. With the tornado she set out to beat it with determination. Tonight, she wasn't simply happy, she was ecstatic. What kind of person would drag her away from this? I plastered a campaign smile on my face and felt sanctimonious.

The guy who bought her the water hovered in the distance. As soon as she finished drinking, he appeared and whisked her away to dance. I occupied myself with watching people. I suddenly got the feeling I was the one being watched. I looked around. A tall man I'd never seen before leaned against the bar in the shadows. He wore jeans and a white t-shirt. He was too far away, and the place was too dark to be able to pick him out of a lineup if the need should arise. When our eyes locked, my unease jumped into overdrive. A chill crept down my spine. He didn't break eye contact or pretend he hadn't been watching me. Touching two fingers to his forehead in a small salute, he blended into the crowd and disappeared.

A hand clasped my shoulder. I jumped and screamed.

"Sorry, Sunflower. Didn't mean to scare you."

I looked around.

Lane grinned. "Wanna dance? They're playing our song."

"No," I snapped. "I can't dance, and we don't have a song."

"Yeah, we do." Lane set his bottle on the table next to mine.

He pulled me up and lead me to the dance floor. I just let him. I am such an idiot.

He found an empty space and drew me into his arms. He smelled like clean mountain air. He'd shaved. That melon-colored shirt accentuated his tan. He looked nothing like the man in the courthouse or the one under his Jeep the day I arrived in town or the one I drove to town from the cemetery.

"Where's your girlfriend?" I asked pointedly.

"Who?" He tried to look confused.

"Stormy isn't going to be happy about this."

"She'll get over it." He didn't deny it.

"I saw you dancing. You two are good."

"We're rusty. We won a dance contest in high school."

"High school? You've known her since high school?" I stopped dancing and stared.

"Since she was two, actually." The scent of cinnamon gum was familiar. He must buy it by the truckload.

"So why are you dancing with me?"

"You call this dancing? Your feet aren't moving." He grinned. White teeth in a tan face. I've heard the term 'dazzling smile'. I've just never seen one. Until now. I felt faint.

"I told you I can't dance," I gasped.

He gently traced the cut on my cheek with the back of his finger. "You didn't tell me what happened."

"I tripped," I said.

He smiled. "Come on, City Girl, what happened?"

"I am not a city girl."

"No? You're not from Dallas?"

"How did you know that?" I didn't know whether to be flattered or worried.

"You're here because...?"

"Lexy wanted to come."

"Ah, and Lexy would be your, uh… twin?"

"Right."

"Well, she seems to be having a good time." Lane chuckled.

Lexy danced by waving as though flagging a train.

"Subtlety isn't one of her virtues, is it?" Lane grinned.

I shook my head. "Apparently not."

"She's enjoying herself," Lane said.

"She always has a good time." And that, I realized, is the reason Lexy is so striking. Our features are alike but Lexy's love affair with life dances in her eyes.

"Hey, Ali," she called, craning her neck to see around the broad back of a man jitterbugging between us, "Are you safe with that guy?" She jerked her head in Lane's direction. "Or do I need to bust his kneecap?"

Lane answered for me. "She's safe. For now." He pulled me closer. His steps were smooth and sure. "Listen to the words of this song," he whispered. "I requested it. I've always loved it. The day you stumbled into the courthouse I knew I was in trouble."

"I did not stumble."

If you're lucky there will be a moment in your life that is so astounding you would give up all other moments in order to go on living that one forever. This was the moment. I never wanted to leave Lane Lanigan's arms. Until he showed up my life had been monochromatic. His arrival flipped a switch which flooded my universe with rainbows. I sound like a love-sick thirteen-year-old. But did I tell you about the rainbows? And that melon-colored shirt? He'd danced us close to the stage. The lead singer looked down at Lane and winked.

"You know Tracy Byrd?"

Lane grinned.

The words to *Keeper of the Stars* swirled in my head. I listened to them so intently, I stumbled, but managed not to trip Lane.

Chapter Twenty-Four

The words of the song echoed after the music stopped. The times Lane snubbed me in town flashed through my mind. I'd think about that later. This moment was too good. His face was mere inches from mine. His hands left my back and moved up. With my face cupped in his hands, he looked deeply into my eyes, as though reading everything written on my heart. Tonight, he had no mirrored sunglasses to hide behind. The answers to my questions were there. No man had ever looked at me with the intensity I saw in Lane's eyes. His dark lashes closed over the raw passions behind them. His eyes lowered to my lips and his mouth followed. In slow motion he lowered his head. His lips met mine, then melted into them. The kiss was exquisitely tender, but I felt it down to my toes. Our feet stopped moving. In fact, I'm pretty sure mine didn't touch the floor. I floated through time and space and …

"Lanigan. What the hell are you're doing?" Stormy demanded.

I crashed back to earth. Lane's head snapped up, tearing his lips from mine.

Feeling robbed, I rubbed my still tingling lips. Stormy stood three feet from us, hands on hips, looking fiercely gorgeous. She looked back and forth between us, not sure who to blame. Lightning flashed from her eyes leaving no doubt of how she got her name.

"Hi, Stormy," Lane said lamely. "You're, uh, back."

"Boy, Lanigan, nothing gets by you." She'd decided to throw her anger at Lane

"Except those three goons you're supposed to be watching. Remember? Where are they?"

"Uh, over there, talking to that guy at the bar?" Lane asked more than said.

"What guy? Isn't that the reason we're here? Aren't you supposed to be finding out who he is?" Stormy challenged. "Why are you over here kissing this blond bimbo?"

Lane looked around. "Uh..."

"Blond Bimbo?" I Pulled myself up to my full height, which was not too impressive since I'm a good five inches shorter than she is. "I resent that." I didn't know where to go from there. I should've added something scathing but couldn't think of anything. What I should have said will come to me at 3:00AM when I can't sleep because I'm still seething.

Stormy didn't dignify my retort with an answer. She looked at me as though she had scraped me from the bottom of her cowboy boot and turned her attention back to Lane.

"Aren't you a little old to be playing with Barbie dolls? Those guys are leaving, Romeo. Come on."

"She scares me," I said watching her stomp to the door. Boy, could she stomp. Very impressive.

"She scares me, too," Lane said. "I'll get over it in 20 years or so. Be careful, Sunflower." Lane slipped through the crowd and was gone. He instantly reappeared. "Go home," he said, "now." He kissed my nose and was gone again.

After several people grumbling obscenities bumped into me, I tottered back to the table. I should have been angry about him ordering me to go home. But for some reason I wasn't. He came back to tell me that. He also told me to be careful. Why?

"Who's the hunk?" Lexy demanded. She slipped into the chair across from me.

"Hunk? Where did you hear that expression?" I took a long pull on my beer.

"The lay-deees room." She enunciated each syllable and laughed.

"I should have known. You can't go in there ever again."

"What? What if I have to…"

"Kidding," I said.

"Who is he?"

"I wish I knew." I took a sip of my beer. It was getting warm.

Lexy stared.

"His name is Lane. Long story. Okay, not long, but hard to explain."

"I have time." Lexy crossed her arms.

I think the fact that I began with the Marlboro Man at the bus stop in the 7th grade and how much Lane reminds me of him proves my elevator doesn't go all the way to the top. I went on to tell her about seeing Lane at the courthouse and how empty I felt when he left—how empty I always feel when he leaves—I told her everything including the embarrassing under-his-Jeep incident.

In spite of all the noise going on around us and the guys who kept asking her to dance, Lexy listened with rapt attention. She is the best listener I know.

When I finished, I sipped my beer and waited for her reaction.

Lexy made wet circles on the table with the condensation on her bottle. "You are smitten because he looks like someone who doesn't exist? Are you plumb addled?"

"Yes. I'm sure I'm 'plumb addled'. When you put it like that, it does sound lame." To be honest, it was difficult to think about anything with Lane's kiss still on my lips. Oh. Maybe that's the reason. Or maybe I don't need a reason. He hadn't faked what I saw in his eyes. So, why did he go running off after Stormy like a whipped puppy?

"What about your beau? David. You do remember you have a beau?"

I felt a stab of guilt. "Well, of course I do." I took another drink and grimaced. Warm beer is only good if you're cooking a pork roast.

My head was beginning to pound in time with the music.

"I can't explain this," I said. "I've always felt invisible. People pass me on the street without seeing me. Lane sees me." I sipped my beer again. "Except, of course, when he doesn't."

"What?"

"Well, when he sees me in town, he pretends he doesn't..."

"Sounds like love to me." The raised eyebrow and sarcasm in Lexy's voice reminded me of David, which was sort of weird.

I rubbed a cold bottle across my head. "It's so hot in here." I took another drink. "This one must not be mine. It's almost full."

"The hunk set it there when he asked you to dance."

"This is colder than mine." I took another drink. The room spun around me. I shook my head to extricate the cobwebs. Lexy's face swam out of focus and changed size and shape. I blinked rapidly. It didn't help. She slipped away.

"Ali? What's wrong?" Her voice echoed.

"Lexy, where are you? I—feel—weird..." The table rose to meet my head.

Chapter Twenty-Five

An image of my worried face hovered above me, slightly out of focus like a watercolor left in the rain. Like a reflection in a well. The mouth opened.

"How do you feel?" Lexy asked. Her voice reverberated.

"My head is going to explode. The room is spinning."

Lexy brought me water and a straw. She sloshed it all over me as she gave me a drink. She set the glass on the nightstand. Wait. Nightstand?

I sat up. Fireworks exploded in my head. I closed my eyes to keep the room from spinning. It didn't work. Lexy perched beside me on the edge of the bed. Worry lines puckered her brows. She washed my face with a cool wet cloth.

"How did we get here?" I asked.

"I drove."

"You drove? What?"

"Driving is easy." Lexy grinned.

"How did you know where to go?"

"I paid attention."

I was too blown away to respond.

"I didn't know how to back up. Bill backed out for me and turned on the lights."

"Who is Bill?"

"I danced with him a lot. Remember? He carried you out to the car. He slung you over his shoulder like a sack of feed."

"Over his shoulder?"

"Yeah, you said he had a nice ass."

"I did not. I would never say that."

"You did." Lexy doubled over laughing.

"He didn't think it was strange that you could drive, but not turn on the lights?"

"He did," she said, when she stopped laughing. "But he kept asking for my number. I think he was smitten. What's my number, Ali?"

"Phone number. You don't have one. What did you say?"

"I told him I don't know my number, but I would ask you. He said you looked like you wouldn't be talking anytime soon. He gave me his. See?"

A phone number had been written on her palm, in red ink no less, beside a red heart. I wondered if the guy always carried a red ink pen. Just in case.

"He made me promise to give him a ring," Lexy continued. "I told him I don't have one that would fit him. He had really big hands."

"He wants you to call him, Lexy. What did I tell you about talking to men you don't know? This could have turned out badly."

"Well, it didn't. You aren't gonna lecture me again about how dangerous the world is, are you?"

"It is dangerous. I could have died last night. If I had, what would you have done? How would you have gotten home?"

"I don't know. You're right. I need to plan on you dying." She grinned.

"Think things through," I pleaded. "You can't always see around corners. Especially in a century that you don't live in."

"You're right. I was scared last night. You needed medical care. I didn't know where to take you. So, I brought you here."

"What happened? We were talking and everything went black."

"You were drinking Lane's beer and fainted. And threw up."

"I threw up? Yuck."

"It wasn't terrible. I cleaned it up."

"I'm so sorry."

Lexy grinned. "What are friends for?"

"It almost makes up for you nearly getting me killed in a tornado. Of course, we wouldn't have been at Blue Sage either, if you hadn't wanted to go. I need to watch what I let you talk me into. Do you think Lane drugged me?"

"No. Why would he do that?"

"I don't know. But then I don't know who wants me dead either. Apparently, someone does."

"I don't think Lane would harm you." A crease formed between Lexy's brows as she thought. "He seems to fancy you. I saw a man standing beside our table while we were gone. Maybe he did it."

"When?"

"You were dancing with Lane. There were a lot of people between us and it was dark..."

"What did he look like?" I asked.

"Tall, slim, white under shirt, jeans. I didn't see his face."

She probably meant a white T-shirt. If so, her description fit the man watching me from the bar earlier. I hadn't seen his face then either.

"My head hurts too bad to think." I looked at the clock and was shocked to see it was past noon. "My goodness. You must be starving."

Lexy poured the last of the peanuts we bought last night into her mouth and threw the bag away. "I've been eating these. I love peanuts."

She certainly does. I made a mental note to buy her a Snickers before my next trip to 1891.

"You might feel better if you eat," Lexy said. "There's nothing in your stomach."

"Maybe."

"What can I get you?" she asked, wiping salt from her mouth.

"I'll go. I don't want you running around out there by yourself." I tried to get up. A wave of nausea hit me. Everything went black. I fell back onto the bed.

"Well, that isn't going to work," Lexy said. "We need to get you to a doctor."

"I'm too sick to go anywhere." I thought about having to get in and out of the car, sitting in an ER waiting room answering endless questions. "I'll be okay."

"What can I get you?" Lexy asked again.

"I would love a can of orange pop."

"Does everything you people drink come in a can? Where do I get orange pop?"

"Outside my door there's a restaurant. Right inside the entrance is a vending machine. While you're there, grab something from the restaurant."

"Grab? What's a vending machine? What's a restaurant?" She frowned in confusion as though I'd been speaking a foreign language, which I suppose, I had.

"You put money into a vending machine and pop or candy comes out. A restaurant cooks food."

"Well, Land O' Goshen. You have a place that cooks food for you?"

"Yes. Please hand me the phone." I called in the order, two cheeseburgers, fries, charged to my room.

Lexy sat on the bed, still looking confused.

"You'll see when you get in there," I assured her.

"How do I get pop out of that machine?"

I explained while I fished quarters from my purse. "If you can drive a car, getting pop from a machine will be a piece of cake. You'll see the restaurant when you get inside the door. The lady at the cash register will have the order. I do this often. She'll think you're me and hand you the food. Take the key so that you can get back in."

"I've got this," Lexy said. She slid the key off the table and pocketed it.

'I've got this?' I need to find out what other phrases she picked up at Blue Sage.

Chapter Twenty-Six

It had been at least thirty minutes since Lexy left on a five-minute errand. I told myself the burgers hadn't been ready, but it became obvious that I had to go look for her.

I eased out of bed and stood up. My head began to swim, but I didn't black out this time. I walked around the bed, staying close in case I collapsed. I was weak but still upright when I reached the edge. Lexy had removed my boots and socks, but I wore the jeans and shirt from last night. I lurched to the door and peered out. No Lexy.

I checked my reflection in the mirror. My hair was matted to the right side of my face. Gum might be involved. With mascara smeared under my eyes and no other makeup, I'd terrify small children, and possibly their parents, but I wasn't up to primping. Nausea reminded me I wasn't up to finding Lexy either.

I staggered through the lobby door weak-kneed and dizzy. Lexy stood by the pop machine arguing with David. David? Neither of them noticed me. David's brows jerked down in a fierce scowl. He held Lexy's wrist in a vice grip.

"Take your hands off me." Lexy spat the words. "Are you insane? You made me drop that can." In a deft move, she twisted her arm from his grasp. "Get down there. Pick it up. Now." She tried to point and nearly dropped the other can.

That girl has moxie. I leaned against the door and watched in fascination. She didn't know David from Adam and didn't care who he was. She was taking crap from nobody.

"Look," he hissed, his face six inches from hers. It would have been closer if he wasn't so tall. "Stop acting as though you don't know me. Have you gone mad?" He spoke rapidly in an even tone. David never raises his voice. The angrier he becomes, the lower the volume. He was angry. "I've driven six hours through hellacious traffic to get here. I want to know what's going on, and I damn well better get answers." He took a step closer, putting the cheeseburgers in serious danger.

"Cool it, David," I croaked.

They both looked at me.

David's mouth dropped open. He stepped back.

"David?" Lexy gasped. "You are engaged to this terrible person? No wonder you're cranky."

"I'm not always cranky," I pointed out.

"Ali?" David asked Lexy.

"Ali." Lexy pointed at me.

"Then who the hell are you?"

"Lexy," I said. "Lexy, this is my fiancé, David Bentley Phipps III. He has a very impressive name, but as you can see, his manners, not so much. Although, he's usually not this bad. Now that we all know who we are, I need to lie down. Coming, David?"

"You owe me an apology. Your manners are appalling," Lexy told David, handing him the cheeseburger sack. She held the door, grasped my elbow to steady me, and guided me through. On our way out she ordered, "Get the can that rolled under the pop machine." The door slammed behind us. She never looked back.

This is going to be good.

Chapter Twenty-Seven

Good grief, Ali, what happened to you?" David grumbled. He set the cheeseburger sack and two cans of pop on the table. He lowered himself into the chair nearest the door. "You look like you wandered off the set of *The Walking Dead*."

"Don't talk to her like that," Lexy said. "She's sick." She didn't understand the reference but didn't like his tone.

I fell back into bed.

"Hungry?" Lexy asked glancing at David. She carried my burger to the nightstand. "Ali can get you one of these on her telephone. She knows how."

"Very impressive," David waved a hand dismissively. "No."

"No, thank you," Lexy prompted. "Ma'am says..."

"No, thank you," David growled.

Lexy unwrapped my food and placed it within my reach, along with my pop which she couldn't figure out how to open. She carried her burger to the table and sat down across from David. "You can lose that attitude, Mister Hunky Big britches."

David gave me his lowered head raised-eyebrow scowl which could mean anything. In this case it meant, 'what did she say'?

"Lexy, honey, don't use anymore of the phrases you picked up in the ladies' room last night until we have time to work on it."

"Okay." She bit into her cheeseburger. A rapturous expression spread across her face along with a dollop of mayonnaise.

"She eats like you do." David opened her pop can.

"Thank you," Lexy mumbled. She wiped off the mayo with the back of her hand.

I suppressed a smile. I love that girl. "Napkins are in the sack, honey."

"Yum. This is so good," Lexy reached into the sack for the napkin. I think that's what she said, her mouth was full.

David scowled. "You'd think she'd never eaten a burger."

"She doesn't get out much."

David is going to wear that eyebrow out before the afternoon is over.

"Well, uh, you know," I elaborated, "some burgers have pickles. Others have onions. Each is a work of art unto itself." I smiled. "A masterpiece. So to speak."

"Are you delirious?"

"Very possibly."

The look of disgust he gave Lexy would have melted me into a puddle of inadequacy. Lost in the wonder of her food, Lexy didn't notice.

David's eyes moved back to me. "What happened to your cheek?"

"A piece of rock flew off a boulder and hit me. On the bright side, the bullet missed."

"What? Who shot at you?" David, the attorney, stared at me in disbelief. "Why?"

"I don't know, David. He didn't hang around to explain."

"Why didn't you tell me? That's weird."

"You haven't heard the half of it."

"There seems to be a lot you haven't told me." He glared at Lexy. Lexy grinned.

David frowned. "Her for instance."

"She's a distant relative," I explained.

Lexy had been taking a drink. She spewed orange pop all over David. "Yeah, really distant," she whooped when she stopped choking. "About a hundred years."

"You're obviously twins." David grabbed a napkin and dabbed at his shirt, spreading an orange stain across it. His scowl deepened.

"Lexy and I aren't twins …."

"Well, we are," Lexy interrupted. "Only, we have different fathers." She lifted a pickle high in the air and dropped it into her mouth, looking like a bored ten-year-old. "And mothers," she finished, with a wink in my direction.

"And there's that bit of time between our births," I added.

"It was a very long labor." Lexy wiped pickle juice from her fingers, laughed and choked again.

"She finds humor in the weirdest things," David observed.

"Everything. You should see her in a tornado. I would kill for her laugh. My laughter is so often forced."

Lexy poked a fry in her mouth. "These are so good. They are gooshy on the inside," she explained to David, "but crunchy on the outside. How did they do this?"

David shot me a questioning look. "She's never eaten fries either?"

"Apparently, not."

"Did she recently drop in from another planet?"

"Close."

David stretched out his long legs, crossing them at the ankles. They looked darkly tanned in white shorts which, unlike his orange pop-stained shirt, were spotless.

"Where were you all night?" he asked. "You still weren't answering your cell at 2:30 this morning. When you didn't answer, I called your room. I was worried." He looked more irritated.

"How thoughtful," Lexy said.

I glanced at the phone. The red light signaled four messages had been left.

"Well?" David's eyes narrowed. "I'm waiting."

"I've been here two weeks. In that time you've called twice. You seem to think I should stay perched by the phone in case you call. As you might have noticed, David, I'm not feeling too well. I've been drugged, maybe poisoned. I didn't think to check my messages, and frankly, your attitude of being the injured party here is wearing thin."

A deep red flush began at his shirt collar, climbed his neck, spreading across his face. He drew a deep breath and let it out in an extended sigh. "You do look like hell," he said in a voice that sounded almost concerned.

"Thank you."

David sprang to his feet and began to pace. "Dammit it, Ali, I want to know what is going on here." He stopped and whirled to glare at me. He seemed more frustrated by the fact that I'm not cowering, than disturbed about the events of last night. I've never seen David this close to losing it. And I don't care. I must be in worse shape than I thought.

"Leave her alone." Lexy placed herself between David and me. "What is wrong with you? Can you not see she is sick? Sit down." She pointed to his chair.

To my shock, David deflated right before my eyes and went back to his seat.

With the tension easing, I bit into my burger. A slice of tomato slid from the bottom of it and plopped onto my chest.

David watched with a look of utter disgust. "Good Lord, Ali. How you manage to get everything you eat all over you is beyond me."

"It's a gift," I said.

Lexy glared at him, daring him to say anything further. When he didn't, she asked, "Should I explain who I am?"

"He won't believe it," I said.

Lexy eyed him speculatively. "You said he was obtuse. Now that I've met him, I think you're right."

"I said he's obstinate."

"What?" David's eyebrow shot up. Again.

Ignoring him, I looked at Lexy, "In all fairness, though, anyone would have trouble believing this."

"I guess," Lexy agreed. Her fingertips tapped against her chin as she assessed him through narrowed eyes. "You know, I don't think he's either of those things," she said finally. "He has a problem listening."

"Exactly. He's not stupid. In fact, he can be quite bright."

"Is he constipated? Ma'am would give him a dose of castor oil or an enema. He looks like he could use one."

I choked and swallowed a laugh. I can't count the times I've crumpled in the heat of the look David gave her. Far from crumpling, Lexy gazed back evenly and smiled.

David had met his match. He squirmed in his seat, looking as though he, too, realized he was losing this set. He lowered his eyes to his hands and scratched at a fingernail.

"If the two of you are through talking about me as though I'm not here," David grumbled, "finish your damn story."

Lexy moved back to her chair and settled in. "Well," she began, "Ali's uncle has this horse. Until Ali came along, I was her favorite person and..."

I listened to Lexy's account with fascination. Hearing it from her viewpoint felt as though I, like David, was hearing it for the first time. Lexy proved to be a natural storyteller. Her monologue was punctuated with colorful words and phrases. She paused for effect from time to time. Her face was animated, and as she talked, her fingers fluttered and darted through the air like small birds. And every so often, she'd look at me, her co-conspirator, and smile or wink.

This is how it feels, I realized when someone has your back. I have nothing to compare our relationship to. She's the only close friend I've ever had. But I know that if the two of us had been a split embryo, shared a womb, and heard the same heartbeat for nine months, I couldn't love her more. I have to figure out a way to keep her from marrying a toad.

Chapter Twenty-Eight

My attention shifted to David. To his credit, in spite of the skeptical expression that often flitted across his beautiful face—I mean the man should be in movies—he didn't interrupt. David too, seemed to be caught up in Lexy's narration. I have never held his attention for more than five minutes. If I had been telling the story, after the first sentence he'd be bored, and I'd be fidgeting while my stomach tried to eat itself. I would've talked faster, my words tumbling over each other in an effort to get out before he erupted in a fit of impatience. Why do I let him do that to me? I've been too caught up in David's charisma to notice what a sycophant I am.

The jarring ring jerked me back to the present and interrupted Lexy's story. As I reached for the phone, I noticed the Indian-head penny, puzzle piece, and the arrowhead lying in the ashtray on the nightstand.

"Hello," I said. I handed them to David.

"Hi, Hon," Jackson's voice boomed. "I tried to call you yesterday evening, but you weren't in."

"I'm sorry I haven't returned your call, Jackson. I haven't been well today."

"What's wrong?"

"Nothing serious, I'm feeling icky."

"Do you need anything?"

"No, thanks. But I appreciate your asking."

"Was Mariah happy to see her old friend, Whiplash?"

"Whiplash?" My mind raced. Who was Whiplash? Then I remembered. "The big buckskin at the barn? Yeah, they acted like old friends."

"They are. I loaned him to a guy last month. We need him now, so I went after him."

I felt a rush of guilt. "I've hogged your horse."

"Glad you are riding her. I need a horse with more size." He paused to exhale smoke. "Anyway, when that lawyer friend of yours is here, you can take him riding. Whiplash's saddle and bridle are in the barn."

"I saw them. Actually, David is here now."

"Yeah? Good. Take him riding this afternoon. Will he be here for the party?"

"I don't think he's planning to stay long." I looked at David. He shook his head.

"Bring him around when you can. I'd like to check him out. See if he's good enough for my niece."

David's frown let me know he'd heard.

"Well, I don't want to keep you on the phone if you have company, Sugar. Bye."

"See you tomorrow." I said to the dial tone. When Jackson is through, he's through.

David sat quietly looking at the arrowhead and penny in his hand, his expression unreadable. He picked up the puzzle piece, gave me a curious stare, but said nothing. The silence dragged on for several minutes.

Lexy broke it. "I really need to get home."

I tried to get up. The sudden movement made my head spin. I crashed against the headboard.

"Good grief, Ali, you can't take me."

"Can you stay another night? I'll be better in the morning...."

David lifted a hand. "Hold it. There's a perfectly logical solution. I'll ride back with Lexy. If I'm supposed to believe this, I need to see for myself."

I opened my mouth, but he cut me off. "Tell me how to get to the barn." He stood up as if it were settled.

122

I gave him directions. "Jackson said we could use the horse we saw yesterday."

Lexy gathered her clothes and went into the bathroom to change.

"She looks amazingly like you." David shook his head.

"Tell me about it."

I'd expected a lengthy tirade, but before he had time, Lexy exploded from the bathroom wearing her own clothes. She looked freshly beautiful.

"Well, that's quite a change," David said. His expression had altered. "If you'd been wearing that garb earlier, your story would've been more plausible."

Lexy ignored him. Running her hands over her skirt, she asked, "What is Ma'am gonna think about this being so clean? Soaking my clothes in that stuff you have took out all the river stains. Would you mind if I do my washin' here from now on? Is tomorrow okay?"

"I wish."

"How do you people keep from getting lazy? I would if I had all this electric stuff. Ma'am says hard work builds character. If she's right, mine must be the size of Pike's Peak." She looked at David. "That's a mountain in Colorado."

"We know." David smiled. His attitude toward her had softened. If he wasn't convinced, at least he was keeping an open mind.

"I'll come day after tomorrow," I told Lexy.

Lexy bent to drop a kiss on my forehead. "I'll wait by the spring. Thanks for the best night of my life."

"I had fun, too," I said. "It almost killed me, but it was worth it to see you having such a good time." I glanced at David. His thoughts were safely hidden behind the mask he donned at will.

He came to the bed, much like Lexy had, and bent to give me a quick kiss. He avoided the mass of whatever was in my hair. "You stay in bed and take it easy. I'll give you a ring."

"You aren't coming back here?" I asked.

"I'm guessing this is going to take a bit of time. I have a long drive back to Dallas."

David was right. He had about ten hours ahead of him.

"I'm glad you came," I said and meant it. "Wandering through that tunnel to 1891 was the weirdest thing ever. Not being able to talk about that almost killed me."

"What almost killed you was in that beer," David pointed out. "You could've told me."

"And said what, exactly?"

"Well, yes," he said. "I see your point."

With a flurry of goodbyes, Lexy and David were gone, and I was alone sorting through my thoughts. David's riding back to 1891 couldn't have worked out better. The attorney in him needed to see for it all for himself. But then, anyone would. So, this was perfect. If he and Lexy didn't kill each other before they got there. I smiled.

I got up and staggered to the bathroom hanging on to everything between the bed and the toilet for support. I took something for my headache, fell into bed and slept.

I woke in terror, afraid to breathe, fully awake and aware of being watched. Who? Where? I turned my head. The nightstand clock blinked 3:05 in large red numbers. David would be back in Dallas by now. Turning my head a bit farther, I could see the silhouette of a man through the flimsy motel drapes. There. Outside my window. Backlit by the vapor light in the parking lot, he stood, his face, cupped by his hands, pressed against my window. He vanished, tested the door. The knob turned once. Twice. But he made no effort to jimmy the lock.

Although I sensed he was gone, I lay paralyzed, too terrified to reach for the phone to call 911. The fact that I should do so didn't register in my frozen brain. Gradually my breathing returned to normal. I managed to sleep, but my dreams were worse than reality.

Chapter Twenty-Nine

I drifted out of a nightmare in which a dark bat-like being appears out of nowhere, swoops down, lifts me up, carries me away. The dreams have changed only slightly through the years. They leave me in a cold sweat, tangled in a mass of damp sheets. As a child I'd been too terrorized to fall back to sleep.

This one had probably been brought on by the scare I'd experienced earlier. I've learned to wait until my breathing and heart rate slowly returned to normal. While I concentrated on taking long slow breaths, it occurred to me that the wheezing shadowy figure in my nightmares might be Margaret. She often wore a black shawl which David called her witch's cape. A newspaper account of my abduction said a witness reported seeing a tall thin woman wearing a black cape lift the child from the back seat of the car. That would have been Margaret who would be wheezing. She had asthma. It all makes sense. Except for the why.

I added talking to Ursula about my breakthrough to my to-do list.

I clicked the TV remote. The weatherperson discussed at length the havoc caused by the heat wave in New York. Small children splashed in the water gushing from a fire hydrant. What time is it? I glanced at the clock. 5:00AM.

I sat up and swung my feet over the side of the bed. My head wasn't pounding, and I wasn't dizzy. Encouraged, I stood up and made my way to the bathroom.

By the time I stepped out of the shower I felt almost normal. I pulled my hair into a ponytail, slipped a T-shirt over my head and rummaged in my suitcase for a pair of shorts and running shoes. As an afterthought I grabbed the can of pepper spray.

I did a few stretches and still felt okay. I opened the door and looked around. The parking lot was empty except for my car and the one always parked in front of the room on the end. There was no uneasy feeling of being watched. I stepped outside. The day promised to be hot, but the pre-dawn air felt fresh. I stretched again and jogged across the parking lot.

Running is one of the things I do for myself. Besides the physical benefits, I feel it's also good for my mind and soul. A spiritual thing. Running allows me to leave behind worries and concentrate on the rhythm of my heartbeat and the sound of my feet crunching gravel. I'm never as 'in the moment' as when I run.

I ran east out of town along the highway, found my pace and settled into it, covering two miles in a matter of minutes. At the intersection of the second mile, a car approached on my right and rolled to a stop about the same time I reached the stop sign. It didn't move on. I recognized Lane's Jeep.

"Hey, City Girl," Lane yelled, "what're you doing, way out here? Get in."

"Huh uh." I took a step toward him.

"Get in."

"No way." I closed the distance. "I'm not getting in a car with you."

"Why not?" He grinned. "I trust you. I got in a car with you. You didn't attack me."

In spite of myself I laughed. "I was driving."

"You call that driving? Come on. Get in."

"Not going to happen," I said.

"Liar." He leaned over to open the passenger door.

Chapter Thirty

I fought with the seatbelt latch. At Lane's touch, it snapped into place.

"There's something I've wanted you to see." He shifted into reverse. The Jeep lurched. "Running into you like this is destiny."

"Density?" I asked, looking over my shoulder to make sure we'd missed the ditch. The wind, combined with the whining of the differential, made hearing difficult.

"Destiny. Things that are meant to be," Lane said.

"I know what destiny is," I said, watching him wrestle with the gear shift. I'm pretty sure I'd been right the first time. Getting in this Jeep is pure ignorance.

"You don't believe in destiny?" The Jeep ground into first gear and shot forward. "I've thought about it a lot. Lately."

"Why?"

"You," he said. "A force takes over destroying any good judgement I might have."

"You occasionally have good judgement? Good to know."

"Yeah, it flies out the window when you're around," he said. "Like the other night."

"About that, where did you run off to so fast?"

"I had a job to do," he said. "I should have been doing it." Frustration vibrated in his voice. "I told you to go home. Did you?"

"Not soon enough."

"Why? Did something happen?" His head turned toward me. His expression unreadable in the dark.

"I got sick. Not sure if it was from your beer or mine. One of them was drugged."

"How sick?"

"Praying-I-would-die sick. I passed out. Lexy drove me home. I woke up at noon yesterday with a splitting headache, too nauseated to get out of bed."

"Oh, man." No mistaking the alarm in his voice. "Are you okay?"

"Better."

"I am so sorry," he said."

I believed him. That kiss at Blue Sage hadn't said, 'I'm going to kill you'. If I thought he'd drugged me, I wouldn't be here right now. I hope. But with Lane, I am so stupid.

A dark shaggy form appeared between the bucket seats. I swallowed a scream. A tongue slapped across my ear. I recognized the big black dog I'd seen at the courthouse. "Hey, you." I laughed in relief. "Keep my ear out of your mouth. That's rude."

"It was an instinctive reaction. Any male would have done the same thing, right, Son?" Without taking his eyes from the road, Lane scratched the dog's chin.

"Hope he didn't pick that up from you," I said. "There's better ways to get a lady's attention."

"Seriously? Who knew?"

"I noticed he has Stormy wrapped around his paw." I congratulated myself on working her into the conversation.

"Yeah. They're tight. She kept him for me when he was a puppy. I had to find another place to live when the landlord realized I had him."

"What breed is he?"

"I don't know. He has that blue eye so he's probably part husky or Australian shepherd, but he's bigger than both breeds."

"How old is he?"

"Five," Lane said, as he dodged a pothole.

Hmmm. Doing the math, I mentally calculated. They weren't living together five years ago when Stormy kept the puppy. I threw tact and diplomacy to the wind and blurted, "Are you and Stormy together now?"

"Together? As in ..."

"Together." I said. "An item."

"We're doing a job."

"Job? As in …"

Lane chuckled at my obvious mimic. "As in job. That's all I can say."

"So, you said. Look, I'm not stupid. I pay to be this blond." I crossed my arms and flounced back in the seat. "This conversation is over. Take me back to the highway."

He didn't stop or turn around. We rode in silence as Lane focused his attention on a rough stretch of road instead of noticing how angry I tried to be.

Finally, he broke the silence, "You're right. She's bossy and she can't seem to help it. But she's sacrificing her time to help me on a job. I need her. She's the best at what she does."

I've had questions out the wazoo, but I've never doubted that Stormy would be the best at whatever she does.

"Stormy's pissed that I'm distracted by you," Lane sighed. "She has every right to be. I need to be focused. She thinks I'm putting her life, my life, and your life in danger. She's right. I need to stay away from you until this is over. I can't."

I couldn't untangle the thoughts swirling in my head. I wished I had a tape recorder because I'm going to be sorting through what he said over and over in my mind. There's no way to make sense of it. I need a reason to—oh, I don't know.

Lane changed the subject. "Does your sister live in Cheyenne Falls?"

"She's not my sister."

"I thought you said she was." The Jeep bucked over a rut, and Lane steered hard to the left to miss a baby rabbit.

"I didn't say that. You did."

"She could be your twin. Who is she? I'm confused," he said.

"We're working on a job," I smirked. "Can't tell you more right now."

Lane laughed. "Touché. You might as well tell me. I'll find out."

"Good luck with that," I said, smugly.

He grinned. "You're still unaware of my persistence."

Lane slowed the Jeep and turned off the dirt road onto a narrow path. It rose so steeply I expected us to roll over backwards at any second. Imagine an amusement park ride on speed. I didn't have time to think about anything but staying in my seat.

"Where are we going?" I gasped.

Lane down shifted, jammed his boot on the gas pedal and threw a glance at me. His jaw was set as he wrestled the Jeep for control. "Up. Hang on."

That answer hardly reassured me. "Up?"

The Jeep vaulted over a ledge and reached a small plateau. A sheer wall rose before us. Lane stomped on the brake, and at the same time he yanked the steering wheel hard to the left. The Jeep slid sideways, throwing me against the door. He killed the engine, pulled the emergency brake, and hopped out.

"We're here," he announced.

"Where?" I looked around.

"There's a spectacular view. You'll see when the sun comes up." Rummaging through junk behind the driver's seat, he pulled out a dented thermos.

"All this to see if there was a view? I'm not buying that." I couldn't see anything but a cliff rising above my window. I fought with the seat-belt latch.

"Here you go," Lane said. He reached across the console to unfasten it. At his touch, it sprang open. "It's all in the technique," he grinned. "You'll have to get out on my side. Climb over."

"Seriously?"

"You can do it. Come on, City Girl."

I managed to get out without being impaled on the gear shift. It wasn't easy.

Lane retrieved a moth-eaten army blanket and spread it out on a level spot.

I looked around. This plateau was inaccessible from the top. Only a crazy person would attempt to reach it from below. Yet here we were. When I realized how sharply the mesa dropped off, I sucked in my breath. I refused to think about how we're going to get back down. No parachutes in sight. Evidently Lane had done it more than once and survived. But why? Either Lane isn't sane—and this isn't the first time I've wondered—or he isn't willing to tell. That last part is getting old.

I had to admit when the sun made an appearance the view would be spectacular. I turned around. The dog sat watching me, his head cocked to one side, looking much like he had the day I saw him at the courthouse.

"His name is Austin?" I asked.

"Yeah. He was already named. I sort of inherited him from a friend." The blanket was finally smooth enough to suit him, and he reached for the thermos. Lane poured steaming black coffee into a cracked mug and handed it to me, then poured some into the lid for himself.

I lifted the mug and sniffed. The coffee looked and smelled like crankcase drippings.

"Why did he get a puppy and give it away?" I asked.

"He was killed by a sniper. Skye never did plan ahead."

I didn't know what to say. "Was your friend a soldier?" I sipped the coffee and almost choked. It tasted worse than it looked. But the ordinary act of wrapping my hands around a hot mug was comforting. I began to relax as the warmth seeped into my fingers.

"No. A federal agent." Lane sat down and patted the blanket in invitation. I lowered myself carefully to keep from spilling the coffee, as if stains could damage the relic.

Austin flopped down between us and laid his massive head in my lap. He gazed up at me before closing his eyes with a contented sigh.

"Are you from Cheyenne Falls?" I asked.

"Nope."

"What are you doing here?"

"Drinking coffee with a beautiful girl."

"I don't mean up here. Cheyenne Falls. What are you doing here?" Exasperated with his evasiveness, I made no effort to hide my irritation.

"Doing a job since the last of July, Sunflower." He grinned, amused by my frustration, which did nothing to quell it. I calculated. He's been in town a short time longer than I have. That answer spawned a whole new set of questions. Where was he before?

"All this cloak and dagger stuff wears me out. You can't answer a simple question?"

"I did." He grinned.

"Wasn't much of an answer," I grumped. "Why do you call me Sunflower?"

"You reminded me of a sunflower the first time I saw you."

"Why?"

"Sunflowers turn a deserted pasture into a golden field. They grow in spite of not being planted or nurtured. They're strong. They thrive in conditions that wilt ordinary plants. They grow in ditches, along fence rows, decorate lonely country roads. They seek light, their faces follow the sun. They're beautiful…"

"Yeah, that's nice. You call me that because you don't know my name."

"Of course, I do. Alexandra Dale Forrest."

I blinked. He even knew my middle name. "How would you know that?"

"I have my ways, Ali." He grinned a bit arrogantly.

He knew my nickname, too. Ali? That had taken effort. I'm a little spooked. "So, you're a stalker?"

He laughed. "Evidently."

Chapter Thirty-One

Silence stretched between us. I broke it. "Make this coffee yourself?" I raised the cup to my lips but couldn't make myself drink it.

"Yeah. It was decent last Tuesday. I forgot how old it is."

"Old as the thermos?"

"Not quite," he laughed. "It's hot though. Darn good thermos."

"Good thing beauty isn't it's only purpose."

"Oh, come on. It has character." Lane observed the dents. "Looks like it's been through World War II, doesn't it?"

"Or run over by a combine. Which war was the blanket from?"

"It's my Grandpa's. He's the one who taught me how to make coffee."

"I kind of wish you'd paid more attention."

"When I was little, we fished a lot. He'd be up before dawn making coffee, so we could drink a cup while we watched the sunrise." He smiled. "Like now."

A ribbon of seashell coral lay silent and still on the horizon, pushing the indigo of night further up into the sky. Now that it was light enough to see his face, I seemed unable to stop staring. But in my defense, he smiles with his whole face. And there's that dimple.

"Pa's a great believer in greeting the day," Lane continued. "Thanking God for it. He says a man's gotta get the day started off right."

"Sounds like you spent quality time with him. He must have loved you."

"Still does. He didn't have much choice. I followed him everywhere," Lane said, fishing a pack of gum from his shirt pocket. He offered me a stick. "He's the best."

"You're lucky." I noticed he hadn't mentioned his father.

"I am lucky," Lane agreed. "These days there seems to be a shortage of people willing to live good honest lives and leave footprints for youngsters to follow. Help them figure out why God put 'em here."

"God doesn't care where I am."

"Sure, He does."

"If He did, He'd be more help. Signs at life's crossroads pointing in the right direction wouldn't hurt," I grumbled. "He could've made it easier."

"But see, that's it," Lane said. "We have to find a path that gives life significance—so we aren't just using up air and taking up space. Most of the time we're all too busy chasing shadows to recognize opportunities." He gazed into the distance. "When we're gone, the world will either be better or worse because we were here. We only have one chance. We have to make it count."

"Making the world a better place. Like heroes. I've always dreamed of being a hero," I said, instantly wishing I hadn't. David would have laughed his head off about that. He knows I'm the biggest chicken who ever lived.

Lane didn't laugh. He sipped his coffee without grimacing. I gave him points for being tough.

"You're stronger than you know, Sunflower. If the situation ever arose, you'd be up for it. I'd bet my life on it."

"I hope you're right. But I don't feel heroic," I said after thinking about it.

"Heroes come in all shapes and sizes. Single moms and fathers who slave away at jobs they hate to feed hungry kids are heroes. They don't ask to be thanked. Love isn't all hearts and flowers. It's more than pretty words whispered in an ear in the moonlight or penned on a fancy card. Love is sacrifice, it's painful, it requires getting dirty. The people who keep truckin' to protect loved ones, they're the heroes. A woman who drags herself out of bed at 4:00 AM to go to work to feed her child. Like my mom, she's a hero, too."

I wondered where his mother worked but didn't want to interrupt.

"Not everyone can save a commuter train in NYC or a battalion in Afghanistan," Lane went on. "But jumping in there to do what we can when the need arises, that's what heroes do. Being willing to sacrifice yourself for what you love, says volumes about who you are."

"So," I asked, "is leaping in front of a bus to save a child love or being heroic?"

"If it's your child, it's love. But it's heroic, too."

What if it isn't my child?"

"That's heroic, but it might be love, too."

I nodded.

"What happened to you, Sunflower?"

"What do you mean?" I stiffened.

"Sometimes your eyes look haunted."

Hmmm. So, he can read eyes, too. Margaret's voice screamed in my head 'Don't tell. Don't ever tell.' But I've seen into Lane's heart. I trust him. I began telling him the horrors of my childhood. I told him what it was like growing up in a Dallas slum. The pain of those memories welled up in my eyes. I rambled back through time remembering the stench of stale smoke, urine and vomit. I choked on it now, as I did back then. I told him of the gangs roaming the streets, gunshots at night, screams of women and children behind cracked doors down the hall.

Lane squeezed my hand, encouraging me to continue. I wasn't aware he'd been holding it. He leaned toward me as I talked listening with the rapt attention Lexy had shown. His brows knitted together in concentration as I told him of the loneliness. Never being able to play outside. Being too shy to make friends, believing nobody would like me because my mother didn't. I described in detail the terror of a small child locked in a dark closet for hours too afraid of the things scurrying across her feet to sit down. I told him about my nightmares.

The secret of being an abused child had dictated my life, colored my view of the world and determined my choices. The fortress I had built around it had become a prison. The shame of my abuse had become the shrine where I worshipped. As I talked, walls crumbled. Light flooded through cracks, destroying the power of secrets. Lexy knew. And now so did Lane. He'd interrupted me a few times only to ask questions.

"Children have no control over what happens to them," Lane said, looking into my eyes.

I moved my head to avoid the intensity of his gaze. With two fingers beneath my chin, he turned my head until I was facing him again.

"But my, how they blame themselves," he said.

"I haven't figured out how to stop doing that."

In his eyes I saw understanding and acceptance. Lane lifted my hand to his lips. He seemed hardly aware of the gesture, but the contact sent currents of electricity up my arm.

"I want to help with that. I know about nightmares," he whispered, my hand still against his lips.

"You?"

He nodded. He released my hand, to reach for the thermos. "My Dad was sheriff in a county near Santa Fe," he said, unscrewing the lid. He poured the liquid into his cup and looked questioningly at me. I covered the mug with my hand. He laughed and replaced the lid.

"Mom had errands to run so she dropped me off at Dad's office. He had papers to serve, but said he'd take me along." A muscle twitched in Lane's jaw. I reached out to lay my hand on his. I started to tell him he didn't have to continue when he drew a ragged breath and went on.

"So, we were way up in the mountains on a road with nothing on it except deer. The mountain went straight up on one side of the road. On the other, the land fell sharply away, and pines grew thick. Two men in a pickup truck came up fast behind us. The driver shot out our back window and a rear tire. Our pickup went off the road and crashed down the bank into the trees."

Lane shivered, reliving the incident. He'd almost forgotten my presence. I shifted my weight and snuggled in close.

"Dad realized what was going down. He threw himself over me." Lane's voice was a monotone. He paused for so long I thought he couldn't go on.

"I heard the shot. Dad jerked and went limp. He stopped breathing. As young as I was, I knew he was dead. I heard a guy slide down the bank. He looked in the pickup and yelled up to the road, 'He's dead. You got 'em.' The guy didn't see me. After the pickup drove away, I crawled out from beneath Dad. We were both covered in his blood."

"My gosh, Lane." Tears flooded my eyes. "I am so sorry."

"We weren't found for two days. Every time I heard a car, I thought the guy was coming back to kill me. I was too scared to walk up to the road."

"Two days?" I gasped, picturing a scared little boy alone with his father's body. "How old were you?" Unchecked tears streamed down my face.

"Dad's funeral was on my fourth birthday."

"Did they find who did it?"

Lane shook his head. His jaw tightened. "No. They didn't. But I will."

I have no doubt that he will. "How do you get over that?"

"You don't. You tiptoe around it. You get better at not letting it consume you." Lane's voice cracked. "You don't let it destroy you."

The lazy sun woke up and peeked above the horizon painting clouds a fiery crimson. The spectacle was wasted on us.

Lane cupped my face. My breath caught in my throat when I stared back into those turquoise eyes. Their color had grabbed my attention in the courthouse. There is so much more to this man than those watercolor eyes. My ability to see into a person's heart through their eyes has often been a curse. However, in Lane's I saw honesty, integrity, and pain too deep to verbalize. No matter how crazy things looked, and boy have they looked crazy, I could trust this man.

His thumb traced my tears, following them to my lips. He leaned forward, moving his mouth over the places his thumb had been. I think he meant to comfort me. Comfort us. But with the initial contact, when his lips met mine, something happened. A lifetime of grief was obliterated in that kiss. And the next one. And I knew. I knew why the earth doesn't spin off its axis. Because in a world filled with war, pain and suffering, there is this. Then after the third kiss, Lane drew a shuddering breath and pushed himself away from me.

"Too soon, Sunflower," he said, when he could breathe. "We'll pick this up later."

Chapter Thirty-Two

Lane's concern we would be seen outweighed his desire to drop me off at my door. A mile from town I got out and finished my run. Actually, I walked. I needed to think.

The sticky web of secrets and lies had strangled me. The walls of my self-imposed prison cracked open. I crawled out when I allowed Lane to look into my heart. The weight I had no idea I'd been carrying was gone. Lane knows about my past and still likes me. In fact, I'm pretty sure he loves me.

Which brings up David. Why could I not trust him with the secrets of my heart? Because David has no interest in knowing the terrified child in soiled panties who shivered in the dark recesses of my soul. So, why have I been engaged to this man for four years? I believed I couldn't navigate life on my own, a myth he perpetuated.

Lane said love is sacrifice. Getting dirty. David doesn't like to get dirty. He wants a fiancé who is clean, tidy, and looks good in the expensive clothes his mother bought her. He wants a girl who keeps her mouth shut, has no opinion of her own, laughs at his jokes, and wears a flashy diamond on a well-manicured finger. I've been all too willing to be her.

Maybe I'm being too hard on David. Lane could understand my scars because he has suffered his own deep wound. Maybe David's indifference comes from never having been seriously hurt. I have to give this ring back as soon as possible.

I showered, found a clean pair of shorts and a shirt that wasn't too wrinkled. I was buttoning it when I heard a knock on the door. As I opened the door, I realized I should have looked to see who was there. I'm a slow learner.

A slim blond lady stood poised to knock again. Impeccably dressed in black capris and a matching sleeveless top, she looked as if she'd stepped out of *Vogue*. I ran my hands over my shirt in a vain attempt to smooth the wrinkles.

She stared at me. "My goodness. You look like Aunt Sharon."

I didn't know how to respond. I stared back.

"I'm April. Your cousin. Jackson's daughter. I tried to call..."

"Oh. April. I've heard of you."

"Well, I would imagine." She pulled me into a hug. I am not a hugger. Why people believe they have a right to be in my personal space is beyond me. But she smelled wonderful. Her perfume was subtle. Expensive.

"Can I come in?" she asked.

"Of course. Sorry." I stepped back.

She breezed past me talking. "Dad was certainly right about you looking like Aunt Sharon. Wherever she is. We have no idea. But then we never know. We have no idea where Abby is either, but she's a bit more dependable. The Dale sisters are both MIA." She giggled. "I can't wait to see Abby's face when she sees you. Tears are going to flow. My goodness, I can't believe you're here after all this time." April dabbed at her eyes.

"Do you know..."

"No. I've totally lost track of your mother. Her phone goes straight to voice mail. She still has the number. It's so hard to reach people on a cellphone abroad. There's the time difference, the lay of the land, and whatever." She waved red-tipped fingers.

It's the 'whatever' that concerns me. I didn't say so.

"I should give you that number."

I waited, but she didn't.

"I've been in Virginia at a women's conference. I speak at these things often. Daddy isn't very patient when he wants to reach me, especially with news this good. He left me fifteen messages." She laughed and shook her head. "I wish he texted. As soon as I heard the lost had been found, I made a bee line, whatever that is, to Cheyenne Falls. I couldn't wait to see you."

"So, you don't—"

"No. I wish Abby stayed in touch better. She used to—in case you returned—she wanted to be close. I guess she gave up. She started traveling with Russ, your dad. He had been so many interesting places in the world that she'd missed out on."

April settled into a chair. My room looked classier with her in it.

"Do you have plans?" Her eyes quickly swept the room as though she hoped tidying up was among them.

Her sudden change of topic caught me off guard. I sort of stopped listening when I realized she didn't know where my parents were.

"Plans?" I'm glad I made the bed.

"For today," she said.

"Oh. Today." She must think I'm a total spaz. "No."

"I thought if you don't have anything pressing this morning, I might take you by the house where you lived before you were—." She blinked. "Before. See if it jogs any memories. You haven't been there, right?"

"No."

"Good." She flashed a dazzling smile. "It's rented. We can't go in. But there's an unused apartment in the back over the garage. Where Abby painted. Dad thought you might like to move in there for the time being, since you won't move in with them. Of course, you won't. He forgets how isolated it is out there. The apartment is small but might work for you for now. It isn't furnished, but that's easy to fix. I could take you furniture shopping. That would be fun."

"I need to run by the bank first," I said in a rush before she started talking again. "But yes, I would love to see it."

"You're going to the bank?" She glanced at my wrinkled shirt. "Well let's go," she said. She stood up briskly. "My car is right outside."

***

April chewed her bottom lip as she eased her Lexus around three single-file bicyclists wheeling along the edge of a tree-lined street. The smallest child, who had more bike than experience, wobbled but made a valiant effort to keep up. None looked old enough to be riding in the street by themselves, but this was Cheyenne Falls, not Dallas.

"I'm hoping that seeing where you lived will trigger memories," April said, when we were safely past the children. "I don't want to be the only one who remembers the time we spent together. I was so crazy about you."

I squeezed April's hand and immediately returned my attention to the view outside the window. "I've always loved beautiful older homes."

April eased the car to the side of the street and parked in front of a large white stucco house with a red tiled roof. "We're here."

My view was partially blocked by a crepe myrtle. A profusion of dark pink blossoms grew between the house and the street. I leaned forward for a better view.

The house, described as Spanish, pretended to be Italian. An ancient, gnarled olive tree shared the courtyard with an ornate fountain. A whimsical statue, a bronze dolphin and elfin boy wearing a grin so roguish it bordered on evil, rose from a pool lined with blue Italian tile and would have frolicked had there been water. I could feel the texture of the boy's sculptured hair beneath my fingertips. I had once splashed in that pool.

"Mom, Dad, and I used to live there." April pointed to the house next door. She turned off the engine and looked down at my leg. "What happened to your knee?"

"My knee? I—" My mind raced through explanations, none of which were as preposterous as what had actually happened. What if I told her I fell running from a tornado in 1891? I imagined her expression and nearly laughed.

"I, uh, fell," I said.

"You don't drink, do you?" April gingerly poked at the raw red area around the scrape. "Have you seen a doctor? You might need stitches. It looks awful."

"Thank you," I said dryly.

"And what happened to your cheek? My, I hope that doesn't leave a scar. We Dales have such delicate skin. We must be careful with our complexions. Your mother is going to wonder what we have been doing to you. You haven't been here that long and you're already a mess. I don't mean a messy mess, but well, you are a bit unkempt. I certainly hope you're wearing sunscreen while you are traipsing around out in those canyons."

I assured her I was.

"Why, as fair as you are you could wreck your skin in no time." April pulled a key from her purse. "Want to see the apartment?"

"Sure."

"That way." April pointed. "It was the servant's quarters when the house was built, but Abby used it for an art studio. She had skylights installed. The apartment is small, but the light is good." She opened the car door, swung around and extended long legs. Over her shoulder she was still talking. "Abby's paintings are up there. Which isn't all that smart if you ask me, but of course no one has. Abby could've stored them out at Dad's and rented this apartment. It's darling. It would've been snatched up in a heartbeat. I'll show you."

While I waited for her to walk around the car, I stood next to the crepe myrtle studying the front of the house.

"What's wrong?" April asked, scrolling through phone messages.

I pointed to a large arched window which wore lacy grillwork like a black tiara. "That was where the picture of us at the piano was taken."

"That's right," April said. She smiled as though I had rattled off the theory of relativity. "The piano sat in that corner because of the light. Remember anything else?"

Unlike the snatches of fuzzily-out-of-focus pictures that flickered occasionally through my mind, a razor-sharp image began to form. A little girl in a pink dress. The child held a small crystal ink bottle up into a shaft of golden sunlight. As she twirled, colors danced on the hardwood floor. Laughing with delight, she spun until she tripped and landed in a heap. As she fell, the bottle flew from her hands, arced through the air, and crashed to the floor.

"Yes," I said. "Did the ink stain come out of the wood?"

"Yay. You're remembering. No. After your abduction, Abby left it as proof that you had once been here."

I followed her around the house, past the stucco-walled back yard, and up the stairs to the apartment. She handed me the key and I unlocked the door. A faint odor of turpentine greeted us. The room was large and airy. Sun streamed through an overhead skylight.

"Oh, I love this light. I wish had a place like this to paint," I said.

"You do, silly. The key is in your hand."

I tried to picture my mother painting in here. A kitchenette that occupied one corner of the room was small but open and equipped with a stove, fridge, and microwave. Two doorways led to bedrooms. They shared a bath. Both were surprisingly large.

"Wow," I breathed. "I love this. It could be so cute."

"I can't believe you're this excited. It's not the Vanderbilt," April pointed out. "It's a garage apartment."

"I want to live here." As the words left my mouth, I realized their truth. I hadn't really thought about the future but knew I didn't want to go back to Dallas. Ever.

I looked around. "I'm going to paint this room Desert Sun, a warm color which will be even warmer with this amazing light. I'll paint the bedrooms a mossy green to provide a backdrop for Abby's landscapes and the house plants I'll put everywhere." I'd already moved on to window treatments and area rugs when April's voice drew my attention to the stack of canvases in the corner.

"These paintings are your mother's."

I pulled out the largest and recognized it instantly. It was twelve-year-old April and a two-year-old me sitting at a piano bench.

"This was painted from the snapshot," I said.

"Yes. Abby painted two. Mine is only slightly different and hangs over my fireplace. She wanted us each to have one. This one is yours. It's been waiting for you."

I dragged an easel to the puddle of sunlight pouring through the skylight, placed the canvas on the wooden frame, and backed away. I scrutinized the painting in shocked silence. I had no idea Abby was this good. Reminiscent of Rembrandt, she'd used bold strokes of dark hues in the corners and foreground. In stark contrast the center of the canvas was done in feather strokes of pastels. Light filtering through curtains backlit the two girls at the piano with an exaggerated halo effect and cast lacy shadows around them. The children were softly abstract, giving the painting a dreamy quality. But Abby's detail, especially in the lace and the shadows, spotlighted her immense gift.

"We look deceptively angelic, don't we?" April's voice was hushed as though she, too, were awed by the work of a master.

"What talent. My goodness. She should be doing art shows. Is she still painting?"

"Probably not." April walked to the canvasses and flipped through them. "She's too busy globetrotting these days. Earlier you mentioned that you wished you had a place to paint. So, you paint, too?" She shot a questioning look over her shoulder.

"I do but I'm not this good. I wanted to major in art but decided I couldn't support myself with an art degree."

"It doesn't look like you have to," April said, looking pointedly at my hand. "That diamond would choke a horse. Dad says you're engaged to a bigshot Dallas attorney."

"I never want to depend on anyone to support me," I said. I didn't want to talk about David. April, for once, was silent.

I nosed around until she reminded me, "We better get you back to the motel to change. The guest of honor can't be late for her own party." I saw a flicker of panic in her expression. "You do have something to wear, right?"

I almost laughed. I should show up in cutoffs.

"Do I have to go? I hate parties."

"Of course." April planted a hand on a hip. "Everyone wants to see you."

"That's kind of the point. I don't want to be seen. I hate parties."

She laughed. "My, that face. What a pout. I'm beginning to believe it."

"I'm not good at parties," I muttered sounding like a petulant child. "I think I'm getting sick. I probably have a fever."

As I locked the door, I looked down into the stucco-enclosed backyard of the house. The overgrown landscape had once been beautiful. A tile patio took up a large portion of the yard. A walk led to this apartment. If my parents lived in the house again and I lived here, we could run back and forth to share a steaming cup of coffee in the morning, or a glass of wine in the evening. Abby and I could paint together and...

"You're going." April was already down the stairs. She didn't look back.

Well. It looks like I'm going. As I followed her to the car, I stopped and looked around. The feeling was becoming all too familiar. A prickly sensation crawled along the back of my neck. I saw nothing, but knew we were being watched.

Chapter Thirty-Three

I hadn't lied about feeling sick when I arrived at Jackson's and saw the size of the crowd milling around the back yard deck. I had trouble finding a place to park.

If I do say so myself, I looked pretty darn good. I wore a lime green sheath by a designer whose name I can't pronounce. David's mother bought it for me during her last trip to Paris. The lines were simple but classy. I almost fainted when I'd seen the price tag. Daydreon liked her son's fiancé to look good. Hopefully, I won't embarrass April by how 'unkempt' I am.

I pulled myself up to my full height, threw back my shoulders, and shook back my hair. I'd seen girls do that at parties. The motion is supposed to convey self-confidence and sex appeal. I tripped and promised myself never to do that again while wearing heels. Or walking. I set out to find April.

It didn't take long. Looking coolly chic in a black sundress with a plunging back, April would have stood out in any gathering. She talked to a small woman beside a picnic table. She saw me, waved, and motioned for me to join them.

"Well, you do have something to wear besides shorts and a wrinkled shirt," April teased, as she inspected my dress. "That color is fabulous with your tan."

Ah, success. "Thank you. I have no idea why I packed it, but I'm glad I did." I enjoyed the surprised appreciation in April's eyes. I laughed. She's so obvious.

"Ali, this is Janet, your Cousin Fred's wife. Janet, this is the long-lost Ali."

145

"I'm happy to meet you," Janet said. Impulsively, she reached across April to give me a hug. "You're beautiful."

"Thanks, Janet." I am so not a hugger. And compliments throw me off balance. I don't believe them but want to appear gracious. And saying 'BS' seems a bit gauche. "It's nice to meet you too."

"My, your resemblance to my mother-in-law is amazing." Janet had an open face. In her eyes I saw warmth, honesty, and generosity. I liked her instantly.

"Where are Fred and the kids?"

"The kids are here…" She looked around. "Fred didn't come."

"He didn't?" April's eyes widened. The conversation must not have gotten around to Fred's glaring absence. "He's the one who keeps demanding to see Ali."

A shadow crossed Janet's face. "He had an accident in the truck this morning. He's really a mess. He said to give Ali his apologies."

"An accident?" April looked more skeptical than worried. "Is he hurt? Fred never misses food." She made little effort hide the fact she disliked her cousin. "Was the truck badly damaged?"

"It's so old and beat up, I couldn't tell," Janet said.

"Well, tell him we missed him." April said, in an effort to sound interested. She turned her attention to introducing me to a group who wandered over. After we chatted for a bit, April and Janet set out on a mission to make sure I met everyone.

"Look. There's Papa Jay." Janet blurted pointing toward the lake. "I'm glad he came."

We made our way through the crowd to where the old man sat under the branches of an oak tree. His wrinkled face creased into a smile when he saw us.

"Hello, April, Ali, Janet," he called as we approached. His eyes were bright and clear. "You ladies look lovely tonight."

"You're still a charmer," April said. She bent to kiss his cheek.

"How smart you are," Janet said. "You have the best seat in the house."

I was thinking how smart he was for knowing who we all were. Even me, whom he had only met once.

"You can see the action from here," Janet continued, "but you're out of the path of the maddening throng."

"It's cool here in the shade. And there's a nice breeze off the lake," Papa Jay said, gazing over the water. "I love it down here. Brings back lots of memories, good and not so good." His voice trailed off as he lost himself in them. He looked up suddenly and winked at me. "Remember when you threw me in there?" He jerked his head toward the lake.

"What? I threw you in the lake?" I looked at April for support.

"No dear, April intervened, "Ali wouldn't think of throwing you in the lake."

"Dang if she wouldn't." He grinned boyishly. "It was right over there. I haven't forgotten it either. She's not a great shot. Don't give her a gun." He laughed and slapped his knee at his private joke. "Where's Lexy?" he asked. "You were like two peas in a pod."

I swallowed hard. I suddenly remembered he'd asked about Lexy the day I met him. Then, I didn't know a Lexy. Now...

"Who is Lexy?" Janet looked confused.

April laughed at my expression and tried to rescue me. "She doesn't know Lexy, Sweetheart. She hasn't met many people. She seems to be spending all of her time riding through the canyons on horseback and ruining her complexion," she said with a pointed look at me.

He gave April a blank stare.

"Well," Janet said brightly. "What a lovely evening."

"There are a lot of people here. Is it my birthday?" Papa Jay asked.

"No, dear, not this time," April said, patting his shoulder. "This party is for Ali."

"Good. I don't need another birthday. I've known Ali longer than everyone here." He winked at me as though we shared a secret.

"How old are you?" I asked.

He chuckled. "I'd tell you if I knew."

"We know he's over 103, but we don't know how much. He doesn't have a birth certificate," April said. "He was born at home without a doctor before statehood."

He's at least twenty years older than I believed him to be. No wonder he got confused. But, for his age, he was amazingly alert.

"You're not Jackson's father?" I asked. "You're his grandfather?"

"That's right," April said. "My great grandfather."

"Incredible," I finally managed to mumble. "You look so young. I hope you'll share your beauty secrets with me."

"Whisky and chewing tobacky." He nodded for emphasis.

I laughed. "Maybe I'll try something else."

"Well, we need to introduce Ali to the others," April said, dropping a kiss on his forehead. "Stay out of trouble, dear. We'll be back to see you later."

"He looks so sharp tonight," Janet said as we strolled away. "Usually, when he gets bumfuzzled about things, his eyes are cloudy."

"Something about Ali confuses him," April said. She shook her head. "The food is out. Let's go eat." And with that, we made our way to the buffet line.

Jackson and Penny insisted that I was the guest of honor and as such should be first in line, so I finished eating before most people. Well, that and the fact that I was starving and snarffed down my food like I hadn't eaten in a week.

Janet had gone to referee a disagreement between her kids and the twins. April had disappeared. I strolled around the yard alone feeling happy and quite smug about how well I'd mixed and mingled. The only thing that could have made the evening better would have been the presence of my mom and dad. I reveled in the fact that I have parents. Parents I haven't met and am already thinking of as Mom and Dad.

The tables of food were being cleared away, and people were converging again in small groups to visit. The yard had been decorated in a tropical theme, and since sundown, the effect of hanging lanterns, candles, and tiki lights was lovely. Penny knows how to throw a party. And all this had been done for me. Me. I'm overwhelmed.

As I weaved my way through the crowd people would stop me long enough to share a story of how cute I'd been as a baby which they'd forgotten to tell me when we were introduced. Surprisingly, I remembered many of their names. They all felt led to comment on my resemblance to Aunt Sharon. Which makes me wonder if I look as much like Sharon as I do Lexy. Jackson wasn't exaggerating about the Dale women having strong genes. I'd heard "I wish Abby was here," and "I can't wait for your mother to see you," so many times I became melancholy. Nobody wished it like I do.

I paused to throw the wildly-colored-paper plate in the trash. Making small talk drains me. I wandered out to the boat dock. Its emptiness offered an invitation to escape from idle chatter. I gratefully accepted. Leaning against the rail, I surveyed the scene.

Strains of island music combined with sounds of waves lapping at pilings below. They seemed to go together. The call of a whippoorwill mingled with songs of the crickets and frogs. I chuckled along with intermittent shrieks of laughter from the twins and their cousins who darted through the woods playing hide and seek much like the children in the Kiowa camp. On a more subtle scale, the adults seemed to be enjoying themselves as much as the children.

My eyes lingered on the trees where the children had disappeared, and I was surprised to see April nearly hidden in the shadows. She was deep in conversation with a man, but a branch obstructed my view of his face until he stepped closer to April. In the flickering light of a tiki torch, I recognized Ron Lang. What was up with that? I have yet to meet April's husband but remembered her saying he hadn't been able to come tonight due to an incredibly important meeting. Hmmm.

I filled my lungs with clean fresh air, and exhaled slowly, savoring the sense of contentment. It occurred to me that I'd been feeling quite peaceful on a regular basis since arriving in sleepy Cheyenne Falls—seemingly a world removed from the stress and crowds of Dallas. I've fallen in love with the people, hills and canyons of this area. And some cowboy.

I checked my watch. No wonder I'm tired. It's late, and my day started with a predawn run. I straightened and stretched, looking out over the lake one last time. Fireflies flitted above. Their reflection, mingled with that of tiki lights, danced on the water. The perfect end to a perfect day. I turned to go.

A blow to my head knocked me to my knees. White-hot pain flashed like an explosion behind my eyes before moving down my neck to my spine. My knees turned to Jell-o and refused to hold me. I fought to open my eyes, but blackness closed around me. I melted down toward the rough dock planks. My attacker lifted me, grunting with the effort, and dropped me over the rail feet first into the lake.

There was hardly a splash as I slipped into the deep dark water.

Chapter Thirty-Four

I sank through the frigid depths totally aware of what had happened but powerless to react. The blow to the head had rendered me semiconscious. Whoever attacked me, counted on my not surviving. Still, I felt no panic. I didn't care. Time stood still.

I settled into a bed of weeds at the bottom of the lake. Sediment, like the confusion of my mind, rose around me in a cloud. Even in an altered state, I knew I had to push myself up, but the more I struggled, the more I sank. Every effort pulled me farther down into the muddy goo. Of its own accord my body tried to float up, but a tangle of vines held my foot. The realization that I would die down here alone in this cold tomb should be no surprise. How fitting that my death would occur in total isolation while a festive party continued above. Nobody noticing the girl on the outside. Again.

Jackson hadn't exaggerated about this water being cold. My whole body grew numb as my mind became more alert. An eerie calm settled in. I stopped struggling.

No. This will not happen. I'm sick of wallowing in this poor-me crap. I can't die now. I have too much to live for: parents, this place I love, and Lexy. I want to see how the thing with Lane plays out. It was the image of my mother learning of my death that gave me resolve.

I clawed at the tangled mass of weeds with fingers too numb to feel. Miraculously, one began to give. I kicked violently with all the force I possessed and dislodged my foot. I was free but didn't have the energy to fight my way to the surface. My throat burned from water swallowed, and my lungs were close to exploding.

I kicked and began slowly rising. I added swimming lessons to the mental list of things to do. I pushed my face through the surface, felt warm air, and sucked it greedily into my lungs with a deep ragged gulp, then sank back down, too weak to scream for help. I raised a wooden arm in case anyone had seen me. At that moment fingers grasped my wrist pulling me upward. They lost their grip and slipped off. I began sinking again, choking on fright and water that tasted like a breeding tank for frogs.

Initially I had been too dazed by the blow to struggle, but now realized the water couldn't be very deep. And I'd been seen. When I sank to the bottom this time, I settled on a large rock. With the last little bit of strength I possessed, I pushed against it and floated upward.

I hadn't broken the surface when a man jumped in and grabbed me. From behind, a strong arm encircled my waist. He held me tightly and kicked his way to the surface. I've heard of victims drowning their rescuers in frenzied panic. I was too weak to struggle.

"It's okay, Babe, I've got you," Jackson said pulling me out of the water.

Jackson had me. Everything would be okay. He lifted me up. Several people leaned down and hauled me out. Ron Lang issued commands. Strong arms laid me on my stomach and began pressing on my back. Water poured from my mouth and ears. Splinters from the dock's rough planks gouged my cheek, and the deck shook and bounced beneath me as people ran around in a frenzy. Everyone shouted orders.

"Has anyone called 911?" A voice screamed close to my ear.

"No time to wait for an ambulance, we've got to get her to town. Tell them we're on the way."

"Ali. Can you hear me?" Jackson asked, dripping water as he bent over me. He scooped me up as though I weighed no more than one of the twins and ran up the hill to an idling pickup. April waited inside the open door and Jackson settled me in practically on her lap. Ron slid into the driver's seat and we bounced toward town as fast as Jackson's rutted road would allow.

"I can't believe you nearly drowned at your own party," April whispered in my ear.

I coughed and gagged. "I told you I'm not good at parties."

151

Chapter Thirty-Five

Where is everyone?" April glared at the double swinging doors as if she could make someone walk through them. Right on cue, they pushed open and someone did.

A large ruddy-faced man in green scrubs bustled into the room. Head tilted back, he peered down at me through smudged bifocals.

"Well, well, what seems to be the problem?" he asked me.

I gave him points for immediately recognizing the patient in our assembled group. But then I realized how I must look. The bandage had come off my cheek revealing an ugly red gash. Mud smeared across my face and caked under my broken nails. Plant life tangled in my hair. At least I hoped it was plants. April had wrapped me in a terrible blanket she'd found in Ron's pickup. Daydreon's expensive dress probably couldn't be salvaged.

"The problem is," April yelled into my ear, "this is an emergency room, or so the sign says. People should hang around in case one occurs. Don't you think?" She tried to jump up to confront the doctor, but since I was halfway in her lap, she couldn't without throwing me onto the floor. Thank goodness she realized that.

Jackson didn't have that problem. He leaped to his feet. "My niece fell into the lake behind our house. She wasn't in there long." The hand he swiped across his face shook. "But it's spring fed and ice cold. She swallowed quite a bit of water."

"The fact that the water was cold could work in her favor," the doctor said.

"She has a huge bump on her head," April added.

152

"I have the headache from hell," I mumbled, although nobody asked me.

"We'll fix that," the doctor said. He found two blankets and tossed one to Jackson who was as wet as I was. He covered me with the other. "You need to get out of those wet clothes," he said to Jackson.

The doctor pulled a light from his pocket and looked into my eyes. "I'm more concerned about the blow to her head," he said to nobody in particular. "Well, let's get you over here and have a look-see."

April helped him settle me into a wheelchair that he seemed to have summoned from thin air. He rolled me into an examining area. A nurse followed us in and helped the doctor move me to a table. She brought in plastic tubes and busied herself hooking up an IV. She gave me two white capsules and helped me lift the water glass.

The curtain had closed when I heard Jackson say, "Tony, glad you're here."

"Ron called me," Tony, answered. "What happened?"

"Jackson's niece was hit over the head and dumped into the lake," Ron explained. "Jackson jumped in and pulled her out."

How nice they could enjoy chatting outside my curtain. And, by the way, who is Tony? Oh yeah, Anthony Checotah, the sheriff.

"Why don't the two of you tell me what happened?" the sheriff suggested.

Ron and April filled in the details of what I'd told them, which wasn't much. Since Jackson had followed in his pickup, he hadn't heard the story either.

"So, this was at a party? Did anyone see it happen?"

"The twins were playing in the trees on the other side of the lake," Jackson said. "Jaci saw it happen and came to get me. I thought she imagined it, but she was hysterical and Ali was gone. So, I went to investigate. I got to the dock as Ali broke the surface. She sank again, but I knew where she was."

"Did your daughter see who it was?" the sheriff asked.

"A man wearing a hoody. She was across the lake and didn't see him well enough to recognize him."

"How old is your daughter?"

"Ten," Jackson said.

153

"I'll want to talk to her."

"Of course."

The doctor left me to talk to the group gathered outside of the curtain. Since he hadn't bothered to tell me the extent of my injuries, I was pretty interested in what was being said, myself, but was becoming too drowsy to keep my eyes open.

"Your niece is a lucky girl, considering the circumstances," the doctor said. "She turned as she was being hit, that probably saved her life. The blow glanced off the side of her head. I'm going to run tests. I'm guessing there's no fracture and I'm hoping the swelling is all on the outside. She has a nasty bump."

"What with?" Jackson asked.

"A blunt object."

"An oar," Jackson said. "There would be several close by."

"Possibly," the doctor replied. "Her attacker didn't intend for her to survive."

I could have told them that.

"I'm admitting her," the doctor continued. "I want to keep an eye on her tonight.

"He intended to kill her?" April's voice was a hushed whisper. She sounded shocked at the news. I'd rather not believe it either, but seriously, did she think he threw me in the lake to teach me to swim? Come on.

"Her brain could swell from an injury like that. She'll need to be checked every hour. In spite of all the water she swallowed, her lungs sound clear. We'll get x-rays in a bit. I'm concerned about dry drowning. She's in shock, both from the trauma and the temperature of the water. We need to keep her warm and quiet tonight."

"Dry drowning?" April asked. "What's that?"

"If a person has been submerged for any length of time or swallowed water through their nose or mouth, there's a danger of their throat swelling shut later. A near-drowning victim should always be checked by a doctor. Especially a child."

"Can someone get a prescription filled before you pick her up in the morning."

"I'll get it filled," April said, "but I'm staying with her tonight."

Chapter Thirty-Six

Ron and Jackson had been assuring the office person that I do, in fact, have insurance. And although I had been a bit remiss for not having verification on me as I sank to the bottom of a lake, it would be brought by the office first thing in the morning.

Do I have insurance? I tried to remember if I had mailed the forms David had his undies in a wad about. I was too confused to think. Yeah. I had. Lane had practically knocked me down as he barreled into me coming out of the post office.

Leaving Ron and Jackson to wrangle with all that, I was wheeled away for a battery of tests. After the CAT scan, I was moved to a room. April had already settled in, looking perfectly groomed and unruffled. I looked like something up from the swamp and she could've passed for Claudia Schiffer. If I didn't love her, I'd hate her. She glanced up from her book as the nurse wheeled me in.

"How is she?" April asked.

"Her oxygenation is good. We'll know more tomorrow. You should go home," the nurse said in an effort to dislodge April from the chair beside my bed. "And close that window."

"It was cold in here," April informed her. She made no move to close the window.

"Do you think the hospital can afford to air condition the whole town? It's 90 degrees out there."

Only a town the size of Cheyenne Falls would have a hospital with windows that open, I thought. The hospital was not only small, but it was also ancient. I smiled at the battle of wills raging around me. I don't know the nurse, but my money is on April.

"How do you feel?" April asked me, ignoring the nurse.

"Like I've swallowed ground glass. Thirsty. I need orange pop."

"I'll get you a can," April said, digging loose change from a designer purse.

"There's a soft drink dispenser at the far end of the hall," the nurse told her. She hurried out the door and April followed her.

The warm breeze blowing through the open window felt good. I stopped shivering. On their way out of the hospital, Ron and Jackson came by my room to say goodbye, then left by the front door. They chatted as they walked along the sidewalk right outside my open window. Jackson stopped to light a cigarette. I heard the click of his lighter.

"You smoke too much," I muttered.

"I hope you don't mind that I called the sheriff," Ron said. "A report needed to be filed. In view of the situation..."

Jackson cut him off. "What situation?"

"The hearing next week," Ron reminded him. "I'm guessing somebody wants to make sure she doesn't get her inheritance. Maybe the same person who shot at her in the canyon."

What were they talking about? Hearing? I sort of remembered Jackson mentioning a hearing. But I was so sleepy...

Jackson exhaled forcefully. "She thought she was shot at in the canyon. But I didn't take it seriously. Maybe it's time I did."

"If a piece of rock grazed her cheek, that bullet missed her by inches, Jackson. And, as for the why—who might want that land?" Ron asked pointedly. "Besides you?"

"You don't think I did this?" Jackson huffed.

"I think," Ron said, "you need to keep Ali safe."

"You got that right. I don't want to explain to her mama how I let anything happen to her," Jackson said. "Eternity wouldn't be long enough to get away from that woman." He softened. "Besides, Ali's kind of growing on me."

They resumed walking and left me sorting through what I'd heard. Someone doesn't want me to live long enough to inherit my land. But that someone isn't Jackson. He saved my life. Then who? My head pounded.

The nurse returned, closed the window, and left without a word.

April breezed through the door with my orange pop. She popped the top, handed it to me, opened the window, and sat on the side of my bed. "Did Dad and Ron leave?"

"Yes," I said. "Just now."

"Oh." She sounded disappointed. She looked as though she wanted to say something but didn't. Which is so totally unlike her. Her eyes were red-rimmed. She sniffed.

"April, you've been crying. What's wrong?"

"I, uh…"

"You're scaring me. What's wrong?"

She laid a hand on my knee. "Promise you won't marry the wrong man."

"Okay," I said. "I'm working on that."

"When you get married then realize you've never stopped loving your first love, there's no way to fix it without hurting people. No matter what you do, it's wrong." A fat tear rolled down her cheek. "Especially when you have children who love their father." Her lip trembled. "You're stuck."

Although I fought sleep, I couldn't keep my eyes open. April took the pop can from my hand and set it on the nightstand.

"I don't understand," I yawned.

"Never mind. We'll talk about it later." She kissed my cheek.

But we never did.

Chapter Thirty-Seven

I awoke from a deep sleep. My mind, tangled as the sheets, tried to shake off the fogginess of the dream. This one, disjointed and fanciful, left me unsettled. I dreamed that everyone I know was out to kill me for land I didn't possess. It ended with Lexy, riding Mariah, saving me at the last minute. Did it contain a warning? If so, the only thing I can trust is a horse and a girl who lives in another century. Perfect.

I opened my eyes. The window had been closed again, but the sunlight streaming through blinded me. I shaded my eyes and looked around. April was gone. The sheriff stood in the doorway. I motioned him in. He gave me a brief nod, walked across the room and closed the curtain.

"Better?" he asked.

"Yes. Thanks."

"Are you up to answering a couple of questions?"

"That's one."

He smiled. Briefly. "Where have I seen you before?" I looked like a drowned rat, shook uncontrollably, still he recognized me. Impressive.

"That's two," I said. "At the courthouse. There was a disturbance. I came to get you."

"Right. I remember you. You nearly knocked my Collin Bogle original off the wall. How long had you been in town that day?"

"Twenty minutes. Maybe." My eyes closed.

"And already showing up where you shouldn't. You're going to be trouble."

"Evidently I already am," I said. I opened my eyes and studied his face. "You can't be a sheriff."

He bristled. "Because I'm Chickasaw?"

"No. A sheriff should be old." I yawned. "Have life experience. Battle scars. Wrinkles. Why would anyone vote for you?"

"I'm older than I look. I campaigned hard. I can be very charming. Maybe they thought I'm the best man for the job."

"Must have been the hard-campaign thing," I said through another yawn.

"You're a tough crowd. What's in that IV?"

"Not enough," I said. "My head is splitting."

He repeated the story he'd heard last night. "Did I get it right?"

"Yeah." I massaged my temples.

"Sorry. I'll be through in a minute. Did you see your assailant?"

"No." My teeth chattered.

"Do you have any idea who it was?"

"No. He was tall. Strong. Muscular. But he grunted when he lifted me."

"You said he. You're sure it was a man?"

"Do you know any women strong enough to lift me over that rail?"

"Guess not. If I remember correctly, it's about three feet high, right?"

"There I was without a yardstick." My eyes closed. "He smelled like a man. Musky. Sweaty. He hadn't been at the party."

"You're sure it was no one from party?"

"Nobody at the party smelled like that."

"How'd you get that gash on your cheek?"

"A man shot at me in the canyon. A bullet hit a boulder and a piece of rock flew off and hit me." I willed my eyes back open.

He looked up from his notes. "When?"

"After I saw you at the courthouse. I don't remember what day. They all run together when I'm dodging bullets."

"Why wasn't it reported?"

"Jackson said it was a hunter.'"

"Do you think it was?"

"No. He shot at me twice. It was no accident."

"He?"

"I was shot at twice. Good grief, you sound like Jackson. It wasn't a woman who shot at me in the canyon or dropped me over the rail last night. Okay?"

"You have a talent for being at the wrong place at the wrong time. Anything else I should know?" His eyes narrowed.

I thought about it. I should probably mention being drugged at Blue Sage, but I don't think it was meant for me or had anything to do with last night. And I'm so sleepy. "Uh, I guess not," I said.

"What about Blue Sage?" he asked.

Whoa. I'd hate to be interrogated by this guy. Wait. I am.

"You already know what happened," I grumbled.

"Let me see if I have this straight. You've been in town five days and you've been shot at, drugged, and practically drowned. Right?"

"Six."

"What?"

"I've been in town six days. You think it was something I said?" The lines around his eyes tightened. He's right. He's older than he looks.

"If you think of anything else, call me," he ordered.

"Well," I said, "I'm being watched."

"By whom?"

"Well, I don't know. I keep getting this feeling I'm being watched."

"Where?"

"In my motel room I saw a man at my window. He tried my door. When it didn't open, he left. He's out there watching my room. Other places, too." I expected him to think I'm paranoid, but he didn't seem to. He made more notes.

"Next time it happens, stay inside and call me. Anything else?"

"No."

"Okay, that should do it for now. Be careful until we catch this guy. Evil seems to be following you," Sheriff Checotah said, snapping his notebook closed. He turned to go.

"That's what James White Eagle said," I mumbled.

He whipped back around. "What did you say?"

"James White Eagle. He said evil followed me."

"James White Eagle is a legend. He never existed."

"Don't bet the farm on that."

"You think you saw James White Eagle? Where? When?"

"I don't know." My teeth chattered.

"You don't know where or when, but you talked to James White Eagle?"

"Mostly he talked to me."

"According to legend, he never spoke to women," the sheriff said.

"Yeah, that's what Moonflower said," I muttered.

The sheriff flipped open his notebook. "Who is this Moonflower?"

"She's, uh… I don't know."

"I'll want to talk to you about this again when you're not full of drugs." He pulled a blanket from a nearby chair and spread it over me. "Where's your phone?"

"I don't know." I realized it could be at the bottom of the lake but was too drowsy to think it through or care.

He handed me a card. "When you find it, put this in your phone. It's my cell number," he said. "I always have mine with me. Make sure I'm in your contacts."

I nodded. I don't always do what I'm told. But I would this time.

"Don't forget." His expression was kind, but I sensed his anger. What happened to me last night upset him.

"That was more than a couple of questions," I mumbled, "by the way."

"Check." He smiled and was gone.

Chapter Thirty-Eight

Later that afternoon the doctor signed my release with strict orders to stay quiet. Ron had driven my car from Jackson's to the motel where it was parked when Jackson and Penny dropped me off. Two days of people bustling around me in the hospital had worn me out. Penny tried to talk me into going to their house, but I longed for solitude. And wanted to spend it with my mother's journals.

Abby began writing her journals to chronicle the events and her emotions of my abduction. Through the years the journals became letters to me. I'm on the third one, no longer surprised to see my thoughts penned by my mother's hand. I know Abby, whom I've yet to meet, better than I knew Margaret who raised me. I kept returning to one particular passage. I'd read it so often the book fell open there. Throughout my childhood I'd fantasized that I was loved by somebody. I was.

Somewhere

Sometimes when the sun sinks below the sycamore
painting a crimson sky, and dusk settles in
comfortable and close like an old friend,
I lay my book of Keats aside
and feel my daughter's breath,
sweet puffs of air, on the back of my neck.
Child of my heart now gone.
Beyond my vision, but not beyond my love,
I know she lives. Somewhere.

~ Abby Forrest's journal

I heard a knock at my door. I wiped tears from the page, laid the journal aside, grabbed my robe and tied it tightly around me.

"Who is it?" I asked, through the closed door. I'm more cautious these days.

"Debbie. Hurry."

Debbie and I have become friends. She's a waitress at the restaurant. When she's not busy, she keeps me company while I eat. She's funny. I like her a lot. Her husband, a long-haul truck driver, was often on the road.

As soon as I opened the door Debbie thrust a plate through it. "A guy ordered eggs Benedict and left. I remembered you're a big fan, so here they are. I smuggled them out. Have you eaten?"

"No, and I'm starving. Debbie, you're an angel." I hugged her. I'm getting better at that. She remembered I love eggs Benedict which meant as much as her bringing breakfast.

After I dropped the dishes off at the kitchen, I ran by Ron's office to sign some papers. Being there felt weird. I'm rather embarrassed about the nearly drowning thing. I hate being the focus of everyone's attention especially when I'm a soggy mess. I had done so well at the party. Looked good, felt confident, talked to a stranger and then got thrown into the lake. I've done so many stupid things in my life, it just felt like one more. I also felt weird about seeing Ron and April in the trees that night. And then there's that strange thing April said at the hospital about marrying the wrong man. Jackson had mentioned that Ron and April dated in high school and most of college. Everyone had assumed they would get married. Except, they didn't. There's a story there. They both married other people soon after their breakup. Ron's wife recently died of cancer after a lengthy illness.

Since Ron had the key to Abby's safety deposit box at the bank, he accompanied me across the street. I took two more journals and the necklace. Now that Ron is more interesting, I checked him out in that surreptitious way that I have, wanting to see him through April's eyes. It didn't work. He's not movie star handsome, like David and Lane, but good looking. I guess. In a nerdy sort of way.

Back at Ron's office, I went to the ornate mirror behind his desk and put on the necklace. I expected I'd feel different wearing my mother's necklace. Lexy's necklace. Who knows how many other women? I stared through my reflection to the generations before me. I touched the gold heart. Wherever Lexy was at that moment, she was wearing it too. Mind boggling.

Ron cleared his throat.

I'd forgotten he was there.

He watched me with a curious expression. "You Dale women are so pretty, April."

"Uh, I'm Ali."

A flush crept up his neck. "Yes, of course." He glanced at his watch. "Hate to rush you, girl, but I have to be in court in twenty minutes."

"Sorry." I hurried out the door.

I went to the apartment and began painting the living room. The color—picture a sand dune at sunset—was perfect with the light pouring through the skylight. I'm going to love living here. Jackson had already turned on the utilities.

I've become quite the history buff. Each trip to visit Lexy left me more impressed by the tenacity of her family. Very few people I know today would have survived back then. Which is what David said when he finally called. He was as awed and confused.

"David, this is so weird. I climbed the cliff to see where all the water comes from that covers the opening in 1891. I got to thinking, it's like Niagara Falls. Not really, but it takes a lot of water to completely cover an opening that size. The canyon is arid on this side but that giant cottonwood that hides the opening needed water at some point."

"You're right. What did you find?"

"There was not only no water. There was no opening. The rock wall was solid."

"That is weird. Almost amazing as your climbing a cliff." David laughed.

"Yeah. You should have seen me staring down a rattlesnake."

He was quiet for a minute. "Ali. You aren't the same person who left Dallas."

"I know," I said.

"There's a reason why the cave only exits into that particular year."

"Maybe in order to meet Lexy. She's the best friend I've ever had and..."

"Yeah. Well, as crucial as that is to the cosmos, there has to be more to it. We need to find out what happened in 1891. How many generations are between you and Lexy?"

"Four. I'm the fifth from her father."

"Can you get your hands on an Oklahoma History book?"

"David, my gosh. Thank God you thought of that."

Silence. My sarcasm shocked him.

"I have a stack of them in my room, David. I told you that. The big deal seems to be the land runs and lotteries. But I'm supposed to help these people somehow."

"How nice you're in a place which allows you to bring help to the less fortunate," he said after a long silence.

I smothered a laugh. When had he become so concerned about the less fortunate? I told him about my near-drowning experience. He said all the right things and didn't demand that I come back to Dallas like I expected. He reminded me how busy and important he was and how grateful I should be that he found time to call. I promised to do more digging in the history books. We ended the conversation.

I think it was John Wayne who said, 'Courage isn't a lack of fear, it's being scared to death but saddling up anyway'. I should get back in the water. I pulled my two-piece from the suitcase and went for a swim in the motel pool.

'Going for a swim' sounds cool like I perfected a swan dive and made several laps in an Olympic-sized pool. Actually, I dog paddled, carefully avoiding the deep end. Then I laid in the sun. Don't judge me. I know sunlight is bad for my skin. I need vitamin D, okay? I soaked up those rays like a sponge and thought about what Lane had said about sunflowers' faces turning to follow the sun. He'd called me Sunflower from the first time he laid eyes on me. He'd said sunflowers are strong and thrive without nurture. That part doesn't sound like me, but I do crave sunlight. Probably from years of being held captive in a dark apartment.

In Dallas I'd assumed I'd die every time I left the apartment. I'd never even had a close call. Since I arrived in sleepy Cheyenne Falls, I've been shot at, drugged and nearly drowned. I've been up close and personal with a rattlesnake and I've out-run a tornado. The old me would've been locked in my room in a fetal position reciting mantras or hail-Mary's. The new me has never felt more alive.

Chapter Thirty-Nine

I groped for the ringing phone. By the time I found it, I was awake.

"Hey, City Girl."

"Lane?" Fully awake now. "Lane." Okay, too late to play it cool.

"If you were expecting Bradly Cooper you're out of luck."

"He usually calls later in the day." I yawned. "It's—" I checked the clock on the nightstand. "Good grief, it's 5:00 AM. I wasn't expecting anyone."

"I have breakfast. Can I entice you to go back to the plateau?"

I thought about the suicide drive up that cliff. And even worse, the drive back down. The only thing between safety and being hurled through a windshield is a seatbelt that looks like a relic from WW II.

"I have to admit the terror of impending doom is intoxicating," I said.

He waited.

"Still thinking. I like the breakfast thing. Not the ride."

"Did you know that one out of eight deaths occurs in bed?"

I yawned again. "I didn't."

"You'd be much safer if you get out of bed and come with me." He laughed.

I'm realizing how much I love his laugh. Unfortunately, he seems to be able to entice me to do anything. Good thing he isn't a bank robber. I hope.

"I doubt it," I said. "Where are you?"

"In the lobby. But if you don't mind, I'll meet you east of town."

"Okay," I said, grabbing my toothbrush and looking through a pile of clothes for my running shoes, shorts, and a clean shirt. I am so easy.

***

Thirty minutes later we were back on the plateau.

"Why are we here again?" I asked.

Austin leaped from the jeep behind me.

"Making memories," Lane said. He poured a steaming cup of coffee from his thermos and handed it to me. "I've worn out the old ones."

"Me, too," I said.

"When the weather conditions are right, magic happens. The moment cries out to be shared. *Kairos* in Greek. You're who I want to share it with." He spread out the blanket, smoothed the wrinkles and grinned. "Okay?"

"Okay." I wanted him to kiss me, but he didn't.

Austin ran around us in circles while Lane poured coffee into his cup. I braced before sipping mine, but it was actually good.

"I'd love to sketch that." I pointed to a rustic barn nestled in the valley.

"You like being outside, don't you?" Lane gave me a sidelong look that I might have wondered about if I hadn't been so busy mixing paints in my mind.

"I crave fresh air and sunshine. I didn't get enough growing up."

He handed me a pair of binoculars. They brought the barn within reach.

"It's beautiful up here." I handed them back and sat cross-legged on the blanket.

The scene below had a mystical quality. The rising sun and breeze turned the dew on trees into dancing diamonds.

Lane handed me a still-warm gooey cinnamon roll.

"This is wonderful," I said, biting into it. "Where did you get it?"

"Buggy Creek Restaurant. Cinnamon rolls are their claim to fame."

"Good to know." Austin flopped down beside me. I scratched behind his ear.

"Sorry I forgot napkins." Lane bit into his cinnamon roll. "Your friend, Debbie, looked like she hasn't slept in a week."

"I've seen that look on you," I said, not surprised he knew Debbie and I are friends. "Poor Debbie. Planes probably kept her awake again last night."

"Planes?" Lane asked. The mug he was raising to his lips stopped suddenly in midair, sloshing coffee onto his lap.

I licked icing from my fingers. "Uh huh. She lives behind the airport. She said planes fly in late at night."

"Do you know what days?"

"No. Wait. Yeah. Thursdays. Her husband is gone Thursday nights. He's a truck driver." I brushed a stealth ant from my cinnamon roll.

"She lives behind the airport?" Lane's eyes bore into me. "Where behind the airport?" These were not idle questions.

"There's a road, practically hidden, past the cemetery. Her car wouldn't start one afternoon. I drove out to get her and nearly missed the road. I wouldn't want to live out there. She doesn't either, but they have big dogs. Nobody in town would rent to them."

"And yesterday was Thursday," Lane said. "Interesting. What else did she say?"

"Umm—," I squinted into technicolor clouds. "She doesn't sleep well on those nights because her dogs bark at the traffic. That road is practically a cow path. How can there be that much traffic?"

"Where past the cemetery?" Lane pulled a receipt from his pocket and handed me a pen. "Can you draw me a map?"

I began sketching. "This road was the reason you were in the cemetery the other night, wasn't it?" I glanced up.

"Yeah."

"You couldn't find it?" I finished the sketch and handed it to him.

"I got interrupted. Remember?"

"Like I'll ever forget that crazy drive to town. I'm guessing you aren't going to explain."

"Later. I can't now."

"Well, of course not." Austin gazed up at me with that one blue eye.

Lane grabbed my wrist and pointed. "Look. There it is."

Fog rolled through the canyon like an angry river. When it reached a spot right below us, a shaft of sunlight stabbed through the break in the cliffs turning the tumbling mist into an explosion of gold, pink, and rainbow fragments.

I gasped. "I've never seen anything like this."

Lane slipped an arm around my shoulder and pulled me close. "I know. Right?"

Joy enveloped us. He held me against his side. Intoxicated by the nearness of Lane and the spectacle below, tears streamed down my face. I cry at the weirdest times, but the glory of the moment overwhelmed me. The sun climbed higher and the spectacle faded. Lane dropped a kiss on the top of my head and released me.

"A bookmark moment," he said. "Every once in a while, an experience comes along that's so special, you need a bookmark because you'll be going back in your memories to find it."

"I like that." I said, realizing there is so much more to this guy than dimples and watercolor eyes. That moment dancing at Blue Sage would be a bookmark moment, too.

I picked up the binoculars, idly aiming them at the barn.

"I see people down there." I watched several armed men hurry from the barn to meet an approaching truck. "Lane, they're unloading men from that cattle truck and taking them into the barn. Look."

He set down the cup and sticky bun, wiped his hands on his jeans, reached for the binoculars, adjusted them, and focused on the barn. "I don't see people. Only a truck."

"Guys with guns came out of the barn and unloaded about ten men from that truck and took them into the barn at gunpoint. And bags. They were carrying sacks." I grabbed the binoculars. There was no sign of anyone. "Lane, they were there. Moving fast."

"I believe you," he said briskly, as he rose to his feet, "Party's over, Sunflower. Time to get to work."

"What's going on? What's happening?"

Lane whistled for Austin, scooped up our belongings and chucked them into the Jeep. He picked me up like I weighed nothing—I seriously shouldn't have eaten that second cinnamon roll—and tossed me into the driver's seat. I scooted past the treacherous out-to-get-me-gear-shift knob, sank into my seat and fastened my seat belt. Tight.

If the drive out to the plateau seemed fast, the drive back to town was more so. I gripped the sides of my seat. "So, this Jeep was manufactured before shocks were invented?"

Lane grinned. "It had good shocks. Once."

All too soon, we were at the edge of town. Realizing he was in a hurry I was ready to hop out before the Jeep rolled to a stop. Lane grabbed my arm.

"Wait, I need to talk to you." His eyes roamed over my face, as if memorizing my features.

"This can't be good," I said.

"I won't be seeing you for a while."

"What does that mean? I don't see you every day now."

"Not because I don't want to. I gotta get done what I'm here to do. I can't be distracted." He ran a hand across his face. "And you are such a distraction. I can't put you in any more danger than I already have."

"I seem to find it without any help from you."

"Copy that. Be more careful."

"I can't think when you're looking at me with those eyes," I said.

"I'm on my way now to Chief's office to tell him what you saw. Don't say anything to anyone else. Got that?" He waited for me to nod. "You have no idea how helpful you've been." He leaned over and kissed the tip of my nose, then below my nose. His lips lingered.

I wrapped my arms around his neck and kissed him back. I hopped out and jogged several yards toward town. He hadn't driven away. I stopped and looked back. Lane's eyes were glued to me. His hand lifted in a small salute. He put the Jeep in gear and drove away.

Nothing about this relationship has been easy. Why can't I be in love with a good-looking predictable Dallas attorney? The one who couldn't care less what I think. The one who believes I'm too stupid to have anything worthwhile to say. Oh yeah, now I remember.

I jogged into town with tears spilling down my cheek. Seeing those men herded into a barn like cattle really upset me. A terrible feeling of dread washed over me. What if I've seen Lane Lanigan for the last time?

Chapter Forty

Incredible." Lexy enthused. I mean, the girl speaks in exclamation points. The couple at the next table watched her with amusement. Lexy leaned back in her chair.

"The special effects were good." I took a bite of cheesy sourdough bread. "I wanted to go to a movie the night we went to Blue Sage."

"Sakes alive. We were right in the middle of that train wreck." Lexy speared a piece of steak and waved it in the air as she talked. "Screaming people, flying luggage. Noise from all directions. Whooo weee."

People stopped eating and stared. I didn't care. Lexy's speech had become a combination of modern-day slang and quaint expressions I'd never heard.

Lane had been gone for a week. I missed him. And still there was no word of my parents. My concern for the three of them grew daily. I channeled my anxiety into working on the apartment. I painted the walls, framed and hung two of my mother's paintings and the prints I'd bought at Tribes.

The rest of what I needed couldn't be found in Cheyenne Falls. I scheduled a shopping trip to Oklahoma City with Lexy. I bought a leather sofa, a recliner, an easy chair, a bedroom suite, an area rug and window treatment for the living room which will be delivered next Monday.

I needed more clothes than I'd tossed in a suitcase when I left Dallas. My wardrobe embarrassed April. I bought clothes for myself and Lexy. She won't be able to wear them at home but they're perfect when she's with me. She loved trying on clothes. Especially the cowboy boots. They were cute with the calico dress she wore. They looked so good on her I bought a pair for myself. If we go back to Blue Sage we're set. I hate shopping, but Lexy made it fun. We laughed and caused such scenes that several stores will probably ban us. But we both needed that respite from our lives.

After the movie, I took Lexy to a fancy restaurant. It required two elevators and some stairs, but getting there was worth the effort. Lexy's expression was priceless and so was the incredible view.

Thank goodness April lives fifty miles away or she'd be having a fit about how often I'm 'out in that old canyon wrecking my skin'. From a distance I've watched Lexy's brothers work in the fields with their father like grown men. They planted crops in land that's not yet theirs, and may never be. Their courage in the face of the adversity makes me proud of the stock I'm descended from.

Lexy leaned forward, elbows on the table. "I'll never forget this day."

"I won't either." I meant it more than she knew. After shopping, we had pedicures and facials. Lexy had never had either of those luxuries. But then, neither had I.

I savored a succulent scallop. "How's your steak?"

"Wonderful. We had beef when Pa helped a neighbor butcher. But it was tough and stringy. The longer you chewed it, the bigger it got." She laughed. "Which is good, I guess. We don't always get a lot to eat."

"It doesn't bother you that your life is difficult?"

Lexy tilted her head. "Difficult? But it isn't. I love Emily Dickinson's quote, *'That it never comes again is what makes life so sweet.'*" A smile crossed her lips as she gazed through the window into the beauty of the night. "I want to be aware. Totally alive."

Lexy wasn't familiar with wine. Her parents probably didn't chill with a glass of Merlot after a day of plowing and butchering. She tasted my wine, wrinkled her nose, and told the waiter she 'fancied' something else. He didn't bat an eye. His expression would have been the same if she'd ordered vintage *Chateau Haut–Brion*. He brought her root beer in a cut-crystal wine glass. He's going to get a big tip.

"Have you seen your cowboy since Blue Sage?" Lexy's gaze wandered from table to table taking in the elegantly dressed diners around us. I wondered what she thought of these people so different from those of 1891. We were a bit underdressed.

I nodded. "He didn't drug me."

"I didn't think so. He fancies you. Does he know you have a beau?" She glanced up, caught my expression, and laid her fork aside. Her eyes searched my face.

How could I explain something I couldn't understand myself? I groped for words. I didn't need them. She knows me so well.

"You love him." she said.

"Yes. I mean no...."

Lexy raised an eyebrow the way David does.

"Don't look at me like that." I felt my face get hot. "Doesn't matter. He's gone."

"Is he coming back?"

"I think so."

"Gone where?"

"I don't know."

"What *do* you know?" Her tone reminded me of David again.

"His truth. I know his heart. I've seen strength and honesty in his eyes. And..."

"And?" She raised that eyebrow again.

"And he loves his dog."

I expected her to laugh. But she didn't. She understood. We gazed out the window watching headlights snake along the street far below. Lights blinked on in windows across from us and stars began making an appearance above.

"What's your take on David?" I asked

Lexy's brow furrowed in confusion. "I didn't take him anywhere. Is he lost?"

I laughed. "No. You've spent time together. What do you think?"

"Oh," she said, relief evident. "He knows a lot."

"That wasn't in question. What do you think?"

Lexy gazed at the ceiling. "He isn't prideful."

"Well, of course he is. He's very prideful."

Lexy shook her head. "He's blustery to make up for a lack of confidence."

"David? Unsure of himself? What?"

"You asked me what I thought. I told you."

"He's an arrogant snob. Surely you can see that."

"It's an act. But he's not, really."

"I'm ending our engagement."

Lexy choked. "What? No. He loves you."

"I don't think so." I circled my glass rim with a finger to avoid her penetrating gaze.

"Of course, he does. You're throwing away a man who looks like Adonis? Adonis is a Greek god," she said. "I've seen pictures of him in Aunt Mattie's book. For a guy you barely know?" Lexy shook her head. "Lawsy me, if that don't beat all."

I stabbed a shrimp with unnecessary force. "It's not because of Lane."

Her stare intensified as though trying to decide if there's anything inside my head.

"David is the only guy I've ever dated. He moved me out of the hood. Nobody had ever cared about my safety. I confused gratitude with love. I knew nothing about either. I have been too shocked that David chose me to wonder if I love him. I'm terrified he'll realize he made a mistake and dump me."

Lexy 's confusion was evident. I hurried on needing her to understand.

"If I got a Christmas gift as a child, it was socks or underwear. I never had a birthday present or party. I went from extreme poverty to David who bought me a car because it was dangerous to walk to the bus stop wearing this honkin' huge diamond he bought me. I was blown away by his generosity. And grateful." Grateful. There it was again. "Still, I resent people like David who float through life so unaware."

"Unaware of what?" Lexy set her glass down and leaned in, trying to understand.

"Their good fortune. David's gifts were nothing to him. He barely missed what they cost. His family breezes through life as though their wealth is due them."

"How is David at fault?"

"He isn't." I avoided her direct gaze.

"Then, obviously, God isn't doing his job," Lexy said. She scratched her nose.

"I didn't say that."

"Yes, you did. Be careful, Ali. Not being happy with your circumstances is saying you are smarter than God. Why He doesn't ask you for advice is beyond me."

I scowled, leaned back in my chair and folded my arms.

She wasn't finished. "Circumstances shape us. Challenges make us stronger. Nobody chooses the family they're born into. We have to play the hand we're dealt. David hasn't faced the challenges we have. Maybe he will at some point. Or maybe God's plan for his life is different."

She gave me time to think about what she said. I wondered why I like her.

"David has no idea who I am," I said finally.

"Good grief, why didn't you say so? For pity sakes. Shoot him." She raised her water glass to her lips, paused in mid-air and glared at me over it. "Just shoot him."

"Sarcasm doesn't become you. You're as bad as David."

"In 1891 a husband is too busy feeding his kids, plowing, fighting to keep crops from dying, grasshoppers from eating them, and praying for rain." Lexy set down her glass, picked up a fork and waved it at me. "He's too tired to talk to his wife. She's been chasing toddlers, changing diapers, washing clothes, and trying to make a meal out of nothing. She doesn't wonder if he 'knows' her. Heck, she's happy if he takes a bath once in a while."

I stared.

"Have you told David?" She took a bite of steak, her eyes considering me as she chewed.

"Of course not. He..."

"No. You're afraid to talk to him." She cut me off with a dismissive flippy-hand thing. "You've never talked to him about being overbearing. If you don't like it, change it."

"I have ulcers from being afraid he's mad at me," I huffed. "That's not love."

"Your fault, not his. You've taught him it's okay to treat you like that."

I seemed to deflate with the long stream of air I exhaled. "You're tough."

"In 1891 people don't have the luxury of marrying for love. A man needs a wife to cook, clean, and wash his clothes. A woman needs a man who will put a roof over her head, keep her safe, fed, and help raise all the kids they made."

"So, he's too tired to talk, but not too tired to make kids," I grumbled.

Lexy ignored me. "It's enough that he works hard, doesn't drink too much, and is hopefully kind. If he has teeth, that's a bonus."

"Well, that puts it in perspective." I wiped my hands and tossed my napkin aside.

Her expression softened. She stopped talking and we both gazed through the window in silence. I realized I seriously lack depth.

I sighed. "David deserves someone who loves him. I don't. I don't think I ever have. I didn't know how love feels.

"And now you do?" she challenged.

I nodded. "Most of the time it feels like you are going to be sick." I thought about it. "David is a good honest man. He deserves someone who will love him with their whole heart. That will never be me."

The sky had turned deep indigo. I glanced at my watch. "David's plane will be leaving Dallas about now. He'll be in the air for about thirty minutes. By the time we get across town he should be landing."

"Are you going to tell him what happened yesterday?" Lexy asked.

My stomach tightened. "I have to. It'll be okay. I hope."

Chapter Forty-One

Y ou shot a man where?" David wore an expression of disbelief. "Next you'll be telling me you're moving to Mars to raise pygmy goats."

"Not a bad idea, actually," I said. "It was an accident, David."

"What is wrong with you?" David was holding it together, but barely.

"We don't have time to get into all that right now, and I'm not sure I'm the person to ask. Talk to Ursula."

"I have. I pay for your therapy and she won't tell me a damn thing." David's jaw tightened. "I meant more specifically, Ali. I need details."

Of course, the attorney in him would need details. I wanted to get up and pace, but I was crammed into a booth. With Lexy sitting beside me, I had no way of escape. Which triggered my claustrophobia when I thought about it.

"Go through it again. When did this happen?" David's voice softened, but his expression didn't.

"Yesterday. I already told you." I picked at a hangnail.

"Ali didn't mean to shoot his private parts. She came to see me…" Lexy offered in an attempt to defuse David and get me started.

"Lexy was washing clothes by the lake. I was keeping her little brother occupied by tossing him into the water. He was screaming, laughing, and splashing. So, I didn't hear Lexy scream. At first."

Lexy picked up the story. "Elmer rode by and saw me. He's been looking for a chance to get me alone and thought he'd found it. He jumped off his horse and grabbed me. He tore my blouse. I bit his hand. He hit me and began to choke me."

David's lips compressed into a tight line of fury as he gently probed the bruises on Lexy's cheek and neck that my makeup techniques couldn't conceal. His hands shook. I had never seen him so angry, but I realized, his anger wasn't directed at me.

"I heard Lexy scream," I continued, talking fast. "Elmer was cussing a blue streak. I told Johnny to stay put and went to help her. Mariah charged out of the woods. Elmer saw me and pulled out his gun. He was going to shoot me. But he didn't have time."

"Mariah knocked him down. The gun flew out of his hand," Lexy interrupted. "Ali picked it up."

"It was heavy," I said. "A pistol with a long barrel."

"Elmer's eyes bugged out," Lexy said. "He looked at her and back at me as though he'd seen a ghost."

"But then he lunged at me, roaring like a bull crammed into a rodeo chute," I said. "He grabbed the gun barrel, which you gotta admit was stupid, right? No way was I going to turn loose." I shrugged. "Somehow it went off."

David rubbed his temples. "You aimed at his...?"

"I didn't have time to aim at anything. I told you."

"Have you been arraigned?"

"What?" I didn't intend to laugh. It kind of exploded. "Arraigned? David, it happened in Oklahoma Territory. 1891. Not even a state."

"Surely you don't think you'll get away with this?"

"Judge Judy hasn't called yet."

"The law is the law, Ali. You shot a man." He grabbed the back of his neck massaging the tension.

"That's very profound, David. How are they going to find me?"

He blinked.

"If there was any law on that side of the tunnel," Lexy informed him, "Elmer wouldn't get by with this stuff."

"I don't think he's hurt too badly," I said. "I only disarmed him."

Lexy choked on her cola. "It wasn't an arm," she said.

"Well, I was never good at anatomy," I grumbled.

David gaped at me like I'd stepped off a spaceship. "I don't know you anymore."

"Ali doesn't think you ever did." Lexy chopped at ice in her glass with a fork. It splattered across the table.

David glared at both of us. He scooped up the splattered ice and dumped it into an ashtray. "A man could bleed to death in a matter of minutes. Do you know how many blood vessels encase...?"

Lexy and I stared at him.

"I guess you don't," he finished lamely. "We have to find out if he's alive."

"He's too mean to die," Lexy muttered.

"I take it you didn't examine the wound," David said.

"Uh, no. I didn't touch the wound." I shook at the thought.

"And he didn't stay around to visit," Lexy added.

"Did you call for help?"

"There wasn't time to dial 911."

"Don't be sardonic, Ali."

"Well, don't be asinine. There is no phone service, David. Who would I call?"

"The nearest law is Ft Reno," Lexy informed him. "It's forty miles away."

"Hanging around until the cavalry arrived hardly seemed feasible," I added.

David shook his head. "Lexy, your parents want you to marry this guy?"

She nodded. "Ma'am does."

"I hope you didn't have your heart set on a big family," I said.

David's brows pulled down into a scowl as he glanced at me. "Does he want to marry you?" he asked Lexy.

"He wants what he wants without marrying me," Lexy said. "Ma'am says men don't buy the cow if they can get milk through the fence."

David slammed his mug onto the table. "You will not marry this guy.

I stared at him in shock.

He turned to me, sloshing more coffee. "Stay away from there until things blow over." He frowned at the menu he'd been examining for the past half hour as though it were at fault for not offering *cordon bleu*. He slapped it closed and crammed it behind the napkin holder. "Surely they've found my suitcase by now. It didn't walk off the plane."

Lexy and I had arrived at the airport late and breathless due to an accident which snarled traffic. David's plane had been late, too, and he was the last one off. His only suitcase had been misplaced. We were stuck in the airport snack bar while the airline searched, and David's bad mood escalated.

"You said you have a plan. We want to hear it," I said in an effort to distract him.

"It may not work since you've taken matters into your own hands," he said.

"I didn't take it into my own hands," I huffed. "If you think I'm going to stand by and watch anyone hurt Lexy, you can think again."

David crossed his arms. "Testy, aren't we?"

"You weren't there. But I don't think Elmer is much into deliberation. Which you do so well," I finished sweetly.

He shrugged. "You're right. I wouldn't have been deliberating either."

"Can we hear your plan?" Lexy asked. She batted those long lashes and David's demeanor visibly softened.

He sipped what was left of his coffee as he thought and leveled a look at me. "What was that story your uncle told you about your family's land?"

"I don't remember the details. An ancestor was robbed at gunpoint and his horse stolen. A rider came out of nowhere to save the day."

"You don't know any more than that?"

"It probably wasn't Mighty Mouse."

"I think Lexy's father is the ancestor," David said.

"They have land now. Everything must have been okay," Lexy pointed out.

"Not necessarily." David's brow furrowed as he thought. "Your father might need help. There's a reason why the tunnel took Ali to that year. I'll go to the courthouse tomorrow and check out the laws that were in effect in 1891." He winked at me, "In case I have to defend you in court."

"Funny," I said. "What are you really looking for?"

"I've dug through early Oklahoma history. You can Google anything," David said.

Lexy frowned. "What's a google? Weird word. Google."

David ignored her. "A few ranchers had legitimate contracts with the Indians. I suspect this Elmer is a squatter."

Lexy had pushed back in the booth, crossed her arms and was quietly singing, "Yankee Google went to town riding on a..." She interrupted her singing to ask, "Is a squatter like a Google?"

David actually smiled. "A squatter is someone who illegally possesses Indian land. We need to know exactly what the law says. We may have to evict him."

"Know where we can get an army tank?" I asked. "I want a life-sized picture of that."

"There was a Homestead Exemption Act. We need to learn more about that, as well as how the land lottery worked. There were land runs that year, too. We need to get names of the people who got land." He looked up at me. "Can you do that?"

"Of course."

"Talk to your uncle again. Get more details. While you're at it, ask if we can keep a horse in the canyon with Mariah and Whiplash. We can't get it to Lexy's father too early and take a chance on getting it stolen. If it's okay with Jackson, I'll bring one from North Haven next week."

"Can you get a decent horse without arousing your mother's suspicion?" I asked.

"I think so. Emerson wouldn't be missed."

He was right. Emerson, a retired racehorse in the back pasture, would never be missed. I felt a warm rush of gratitude that David was taking this on.

David turned his attention to Lexy. "You're going to have to find out about your boy, Elmer. My guess is he's too embarrassed to let anyone know what happened. If he's, uh, disfigured, he might be after revenge."

"He's mean as a bull snake now," Lexy said. "This won't sweeten his disposition."

"I did it." I shouted. Heads turned, so I lowered my voice. "Surely he won't take this out on your family."

"If he's as mean as Lexy says, he'll take it out on whoever he can. And, as you pointed out, you're not available," David said. He patted

Lexy's hand and added, "Don't worry." He gave her an encouraging smile.

I stared at him. Who is this guy?

A woman hesitated beside our booth. We all looked up. "David Phipps?" she asked.

"I'm not sure who he is," I mumbled.

"Yes," David answered.

She smiled. "Your bag is at customer service. I'm sorry for the delay."

"Thank you," David said. He stood up. "Let's get the bag and get on the road. We can talk in the car."

Chapter Forty-Two

David's knees would have been under his chin in my Mustang's practically nonexistent rear seat. So, he drove back to Cheyenne Falls. Being the alpha male, he would have driven anyway. I curled up in the back and dozed. Up front, David and Lexy chatted away like old friends.

When we arrived at my motel room, I brought a pot of coffee from the restaurant, then changed into sweats and a t-shirt. We all talked late into the night. Finally exhausted, we turned in. David went to his room. Lexy slept in my spare bed.

The paradox is, after I stopped caring what David thought, he seems to like me. At least he's stopped treating me like a deranged toddler. I almost enjoyed his company. Working together to solve Lexy's problem, we formed a common bond. Us against—whatever.

The next morning the three of us made plans as we lingered over breakfast. Lexy enjoyed her waffle as much as she'd enjoyed her expensive dinner last night. David convinced me to stay away from 1891 until we find out more about what is going on with Elmer. Because he hoped to learn more, he rode Whiplash back through the canyon and tunnel with Lexy—again. A three-hour ride each way, I knew he would be gone at least six hours. But when he hadn't returned after nine, I grew concerned and drove out to the barn to wait. An hour later I was relieved to hear horses approaching through the evening dusk. David was in an unusually good mood and said everything went 'swimmingly' and I shouldn't have worried. By the time we brushed and fed the horses, it was late.

David didn't seem irritated about missing his flight back to Dallas, which was seriously strange. He's not one to handle setbacks with calm acceptance. He'd already made provisions to keep his room another night and had scheduled a flight tomorrow. Hmmm. He had to have done that before he left—no cell service in the canyons—which means he'd planned to be gone that long but failed to share that information with me.

Before he went to his room, I got the ring box from the nightstand drawer and handed it to him. He looked in the box, saw the ring and looked at my bare hand.

"What's up, Ali?"

"David, I'm not going back to Dallas. I knew I belonged in Cheyenne Falls from the moment I arrived."

He nodded. "I know. You hate Dallas." There was no anger. No big scene, although I didn't expect one. David isn't into big scenes, but he understood. I could see it in his eyes. They were warm like melted chocolate. Not hard like they can be.

"I knew this day would come, that you would leave me," he said.

"You thought I would leave you?" I asked. "Why?"

"You've never trusted that I love you. I knew when you were strong enough, you'd be gone. I've talked to Ursula about it."

"You have?"

"She wouldn't tell me what she thought, of course. I wanted to know if I was right in thinking your childhood kept you from believing you were worthy of love."

My brain went into shock. He paid for my counseling knowing I would leave when I got well. I didn't know what to say. Love has many forms.

"What about law school?" he asked.

"I can transfer to Oklahoma University. They have a great law school."

"You've already taken steps in that direction?"

I nodded. I'd braced for cold anger. His gentleness threw me a curve. Tears welled in my eyes and spilled down my cheeks. He wiped them away. Okay, that did me in too. My tears irritate him. He has always seen them as a sign of weakness.

"I can't thank you for all you and your mom have done for me," I sniffed.

"No thanks necessary."

"Daydreon has been so kind. I'm not the wife she would have picked for her son. But she never made me feel that way. You helped me out of a pit and set me on solid ground," I said. "You gave me a gift I'd never had. Hope." There should be a song lyric in there.

"I'm glad it was me."

Neither of us knew what to say next. Rare for David. Normal for me.

"Will you still help Lexy?" I asked, afraid to hear his answer.

"Of course. I have to take care of my girls." He raised my chin with two fingers until I was looking at him. "Get this, Ali. This affects more than Lexy. From what I can figure, without the land Lexy's father needs to claim, you have nothing to inherit. We have to make sure he gets that land."

"But it's been in the family for years."

"It won't be if we don't help him. If you had listened to me and not come to Cheyenne Falls, generations of your family would have lived different lives. You didn't accidentally happen across that tunnel. This is why you came." He pulled me to him, wrapped his arms around me and just held me. He's never done that. Ever. Well, bugger. Now we're through, he likes me. I will never understand men.

"This whole thing is so weird," David said.

"What?" I mumbled into his shirt.

He released me. "You and Lexy. This twin thing going on. You finish each other's sentences. You think alike and both chew your lower lip. Lexy even has your unique speech cadence."

"She does things like me, but we're different, too," I said. "She's self-confident, spontaneous and fun."

"You would be too if you hadn't been raised in a closet. But you're changing. Coming out of that." He scratched his head as he thought. "Different. We'll talk more in the morning," he said. "Get some sleep."

But of course, I couldn't. After he went to his room, I stared at the ceiling for hours. I had arrived in Cheyenne Falls exactly three weeks before the 1891 land lottery. Exactly three weeks before the hearing that would have declared me dead and thrown my inheritance up for grabs.

David is right. This is not random. Not mere coincidence. My arrival was carefully orchestrated. Like the words to the song Lane and

I danced to at Blue Sage. *Keeper of the Stars*. Had God planned this? For the second time tonight, I pondered his plan for my life.

When I met David for breakfast the next morning, he'd received several calls from Dallas and was in a bad mood. If it had been anyone else, I would've said he was frazzled. But David doesn't frazzle. His suitcase had been misplaced on the plane and the airline had given him the wrong one. Having no toiletries or clean underwear made him cranky. So, we were back to the irresponsibility of the airline.

When we'd arrived at the motel yesterday, he discovered instead of a change of clothes, he had a bookkeeping system, along with a .457 Magnum and fifty grand in Franklins. That brought on a whole new tirade about lax security. Peeved by the situation, he decided to hang onto the suitcase. In his infinite wisdom David decided whoever lost it would be even more irate than he'd been over lost underwear and toothbrush. Dealing with that, he concluded, might teach the airline to be more careful. That's how he thinks. Sigh.

But he lightened up a bit on the drive to the airport. I drove so he could spend most of the time on the phone. Now that he was on his way home, it was business as usual. He got things straightened out and was in a better mood when I dropped him off in front of the Southwest departure kiosk. He went over the 'to-do' list he'd given me. He leaned over, gave me a quick kiss, and was gone. In other words, he acted pretty much like he would have if he hadn't been carrying my diamond back to Dallas in a box.

I had prepared myself for the reality of my new-found freedom looking different on this side of goodbye. I'll probably go through rough patches of sadness and confusion, but right now I feel liberated. I put down the top of my car, enjoying the sunshine, warm breeze, and the intoxication of knowing, for better or worse, I've taken control of my destiny.

I cranked up the radio as soon as I hit the highway. Waylon was singing *Mamas Don't Let Your Babies Grow Up to Be Cowboys*. I adjusted my rearview mirror. That's when I noticed a truck following me.

Chapter Forty-Three

Ten miles from Cheyenne Falls I realized the truck was still there. It had been several cars behind me but had gradually closed the distance and now hugged my back bumper. It's headlights, on high beam, blinded me which I'm guessing was the driver's intent. It's not dark enough to need headlights, and not like he couldn't pass me. There hasn't been another car on this road for miles. This can't be good. At all.

I reached up to adjust the rearview mirror. The truck had followed when I exited onto Highway 62 and headed west. Vehicles on this stretch of road, except for an occasional pickup, were few and far between. The truck driver was stepping up the intimidation, which his two passengers found hilarious. They were now practically in my back seat and, as I've mentioned before, my back seat is not roomy. The clock on my dash glowed 8:00PM.

"You're okay. Your stupid imagination is playing tricks on you." I'd been repeating the mantra over and over. That's a lie and I know it. I'm losing credibility with myself. A wave of panic washed over me, but I refused to give in. People who panic make stupid mistakes. I know that from experience. I had to stay calm and think. The vehicle, not big enough to be a tractor trailer rig, was probably a farm truck. This stretch of highway is four-lane. Not only does the driver have plenty of room to pass, but there's the afore mentioned lack of traffic. Whatever he's doing is deliberate.

I glanced at the console where I usually keep my cell phone, knowing it wasn't there. Because the top was down, David had placed the phone in the trunk, along with my Smith and Wesson Bodyguard .38 special, when we stopped to eat. Rather ironic, I thought grimly.

He'd bought them both for my protection and insisted that I keep them close in case of emergencies, but now that I'm in a crisis, they're out of reach.

Before I had time to think about that or anything else, the truck crashed into my rear bumper. My heart jumped into my throat. The car lurched. My head snapped back then forward. A billboard rushed toward me with dizzying speed.

I lost my bout with panic. It swirled in my stomach along with the linguini Alfredo and wine I'd had at Zio's. Tears misted my vision, making the landscape look like a watercolor left out in the rain. I choked and swallowed convulsively. I had no idea what to do. Jerking the steering violently to the left, I barely missed the sign. Before I could straighten the wheels, the truck hit me again with more force. As the car shot forward, my foot instinctively stomped on the brake. The Mustang went into a skid.

"Big mistake, Ali, I thought to myself. A ravine slid toward me sideways.

Using knowledge I didn't possess, my foot lifted from the brake and stepped on the gas. At the same time, I steered hard to the right. Miraculously the car missed the ditch, but I over-corrected in an attempt to get back on the highway which threw me onto the center median. I took my foot off the accelerator and eased the steering wheel back to the right. The wheels straightened and made contact with the hard surface of the highway once more. The car was under control. I didn't have to be reminded that my survival chances would be poor if the convertible rolled.

I gulped. This guy wants me dead. See how I figured that out? I pick up on these things. Has the world gone mad? Is everyone in it is out to kill me? I've done nothing to these people. I don't know them. I stole a quick peek at the rearview mirror to determine the truck's location. It seemed to be dropping back. I resumed breathing, but then realized the driver was giving himself room to gain enough speed to destroy me with the next crash.

This day is not going the way I planned. At all.

White hot anger flashed through me. I've had it with people trying to kill me. I stomped on the gas pedal sending my car fishtailing forward. I risked a quick glance in the rearview mirror and laughed at the look of astonishment on the faces of the three Hispanic men in the truck. This car can fly.

David enjoyed boasting about the speed my car could achieve if pressed to do so, as if I'd want to work that into a conversation around the country club pool. He took great pride in the 5.0-liter V-8 460 HP engine in my birthday present. I'd have picked a car that got better gas mileage. Right now, I'm convinced he did just fine.

The chase covered several miles in a matter of minutes. The truck didn't have a chance of catching my Mustang GT. I tried to swallow but couldn't. I had never ridden in a car going this fast, much less driven one, but I'm not rolling over and playing dead. I'm sick of being a victim. If that jerk intends to kill me, he'll have to catch me first. The speedometer numbers end at 120 but the needle had disappeared past that. "I should have been a race car driver. I'm just wasting all this talent." The wind blew the words back in my mouth.

I let out a whoop of pure joy as the little car crested the last hill and fairly flew toward the welcoming lights of Cheyenne Falls nestled serenely in the valley below. This time when I checked the rearview the truck was gone. I slowed down.

Chapter Forty-Four

Sheriff Checotah sat at his desk thumbing through papers. He looked up when I exploded into the office much like I had the day Lane sent me after him. The door crashed against the wall.

I looked for the wolf painting I'd nearly knocked down last time. It was gone.

"I took it home in case you came back." The sheriff answered my unasked question.

"Were you absent from charm school when they taught how to make an entrance?" He stood and pulled out a chair for me. "Seinfeld's Kramer could take lessons from you. Sit down before you collapse."

I sat.

He looked at my face and said, "Take a deep breath and talk to me."

I took several. When I could speak, I told him what happened, and amazingly, once I began, the words came out coherently. I finished with, "It was blue, bigger than a pickup, but it wasn't a semi."

He glanced at me. "One ton?"

"Won ton? No…. Thank you, though," I added, remembering my manners.

He shook his head and moved across the room to the radio and barked out my description of the truck. But as I listened to him relay the sketchy details, I had little faith it would be found. He replaced the mic and turned to face me.

"Well, Hon, I don't think we have a snowball's chance in hell of finding your truck, but if we get lucky, I'll let you know. You're out at Jackson's, right?"

I shook my head. "I'm still at Buggy Creek Inn."

"Stay close to the room. You were shot at in the canyon. It's only been a week since you were fished out of the lake, and now this. Someone has it in for that pretty blond head of yours."

"I'm growing on you, aren't I?"

He laughed. "Well, I don't want to see you dead. It wouldn't look good on my resume. Could you pick those guys out of a lineup?"

"Probably not."

"Come on. I'm walking you to your car."

We walked out of the courthouse into an evening too warm to be comfortable. I'd parked near the front door. The sheriff went to the rear of my car to inspect damage. Something I'd neglected to check before racing into his office. I followed him. A taillight was broken, the chrome bumper was bent, and the trunk was badly smashed. I burst into tears.

The sheriff ran his fingers over the depression and dislodged a flake of blue paint. He placed it in a handkerchief.

"Hmmm, look at this," he said.

"What?"

"A bullet hole. I'm guessing this wasn't here before today."

Stunned, I shook my head.

"When I find these guys, and I will, I'm charging them with attempted murder. See if the trunk will open."

I knew they intended to kill me. But by the time I got to the sheriff's office, I'd convinced myself they were trying to scare me. The bullet hole was visible proof I was right the first time. My hands shook as I pressed the button on my key. To our surprise the trunk popped open. The sheriff clicked on a flashlight.

"What are you looking for?" I wrapped my arms tightly around myself.

"This. Looks like you need a new spare," he said. He fished a pocketknife from his khakis and dug a bullet from the tire. He picked it up with the handkerchief and closed the trunk.

"Al's Body Shop near your motel does good work," he said. "He'll get your car looking good as new. I'm guessing this is a custom paint job."

I nodded.

"Do you know who did it?"

"A custom shop in Dallas." Tears streamed down my face. "My fiancé…." I corrected myself. "David ordered it. He'll know." I sniffed and wished for a tissue. "I'll call him."

"Good. I'll tell Al you'll be coming in and needing a loaner." He looked at me and realized I was shaking like a leaf. "Can you drive?"

I nodded.

He opened my car door and I slid in. "The shock is wearing off. Go straight to your room, pour yourself a glass of wine, take a bubble bath. That's what my wife does when the kids stress her out. With our brood, it's a wonder she's not a wino."

I nodded, thanked him and drove away. He would have been proud if he'd known how well I followed his orders. I didn't have wine, but I filled the tub and poured in aromatic bath salts. After soaking for an hour, I'd stopped shaking.

I padded barefoot to the window and peered through a crack between the drapes. A car marked 'Sheriff' was parked beside the light pole in the parking lot. The driver, too large to be the sheriff, was inspecting the damage to my car. It must be the deputy. What was his name? Danny, I think. Sheriff Checotah must have sent him to check on me. Knowing I was protected, I crawled into bed and slept like a hibernating bear.

Chapter Forty-Five

April had driven in for the day, so Penny threw together an impromptu lunch on the veranda overlooking the lake. Janet, April, Penny and I lingered over Penny's scrumptious food enjoying each other's company, the gorgeous weather, and scenery. The big topic had been my latest close call.

I'd rather not take all this personally. The truck episode, near drowning, being drugged at Blue Sage and ambushed in the canyon convinced me. Somebody doesn't like me. I sound calm. But I'm terrified. And angry. This is getting old.

"My goodness," Penny said as though reading my mind, "you must be afraid to walk out your door."

"Almost. I've been hanging at the motel, mostly in the pool. I'm gloriously tan, but practically a hermit."

"Good thing I came today to drag you out," April said. "I'm here for you."

We'd discussed the local gossip. April, who had an impassioned opinion on practically every topic, had done most of the talking to the surprise of no one.

I pulled my eyes from the diamonds the sun created on the lake. The breeze sent them dancing across the surface. I realized that Janet, who sat beside me, had been twisting the napkin in her lap for the last twenty minutes.

"Are you okay?" I asked.

Worry lines puckered her brow. "I'm concerned about Fred."

"What's the matter with him, dear?" Penny asked. She patted Janet's arm.

"I don't know," Janet stirred sugar into her tea. "He's never home and when he is, he's awful. He snaps my head off and has no patience with the kids."

"Well, with your kids, no wonder," April said. She smoothed champagne-blond hair into an already perfect updo. "It's probably another woman."

"April." Penny chastised her stepdaughter.

April's eyes widened. "What?"

"Fred would never do that to Janet." Penny's voice was louder than necessary. "Would he, Ali?"

"I guess not," I said. "I've never met him." Which is weird, now that I think about it.

"Jackson has been edgy, too." Penny said.

"He has?" April's concern for her father was more evident than what she'd mustered for her cousin. And everyone except Janet, forgot about Fred.

"It's probably Tribes," Penny said. "Profits have drastically dropped off."

"That happens from time to time," April reminded her.

"Not in the middle of August. Tourist season carries Tribes through the winter months. This is summer break. Kids should be swarming all over the place."

"How bad is it?" April asked.

"It can't get much worse." Penny pushed away her plate, her lunch barely touched. Penny's ample body proved she was not one to waste food.

"He has good ideas," I said, looking through the spinach salad for a mushroom.

Penny nodded. "He wants to add a small lake for fishing and boating, build a restaurant, and add landscaping around it all, which would be lovely."

"It always feels cooler by water," Janet said. "But where would he put all this? There's not much room for expansion, is there?"

"It would depend on Ali selling part of her land," Penny said.

"Which land?" I asked.

"The land adjacent to Tribes is yours. Or soon will be," April said.

"So, Jackson could enlarge Tribes if he had my land and a water source?"

"Well, yes. But it would cost a lot to get it directed to the right place."

My head spun. I remembered my conversation with Jackson the evening I arrived. He'd said I'd be inheriting land and a sizable trust fund from my grandmother on my birthday. I'd been too overwhelmed to think about it. Now, I'm wondering how sizable.

"Where did you get Grandma's hollyhocks?" April asked suddenly.

"Ali found them," Penny said. "She's been landscaping my yard."

April's eyes widened. "It's beautiful. How did you get those boulders?"

"I saw them in the canyon. Jackson sent a crew after them."

"You didn't do all this digging." April was aghast.

"Yes, she did." Penny raised my hand showing April my calloused palm.

"My word." April appeared poised to dial 911. "I have to get you to a manicurist immediately. Surely there's one in this one-horse town."

"No, thank you," I said.

"What?" April stared at me as though I had walked away from 'Deal or No Deal' with nothing.

"My hands prove I haven't been sitting on my butt all summer." I picked at a callous. "It was therapy. I've always lived in apartments."

"Right." April rolled her eyes.

"Isn't it fun watching plants grow?" Janet asked, unaware of April's frustration.

"Thrilling," April said. "Back to my question. Where did you get Nana's hollyhocks?"

I stirred my lemonade, stalling for time.

"Ali found little plants," Penny the rescuer jumped in to explain. "Didn't you, dear?" she asked as she aimed a spoon of strawberry chiffon at her mouth.

"Where?" April demanded looking pointedly at me.

"Uh, a little old lady gave them to me." It wasn't a lie. If Lexy lived in this century, she'd be old. Really old.

"There aren't any anywhere. I haven't seen them since Nana died. I've looked." April deliberately laid her fork aside, folded her arms and stared at me. "Where did she get them?"

"Who?" I gave her a round-eyed stare.

"This little old lady of yours. Don't be asinine."

"I don't know." Amused by April's irritation, I grinned. When did I get like this? "Well. Where is she? I want to ask her."

"She was in a canyon."

"Which canyon?" April demanded.

"I don't know." I waved a fork in the general direction. "They all look alike."

"Let me get this straight. You met an old woman in a deserted canyon planting hollyhocks? She'd have to be demented in this heat."

"It wasn't this hot then."

"Right." April pursed her lips. She tilted her head to the side. "Next you'll be telling me Snow White ditched the prince and ran away with Dopey."

I winked at Janet. "Oh, you know about that. They moved to D.C. and had kids. Have you really looked at Congress? Especially that one guy. The one with the big ears…."

"My heavens, April," Penny admonished. "Leave her alone. She's transformed my backyard into a show place. I don't care where she got the damn hollyhocks."

We all stared at Penny. She never cusses.

"Well, I want some," April announced.

"No kidding," I said.

"Well," Penny said quickly, "these are starting to bloom. We'll have enough seeds for everyone in the county. I'll make sure you get yours."

April continued to study me. "Thank you," she said, "that would be nice."

What is wrong with this picture? I shot a man and got in more trouble for planting a few stupid old flowers.

"Good grief." I stood up. "Where is Jackson? I need to talk to him."

Chapter Forty-Six

I found Jackson down by the lake bent over the twins' paddleboat. He looked up with a welcoming grin. He doesn't act like he wants to do me in.

"I wondered when you'd get bored with women talk," he said.

"I stuck it out way too long." I smiled. "I'm curious."

"Sounds serious." He straightened up, laid down the screwdriver and wiped his hands on a red rag. "Okay, shoot."

"Tell me that story again of how our family got this land."

"It's a legend. Don't know how much is true." He stretched his back. "The big land run happened up by Guthrie. This part of the state wasn't in it. 'Course it was Indian Territory back then. Our area was parceled out in a lottery."

"What year would that have been."

He gazed across the lake as he thought. "1891 I think."

I concentrated on not reacting. "How did that work?"

"They had to go to a fort to sign up. So, one of our ancestors…"

"Which one?" I asked.

"His name was John. John Dale. He was on his way to Ft. Sill. Maybe it was Ft. Reno. That was before my time, you know." He grinned.

That confirmed it. It happened in 1891. The 'ancestor' was Lexy's father, John Dale. My heart skipped a beat.

"Two guys," Jackson went on, "stole his horse, robbed him, and took his shoes. There he was, miles from home in the middle of nowhere, horseless and barefooted. He wasn't familiar with the trail and not sure he was going in the right direction. He was in a bit of a bind, I'd say."

I made a mental note to locate an old state map. Jackson lit a cigarette.

"To make matters worse," Jackson continued, "it happened during a storm. According to folklore rain came down in buckets. The weather gets worse every time the story's told. It would've been more plausible if he'd been rescued by Noah." Jackson grinned at his joke. "A guy rode out of nowhere dressed in all black riding a big black flashy stallion."

"Flashy?"

"It had a jagged blaze shaped like a lightning bolt. The guy's clothes were shiny with metal teeth. Sounds sci-fi, right?" He took a drag on his cigarette.

"Sounds like a zipper to me," I said.

"I guess it does. Did they have zippers back then?" He selected a screwdriver.

"Don't know," I said, laughing. "That was before my time, too. But if zippers were common, it wouldn't have been mentioned in the story through the years."

"I guess not. Anyway. This guy has John's stolen wallet with the papers he needs to prove who he is, his shoes and his horse. Nobody knows who he was, where he came from or how he got that stuff away from the robbers, but he rode the rest of the way to Ft. whatever with John to make sure he got signed up for the section of land he wanted. And, by George, he got it. But he wouldn't have if it hadn't been for the mysterious stranger who was never seen again. Or the guy with him."

"Anything you can add?"

"The jacket had a white emblem. Oh, and he had blond hair. I guess not many men had blond hair back then." Jackson scratched his head. "I wonder why he wasn't wearing a hat in a rainstorm. And the horse was flashy."

"So, you said." I watched Jackson exhale a stream of smoke.

"Yeah, it was spirited. Supposedly it was seventeen hands. Like the rain, the horse got taller with the telling. With that lightning bolt blaze and..."

"Knee-high stockings on the rear legs," I said.

"Yeah. How did you know?" Jackson asked.

"Lucky guess." Jackson had described Jupiter, David's horse.

"I don't know how factual that story is," Jackson said. "It's quite a tale."

"Sounds like we owe everything we have to a guy on a big black stallion," I said.

"The story might have changed through the years but, nobody forgot that horse. Taught me a valuable lesson." He bent to tighten a screw.

"What's that?"

"Don't ride a flashy horse if you're robbing a stagecoach."

"Sounds like good advice," I said.

"Clothes can be changed, but witnesses don't forget a flashy horse." He glanced at me and grinned.

"Good to know." I laughed and changed the subject. "I think I'll drive out to look over the section in the canyon. Can you tell me how to get there?"

He nodded. "Pretty out there. There's an old house on it. You'll probably want to tear it down." He gave me directions. "Take lots of water. It's going to be a scorcher. Be careful."

"I will," I promised.

I stopped by my room to change into jeans and call David. He answered on the third ring sounding rushed and distracted. I kept it short. I relayed my conversation with Jackson. "He couldn't have described Jupiter more accurately if he'd been looking at him," I said. "It sounds like you're going to make a ride, Paul Revere. Wear your water-proof black Nike warm-up suit. You might run into rain so wear a hat. And don't rob any stagecoaches."

"Excuse me?" David said. He wasn't in a joking mood, so I didn't explain.

"In time travel books I've read," I said, "people go back in history to change it."

"I've got to go," David said.

"We're going to make history happen that has already happened."

"Goodbye, Ali,"

"Isn't that fascinating?" I said to the dial tone. "Guess not."

As I drove out of town, I remembered what Jackson had said. "Another guy was with him." He hadn't mentioned that before. I'm pretty sure. Who would David take? Jackson must be wrong.

Chapter Forty-Seven

Jackson said to watch for an old windmill missing a blade. He hasn't been out here in a while. It's missing three or four. As I turned onto the unpaved road, I couldn't shake a feeling of *déjà vu*. I've never passed the old grey barn or the landmark windmill, never been on this road or driven out of town in this direction. Still, as I dodged a rock large enough to derail a freight train, the certainty I've been here before stayed with me.

Sunflowers, growing along a rusty barbed-wire fence, looked as hot and wilted as I felt. A strand of wire curled around a weathered post. The sunflowers reminded me of Lane. He's been gone over a week now and I have this aching need to see him. It's way past missing him.

Jackson had been right about the day being a scorcher. I should have had the top up and the air on. But I love the feel of the wind in my face. I sang lustily along with an old Wynonna song, *Heaven Help My Heart*, which of course made me think of Lane, too.

Sienna bluffs rose in the distance giving the area a feeling of remoteness. The August sun took its toll on clumps of wilted love grass, but trees provided shade for grazing cattle. The Angus and I were the only inhabitants of the valley.

But that changed when I topped a hill and saw a lone figure shuffling toward me. I was almost past before I realized who flagged me down. Dust swirled around the car as it slid to a stop. I choked.

"It will be a month before another bus comes through here. Need a ride?"

Stormy staggered through the dust, opened the door and sagged into the seat. She eyed my Sonic cup in the holder. "May I?" she croaked.

"It used to be a cherry lime. It's mostly water now. Why are you out here?"

Stormy downed it in one gulp and wiped the moist cup across her forehead, leaving smudges on its surface. Sweat and dirt had plastered her normally bright bouncy curls to her head framing a face nearly as crimson except for the white ring around the mouth. Her eyes were haunted. She resembled a death camp refuge who has seen too much.

"Where's Lane?" I asked.

She stared at me as though English wasn't her first language.

"Where is Lane?"

She mopped her face with the bottom of a grubby T-shirt. "Do you have a phone?"

"Oh, so you can talk." I handed over the phone. "Where is Lane?"

Ignoring me, she jabbed in a number and waited impatiently for an answer.

I squinted down the road at heat shimmering in the distance.

"Danny, thank God." she shouted. "We need help."

"Who needs help?" I yelled.

"Stop." Stormy interrupted Danny's rambling. "They've got Lane."

"Lane?" I screamed. "What? Who has Lane?"

Stormy waved me away. "Those three goons we've been trailing. But they're expecting company." She paused as Danny asked a question. "No. They've been beating him, but he honestly doesn't know. He's in bad shape. Hurry. Bring an ambulance."

"An ambulance?" I shouted in a full-blown panic attack. "Who has Lane?"

She scowled in an effort to shut me up as she listened to Danny.

"What? Danny, we don't have time for this. Lane could be dead before you get here." She gave him directions and added, "Of course, I'm going back." Stormy's voice rose shrilly. "Lane wouldn't leave me. Get off your butt and get out here." She viciously punched the end button and mumbled. Fortunately, I couldn't hear. It wasn't the words that terrified me. I could smell her fear.

"You show up in the damnedest places," Stormy grumbled.

"So, I've been told. Who has Lane?" I couldn't breathe. The words 'dead', 'beaten', 'ambulance' ricocheted through my brain. I couldn't think.

"I don't know how much longer he can hang on." She drew a ragged breath.

"Look, I need details," I said. "I think I'm being patient here considering I seriously want to scratch your eyes out. Where exactly is Lane? Who has him?"

"Go back to town," Stormy ordered. Her eyes raked over me, assessing and dismissive. "You'll be in the way."

My chin jutted defiantly.

She dug in. "I don't have time to babysit you."

"We're wasting time. I have a phone and the sheriff is on the way. You can't walk back there in this heat." But she was looking a little better.

"Do you have any water?"

"There's a bottle in the back seat." Jackson was right. I should've brought more.

"You should've brought more." Stormy accused. Her expression indicated she thought I was overdue for a brain transplant. "Why are you out here without water?"

"I didn't know I'd be on a recon mission. What's your excuse?"

I've seen Stormy bring a man to his knees. Even now half dead, if she battled Attila the Hun, I'd bet on Stormy. She scares me. But today my concern for Lane overrode my fear. I desperately tried to clear my mind and concentrate on the task at hand. I put the car in gear and drove down the hill.

Stormy drained half the water bottle and recapped it. "Gotta save a little for Lane," she muttered. "He's tied up in a shack. Slow down so they won't see our dust."

My foot eased off the accelerator. "What? Lane is tied up in a shack? Where should I park?"

Stormy pointed to an abandoned well-site road. I concentrated on breathing and turning. Foot off the gas. Foot on the brake. Turn the wheel to the right. We rattled across the cattle guard and followed the road. I parked behind a small grove of trees and we got out.

"This is suicide," Stormy mumbled. "We have to get to that stand of trees."

"You did it once, right?" My voice was surprisingly calm.

"I made it from the house to the road. Not to where we are."

"Let's do this," I said not knowing what 'this' entailed. A hawk circled above. We followed it to a dry creek bed that would barely conceal a coyote, then to a grove of trees. We fought our way through underbrush to the house. Nobody had mowed this yard for years. Stormy's bare legs were scratched and bleeding. She peered through a broken window.

"What's happening?" I asked, sliding in behind her.

Chapter Forty-Eight

H e's either asleep or unconscious," Stormy said. "He's alone."
She didn't say 'or dead', but that's what I heard. I licked
my parched lips. I'd kill for a drop of water, but Lane would
need it. Thirst couldn't compete with my urgency to get him
out. Being this close and not able to help him was hell. None too
gently, I pushed Stormy out of the way and peered through the broken
glass. Lane was tied to a chair, his hands behind him. His head drooped
forward. He wasn't moving. I stopped breathing.

"We've got to get him out." I glanced over my shoulder.

"Well, what do you suggest, Cinderella? You got a pumpkin
coach?"

I thought fast. "Do you have matches?"

"Yeah, why?"

"You do?" She doesn't smoke. Why would she have matches?
"We could start a fire and get him out while they're fighting it."

"That's not totally stupid," she said.

"Thank you," I said, blinking sweat from my eyes.

"Three men are in the house." Stormy slapped a fly on her knee.

"You guys were trailing three men at Blue Sage," I said. "I'm
picking up on a trend here. It's probably the same three who ran me
off the road. I'm guessing they won't be any happier to see me now."

"More are on the way. We've got to get him out before they get
here."

I swallowed hard. "They're armed. We aren't. I fail to see how the
number makes a difference." Sweat trickled down my spine.

"Can you get through that window?"

"Yes." The broken window was small and higher than most. Shards of glass stuck into the frame. But I would get through.

"Okay. The fire needs to be far enough away to buy you time," Stormy said. "But close enough for them to see. I'll set that shed on fire and make a lot of noise. When they run out, cut Lane loose."

"With what?"

She handed me a small pocketknife. "It's not very sharp. Make sure they're all out of there. You can count to three, right?"

"What if Lane can't walk?"

"I don't know. This is all we got. It has to work. We'll meet at your car. Ready?"

"Wait." I grabbed Stormy's arm. "What if they get you?"

"No matter what happens to me, get Lane out of there and keep going as long as he can make it. Don't stop. Don't look back."

"But..."

"Don't argue. Do it." Her face was fierce.

"Okay." My mind reeled. *She knows this won't work. She's sacrificing her life to save Lane. I'll think about that later.*

Stormy turned to go. Her shirt plastered to her back, she glanced over her shoulder. "You're going to barf, aren't you?"

"Of course not," I said to her back. She was gone, and I was doing exactly that. I straightened, wiped the back of my hand across my mouth, and clutched my stomach with both hands. My breathing was fast and shallow, on the verge of hyperventilating. No one accused me of being brave. I inhaled deep and slow. Concentrating on my breathing took my mind off the fact these men tried to kill me.

The first morning on the plateau with Lane, he'd said, "If the opportunity to be a hero arises, you'll do fine, Sunflower. I'd bet my life on you." If he'd known this day was on its way, he might not have been so certain.

A shout from inside the house pulled me back to the present. The door flew open and banged against a wall. Men ran out yelling instructions to each other in Spanish.

A cloud of pungent smoke filled the air. I looked in the direction the men had gone. The shed was engulfed in flames. Stormy must have found gasoline. She couldn't start a big fire that fast with a puny book of matches. Lane said she's the best there is at what she does. Only a fool would underestimate her.

A man raced back into the house and came out with an armload of blankets. I waited until he reached a battered stock tank and dropped them into it. Another man grabbed the rusty handle and began pumping furiously. I had considered sneaking in the front door, but with the stock tank so close to the house I couldn't risk it.

Waist-high dead grass around the shed had already started burning. The fire spread fast in the constant Oklahoma wind. We hadn't taken that into consideration. Flames raced toward the house. If I don't get Lane out—don't want to think about that.

Later, I wouldn't be able to tell anyone how I shimmied through the tiny window without slashing a vital organ. Once inside the house I began hacking at the cords binding Lane's wrists. His hands, swollen and purple, resembled over-ripe plums. I've never seen skin that color on anyone. He hadn't made a sound or movement, but he was breathing. I sobbed in frustration. Stormy hadn't lied about the dullness of the knife.

Finally, a cord broke. Lane's hands were loose. His arms fell to his sides. I hurried around and squatted in front of him. The smell of smoke was stronger. I had sawed through one of the ropes around his ankles when Lane groaned, raised his head, and opened a swollen eye. His face looked like something out of *Nightmare on Elm Street*.

"What the hell are you doing here?" he demanded in a harsh whisper.

"I was on my way to knitting class and seem to have made a wrong turn," I said, glancing up. "I'm glad to see you, too, precious." I turned my attention back to hacking at ropes with a tiny knife.

"Get out of here." Lane growled.

"Not without you." With one final tug, the rope fell to the floor. Whimpering in relief, I rose, pulling Lane up with me. "Can you walk?"

None too steady, he stood and rubbed his wrists. "I don't know." He dropped an arm around my shoulder and took a tentative step. "Yeah. I think so."

I held on to him in case.

"Where are they?" He coughed. Smoke was getting thick.

"They went to check on a burning shed," I said.

"There's…" He was interrupted by the banging of the outside door. The floor shook with heavy footsteps.

My eyes flew to Lane's face.

He put a finger to his lips. Grabbing the chair he'd been tied to, he lurched toward the wall and flattened himself behind the door. "Distract him." he mouthed.

"How?" I asked.

"You're a girl, you should know."

The man stopped before the doorway when he saw me. Under different circumstances, his expression would have been hilarious.

"Que Pasa?"

"Hola," I said, working frantically to remember any Spanish I might have heard. *"Broken nachos por tacos una hormigas? Por favor?"* Lane said a girl should know how to do this. I gave my head a coquettish toss and tripped. Look seductive. I managed a pout. I'm not good at this at all. I pointed to the burning shed. "I brought wieners. What good is a fire without wieners to roast?"

A look of murderous rage crossed his face. *"Gringa Chica Loca."* He stepped forward, hesitated, and realized Lane was gone. Lane brought the chair down over his head with surprising force. The guy crumpled, chair parts clattering to the floor around him.

"Dang. Not bad for someone I thought was dead," I said.

Lane stepped over him and looked out the door.

"Did you kill him?" I asked.

"Don't know," he muttered. "Gave it my best shot. What did you say about ants?"

"Ants? I said friends."

"You said hormigas, that's ants."

"Whatever. Do you see the other two?"

"Yeah, they went behind the shed. There's so much smoke between us I don't think they could see us anyway." He grabbed my arm. "Come on."

Chapter Forty-Nine

Lane managed to hobble to the cedars where Stormy and I had hidden. Our progress was agonizingly slow. Flames lapped at the underbrush at the trees edge. Cedars explode in a fire. Really. We couldn't stay there, but Lane needed to rest. We stood beside the house, Lane sagged against it, clutching his side.

"Think my ribs are broken," he said between gasps. "Hurts to breathe."

On the wall beside his head a paint curl clung tenaciously to an otherwise bare board. Jackson said I'd probably want to tear this house down. I won't have to. It'll be gone within the hour. The smoke, a white plume against a cerulean sky, should be visible for miles. Where are the firetrucks?

"You didn't really bring wieners, did you? I'm starving," Lane said.

"No. I would have, but my invitation said nothing about wieners."

Two crows squabbled on a sagging strand of rusty barbed wire which served as a fence. Behind it several cross-bred Angus regarded us with mild curiosity, slapping their sides with burr-tangled tails. This could be the final five minutes of our lives, but for them it was another lazy summer afternoon.

"We've got to find Stormy," Lane said.

"She'll meet us at my car. You can't make it that far."

"Where is it?" Lane asked. He'd taken my words as a challenge.

A gunshot interrupted the crows' dispute, sending them up into a tree.

"That can't be good." My heart leaped into my throat. We waited, listening intently. There were no other sounds but the scolding of the incensed crows.

I looked up. The hawk circled above us. James White Eagle had said, 'always follow the hawk.' At the trees edge I nudged Lane. "Follow the hawk."

"Have you lost it?" he said.

"The fact I'm here pretty much proves it. What do we have to lose?"

He nodded.

Flying above our heads, the hawk headed south. Edging away from the protective cover of the trees we followed. If either of the two guys looked our way, we'd be in trouble, but they were making a frenzied effort to keep the fire from reaching the house. I realized they must be living there. This is probably not a good time to collect rent.

The hawk led us to the creek bed and then in the direction of my car. We stayed low. The heat and humidity, thick as the smoke, made it difficult to breathe. Lane's every breath was a struggle. He staggered to the car and slumped over the hood. I opened the door and moved him to the seat. He sank into it. I found a protein bar in the dash and the half bottle of water we'd saved. He downed the water in three gulps. I'd tried to believe Stormy would be waiting beside the car. She wasn't.

"I'm going to find P.J. Get in your car and go for help," Lane said.

"You can't. You can barely walk. I'm amazed you made it this far."

Without another word or backward glance, he lurched to his feet and staggered into the woods.

I'd left my phone in the car. I grabbed it and punched in the number Sheriff Checotah gave me. His personal cell. He answered on the first ring.

When I heard his voice, I burst into tears. "Where are you?" I sobbed. "Why aren't you here?"

"Ali, what's wrong?"

"The three guys who ran me off the road had Lane tied up in a house," I choked. "I saw their truck. We got him out, but now Lane and I can't find Stormy. Lane's in bad shape. I think Stormy's been shot."

"Damn. Where are you?"

I quickly gave him directions. "Stormy called Danny half an hour ago. He said you were on the way."

"Danny? Are you sure? He didn't tell me."

"They're expecting company. Bring an army. And an ambulance. And, oh yeah, a fire truck. Hurry."

"Copy that. On my way. Stay where you are."

"Okay," I hiccuped. But I didn't. I needed to find Lane and Stormy, but I didn't know where to start. I looked for the hawk and found it circling above. I followed it to a wooded area and found Stormy half sitting on a boulder. Most of her weight sagged against Lane who braced himself against a tree. A splotch of red spread across his shirt. His stricken expression broke my heart.

"Come on, stay with me," Lane crooned in Stormy's ear.

I raised Stormy's sleeve. She'd been shot halfway between her shoulder and elbow. Lane's thumb pressed against the wound. I cut a strip of material from the bottom of my shirt and tied it tightly above Lane's thumb. The bullet entrance and exit wounds were low enough for a tourniquet which seemed to be the only thing we had going for us. I tore off more strips and wrapped them around her arm. When I became indecent, I cut a strip from Stormy's shirt. We weren't wearing much but the bleeding stopped.

"Can we get her to my car?"

Lane shook his head. "She's too weak. I can't carry her."

He was right. He could barely walk. I straightened, listening for sirens. Nothing.

"Help is on the way," I promised Stormy.

She raised eyes filled with pain and exhaustion. Her expression said it all.

A car door slammed. Hopeful, I ran to peer through the trees. It wasn't the police. Two men got out of a late model car.

I hurried back to Stormy and Lane. "It's not the police, it's two guys in suits." I heard voices and stopped talking.

I ran to look through the branches again. The newcomers waited by their car as the two Hispanic men walked toward the road. The guy Lane clobbered wasn't with them. Surely, they would have missed him by now. Both groups of men drew guns and started toward our grove of trees from opposite directions. We were surrounded and cut off from my car.

They knew we could only be in one of two places on the property. The stand of cedars beside the house which was now engulfed in flames or the grove of trees a hundred yards from the house. It didn't take a brain surgeon to figure out where we were.

"We're trapped," I told Lane, surprised by my lack of panic.

"Come here. Hold Stormy for a minute while I go look," Lane said.

As he stepped away, I saw numbers scratched in the boulder where he'd been. My initials A.D.F. And the date 8.16.1891. "I don't believe it," I gasped. We were at Aunt Mattie's homestead. Right in front of the root cellar. Maybe it's still here. I peered up at the trunk of the cottonwood tree. Above Stormy's head the message Aunt Mattie's husband had carved so long ago still rang true. "Love will guide us," I murmured.

"Lovely, Sunflower," Lane said, "but this is no time to wax poetic."

No wonder I'd had a feeling of *déjà vu* driving down this road. The road hadn't been here then, but I had. Since Lexy and I outran the tornado last week in 1891, everything here had aged over a hundred years. We'd slid down the sandstone cliff in the distance. Aunt Mattie's sod house had been built beside the same creek downstream from the Kiowa village. The draw we'd used for cover is where the creek had been. The house I rescued Lane from had been built where Aunt Mattie's sod house once stood.

"Help me move this rock," I snapped. I moved Stormy to a tree stump, grabbed a branch of a cedar tree and sawed furiously with the dull knife.

"You can't cut anything with that," Lane told me.

"No kidding," I said.

He pulled a hunting knife from his boot, grabbed the branch and deftly removed it.

"Wish I had known you had it an hour ago," I said.

"Glad they didn't."

"Yeah, me too. We've got to move the rock."

Lane eyed it skeptically. "Do I look like Roman Reigns to you?"

"He can't," Stormy mumbled. "He's a wuss."

"Your confidence warms my heart," Lane said.

"There used to be a cellar behind this boulder. It's our only chance," I said. "Lexy and I moved this boulder during a tornado."

"It wasn't last week." Lane said. "This rock has been here for years."

It had been over a week, but in 1891. No time to chat about it now.

At the edge of the clearing, I backed toward Lane and Stormy sweeping our tracks and Stormy's trail of blood with my cedar broom. As I swept, I remembered learning the Kiowa method of escaping enemies by erasing tracks with a cedar branch. I thought it was worthless information I would never need. I'll apologize later.

"I thought you were going to help," Lane whispered. "What's this 'we have to move the rock' stuff?" He put a shoulder to it and grunted with pain and effort. It didn't budge.

I hurried to the other side of the clearing and backed toward Lane sweeping as I went. "Did it move?" I hissed.

"You could help if you weren't so busy tidying up."

"Shhh. Move it," I said through gritted teeth. I shoved my shoulder into the boulder and with our combined effort, it yielded. Our next effort moved it more.

The voices were getting closer. The underbrush crashed as the men reached the grove of trees. They would be in our clearing in a matter of seconds.

Chapter Fifty

I glanced into the dark cellar. "The stairs are gone. Can you get in there?"

Lane started to argue about going first but realized this was no time for manners and squeezed in. I helped Stormy down and handed her to Lane. Using the cedar branch as a broom, I backed to the edge sweeping away our tracks as I went and wedged myself behind the boulder. Lane steadied me as I landed. I pulled the branch to the opening and held it upright hoping it looked like a small tree.

The two suits met the Hispanic men in the space we'd occupied just minutes ago. One of them practically stood on my hand. Rays of the setting sun slanted through tree branches bathing him in light. His dress pants had picked up burrs and grass seeds. Wet stains crept from under the arms of a long-sleeved white shirt. He'd loosened the tie. His mouth compressed into a line of tight-lipped fury. He was so close I could see red hairs on his fingers which held a gun loosely at his side. A wedding band on the ring finger shocked me. Like I couldn't believe evil men got married. The gun held my attention. I stared at it and had to remind myself to breathe, praying he wouldn't look down or notice the shaking branch.

"Where'd she go?" he asked.

"She got by you." said a strong Spanish accent.

"Nope. We would've seen her."

Lane and I looked at each other. They hadn't realized he was gone.

"She disappear like coyote," one of the Hispanic men said. He did a raised-hand thing like releasing a butterfly. "Poof."

"What did Danny say?"

"He say redhead come rescue boyfriend. Get her."

"He'll be pissed if you don't."

Stormy looked at me wide-eyed, realizing why help never came.

"It's me you need to worry about, you idiot," the man with the gun growled.

A car door slammed.

"Danny's here."

"Hey, Danny, we're back here," a voice yelled.

"You 'splain to him," another one said.

If Danny is one of the bosses, I wondered, how bright these people could be.

"Explain what to me?" Danny asked as he swaggered into view.

"Nada."

"Where's the redhead?" Danny asked.

"Your boys here have been fighting a fire," Mr. Business Suit said. "Instead of looking for her."

"I shoot her," one of the Hispanic men said. "She not far. Ees probably dead."

"If she were dead, she'd be easier to find. Wouldn't you think?" Danny said. "Did you unload the barn?"

"Si. We take care of eet."

"Well, forgive me if I don't trust your ability to follow orders." Danny's voice held heavy sarcasm. "You haven't given me much to work with here."

"Did you get anything out of that guy?" Mr. Business Suit asked.

"Nada."

"Yeah, that's what I thought. Get rid of him," the guy holding the gun said. "Find the redhead and finish her off. Now."

"Your boss was supposed to meet us here. I'm not waiting around all night," Mr. Business Suit said. "Dang, that helicopter is flying low."

In the root cellar we listened as intently as they did. The sound of rotary blades grew louder as the copter drew closer. It stopped overhead and hovered barely above the trees. The upper branches of the cottonwood whipped into a frenzy. Light flooded the small clearing.

"What the...?"

Then we heard sirens. Lots of sirens. Checotah believed me. He'd brought an army.

An amplified voice demanded, "Throw down your weapons. Come out with your hands up." Just like in the movies.

For several agonizingly long minutes, nothing happened.

"Damn." Danny said.

Guns began dropping. The guy above me threw his down with force. It hit the ground and bounced into our hole, striking Stormy's face. Her head jerked, but she didn't utter a sound. That girl was tough.

The men shuffled away, cussing as they went. Lane and I stared at each other, not believing it was over.

"Renegade, can you hear me? Where are you? You guys okay?" the sheriff yelled.

Lane tossed my cedar branch aside and looked out. "We're here, Chief." He climbed out and reached down to help Stormy. But with broken ribs, he didn't have the strength.

"Tony is here?" Stormy asked.

"Apparently," I said, helping her out. "I called him from my car."

She moaned as I moved her. "You didn't leave us," she said.

"Of course not. Once I knew the sheriff was on the way, I came to find you."

A deputy appeared and reached down for Stormy. Before I followed her out, I looked around. It was too dark to see much. The roots of the cottonwood had taken over the area where shelves once held sparkling jars of Aunt Mattie's jewel-toned sand plum jelly, perfect tomatoes and green beans. Only the area we'd crowded into near the opening remained. I doubted the people who had once lived in the house had known the root cellar existed.

"How did you know about this hole?" Lane asked.

"You wouldn't believe me if I told you."

Sheriff Checotah walked into the clearing. "You look like hell," he greeted Lane. "How'd those guys miss you?" He turned around and motioned for the EMSA crew.

"We hid in that hole," Lane said. "Ali swept our tracks away with a cedar branch."

"Ole Indian trick," Sheriff Checotah said. "You learn that from White Eagle?" he teased me. His smile disappeared when he saw Stormy.

"Chief, there's a gun down in that hole. Should have some good prints." Lane said.

James White Eagle. With the mention of his name his words came back to me. 'You will save lives. You will find strength to fight evil. You will show signs of greatness.' I hadn't believed him. He had predicted today.

"He doesn't talk to women," I said automatically, too stunned to think.

"Who's White Eagle?" Lane asked.

"A Kiowa legend," Checotah said.

The emergency crew placed Stormy on a stretcher. As they carried her past me, she mouthed the words, "Thank you."

"Give me the flashlight, will ya?" Lane asked the sheriff.

He squatted by the boulder and aimed the beam at the faint marks in the rock. "A.D.F. 1891," he read slowly. "Alexandra Dale Forrest?" He looked up at me.

I nodded, still thinking about White Eagle's prophecies. What else had he said?

Lane's finger traced the faint letters and numbers that time and the elements hadn't erased. He looked up at me again, his face a question mark. "1891? You're going to explain this to me. Soon."

"Okay," I said.

"Hey, Bro, looks like you need a stretcher," an E.M.T. told Lane. Besides his swollen bruised face, Stormy's blood covered his shirt. He looked bad.

"I can walk," Lane insisted.

"A man inside the house might need attention," I said. "Get him out before it burns."

Walking single file through the trees, we fell in behind the emergency crew carrying Stormy. When we exited the woods, Lane waited for me. I wrapped an arm around him. Checotah got on the other side and together we walked him ever so slowly up the hill.

A siren grew stronger as another ambulance approached, music to my ears more beautiful than any symphony. With the danger passed, I was utterly exhausted. But alive. We survived because of what I learned from Lexy and the Kiowas in 1891.

Chapter Fifty-One

More fire trucks followed the ambulance through the gate, passed the flashing lights of law enforcement vehicles and joined the first fire truck. I watched Sheriff Checotah's deputies cuff the Hispanic men and load them into a county car. They had a bit more trouble with their former colleague, a raging Danny who tried to convince anyone who would listen he'd been called by Stormy. He wasn't going down easily.

Checotah looked at me, his brows raised in question.

I shook my head.

"I came out here to arrest these guys," Danny bellowed with a broad sweep of his arm which seemed to indicate everyone in a five-mile area.

"That won't fly, Danny," Lane said. "You sent those guys to get me."

Danny's expression was priceless when he saw Lane with Checotah. "I can explain," he said. He wasn't swaggering now.

"Not this time," Lane said.

The times I'd seen Danny outside my room I'd thought the sheriff had sent him to protect me. If Tony hadn't sent him, then who?

Lane hobbled to the ambulance to talk to Stormy. They conversed quietly. Lane brushed hair from her eyes, his face close to hers. I wondered if he'd kissed her. The emergency crew reminded Lane they had a job to do. He stepped back. They attached an IV to her arm as the doors closed.

Sheriff Checotah ignored Lane's protests and forced him into another ambulance.

"Come here, Sunflower," Lane said.

I moved to the door. He pulled me close. "I'll catch up with you tomorrow. You did good," he whispered. "My little hero." Then he looked past me, his eyes searching for Checotah. "Hey, Chief, take care of my girl."

Lane kissed me. It wasn't a kiss on my nose or a peck on my cheek. His lips met mine in a kiss that lingered and didn't care who saw it. That was not a kiss that said, 'I'm in love with Stormy'. I'm so confused.

Taillights bounced as the ambulance bucked over love grass clumps on its way to the gate. I suddenly realized how much of my shirt was gone and wrapped my arms around myself to recover a shred of modesty. Firemen carried the man out of the house as flames licked near the door.

"He'll make it," Checotah said. I wasn't sure if he meant Lane or the Hispanic dude. Glancing at what was left of my shirt, he reached into his car, pulled out a sweatshirt and tossed it to me. *Caddo County Jail* was stenciled across the back. He studied me. "Are you okay?"

I slipped the shirt over my head. "Yeah," I said. I shook uncontrollably. He knew I was lying. I was a mess.

"Come on," he said. "I'm taking you home." Placing a hand on the small of my back, he ushered me around his car. "Can't believe I nearly let you get killed again. I'd never hear the end of it from your mama."

"You know my mother?"

"Honey, everyone knows your mother. Nothing gets done in this town without her. I'll drive you to your car." He motioned for a deputy to come with us and we waited while he climbed into the back seat. The sheriff followed my directions to where I'd left the Mustang in a previous lifetime. "Give me your keys."

As we waited for the deputy to adjust the seat and find the lights, I thought about how bizarre this day had been. Had it only been shortly after noon when I drove out here? Seemed like eons ago. The day started so normally with Penny's delicious brunch. But what a turn it had taken. You never know what a day will hold when you get out of bed in the morning.

Headlights swept across my door at the motel as the deputy angled my Mustang into a parking space. The sheriff waited, his engine idling.

The deputy put up the top on my car, got out, locked it and handed me the keys.

As I slid out, the sheriff said, "Could you drop by my office in the morning at nine?"

I nodded. "Thanks for coming."

He gave me the shadow of a smile. "That's kind of my job. I'm glad you kept my phone number. Wasn't sure you would."

"Me, too," I said, "You have no idea."

As I unlocked my room, I realized my fingers were glued together with Stormy's dried blood. I staggered through the door, closed it, and leaned against it.

In the glaring light of the bathroom, I stared at my hands. Blood had caked under my nails and into my cuticles. I turned the shower on full blast. I tossed what was left of my bloody shirt in the corner, shimmied out of my jeans and stepped into the steam. As water pounded my body, I tried not to think.

Chapter Fifty-Two

Giving up on sleep at dawn, I dressed, pulled my hair into a ponytail and slipped out the door. As I passed the news rack, the morning paper caught my eye.

Two-inch headlines screamed *HOMETOWN GIRL PROCLAIMED HERO*. The story framed a picture of me. I have no idea when it was taken, but I couldn't have looked worse if the photographer had caught me during the tornado. Mascara smeared under one eye. Leaves and twigs tangled through my hair. I looked like I'd been crying, throwing up, or both. I had. My lifetime-achievement-award picture looked like I'd dug out of Folsom Prison.

But I loved the sound of 'Hometown Girl'. I arrived in Cheyenne Falls less than a month ago. I still have a job in Dallas, I think, and I'm enrolled in law school there. I have a Dallas address which reminds me I need to terminate the lease on my apartment. I live in a motel but I'm a 'hometown girl'. *The Cheyenne Falls Times and Free Press* is never wrong. A little humor there.

Nobody bothered to interview me. Lane and Stormy are hospitalized, so how authentic can the account be? I plunked quarters into the box and pulled out a paper.

Scanning the story, I learned my "heroic actions" saved the lives of two out-of-town police officers. Police officers? The reporter must have been smoking crack. I took the paper with me.

The motel parking lot was jammed because of the Junior Livestock Show at the fairgrounds. As I threaded my way through the maze of pickups and stock trailers, I thought about my prophetic conversation with Lane about heroes.

The morning on the plateau when I naively told Lane I'd like to be a hero I didn't think it would feel icky and disjointed. Heroes have it all together. They instinctively do what needs to be done. They're John Wayne brave, not throwing up petrified like I was yesterday. I hadn't believed James White Eagle's prophecies.

Lane had said love isn't always hearts, flowers, moonlight and love songs. Love is messy, dirty and painful. You put on your big-girl panties and wade through it. That's my version of what he said, but I got what he meant about love being sacrificial. Being heroic is close to the same thing. Wouldn't you think? In both instances one person puts the well-being of another above their own.

I wanted to be thought of as heroic without having to *do* anything. Like one day I would casually gesture to my Nobel Peace Prize on the mantel and say, "Oh, that old thing? I get tired of dusting it." Being a hero was not glamorous. It was terrifying. Chaotic. Another thing I failed to accurately calculate. Still, I gotta admit, knowing I kept Stormy and Lane alive feels pretty good.

The morning sky blazed with glorious colors I barely saw. With only three hours of sleep I barely saw anything.

I drove to the hospital and learned Lane hadn't been admitted. I found Stormy's room, but a nurse bustling toward me kept me from going in.

"Excuse me, Ma'am," she said. "Are you a friend of the lady in this room?"

My hand still on the doorknob, I considered the question. Stormy and I have definitely not been friends. I'm not sure how things stand now. I assumed the nurse wasn't going to let me in unless I was a close personal friend.

Before I could answer, she rushed on. "The reason I'm asking is she needs more blood, and I was wondering if you might donate. Do you know your type?"

"O positive," I said.

"Perfect." She beamed a smile in my direction. "Now?"

"I guess," I said. "Sure."

I followed her back down the hall to a small sterile-looking room lined with white metal cabinets. The paperwork took longer than giving blood.

"What kind of juice would you like?" she asked, as I sat up. I started to tell her I didn't want any juice, but she interrupted me with an upraised hand.

"You need to hydrate to keep from getting woozy."

"Orange juice," I said.

She hurried out the door and quickly returned with a carton of apple juice. Neither of us mentioned the discrepancy. I sipped it on the way to Stormy's room.

Stormy, dwarfed by piles of pillows, looked nothing like the person who could destroy me with a glance. I stepped into the room and hovered near the foot of the bed. Around the cheek which resembled a plum, her skin was alarmingly pale. She hadn't made a sound last night when the gun bounced off her face. The pain must have been excruciating.

Stormy opened her eyes. I was ready to bolt but saw welcome in them. She gave me a weak smile and motioned for me to come closer.

"Ali, come meet Lyle."

I hadn't noticed the nice-looking man who stood and offered me his chair. His clothes were casual but looked expensive. You can tell. His thick brown hair, longish on top, was cut short around his ears and neckline. Laugh lines crinkled around his warm brown eyes when he smiled. Which he was doing now. Who was he?

"Lyle, this is Ali." Stormy waved an arm in my direction. "Ali, this is Lyle."

Well, that told me nothing. Again, he offered me his chair.

"No thanks," I shook my head and backed toward the door. I hate hospital smells. And Stormy scares me. "I can't stay. I just came to check on Stormy." My eyes moved to the plastic bag of goo hanging above the bed and followed the liquid through the tube into her arm.

"Stormy lost a lot of blood yesterday," Lyle said.

"She knows," Stormy said. "She wore most of it home."

"And little else," I added.

"Ali tore up her shirt to keep me from bleeding to death."

"This is the girl who saved your life?" Lyle asked.

I was offended by his surprise.

"Yes. Lane's, too," Stormy said.

"Thank you." Lyle extended his hand. I stepped forward and shook it.

"I was..."

"Quite astounding," Stormy finished. "I haven't the foggiest idea why you showed up, but if I'd known how much I'd need you I'd have been nicer."

"You're the girl Lane is gaga over?" Lyle asked.

There was that surprise again. But then I remembered how I must look.

"Wait. What did you say?" I decided I better sit down.

"You can't have him until I kick his butt," Lyle said, through an enormous yawn. "I intended to last night but couldn't find a spot that wasn't already bruised or broken."

"What?" I asked again. I'd been lowering myself into the offered chair, but at his words, my knees collapsed, and I sort of plopped into it.

"I said I was going to..."

"Not the butt-kicking part, the other thing."

"You can't have him until I get through with him."

Yesterday I hadn't just imagined that Stormy and Lane loved each other. Stormy took a bullet for Lane. So, who is Lyle? And what did he say?

"He knows Lane loves you," Stormy said. "That's the problem. The whole world knows." She rolled her eyes.

"Where is he?" I asked. Lane loves me. I couldn't think about anything else.

"I hope he's sleeping. The doctor wanted to admit him. He was in bad shape," Stormy said.

"How bad?" My heart leaped into my throat.

"He was dehydrated. He has broken ribs, a broken cheek bone, and a bruised something. Spleen maybe. It's a miracle one of those ribs didn't puncture a lung. He owes us big time."

I liked the way 'us' sounded. Stormy and me—a team. An unlikely team, but a team, nonetheless. Neither of us could have done it alone.

"ER got fluids in him before they let him go," Lyle added. He perched on the edge of Stormy's bed and placed a hand on her knee.

"I've seen many a woman fail to rein in ole Lane. Didn't think I'd live long enough to see it."

I fought a ridiculous urge to cry.

"If you will excuse me, I'm going down the hall." He stood and stretched. "You girls probably need a chance to talk." He looked directly at me. "Don't wear out my wife."

"I won't," I promised. "Wife? Wait. Did you say wife?"

Lyle opened the door. Light poured in illuminating me. "You're better looking than your picture." He grinned.

At my blank stare, he added, "I've seen the paper."

I groaned.

He laughed as he walked out.

With questions spinning through my head, I waited for the door to close.

Chapter Fifty-Three

Lyle is your husband?" I asked, still dazed by the realization.

"Who did you think he was?" Stormy's tone sounded more like the old Stormy.

"He's nice," I said. "So, you must not be a total bitch."

"I'm not good at apologies. I haven't treated you well."

"No kidding."

"There's no excuse for the way I acted."

"I can't argue when you're right," I said.

She smiled. "You aren't making this easy."

"Well, you haven't exactly apologized." I sipped the apple juice.

"I am sorry." Stormy tugged at the neck of a lacy lavender gown. It definitely wasn't hospital issue. "This is Lane's fault. He talks me into leaving my comfy home to come here and live in a shack. 'It'll be fun,' he says. 'Like old times', he says. 'Chief needs help', he says. Then every time I turn around, he's running off after you."

Stormy grimaced as she tried to get more comfortable. "In my defense," she went on, "I thought you were chasing him and getting in our way. He's always had women falling all over him. In school, girls pretended to be my friend to get close to Lane. Running interference for him is an ingrained habit."

"I thought you were a ditzy blond having a good time with Lane," Stormy continued. "Yesterday when I realized how far you'd go to save him I knew you were solid. Not much scares me but depending on you to get him out of that house terrified me. I was certain you couldn't do it."

"So, to make sure I failed you gave me a knife that wouldn't cut butter." I grinned.

"Distracting them was too dangerous. I couldn't take a chance of your getting shot."

I thought about that. She didn't like me, but she risked her life to protect me.

"I totally underestimated you," Stormy continued. "In the end, you rescued us all. Seriously, I am sorry."

"Apology accepted." I smiled. "What were you doing here?"

"Working undercover. Tony called Lane for advice when he realized the extent of the drug problem in his county." Stormy licked dry-chapped lips.

I handed her a glass of ice chips. "The newspaper said you and Lane are cops."

"You didn't know?" Stormy nodded. "Lane is a Federal Agent. DEA. Since he works in DC, nobody around here would know him."

"I'm stunned. Why would Lane come to Oklahoma?"

"Several reasons. If Lane is your friend, he's in it for life. If he can help, he's there. Tony had lost his county. Any third grader could get drugs. Burglaries and robberies were through the roof. Addicts were stealing anything not nailed down for drug money." Stormy tipped the glass. Half of the ice splattered on her face.

I handed her a towel.

"Thanks. Every time Tony's men made a bust, the perps were back on the street before the ink dried. Evidence disappeared from a locked room before trials. Another problem was Danny. He realized we were cops the afternoon we collared those guys at the courthouse. Why were you there?"

"Wrong place at the wrong time," I said. "Story of my life."

"Lane didn't trust Danny. But Danny is related to Tony's wife. Tony wouldn't listen. Anyway, once he knew we were cops, we got nowhere. So, we trailed the three stooges, hoping they'd lead us higher up the ladder."

"I wish you'd been there the night they chased me into Cheyenne Falls," I said.

A nurse came in, replaced the depleted bag of red goo with a new one, and checked the drip. Stormy waited for her to leave before resuming her story. "Victor Ruiz is a drug lord who has a larger army than small countries, and a compound near Tijuana. He also has a private air strip. The DEA has been watching him. He's been a thorn in Lane's side."

My head was spinning. "So, Victor Ruiz is the other reason Lane came?"

"This has his name written all over it. Lane is sure Ruiz is running operations in other states but can't prove it."

"Operations?"

At my blank stare, Stormy explained. "It's easier to fly drugs into central states like Texas, Oklahoma and Arkansas than to smuggle them across the Mexican border. Small town airports are usually located outside of town with little or no security. The Cheyenne Falls airport was perfect. The back road which leads to the far end of the runway makes it easy to unload and refuel a plane without being seen."

"That's why planes flying over Debbie's house grabbed Lane's attention," I guessed.

"Right," Stormy said. "Lane knew the road existed but couldn't find it."

Lyle slipped back into the room and reclaimed his seat on Stormy's bed.

"Where do you come in?" I asked Stormy.

"Lane didn't have time to form the rapport it takes to infiltrate a drug ring. Druggies are skitzy. He thought a couple might look more innocuous. He needed my eyes and ears. It's amazing what you can pick up when you're invisible."

"Why would you agree to her going undercover?" I asked Lyle.

"You know her well enough to know I couldn't stop her," Lyle said. "She loves undercover work. Lane and Tony were both here. She's been in more danger in Santa Fe with less protection. She left her job with the police force a couple of months ago and had time to do this. When the baby comes, she won't have time for anything else."

Lyle and Stormy looked at each other and smiled.

"Baby? You're pregnant?" I looked at her flat stomach in shock.

Stormy laughed. "We're adopting. Her mother is in prison and putting her baby up for adoption."

"Wow. Congratulations," I said.

Stormy sipped ice chips without spilling any.

"So, you've both known Lane for a long time?" I asked.

"I don't remember when I didn't know him. I was two when Lane and his mother moved in next door," Stormy said. "Lyle lived down the street. Lane, Lyle, and my brother Larry called themselves 'The Three L's.' Everyone else called them trouble. They had a silly ritual when they were ten. They became blood brothers by cutting themselves with a rusty knife."

"What was silly about that?" Lyle asked.

"They wouldn't let me in on it because I'm a girl. It's a wonder they didn't all die of tetanus." She frowned. "I might have wished it on them."

Lyle laughed. "Well, she is a girl, but it wasn't the only reason. She was two years younger, but she could outrun, outclimb, outfight any of us. It was embarrassing. Thank goodness she didn't play football."

"They played football in high school," Stormy said. "Tony was quarterback. Go Scorpions." She did a weak fist pump. "Everyone on the team had a nickname. Larry was The Limp. He was always hurt. Lane was Renegade because he drove an old Jeep at the time. Oh wait, he still does." Stormy smiled. "And the name fit. Tony, being Chickasaw, was Chief and Lyle was Piston because he was good on the line. I don't understand it, I just go with it."

Lyle smiled and didn't explain.

"Were they good?" I asked.

"Not so you'd notice. Larry was terrible."

"Well, wait a minute," Lyle said. "We were state champions our senior year. Lane and Tony both got football scholarships. Tony's brother, Sixx, skipped college and went straight to the NFL. He's still playing. All pro kicker last year."

"Whatever," Stormy said with a dismissive handwave.

"Stormy thought football was an excuse for her cheerleader routines," Lyle teased. "She saw it as an opportunity to get in front of a crowd and shake her, uh, pom-poms."

Stormy threw a box of tissues at him. Lyle ducked and laughed.

"Speaking of nicknames, Stormy is probably a nickname, but Lane calls you PJ."

"My birth certificate says Paula Jo. My father started calling me Stormy when I failed to outgrow the terrible twos. It stuck."

"I'm glad Lane didn't fall in love with you a long time ago," I said.

Stormy laughed. "He knew me too well. He's like my brother. Most of the time I want to kill him, myself. He can be so irritating. You'll see."

"I didn't give him a chance," Lyle countered. "When she turned sixteen, I staked my claim. Truth be known I've probably loved her since she was ten." He looked at Stormy with so much love in his eyes I looked away.

Embarrassed, I stood up. "By the way, you may not have blood brothers, but you have a blood sister. I wore so much of your blood home last night, I'm sure some seeped in somewhere."

"But I don't have any of yours," Stormy pointed out.

I motioned to the bag hanging from the IV pole. "Actually, you do." I backed toward the door. "I'm supposed to be at the sheriff's office. I better go. Nice to meet you, Lyle."

"Come back," Stormy said, "If Lane isn't a total idiot, you and I are going to be stuck with each other. We need to work on this 'friend' thing."

Lyle laughed. "I think she just told you she wants to be in your wedding."

Chapter Fifty-Four

Lane's eyes lit up when I walked into the sheriff's office. One eye lit up. The other was swollen shut. "Hey Sunflower," he said.

"I thought you would be asleep." I couldn't stop staring at him. His face was bruised and so swollen he would probably scare small children. He had a gash on one cheek and a busted lip. Still, he was the most beautiful thing I'd ever seen.

"He might as well be asleep. He's useless here." Sheriff Checotah pulled out a chair for me. "I had no idea you could walk into this office so sedately."

"I've been practicing." I sat down.

"How are you today?" he asked.

"Nobody has tried to kill me yet."

"Well, that's a plus. Thanks for coming in."

The sheriff sat across from me. Lane leaned against a nearby window. Austin had been lying by his feet. He got up, came to me, flopped down beside my chair, and exhaled loudly.

"Traitor," Lane said. His stance reminded me of the first time I saw him. But with cleaner clothes and a battered face.

"I thought your 'accidents' were related to your inheritance," the sheriff told me, around the toothpick clamped between his teeth. "I didn't realize, thanks to Renegade, you're connected to this case."

"I'm more involved than you know," I said. "The suitcase those guys thought Lane had, I know where it is."

My chair squeaked when I moved, threatening to throw me backwards. Danny's weight must have sprung whatever held it together. I wondered who would be using it now that Danny had relocated to a cell down the hall. Talking too fast, I launched into the story of David's switched luggage.

"Where's the suitcase now?" Sheriff Checotah leaned forward, listening intently.

"Dallas. It might be what you need to tie this to Ruiz," I told Lane. Austin looked up at me. His tail thumped the floor.

"Ruiz?" Lane asked.

"I've been talking to Stormy," I said.

"Your fiancé still has the suitcase?" Lane asked.

"Ex-fiancé. Yes. I talked to him last night." I scratched behind Austin's ear.

"Do you think the guys in the truck connected you with the suitcase?" Chief asked.

"No. If they thought I had it, they wouldn't have grabbed Lane. It wasn't with me when they tried to push me off the road. By the way, that truck was parked by the shack where they held Lane. Last time I saw it, it was engulfed in flames."

The sheriff made notes. "Yeah, I saw it, too. We got those guys, but we still don't know who shot at you in the canyon or tried to drown you. Whoever it was is still out there. Until he's apprehended, I'm posting a deputy to keep an eye on you."

"I wish this was all over."

"And I wish you would be more careful. No more predawn runs." The sheriff looked sternly at me and more pointedly at Lane. "Lanigan, I'm surprised at you."

Lane nodded. "You're right, Chief. I used terrible judgement."

"Well, wait a minute," I said. "There's enough blame to go around. I was an idiot."

The sheriff didn't smile. "You wish this were over? So, do I. But the truth is, it's not. You've got to be more careful, Young Lady."

After a long silence, I ventured, "Last night before you arrived those guys were talking about a boss who wasn't there. Any idea who it might be?"

"Chief hasn't interrogated them yet," Lane said. "They won't give him up."

"Do you think you got everyone else?" I asked.

The sheriff shook his head. "We'll be rounding up dealers for weeks. We got the guys in the DA's office. I'm pumped about it." He said nothing about Danny.

"The ledger in the suitcase should help," I said. "The entries are meticulous."

"You've seen it?" the sheriff asked.

"Yes."

"What else is in there?" Tony asked.

"$50,000. And a .457 Magnum."

Tony whistled. "No wonder they're intent on getting it back. Business and bucks."

I looked at Lane. "What were you doing up on the bluff?"

"Kissing a pretty girl." He grinned.

I glanced at the sheriff and we both glared at Lane.

"Watching the barn," Lane said. "We were sure they used it to stash whatever they unloaded from the plane. It's not far from the airport, but remote. No nosey neighbors for miles. I had a bird's eye view from the plateau without being seen. But I didn't know when to be there until you told me which night the planes flew over Debbie's house."

"The owner of the barn has to be involved," I said. "Why haven't you arrested him?"

The sheriff coughed and averted his eyes.

"What?" I asked.

Lane laughed. "Far be it from me to say I told you so, Chief."

"What?" I demanded, beginning to get angry.

"That would be you, Sunflower," Lane said.

"The barn I'd like to paint is mine?"

"You own the land. Or you will next Wednesday." The sheriff grinned.

"Wait a minute. Lane, you thought I'm involved?"

Lane laughed. "I was keeping an eye on you. Multitasking."

"I'm out of here." I stood up and headed for the door.

Lane blocked my path. "Come on, Ali. A joke. A little humor there."

"Not funny," I grumbled.

"Lane swore you didn't know." The sheriff flicked a badly mangled toothpick toward the trash can. Spent toothpicks piled near the can bore evidence this wasn't a rare occurrence. "Until recently," he added, "most of the area has been planted in peanuts. The barn hadn't been used in years."

"That land is mine?" I asked.

The sheriff nodded. "Along with the land where Lane was held."

"You might want to plan a fire sale," Lane said.

"Good grief. My land was being used by a drug ring?"

"You weren't around," Sheriff Checotah shrugged.

"Until I was."

"Right. And they needed to get you out of the way," the sheriff added.

I let it sink in. "Who's been planting peanuts on my land?"

"Your cousin Fred."

"Have you talked to him?" I asked. "Wouldn't he know what's going on?"

"It's on my list," the sheriff said, "he's been a bit hard to locate."

"Did you catch those guys unloading men from the cattle truck?"

"No. I sent Danny out to look around, but he didn't see anything."

"You sent Danny?" Lane looked pointedly at the sheriff.

Sheriff Checotah nodded. "I better get out there."

"A lot more than drugs could be coming in on those planes," Lane said.

"What do you mean?" I asked.

"The number of people being bought and sold into slavery is higher now than at any time in history," Lane said. "It would explain the trucks meeting those planes. They wouldn't need trucks to unload drugs." Lane looked at me. "Girls aren't the only ones forced into slavery. Men will do anything to escape their country. They come here to work thinking they'll make enough to send for their family. But when they arrive in Mexico, they're taken captive, forced to work for nothing, and usually sent to California."

"Was Fred at the party when you were thrown into the lake?"

"Well, that was random. No. Janet said he'd been injured in a wreck. Wait… I remember. When the guy picked me up and threw me over the rail, he sounded like he was in pain. You think it was Fred."

Chapter Fifty-Five

Fred is certainly becoming a person of interest," Checotah said. "When will you talk to him?"

"When we find him. As I said, he's been scarce. By the way, do you remember telling me James White Eagle said your life is in danger?"

"Who?" I stalled.

"James White Eagle was a legend circulated by the old people," the sheriff said. "He never existed. But you said you talked to him."

"Sounds like I said he talked to me."

"Supposedly he died in a massacre in 1818."

"What? 1818? He did not. I mean, uh, ... How could he die in 1818 if he never existed?" I asked. Checotah was wrong on both counts. James White Eagle existed and was alive and well in 1891. I used rare, good judgment and kept my mouth shut.

"I thought we were talking about who wants kill me," I reminded him.

"Where did you hear that name? You didn't make it up."

A phone rang on his desk. Saved by the bell.

Sheriff Checotah dug through a pile of papers sending them drifting to the floor. He finally found the phone and answered it. His eyes widened. "It's David Phipps," He whispered. He clamped a hand over the receiver. "He wants to talk to Ali."

"David Phipps? The attorney in the Branch Barlow murder trial?" Lane asked me.

"The movie star who murdered his wife?"

"Allegedly," I said.

"The media is all over it," Lane shook his head. "It's bigger than the O.J. Simpson trial. The witnesses have been the who's who of Hollywood."

"When would you have time to watch the news?" I asked.

"I've seen Phipps on TV. Dang, he's better looking than Barlow." Still holding his hand over the phone, the sheriff stared at me. "How did he know you'd be here?"

"I talked to him last night," I said. My claim to fame seems to be knowing David.

"Branch Barlow is a movie star who killed his wife," Lane explained to Jake, a young deputy who had walked in. Jake looked at me and shrugged, unimpressed.

"Allegedly," I said.

"And dumped her body…"

"Allegedly," I said.

"She was drop-dead gorgeous. Why did he kill her?" the sheriff asked.

"Allegedly," I corrected.

"Poor choice of words," Lane grinned. "I heard he told her the spark was gone, so she tazed him. There's probably more to it. He was in that movie…"

"Excuse me." I interrupted. "May I please speak to David?"

"Sorry." The sheriff handed me the phone.

"Hi, David," I said.

"Your phone is dead."

"Yeah. I forgot to charge it last night."

"Again." David exhaled his exasperation. "Your picture was on the front page of the Dallas Star this morning."

"You're kidding."

"It wasn't very flattering. You looked like Jane Goodall on speed."

"Thanks."

"I'm impressed, Ali. You, of all people, involved in busting an international drug ring. You don't even go out alone after dark."

"It wasn't dark yet," I said.

"Are you feeling better this morning?"

"A little. I'm exhausted and every muscle in my body is reminding me of its existence. Uh, David, the mystery suitcase may be the evidence the sheriff needs to put these guys away."

The sheriff, who wasn't too busy gossiping with Lane to listen to my conversation, said, "Tell him, I'll send a plane after it."

I relayed the information.

"I've chartered a plane," David said. "I want to arrive before the horses get there. I'll bring it with me. Tell him I'll hand it over in exchange for underwear."

Good. David is joking. I laughed. "Should he guess at the size?"

"I'm shipping the horses to Cheyenne Falls tomorrow. One is Jupiter."

Of course, he'd want to be here. Jupiter is worth a fortune. Above and beyond that, David raised and trained Jupiter. He's gorgeous and soon to be a legend. Five generations of Dales are still talking about that 'flashy horse'.

Behind me Lane and Tony were still talking about David. I head the sheriff say, "Good grief, Lanigan, you finally fall in love and her fiancé is David Phipps? What is wrong with you?"

"Ex-fiancé," Lane insisted."

I missed the rest of Lane's answer because David was saying, "Ali, are you listening? I said I've rented stalls for the horses at the fairgrounds."

"Sorry, David. Right. Thank you for doing this. Lexy will be so happy."

I looked at the sheriff. "David is coming, too."

"Great," he beamed. "Tell him…"

"You tell him," I said, handing him the phone.

Sheriff Checotah spoke briefly with David and handed the phone back to me.

"I've reserved a room at Buggy Creek Inn," David said. "But I may be sleeping at the fairgrounds. It depends on how good their security is."

"What about this case you're in the middle of?" I asked.

"The DA's star witness had emergency gall bladder surgery. He asked for a continuance."

"You're coming here instead of preparing for trial? This isn't the David Phipps I know. Who are you?"

"We're prepared. I'll work on it there. You sure you're okay?" David asked.

"I'm a bit rattled, but I will be."

"Okay. Gotta go," David said.

"See you tomorrow."

This ride is really going to happen. We're going back in time to change history. Actually, to keep history from changing. Dazed, I hung up and turned around. Lane and Sheriff Checotah both stared at me.

"Well, I said, smiling brightly, "How about those Cowboys?"

Chapter Fifty-Six

I shimmied out of my clothes and sank into the bathwater's velvety warmth until bubbles tickled my nose. I closed my eyes and felt tension and stress drift away. Twenty or thirty minutes later, seriously, who keeps track of time when one is languishing, I rose out of the water like some ancient sphinx, which wasn't as graceful as it sounds. It involved slipping and splashing. A knock at the door startled me. I was not expecting company. I grabbed my robe, wriggling into it on the way to the door and peeked through the drapes.

Lane's Jeep was parked beside my Mustang.

I opened the door and there he was. Nothing to separate us. No David, no Stormy, no misconceptions, no wrong conclusion, or stupid mirrored sunglasses for him to hide behind. Lane no longer tried to conceal what I read in his eyes. It was all there.

"Well? Can I come in?" he asked.

I backed away from the door, pulling him with me. He closed it with his foot.

My eyes roamed over his face. "You have a gash on the same cheek as mine," I said.

"I hope it's not hereditary. Our kids will all have scars."

"We're going to have kids?" I asked."

"Lots."

"Is this a proposal?"

"I'll do better when I'm not half dead." He sank into the chair beside the door. The lines of exhaustion around his mouth erased when he smiled. "We have to give people time to know that we know each other first."

"Good idea," I grinned.

"I gotta tell you I'm scared."

"Why?" I sat on the chair across the small table from him.

"I swore nobody would ever get this close to me again."

I waited to see if there was more. There was.

"My first love vowed she'd love me forever then dumped me for some rich guy she met in college." He paused. "You probably won't believe me since this happened so fast, but I don't love easily."

"That's what Stormy and Lyle said," I told him.

"I finally fell in love again. We'd been married eighteen months when she died in a car wreck. She was six months pregnant. Our baby was a boy."

"Lane, how horrible. I am so sorry. How long ago?"

"Three years."

"No wonder Stormy was so protective. Lyle, too."

"Stormy's like an ole mother hen." He reached for my hand and raised it to his lips still looking at me through those dark lashes, wasted on a guy. "I came to seduce you. But I'm too tired. And have broken ribs."

"Lane, we've gotta talk." I paused and chewed my lip.

"Oh, damn. It's never good when a woman says that."

"I'm a virgin," I blurted.

"You're what?" He laughed. "Oh. You're serious. How long were you engaged?"

"Four years."

"Four years? And in all that time you never…"

"No."

"And Phipps was okay with that?"

I thought about it. "Umm, not always."

"Wow. The guy deserves a medal. Not many men would honor your conviction."

"You're right. Gee, never thought about it." I went on in a rush. "In high school guys bragged about their conquests in the locker room. I didn't want to be another notch on someone's belt, didn't want anyone bragging… You know."

Lane laughed. "You thought you could stop them?"

I blinked. "You mean they would lie?"

"Your refreshing air of innocence is what I was drawn to." He grinned. "But we gotta get married. Soon. I'm not Phipps."

"Okay. As soon as my parents are found. I want them at my wedding."

"Fair enough. How long is Phipps planning to stay?"

"I don't know. Through the hearing. He's worried about me. You okay with that?"

"I guess. As long as he's not planning to stay with you."

"He booked a room." Normally David would've asked me to do it.

"Does he know about me?"

"No. Not yet. When I ended our engagement, there was nothing to tell. I didn't know where you were or if you were coming back. You almost didn't."

"How's he going take it?" Lane asked.

"Okay. All the great actors aren't in Hollywood. That's why he makes big bucks."

"I had no idea who you were engaged to. I merely knew someone paid a fortune for the rock you had." As if to erase it, he rubbed his thumb over the white line on my tan finger where the ring used to be.

"Everything is a contest with David's friends. The fiancé sporting the biggest diamond wins. David won. It had nothing to do with me."

"Ali, I'll never have that kind of money."

"Being that wealthy is obscene," I said. Lane started to say something. I held up my hand. "I grew up in poverty. If I got a pair of panties or socks for Christmas, I was excited. I don't need much. I don't know what your world is like, but if you're in it, I'm there."

"You're sure?"

"I never fit into David's life. I ended our engagement because I realized I no longer wanted to make the effort." I paused to collect my thoughts. "David is the only man I ever dated. I had nothing to compare that relationship to. Now that I know how love feels, I won't settle for less. If we live in a tent, Lane, I want to be with you."

"Is this a proposal?"

I laughed. "You already proposed. I think. Do you believe in love at first sight?"

Lane yawned. "I believe when someone important grabs your attention, you remember everything about that moment—sights, sounds, smells—and after that attraction grows into love, it becomes love at first sight. What do you think?"

I nodded. I thought back to the day at the Courthouse. When Lane Lanigan thumbed up the brim of his Stetson and looked at me with those watercolor eyes, he consumed my every waking thought since. But he doesn't have to know it. Yet.

Lane grimaced as he stood up. He yawned again. I got up, too, and kissed him, carefully avoiding the gash on his lip.

"Can I crash on your spare bed?" he asked. "I've got to lie down. I promise to behave. I want to know you're close."

"Of course," I said. I helped him to the bed. He winced as I eased him down on it. I took off his boots and covered him with a blanket. "Do you have a prescription for pain?"

"Yeah. In my shirt pocket."

I retrieved the prescription and went to the bathroom to dress. Lane was already asleep when I came out. I heard a noise outside. Cautiously, I pulled back the heavy drapes. Austin scratched at the door. He saw me and his tail waved. I opened the door and waited while he, in no great hurry, stretched and ambled in.

I laughed. "Don't rush into anything."

He padded to the bed where Lane snored softly, dropped to the floor, lowered his head and heaved a sigh.

I drove to Walmart, filled the prescription, and picked up some other things. Back in the room I checked the dosage instructions, woke Lane and gave him two pills, managing not to spill water all over him. He smiled, thanked me, and was back asleep before I could say "You're welcome."

Chapter Fifty-Seven

The next morning, I stretched and smiled, working on waking up. Austin sat beside my bed panting in my face. When I opened my eyes, he licked my nose.

"Why do you smell like fish?" I asked.

Lane was sitting in the chair beside the door. He grinned and put a hand over the phone. "The cook gave him a can of tuna." He finished his conversation and brought me a steaming mug of coffee.

"I could get used to this," I said, scooting into a sitting position before accepting the cup. "You shaved. Bet that hurt." I glanced over at the spare bed. "How long have you been up?"

"A while," he said. "I'm an early riser." His hair was damp, and he'd changed clothes.

"Good to know." I sat up higher in the bed and pushed the pillow behind my back. "I need some answers. How did those guys get you?"

"Let me back up. You know I'm with the DEA, right?"

I nodded. "Stormy told me."

"Victor Ruiz has eluded me for years. My partner nabbed one of his known cohorts. I'd gathered the evidence against him, so my boss insisted I do the interrogation and I wanted to be there. When we came down from the plateau and I dropped you off, I headed to Will Rogers Airport and caught a flight to DC." He chuckled. "Only Oklahoma would name two airports after men who died in a plane crash." He shook his head.

He sipped his coffee and collected his thoughts. "We knew Jenkins was the weasel in the D.A.'s office. Stafford was the organizer. Bagging him was huge. He sets up the operation, then leaves it in the

244

hands of someone capable—in this instance Jenkins—and moves on. I need something to tie him to Ruiz. I'm hoping it's in that suitcase."

"Jenkins ran into a problem," Lane continued. "A thriving drug business had already been set up here. The guy running it took exception to them moving into his territory. Jenkins' men can be very persuasive. I know from experience." Lane ran a hand across the bruises on his face. "We don't know who he is yet. I'm betting it's your cousin."

"I'm getting used to the idea," I said.

Lane grimaced as he shifted his weight. "When I got back to town, they ambushed me at the house where you dropped me off the night we were at the cemetery. Stormy had gone back to Santa Fe while I was in DC. I wasn't sure she was back. Fortunately, she was not only there, but she was also awake."

"You guys are cops. Where were your guns?"

"We had both gotten off planes. They were packed away. Unfortunately."

I wrapped my fingers around the coffee mug enjoying its warmth. "How did Stormy know where they took you?"

"I didn't go down easy. She slipped under a tarp in the back of the truck while they were wrestling with me."

"Good grief. Stormy went with you? No wonder she was so tired. Where did she sleep?" Without her courage, Lane would be dead.

Lane saw my shudder and read my mind. "Knowing I would die without telling you I love you hurt more than these broken ribs." He grinned. "When I saw you hacking away at those ropes, I thought I was delirious."

"Wish I'd known you had that knife in your boot."

We were interrupted by a loud knock on the door. I jumped.

"Breakfast," Lane announced. He went to the door, handed the man some money and brought the sack to the table. He pulled out two burgers and fed them to Austin.

"It's hard to keep a hungry dog out of your food," he said. He opened a box and handed me a waffle with bacon and eggs then got to work on his sausage, eggs, and hash browns.

"Your turn," he said between bites. "Explain the hole we hid in."

"It's a long story." I cut into my waffle.

"I'm not going anywhere." He waited, not breaking eye contact.

I told him about following Mariah through the tunnel, meeting Lexy in 1891, outrunning the tornado, taking refuge in the root cellar, and carving my initials in the boulder. I considered telling him about shooting off Elmer's penis but decided it could wait until after we were married.

"Exactly when did you carve those initials?" Lane bit into a slice of bacon and washed it down with coffee.

"The day we were at Blue Sage. "

He chewed his hash browns without comment. I went on to tell him about Lexy's friend Moonflower teaching her how to erase tracks with a cedar branch.

"At the time I believed I'd never put that information to use," I said.

He still said nothing.

"I knew you wouldn't believe me." I handed him the ashtray containing the arrowhead, my jigsaw puzzle piece, and 1889 Indian head penny.

"Nobody could make up a story like that. When you wouldn't tell me who Lexy was, I called my crew in DC. If they couldn't find her, she doesn't exist." He turned the penny over. His eyes widened when he saw the date. "It's pretty farfetched. I believe you."

I laughed. "I was pretty smug about you not finding Lexy."

"I collect arrowheads." He examined the one in the ashtray. "So, tell me about this White Eagle that Chief is so skeptical about."

"James White Eagle is a Kiowa shaman. But he doesn't live with a tribe. Moonflower said he travels on the wind. That may not be quite accurate, but he was in her village the day I was there. He predicted I would face danger and save many lives. He warned me my life was in danger, which I already knew by then. I must have mentioned his name to Checotah at the hospital. Big mistake. I was on drugs. He was questioning me about the near drowning. He believes White Eagle was a legend who never existed. But he did. He told me to follow the hawk. It would lead me out of danger."

"The hawk that came out of nowhere and led us from the house?" Lane asked.

"Yes. That hawk saved my life more than once. I'll tell you about the rattlesnake sometime."

"Well, White Eagle was right about you saving lives," Lane said.

"You'll want to see the tunnel, of course."

"Of course. But that's impossible today with your ex-fiancé riding into town with the evidence. Not that I'm in any shape to ride a horse now with a bruised spleen and broken ribs. In those famous words of Dirty Harry, 'A man's gotta know his limitations'." Lane picked up my puzzle piece and tossed it in his hand. "What's this?"

"The symbol of my life," I said. "I found it when I was a child. It didn't fit any puzzles. I didn't fit anywhere either. We are alike, that puzzle piece and me."

Lane dropped the piece in the ashtray, leaned close and cupped my face in his hands. "Your piece once fit somewhere. It became separated from its puzzle like you were separated from your family. You tried to fit into places you were never intended to be. You're home now. You fit perfectly."

Tears blurred my vision. I pressed my palms against my eyes.

"When we were kids," Lane continued, "Chief told me a fable I've never forgotten. An Indian boy found a hawk egg. He couldn't climb the cliff to put it back in the nest, so he placed it in a prairie chicken nest on the ground. The eggs hatched. The hawk grew up with the prairie chickens never knowing it was a hawk. He watched birds riding the wind, but never tried to fly because he didn't know he could. You were taken to a place you didn't belong. But you refused to stay a prairie chicken. Finding who you are took courage."

The more I'm with Lane Lanigan, the more I discover. His wisdom, depth and understanding blow me away. More to the point, Lane listens. He makes me feel valued.

"So, Phipps knows about this tunnel of yours?" Lane asked.

"I should probably tell you the other reason he's coming."

Chapter Fifty-Eight

Your stomach tightened and your breath caught in your throat while the jet, like a pregnant elephant, lumbered across miles of runways. You're reminded of a roller coaster chugging laboriously up the first giant hill. It pauses at the top before careening down the other side. The jet engines whine and wind until they can't get tighter. And you wait, not breathing, until that moment when the plane shoots forward with the speed of a stone released from a slingshot.

That's my relationship with Lane. Since I first laid eyes on him, I've been riding a roller coaster in a state of breathless suspension. Wow, who is that? He likes me. I think. He doesn't know I'm alive. He noticed me. No, he didn't. He loves me. He doesn't know I'm alive. He loves me. He loves Stormy. Well, I've pulled the last petal from the daisy and, as it turns out, he loves me.

That scares the hell out of me. I've never wanted anything this badly. But things never work out for me. My luck isn't this good. Something bad will happen. I can feel it.

Lane called. The meeting with David went smoothly. David handed the suitcase over to Sheriff Checotah. Lane and Checotah were at the sheriff's office checking it out. Lane was elated over what it contained.

David called, too. He was on his way to the fairgrounds to meet the van, and get the horses settled. I'll have to explain Lane to him. I'd rather have a root canal, but I hope he gets here before Lane. David deserves a better explanation than he got the night I returned his ring. Now that he no longer intimidates me, I hope I can explain. I've been practicing.

I peeked through the drapes. Sheriff Checotah had sent Jake, the young deputy, to keep an eye on me. I'd met Jake when we'd been in the restaurant picking up to-go lunches. While we waited, he'd shown me pictures of his two-year-old daughter and pretty wife.

My protector Jake sat in his patrol car outside my motel room reading. He looked up, saw me and waved. I waved back and closed the drapes. I had no idea the sheriff had been posting deputies to keep an eye on me which is why, I realized, he knew about my early morning runs. Obviously, he's been aware of the danger longer than I knew. He's making no effort to hide that from me now.

I'd been keeping myself busy doing laundry. But then I pretty much died of boredom. I'd arranged my clothes according to color three times. I don't have that many clothes.

I picked up the book I'd brought from Dallas. Silly me. I thought I'd have time to read. Until now I hadn't looked at it. I'd only read a few pages when I was interrupted by a loud knock on the door. I tossed the book aside.

"It's about time, Lane," I said as I raced to the door and opened it.

The guy standing there was not Lane.

Or David.

Or the sheriff.

Or Jake.

He was tall. Auburn hair, cut in an old-school flattop, matched a ruddy complexion. His eyes were gray, not blue. What I read in them terrified me. I glanced past him. He stood between me and the patrol car. I couldn't see Jake.

My welcoming smile faded. "Uh, you aren't who I expected."

His eyes widened. He looked like he'd seen a ghost. Beneath his freckles, his face drained of color.

"You have the wrong room." I looked around him. The deputy had gone back to reading his book. He didn't look up. I tried to close the door.

"You're dead." He stuck a scuffed work boot in the door. I killed you."

"You're insane." I slammed the door into his foot and kept shoving.

"Wait." he said, "I know who you are."

Really scared now, I leaned into the door, screaming for Jake.

The guy grinned through the opening with a maniacal expression. It was like the clip from the movie where Jack Nicholson says, "Heeeeeeeers Johnny," and more terrifying.

"You had me going there for a minute, Cuz." He laughed.

"Cuz?" Even as I questioned, I knew. My stomach tied itself in a knot. "Fred." I braced my back against the door and leaned all my weight against it. "Go away."

"Well, that's no way to treat family." He shoved it open, taking me with it like I weighed nothing. He swaggered in, closed the door and locked it.

Trapped, my claustrophobia kicked in. "You were watching me at Blue Sage," I said. Surely Jake had seen him. Maybe he was calling for backup.

"Girl, I've been watching you since you got to town. You happened to see me that night. I've never seen you up close, though. You sure look like my mother."

"So, I've been told. What do you want?"

His face contorted. Fury blazed in his eyes. A muscle bulged in his cheek. Not good signs. I've seen men crazed by anger, but not directed at me. And I wasn't trapped in a motel room with them. A room which seemed to shrink by the minute.

"A smart girl would know." His eyes narrowed.

A chill snaked down my spine. I couldn't think. No way would this end well. Sheriff Checotah told me not to leave my room. He said nothing about Fred showing up here. Major oversight on his part. If only Lane had left Austin.

Fred's mouth twisted into a sneer. "I've hated you from the time you were born. 'Now, Freddy, you leave the baby alone'," he mocked in a falsetto. He leaned into my face. "Do you know how sick I got of hearing it?"

"I'm getting an idea." I licked dry lips and stepped back.

"Even my mother liked you more. She wanted a girl. I was a big disappointment."

I swallowed hard. My heart threw itself against my ribs in an effort to escape.

"I hadn't noticed how little attention I got," he snarled. "Until you were born. Well, Granny or that nosey April ain't here to protect you now, are they?"

"Nope." And neither was anyone else. I bristled at their glaring absence.

I read somewhere that if abducted you should establish a rapport with your captor. Cause him to see you as a person, a potential friend. Find common ground.

"Uh, think it's going to rain?" I gasped.

He stared at me.

"Guess not," I said. I can't hold a conversation with normal people. What do you say to someone deranged? 'Been off your meds long?' came to mind.

I forced a smile. "Your kids are darling, sweet little lambs." I'm not around a lot of kids and I'm near hysteria. Give me a break. What are their names? Great. I don't even know their names. "They're so smart. They must take after you."

He blinked. For a moment his eyes softened. He looked sane and I had a glimmer of hope. But then he remembered he hadn't come to chat.

"Shut up," he growled.

I backed away. He followed me across the room. He slapped me hard knocking my head into the wall. Stunned, I froze. But then rage set in. I head butted him.

He exhaled forcefully and bent over.

I made a break for the door. Frantically I fumbled with the lock. The door opened, but as I bolted out, he grabbed my ponytail and pulled me back inside. The deputy sat in his car with his head down.

"Jake." I screamed. "Help."

Fred laughed. "The deputy?" he sneered. "He had a bit of an accident. Who knew reading could be dangerous? He's not gonna be much help." The door slammed shut.

"What did you do to him?" I demanded. "He has a wife and baby."

Fred laughed. He threw me against the wall and held me there with a forearm across my throat. I gagged and choked. I tried to push his arm away with both hands. My futile attempts amused him. I bit his thumb. Biting off a thumb isn't easy as it sounds. His eyes narrowed and he cussed under his breath. He hit me again, this time with his fist.

When Fred thought I was Aunt Sharon, he'd said, 'you're dead'. The rest of what he'd said came back with bone chilling clarity. 'I killed you'.

He killed his mother. What? If he killed the woman who gave him life, I have no hope. He doesn't even like me. I'm going to die.

Holding me against the wall he dug a cloth from his pocket and shoved it over my face. I breathed in sweet sickening fumes. I kicked him and scratched at his face. Then things got fuzzy. My knees buckled. I slid down the wall to the floor.

He bent to jab a needle into my arm. As the world spun away, his words echoed in my head. Each word. Slowly. Separately. Dripping like raindrops into a well.

"You're... dead. I... killed... you."

Chapter Fifty-Nine

Dying was not on my to-do list. Major oversight on my part. I had no idea how long I'd been here or how I got here. I'd clawed the walls with bloody fingers until my nails were gone. Nobody knew where I was. Not even me.

My tomb was an abandoned well. The stench of rotting flesh had twisted my stomach into knots. My whole body throbbed. My muscles cramped. My head felt as though a cherry bomb exploded behind my eyes. My throat was raw from screaming. Nobody to hear. But panic doesn't listen to reason.

Terrified, I whimpered, "God, I give up. If you exist, please help me." As the words left my mouth the darkness faded. Slowly at first, like dawn swallows night. Light swirled around me. Gold, yellow, orange. The colors spun together, yet each maintained its own integrity. My chilled bones were warmed in the glow. I stopped shivering.

I'd imagined God's voice would sound like Niagara Falls, a roar filled with majestic power. It didn't. The words simply dropped into my mind like fresh rain. As they washed away my panic, they brought peace. And clarity.

"Do you know how much I love you?" He asked.

The question shocked me. I knew the answer was no. Nothing had ever come close to the love I felt at that moment.

He gave me time. I had questions but couldn't form thoughts. I didn't need to.

"You want to know why you were kidnapped," He said.

"Yes."

"Every action has consequences. When Margaret lifted you out of that car, she set you on the path you were meant to follow."

"You're saying being ripped from my family was in your plan. Why?"

"If I had left you in Cheyenne Falls, Fred would have killed you."

"He was just a child. About six when I was abducted," I said.

"Yes. By then he'd already tried twice. I knew his heart. He would have kept trying until he succeeded. His mother could not love him. He blamed you. Ask April."

When Jackson showed me the picture of Aunt Sharon holding a newborn me with an unhappy Fred standing beside her, I had felt sad for him. I shuddered as I remembered the naked hatred in Fred's eyes as he shoved his way into my motel room.

"Removing you prevented him from becoming a murderer as a child," God continued, "which gave him more time to repent. To come to me. He chose not to."

I was stunned by the sadness in God's voice. "You love Fred."

"Of course, I do."

"After all he has done to me? How could you?" I knew in that instant that God loved Fred as much as He loved me. It boggled my mind.

"You can't see Fred through my eyes."

"No. I can't."

"But I'd like you to try."

"So, you sent me to live with someone who hated me," I accused. I immediately felt bad. Did I really think God owed me an explanation?

"Margaret didn't hate you. She didn't know how to love," God's voice was gentle.

I thought about that. I never saw pictures of a family she might have had. We spent every holiday alone. I had never thought about her meager existence. How sad she must have been. Nobody loved her. Not even me.

"Your childhood prepared you for your destiny. If you had remained in Cheyenne Falls you would not have survived. You wouldn't have been in the canyon the day you found the tunnel and met Lexy. Without your intervention many would have perished that day including Moonflower and Lexy at the hand of the Apaches. You would not have met Lane and Stormy. Fred's men would have killed them. You have accomplished work I planned for you before the beginning of time."

God gave me time to digest what He had said. Then He showed me a tapestry. The pattern was exquisite.

"This represents your life. I see the intricate design. For now, all you see from your side are the stitches and knots. Someday you will comprehend its beauty. Not yet. Fred was blinded by greed. He could never understand," God continued, "that if he'd succeeded in killing you, the land he covets would never have belonged to your family. Neither would their wealth."

"I don't get it."

"You have yet to accomplish your mission."

God's tenses were confusing. Even without a brain injury, it was difficult to realize that He's in our past, present, and future at once. Trying to figure it out gave me a headache.

"Everyone you come in contact with is infinitely loved by Me. You have been given the ability to see into the hearts of others through their eyes. It is a gift. Use it wisely. Love the unlovable I send to you."

"That's kind of a lot," I said. "You've sent me some real doozies."

I heard a chuckle in His voice. "See me in all circumstances. Learn to be content."

"You gotta be kidding." I probably wouldn't have said that if I'd been thinking clearly. I hope. "My mission—how will I…"

"Continue to stay on the path I've set for you and watch for the guides I send. The hawk. James White Eagle."

"He's real?"

"Of course. He warned Me about you." There was that chuckle in His voice again.

"Would you tell Tony Checotah that White Eagle existed? He doesn't believe me." I paused. "Can you get me out of here?"

The light swirled, shook, and jiggled. God was laughing. "Can I? Did you really ask that? Of course, I can get you out. Did you forget who you are talking to?"

"Sorry."

"In the fullness of time. Until then I can give you peace. Your work is not finished. My plan is being accomplished through you. You cannot see that now, but you will."

"Stay with me," I pleaded.

"I'm with you always, Ali."

The way He said my name was a love song to my ears. I understood. He had.

"Help is on the way," He said. "And Ali, be more careful. Your guardian angel is begging to be reassigned."

Chapter Sixty

A rock bounced off my head. Dirt rained down. Above me boards were lifted and thrown away. As planks and rocks were tossed aside muffled words became more distinct. The final board was gone. Light flooded into my prison.

I blinked.

"She's here." Sheriff Checotah yelled. "Down here."

People began coughing, choking, and gasping.

"Ali, I'm here." Lane yelled. "Can you hear me?"

"Lane," I mumbled. "Lane…"

"Can you reach her?" David shouted.

"No."

"What's that smell? Ali, can you hear me?" David said.

"There's something dead in there."

"Hang on Sunflower," Lane shouted. "We're going to get you out."

"We can't reach her. We need more help."

"Call Search and Rescue." Checotah yelled.

"Already on the way."

"Ali." someone screamed. "Ali, can you hear me?"

Lexy? I tried to respond. It came out in a groan. How did she get here?

"Hey. Lanigan is going to kill Fred. Somebody get him," the sheriff yelled. He was right above me. "Seriously, cuff Lanigan, now. I don't wanna charge my best friend with murder."

"How are we going to get her out?" someone asked. He must have been looking down. His words echoed around me. He choked and gagged.

"Lanigan's dog has Fred down." another voice shouted.

"Yeah, we'll get to that in a minute."

"Ali, can you hear me," Lexy yelled into the well, her voice bounced around the walls. She sobbed, "Ali?"

"Don't cry, Lexy," I mumbled.

"I heard her. She's alive."

"How are we going to get her out? She's really wedged in there."

"Ali, you're going to be okay. We'll get you out. That smell." That was David.

"Get that dog away from Fred." Sheriff Checotah yelled.

"Come on Checotah, a dog can't be charged with excessive force. Let 'em go."

"Fred won't live long enough to be tried, if somebody doesn't get that dog."

"That's a problem?"

"Huh uh, not me. I'm not touching that dog. I think he's got rabies."

"Shoot him."

"Copy that. The dog or Fred?"

"No." I screamed. "Austin… don't shoot Austin…"

"Hey, Lanigan, I heard her. She's worried about your damn dog."

"Lanigan, get your dog." Checotah yelled.

"He can't," a deputy yelled. "You said to cuff him."

"Well, uncuff him. Lanigan, get that dog."

Gloom swallowed me. Voices faded away.

Chapter Sixty-One

I drifted through mist aware of the rhythmic whooshing to my left and steady hums and electronic beeps. Unfamiliar odors filled the air. The cloying fragrance of roses threatened my queasy stomach. I tried moving my foot. It moved. I'm not in the well.

The next time I rose through the fog I heard voices. Lane was holding my hand.

"She had surgery to remove bone fragments right after she arrived. There's brain activity, but we don't know how much damage has been done. They did another MRI and CT scan this morning."

When the fog rolled back in, I wasn't afraid. I'm not alone. Lane is here.

Fighting my way up to the light was as exhausting as fighting my way from the bottom of lake. If I could break through the surface, maybe I could wake up. I heard snatches of conversation and relaxed. It was enough, for now, to rest in the knowledge I'm out of the well.

"And, of course, his cover was perfect." The sound of Lane's voice flowed over me like warm honey. "Respectable businessman, husband and father. His family founded the town. He was established in a profitable fifth-generation farming operation."

"It couldn't have been Fred who shot at Ali in the canyon," Jackson said. "He was a sniper in the military. He wouldn't have missed."

"He said a hawk attacked him as he fired," Lane said. "Twice. The men who tried to run her off the road worked for him. He drugged her beer at Blue Sage. If she'd drunk more, she might have died. I set my beer on the table with hers and had to leave suddenly. She'd been drinking mine by mistake but drank enough of hers to get sick."

"You were at Blue Sage with Ali?" Jackson asked.

"No. I was trying to tie Fred to the drug ring. But I, uh, got distracted."

"You sound pretty sure it was Fred," Jackson said, unconvinced.

"Here's what we've pieced together. Before Fred tossed her into your lake, he hit her over the head with a sawed-off bat. She turned her head and only received a glancing blow. He used the same bat when he stuffed her into that well, thinking she was dead. We found the bat in his truck. The blood on it is Ali's."

"He's always been a bully. I thought he'd changed." Jackson exhaled deeply.

"Attempted murder charges will stick," Lane said. "Besides Ali, Fred thought he'd killed Jake, the deputy guarding her room."

"Why would he do this?" Jackson asked.

"He'd been using Ali's land like it was his. He farmed some, leased some and pocketed the money. He used her barn to stash drugs he'd been flying in from Mexico," Lane said. "Ali showing up when she did, got in his way." There was a long pause. "There's no easy way to tell you. Someone got in his way before Ali. She wasn't alone in the well."

"Ali was in that well with a corpse?" Jackson asked. "Who? Do we know?"

"Waiting on DNA," Lane said. "We think it's your sister."

"What?" Jackson gasped. "My sister?"

No. My heart raced. I tried to open my eyes. Jackson's sister. My mother?

"We think it's your sister Sharon."

"What kind of monster kills his mother?" Jackson's voice was incredulous.

"According to his cell mate, quite the chatterbox, Fred's mother saw something she shouldn't have."

"Ali was in that well with Sharon's body?" Jackson's voice cracked. A chair clattered to the floor. Heavy footsteps rushed from the room.

"Poor Jackson," I whispered, surprised that something came out. My eyes fluttered open. I could see.

"Well, hello, Sunflower," Lane said with a crooked grin.

"What happened to your face?" I asked.

"You don't remember?"

"No. Thirsty."

"I better make sure it's okay to give you a drink. Don't want you to leak or anything. Don't go away." He raced out the door.

Don't go away? Seriously?

Lane quickly returned with a hoard of people dressed in scrubs. They began poking and prodding me. I cringed as a doctor pulled up my eyelid and flicked on a flashlight.

"Do you know where you are?" He leaned back to inspect me.

"Hospital."

"Do you know what year this is?"

"1891?" I guessed.

"Well, that was random," the doctor said.

"Not as random as you might think," Lane mumbled.

The pain in my head was excruciating.

The doctor raised my wrist, took my pulse, and scribbled on a chart. "Do you know what happened to you?"

"My head hurts."

"Name some of your friends."

"They already have names." Shutting my eyes in dismissal, I went back to sleep.

The next time I opened my eyes the room was full of flowers and balloons. A chain of letters draped across the window spelling 'HAPPY BIRTHDAY'.

"Who's birthday?" I asked Lane.

"Yours. You pretty much slept through it. You weren't a lot of fun."

"I'm not good at parties," I said.

"So, I heard."

"April was here?" I asked.

"Yep. She did most of this." He gestured to the balloons and flowers.

"My first birthday party ever and I slept through it. Story of my life."

"We'll celebrate when you get out of here," Lane promised.

The days drifted by in a blur. I slept a lot, and every time I woke, Lane was close. Jackson and Penny had been here often, doing most of the talking and keeping the conversation light. They seem to know Lane quite well.

Janet came. Several times. Mostly, she cried and held my hand. I wanted to console her but couldn't form the right words. She brought me a soft fluffy blanket which I loved.

I spent the biggest part of the next few days sleeping.

Once, when I woke up, April sat beside me. We were alone.

"Hi, sleepy head," she said. "Lane went to make some phone calls. He's hardly left your side. It's a good thing he hasn't taken a vacation in years. His evidence led to the arrest of Victor Ruiz. Lane's boss is counting the time spent in Cheyenne Falls as work. You sure had us scared. The doctor thinks you'll make a full recovery. It will take time and lots of rest for your skull to heal."

I hadn't thought to ask anyone if I would be okay.

"I really like Lane." April winked. "What other secrets have you kept from me?"

Good. She hasn't met Lexy. I smiled.

"I met David, too. He's around here somewhere." She looked around as though she had absent-mindedly misplaced him. "He and Lane seem to get along well. They act like old war buddies. I can see why you're in love with Lane. He reminds me of someone."

"Marlboro Man."

"The Marlboro Man? No, Silly. Uncle Russ. Of course, with Lane's face so bruised it's hard to tell..."

"My father?"

"Yeah. It's more than the mustache and dimples. They have some of the same mannerisms. You'll see. You made the right choice."

"I did?" I was surprised she thought so.

"Lane's love is a rare and beautiful thing. Everyone should be loved like that." April's smile held a hint of sadness. "But few are."

I remembered God saying nobody had ever loved Margaret. No wonder she didn't know how to love me. She did the best she could.

"I'll let you get some sleep." She rose to go.

"April, wait." I grabbed her hand.

She sat back down and waited.

"April, God was with me—in the well."

Her eyes widened. She leaned in close. "Did he say anything?"

"A lot. He told me to ask you…"

"Ask me? God told you to ask me something? What?"

I tried to remember. "I don't know. Oh, wait. Fred tried to kill me when I was a baby. God said you would know."

April's hands raised to her face. Her fingers splayed across her mouth. Whatever she expected me to say, that wasn't it. For once she was speechless.

"Do you?"

She nodded. "You were just a month old the first time. I found him trying to drown you in the toilet. The second time was right before you were kidnapped. I caught him holding a pillow over your face. I kept thinking he was too young to know what he was doing. A child couldn't be that cruel."

"Thank you for—saving my life." Trying to think was giving me a headache.

"You're welcome." She smiled rather wistfully. "I wish I could have helped you this time. But he'll never hurt you again, or anyone else. I can't believe someone who shares our DNA could do the things he's done. More horrible things are coming to light all the time." April leaned back in her chair, deep in thought.

"Poor Janet," I said before falling back to sleep. "We have to help her."

***

I drifted up out of a deep sleep. Someone held my hand. Lane? No. David.

"Hi," he said when he realized I was awake. "You scared me."

"You don't hate me?" I mumbled. Evidently, not. He was holding my hand.

"Hate you? Ali, you're my best friend. I could never hate you."

Too groggy to speak, I was content to listen.

"I wanted to be good for you. Make your life easier. Protect you."

"You did," I said. "I don't know …"

"I saw myself as some Sir Galahad," David interrupted. "I didn't realize how fiercely you fought for independence from Margaret. Your heart wanted to soar. My love felt like a prison."

My heart wanted to soar? David has never talked like that. There was more to what he said, but even if I could form a lucid thought, I didn't have the strength to have this discussion. We would someday. But not today.

"Lexy made me see that," he smiled.

"Thank you, David," I said. I went back to sleep with him still holding my hand.

After several hours I awoke to the sound of laughter. Rolling on the floor knee-slapping laughter. I've never heard David laugh like that. Ever.

"Almost fell off my horse I was laughing so hard," David said, when he stopped long enough to catch his breath. "When those guys realized you were cuffing them around that tree their expressions were priceless." There was another burst of laughter. David continued, "What do you suppose went through their mind when you made them hand over the billfold, shoes and horse they had stolen. They had to wonder how we knew."

"Their shock made apprehension easy," Lane chuckled.

"When you flashed that badge, their mouths fell open," David said.

"I wonder how much jurisdiction I'd actually have in Indian Territory in 1891."

"I've never had so much fun," David said. "That guy peed in his pants." David was laughing again. "They'll need bolt cutters to get those cuffs off."

"Well, the main thing is we got it done," Lane said. "John Dale has his land, his sister Mattie has hers, and the rest will be history."

"It already is," David said. "The most incredible story of my life and I can't tell anyone about it."

"We know," Lane said. "We make quite a team."

I lay still absorbing what I'd heard. Together David and Lane saved the Dale family land. So, the 'other guy' in Jackson's story was Lane.

Chapter Sixty-Two

Awoman with black '60's poofy hair stood at the window, her back to me. She wore a cotton flower-print dress, a throwback to the days of TV moms. I studied her with more than a little curiosity.

"June Cleaver?" I asked.

Lexy turned around wearing a dazzling smile and Buddy Holly glasses.

"What are you doing here?" I laughed. It was worth the stab of pain.

She bounded to my bed and gave me a hug. With a thumb she pushed the glasses up on her nose and stuck her hands on her hips.

"How do I look?" she demanded.

"Like a near-sighted Liz Taylor. Get over here and sit down," I ordered, patting the side of the bed. "I've been dying to see you." I reached for the control and raised the bed to a sitting position.

"David said I needed a disguise to avoid questions." She did a Vanna White gesture, which included her entire ensemble. "He found it at a Goodwill store."

"He paid too much for it," I said. "Tell me what's going on."

"What do you want to know?" Lexy asked.

"The hearing," I said. "I've only heard bits and snatches. I want your version."

She leaned forward and, with typical Lexy delight, launched into her story.

"Ron Lang waited for us outside and introduced himself to David, who he assumed was still your fiancé. So, I knew who he was. David and I followed him into the courtroom. Evidently Ron and the Judge are friends. The Judge launched into a fish story. He had the papers filled out and ready." Lexy paused before continuing. "There wasn't much to it. I signed them. I've been practicing your name. The Judge handed Ron the folder, and that was that."

"Seriously? That's all?" I asked. "After 28 years?"

"Yeah. But here's something funny. The Judge noticed my hands when he asked to see my birthmark. He said, 'Good grief, Young Lady, where did you get those callouses."

"Before I could say anything, Penny told him I'd been working in her yard."

"How did you fake my birthmark?" I asked.

"It's a good thing David remembered it. He painted it on with dye."

"So everything went well, I take it."

"You take it where?" Lexy asked.

"It's a figure of speech," I answered.

"I thought your cousin April was going to ruin everything. She kept asking where I've been and wouldn't shut up."

"What did you say?"

"I told her I'd been arrested for being drunk in public, and it took longer than expected to break out of jail."

"You did not."

"Yes I did. Boy, can she talk, but that shut her up."

"Wait," I said. "What about Fred?"

"I didn't know which one was Fred. I didn't know anyone, really. He was looking at his phone. We were on our way out when he looked up and saw me. Ali, I wish you could've seen the look on Fred's face." The memory sent her into spasms of laughter. "He got the flesh creep like he'd seen a ghost. And, of course, he thought he had."

Lexy's mood was infectious and soon, we both gasped for air. A nurse peeked in, looked around the room, and abruptly left, which provoked another attack.

"I waved at Fred," Lexy said. "He jumped up and yelled, 'You're dead, bitch, get out of here.' I blew him a kiss like I was glad to see him. He screamed, 'Ali is dead. I killed her. I can prove it.' Then he stomped over everyone trying to get to me."

"What happened then?" I asked.

"He lunged at me screaming 'You're dead.' But David stepped between us. Fred ran out the door, jumped in his pickup and drove straight to the well where he'd left you—that was David's plan. The sheriff and Lane had no idea what Fred had done with you. It was David's idea for me to impersonate you," Lexy said, quite proud of David.

"Lane and the sheriff waited outside. David and I ran out and followed. Fred was throwing rocks off the well when we drove up. Do you suppose he intended to drag a dead body into court to prove he'd killed you? How deranged is that?"

I shuddered. "If this hadn't happened when David was here, I'd still be in the well."

"Lane went crazy when he realized you were in there," Lexy said.

"I remember hearing sirens, but not much else," I said. "Wait. Somebody was yelling something about a dog."

"Yeah," Lexy continued. "Lane's dog jumped out of the Jeep and attacked Fred, who tried to crawl under his pickup. It would have been funny, but we still didn't know if you were alive. Lane wanted to jump in the well but it was too small."

"Is David upset about Lane?"

"He had a problem at first," Lexy said. "But he didn't have a chance to find out about you and Lane in a normal way. Lane lost it when you disappeared. David figured it out then. They've had some serious talks. I smoothed things over."

"He understood?"

"He does now," Lexy grinned.

"David needs someone like you. Thanks for talking to him."

Her eyes danced with mischief. "Well, I didn't tell him the minute you laid eyes on Lane you lost all capacity to reason and every shred of common decency."

"That's so not true."

"I didn't tell him about the public spectacle you made of yourself when you tried to jump Lane's bones at Blue Sage."

"What? Where did you hear that term? I did not."

My adamant denial ended suddenly when someone in the hall cleared his throat. Woops. We both stared at the door.

"Well, well, who's this young lady?" Jackson asked, as he came in.

How long had he been out there? Embarrassed that he might have heard the conversation, I searched for a believable answer and looked to Lexy for help.

She rose and extended her hand. "You must be Uncle Jackson. I'm Lexy. I work with Ali. In Dallas." She glanced at me over her shoulder. "I'm practicing my social skills."

"Good," I said.

"Nice to meet you. Sit back down." Jackson motioned to where she'd been sitting on my bed. He walked around to the other side and kissed my forehead, before turning back to Lexy. "So you're the one Papa Jay keeps badgering Ali about. Where did you meet my grandfather?"

"Huh?" I said, confused.

"Papa Jay." Jackson reminded me. "Remember? He asked you about Lexy." He lowered himself into a chair near Lexy and regarded her with open curiosity.

"I've had a head injury," I mumbled. "He did?"

"I met him at a Coldplay concert," Lexy said. She adjusted her glasses.

"What?" Where had she heard of Coldplay? Jackson and I both stared at her. He looked to me for an explanation.

"She sneaks my drugs when the nurses aren't looking." I cast a threatening glance at Lexy. "She was kidding, Jackson."

"Yeah. It was actually a speed-dating site." Lexy patted her wig.

"What would you know about speed-dating?" Good grief. How long have I been in a coma? "Actually, Papa Jay has never met Lexy," I said quickly.

"Well, I know you've received a blow to the head and there's a lot you don't remember, but Lexy isn't a common name," Jackson said. He took off his ever-present hat to scratch his head. "But you told Papa Jay you didn't know Lexy."

"Well. I didn't know her yet when I told him that. I had just arrived in town."

"But you worked with her in Dallas." His forehead wrinkled in confusion.

I blinked. "That. Yes, of course. I, uh, didn't know her name then." Good grief. I lie as badly as the secret service.

Jackson lifted a brow. "What did you call her in Dallas?"

I glanced at Lexy for help, but Lexy not only ignored me. She enjoyed my discomfort immensely.

Note to self, choke Lexy. "Uh, Gladys," I said finally.

"Gladys?" Jackson looked more confused by the minute.

"Gladys?" Lexy echoed.

"Why did you call her Gladys?"

"Yeah, why?" Lexy demanded. If looks could kill, Lexy would already be dead.

"Gladys is her real name," I said. "How are things in Dallas, Gladys?"

"Peachy," Lexy said, with a big smile.

"Peachy? Did you just say 'peachy'?"

"Yes. Can I not say 'peachy' either? It wasn't on the wall in the la-deees room."

Jackson made a valiant effort to understand the conversation.

"You would love Dallas." Lexy told Jackson. "There are stores everywhere and you should see all the cars. People drive on roads that crisscross and go over each other. The roads, not the cars but sometimes the cars do too. It's amazing."

I've got to shut her up.

"Well, that's nice." Jackson said.

I'm as confused as Jackson. Lexy has been to Dallas.

"She hasn't been in the U.S. long," I said. "She gets excited over big cities."

"I can see that, she doesn't have an accent though," Jackson pointed out.

"She speaks good English. But sometimes she gets words in the wrong place."

"I see," Jackson said. His expression said he didn't. "Where you from, Darlin?"

"France," Lexy said. "That's a place," she informed Jackson.

"Bolivia," I said at the same time.

Jackson scratched his head again.

"Uh, the French section of Bolivia," I explained.

"Yeah, they have showers there and everything," Lexy said.

"Showers are a big deal to Gladys," I added.

Jackson chuckled. "Have they said anything about dismissing you?"

"No. But it should be soon."

"You know you're welcome out at the house." He turned back to Lexy. "How did you know Ali was in the hospital?"

"I called her, and the lady at the motel told me what happened." Lexy lied smoothly.

"Well, I can see her anytime. I'll let the two of you visit," Jackson said, moving toward the door. "See you soon, Sugar. It was a pleasure meeting you, Gladys."

As Jackson left Lexy turned to me. "That went well."

Chapter Sixty-Three

Tell me about Lane and David helping your father. I heard them talking about it earlier, but I was drifting in and out. It sounded like David took your father a horse."

Lexy nodded. "He did. A big bay. Of course, I couldn't tell Pa how he got there. So, I told him he'd been wandering around down by the lake. Pa said he'd keep the horse until his owner came to claim him. He figured it belonged to Elmer and was afraid he'd think we stole it. David bought a used saddle and bridle. He said a new one would raise a red flag. He was right. I didn't see any flags."

I nodded.

"David told you he was shipping horses to Cheyenne Falls when you spoke about the switched suitcase. He told you he wanted to hand it to the sheriff himself. Do you remember any of that?"

"Sort of. How did David and Lane help your father?"

"Well, they followed the route Pa took to Ft Reno. They figured out where the danger spots would be, so they hid there until Pa came through. They waited for the Rafferty brothers to go by and fell in behind them. They planned to intercept them before they got to Pa. But it was raining hard and they lost them."

"Jackson mentioned that rain," I said.

"But if they had caught the Rafferty's before they got to Pa, Jackson's story would have been different. It happened exactly like he said."

"What's really weird is David and Lane working together to pull this off. I haven't had a chance to talk to Lane about it. But dang it, I was supposed to be the one to go back in time and change history. James White Eagle said so."

"James White Eagle missed the part about you being in the bottom of a well."

Chapter Sixty-Four

The smell of coffee woke me the next morning. Jackson sat beside my bed sipping from a Styrofoam cup. I watched him not wanting to break the spell. Strange that I'd become so attached to my uncle in such a short time. But as a small child I must have adored him. He'd been a major player in my early years. Maybe those feelings lingered somewhere beyond my memory.

He felt my eyes on him and smiled. "Good morning, sleepyhead."

"That coffee smells good. Did you bring me some?"

He motioned to the cup on the nightstand. "Lane went out to make a few calls."

Austin lay beside Jackson's chair.

"Austin," I said.

He raised his head and looked at me with that one blue eye. His tail flopped.

"Lane snuck Austin in and talked the nurse into letting him stay. He had to see for himself you were all right."

I raised the bed to a sitting position and reached for the coffee.

"Your color is better today. They'll be kicking you out soon. Thought I better come see you while I can find you." He chuckled.

"I'm glad you're here. I want to run something by you."

"Shoot."

"You need a business partner."

He crossed his legs. "Why? Tribes is barely making it now."

"Just listen."

He sipped his coffee. "Okay."

"I want to be that partner. We can use my land next to Tribes to make the expansion you have in mind. We'll dig a lake and put in a dock. We'll stock it with fish and have a bait shop and boat rental. Imagine a restaurant near the lake with lots of glass to take in the view and a parking area for buses near the road.

"We'll build the villages and campsites along the stream which we'll connect to the lake. Dugout canoes can carry tourists from place to place, and over the canyon, a zip line. I'm pretty excited."

Jackson raised an eyebrow. "I can see that. Where will we get the money?"

"I'll sell that section of land where Lane was held. I never want to see it again. With that money we'll make the improvements. We can borrow the rest if we need to."

"You've been thinking. The problem is tourism has dropped off drastically. I'm not sure we could make this go."

"I think we can," I said. "Your big event is in August when Oklahoma is hotter than blazes. That might have worked forty years ago, but now people are tied to their air conditioners. Spring is cooler. People are tired of winter. They're looking for something to do outside. We'll schedule our event toward the end of April, do a big advertising push at the Guthrie celebration and catch the Land Run crowd."

Jackson gazed up as he thought. "That could work."

"We need to start the ad campaign earlier. Maybe the Houston rodeo in February. We need a riding stable for horseback tours." I stopped to take a breath, then hurried on before he could nix the idea. "I'd like to use a portion of the money from the land sale to do a large international advertising campaign. Something that will draw foreign visitors to Oklahoma. The state will help with advertising once they see our proposal. Cheyenne Falls will need more than one motel. Buses of people will come if we advertise right."

"I'm impressed, Young Lady. How do you know all this?"

"I'm working on a law degree. I have a BS in business with a minor in marketing. You can take care of all the things you do so well. I'll need help. We'll hire Janet. We can take care of the books, the advertising, event planning, booking tours—all the things you hate—I think together we'll put Tribes on the map. Not just state or national, but international. What do you think?"

"That's an ambitious plan. It could work." A slow grin crossed his face. "You have yourself a business partner. I'll have Ron draw up papers before you change your mind."

"First, we have to sell that land, so we have capital. It's legally mine now, right?"

"Are you sure you want to sell that piece? That's the best land you have. Why don't you sell the land overlooking the canyon? It's not worth as much."

"It is to us. Lane and I are going to build a house there."

"You've talked to Lane about all this?"

"He thinks it's a great idea. I want to finish my law degree. If I practiced law, it would only be part time. Law was my whole life in Dallas. I don't live there anymore."

"With all that's happened since you arrived, I was afraid you'd be high-tailin' it back to Dallas as soon as they release you here."

"Nope. You're stuck with me."

"How will Lane juggle this with working in D.C?"

"Southwest Airlines has a direct flight from Oklahoma City to BWI. He'll come home often. I'll go there some. We'll make it work. When my parents get home, I'm staying close to my mama."

Jackson grinned. "Well, hurry up. Get out of that bed. Let's get started."

Chapter Sixty-Five

April had carried out a treasure trove of gifts, flowers, and stuff accumulated during my stay. She waited in her car to drive me home. 'Home' being the apartment. While I'd been hospitalized, she and Penny had cleaned out my motel room. They had been busy getting ready for my arrival. David had shipped the things from my Dallas apartment. The furnishings Lexy and I bought in the city had been delivered.

I was on the way out when my cell rang. My therapist Ursula's face and number displayed on the screen.

"Ursula, hello," I said. "What a nice surprise. I'm so glad to hear from you."

"Ali, are you all right?"

"I'm being dismissed from the hospital as we speak," I said dodging a mylar balloon April had missed. It bobbed and dipped around my head.

"Are you ill?" She sounded alarmed.

"I'm okay now." I realized I hadn't spoken to her since leaving Dallas. Which is a record. Normally I'm tied to her apron strings, so to speak. I thought about all that's happened since I've been in Cheyenne Falls, especially my breakup with David. And falling in love with Lane. Not to mention Fred's four attempts on my life. I don't know what this means, not needing to talk to her.

Ursula didn't pry. Ursula never pries. She lets me reveal as much as I want.

"I was concerned when you missed your appointment."

I never miss appointments. In Dallas I had barely survived between sessions.

"Ursula, you won't believe this. I'm in Oklahoma. I found my family."

"Ali, that's wonderful news. What are they like?"

I thought about that. Jackson, Penny, and April are amazing. But Fred tried to kill me and stuffed me in a well on top of my dead aunt. I'll tell her about that later.

"My parents are out of the country. I haven't met them yet. But I have a supportive extended family. I've gone through family pictures. I was loved and adored as a baby. By a cast of thousands." Minus one.

"Ah," she said. "That explains it. Something didn't make sense to me. You've never exhibited the symptoms of an unloved baby. When an infant isn't nurtured, its brain develops differently, which often causes an attachment disorder. You don't have that issue. You've come through your childhood more emotionally intact than you've realized."

As she spoke, I realized why Margaret couldn't love me. She had the attachment disorder Ursula spoke of. She had been an unloved baby.

"I'm sorry about missing the appointment," I said. I'm not sure where we go from here. I won't be coming back to Dallas. Can we do phone sessions?"

"We can do that if you need to. I'm not sure you will. I hear strength in your voice that's never been there. I also hear excitement. I can tell good things are happening."

"I'll call you and set up a session. I want to bring you up to speed on everything. But right now, my cousin is waiting downstairs in the car. I need to run."

"Okay, dear, call at our regular appointed time. I'll keep it open for you."

Chapter Sixty-Six

Whatever you're painting can't be as pretty as the picture I see from here." Lane lounged in the doorway of my spare bedroom, wearing only sweatpants.

I looked up from the canvas. "Good morning, Sleepyhead."

Large bruises were still visible on his face and upper body, a sheet had creased his cheek, and his hair was rumpled.

He yawned. "I hope your parents are located soon," he said, massaging the back of his neck. "Your daybed isn't all that comfortable. I want a wedding ring on your finger and you in my bed."

"Guess what. Ron just called. He hasn't talked to my parents yet, but they've been located. They've been in Italy all this time. They went on a two-week trip the day before I arrived here. They rented a chalet somewhere in the mountains. There was no cell service. My dad had some vacation coming so they stayed two more weeks. They're on their way back to Naples now."

"That's awesome, Ali. You've gotta be excited." Lane said.

"I am. We'll get married as soon as they get here," I promised. I couldn't stop staring at his beautiful, bruised face. "I don't want a big wedding."

"Good." He looked relieved. "I hate big weddings, but I'd do it for you."

"There's coffee," I said. "Your cup is on the cabinet by the Keurig. Hey, do you think Lyle and Stormy would come back for the wedding. Lyle could marry us."

"Great idea." He padded barefoot into the kitchen. "Need a refill?"

I pulled my attention from the mixture of Payne's grey and cobalt blue I'd scumbled into the upper left-hand corner of the canvas to glance at my cup. "No, I'm fine."

"I know that's right. But do you want any coffee." Cup in hand, Lane walked behind me to study the landscape I'd been working on.

"You're really good," he said. "You've done a great job on Mariah. She has a mystical quality. Where is the waterfall? I don't remember it being in the valley," Lane said.

"It's the canyon of 1891. She's the Ghost Horse. She can be anywhere. Even in two centuries. Did I tell you Jackson gave her to me?"

"I knew." Lane set his coffee down beside mine. Still standing behind me, he wrapped both arms around me. "He might as well. She thinks she belongs to you anyway." He nuzzled my neck and gently bit an earlobe.

I turned around in his arms and kissed him, carefully avoiding his busted lip. We were interrupted by a knock on the door, but before either of us could take a step, the door flew open and Lexy breezed in, trailed by David. They were both carrying grocery sacks.

"Don't mind us," Lexy said, slipping around us and heading for the kitchen. "Guess where we've been," she demanded before I had time to wonder about Lexy being here. With David. She set the sacks on the cabinet and waited. "Guess."

She wore a dress with a short flippy skirt, and the cowboy boots I'd bought her. She looked more like she belonged in the twenty-first century than I did. I looked down at my cutoffs and paint-splattered T-shirt.

"I haven't a clue." I dropped brushes into a jar of water.

"Whispering Pines Retirement Home," Lexy crowed triumphantly.

"A nursing home. Why?"

"I went to see my brother." Lexy said. "Pappa Jay is my little brother Johnny."

"Are you delirious?"

"Uh, think I'll get dressed," Lane said, on his way to his makeshift bedroom.

"You didn't figure it out from what Jackson said at the hospital?" Lexy grinned.

"I've had a head injury, you know. Remind me."

"He said his grandfather asked about me," Lexy said over her shoulder. She pulled mushrooms and celery from a sack.

"You said you met him at a Coldplay concert. I wanted to shoot you. How do you know who Coldplay is?"

Lexy laughed, glanced at David, and ignored my question. "So, I got to thinking he could be my…"

"Brother? What? No way."

"Way." Lexy finished. "David called to see if John Dale was a resident. He was there, so this morning we went to see him."

I collapsed into a chair. "I don't believe this. He must be over a hundred years old. He should be in the Guinness Book of World Records. How old is he?"

Lexy folded an empty grocery sack and thought about it. "I don't know."

"Did he recognize you?"

"Of course. He recognized you."

"That's right, he did," I said, remembering the night I arrived in Cheyenne Falls. "I thought he was confused because he's old."

"We haven't changed quite as much as he has," Lexy said. "It's depressing to think I could look all leathery like that."

"You won't. Nobody else lives that long." I shook my head. "What did he say?"

"He told me that Pa made a fortune on those short-legged cows and calves that David brought to him. The meat was better than the tough stringy meat of those longhorns of Elmer's. Pa couldn't drive them all the way to Abilene with those short legs," Lexy took the mushrooms to the sink. She patted them dry and continued. "By the time he had built up a herd, the railroad came through and he shipped them on trains. People were willing to pay a fortune for one of his Hereford bulls and came for miles to get one. He couldn't breed them fast enough."

"What cows?" I asked David.

"David took three short-legged cows and a bull to Daddy." Lexy said.

"White-faced Herefords," David explained.

"How long was I in a coma?" I stared at them both. "I bet it was fun herding cattle through the tunnel."

'Not so much," David said.

"Johnny said Pa became so wealthy selling his cattle that he bought more land. Lots more land," Lexy went on.

David, rummaging through the cabinets for a skillet, didn't look at me. I'm beginning to suspect it was before I was in the hospital.

I found one and handed it to him. "What else did he say?" I began setting the table. Looks like Lane and I are having company for breakfast.

"Remember the sack of peanuts you brought me to roast? Well, Pa planted them and made money on his first crop. They did so well that everyone in the valley wanted to plant peanuts. Pa sold them seed."

"No wonder this area grows the best peanuts in the country," I mused. "They started out with great peanuts and had a hundred years to get better."

"Do you realize the Dale family owes their wealth to our efforts?" Lexy handed the sliced mushrooms to David. He added them to the sausage and onion in his skillet.

"That reminds me," I said to David. "I've been wanting to ask why you didn't wear a hat. I told you it was going to be raining. And why did I not know you can cook?"

"I did wear a hat," he said looking at Lane. "Your boy here loaned me a cowboy hat. We were in hurricane force wind and it blew off. I was too busy to chase it down."

"He looked goofy in it, anyway," Lane added. "Definitely not GQ."

I retrieved oranges from the fridge and juiced them. "What about Elmer? He must not have been much of a threat through the years."

Lexy doubled over laughing like she had after the tornado. It's one of the things I love about her.

"You won't believe this," she said when she could talk.

"I'm having trouble believing any of it."

"Elmer thought you were an angel sent by God to protect me."

"And actually..." I began.

"He was too scared to harm any of my family."

"Not too surprising when you think about it," David said. "That was the only time he ever saw you. It makes sense he might think you appeared to save her." He winked. "Especially since you're such a good shot."

Not only is Lexy's little brother still living and like a million years old, but David is also making jokes. I have to mark this day on the calendar.

"Especially after David and Lane had a little talk with him. He came to see Pa with a peace offering of a pair of good work horses and promised to be a good neighbor. I guess he kept his word," Lexy added.

"What? You and David went to confront Elmer?" I asked Lane.

He grinned. "We paid him a little visit."

"You went with broken ribs?" I glared at Lane. "Do you know how dangerous it is riding a horse with a bruised spleen?"

Lane did a palms-up gesture. "Elmer's bodyguards were handcuffed to a tree."

David laughed. "We figured we should strike while the iron was hot. Our timing was pretty good."

I looked at Lexy. "So, you don't have to marry a toad?"

"Nope," Lexy said, glancing at David. She began arranging Sunrise Bakery's famous blueberry muffins on a plate and poking birthday candles into them. "We're having a birthday brunch today since you so rudely slept through your birthday."

"How thoughtless of me."

"This apartment suits you," David said, carrying food to the table. "Lots of light." His eyes roamed around the room coming to rest on the large ornately framed painting of April and me which dominated one wall. "That's you?"

"Yeah, with my cousin, April. My mom painted it." I glanced up at the skylight. "She used to paint up here. Living here makes me feel close to her."

"They lived in the stucco house, right?" David asked.

"Yeah. That's where we lived before I was kidnapped."

"Ali, this is the homecoming you've dreamed of. I'm so happy for you," David said.

His sincerity touched me. I believed him. Lexy carried in more food, I poured orange juice into glasses, and Lane brought coffee cups to the table. We'd put this together so effortlessly anyone would have thought we'd been doing it for years.

We sat down to eat. The food was too good for conversation, so we stopped talking and ate. I stood up to get more coffee.

"By the way, Ali," David said. "I've been talking to Jackson. We don't want you to sell that half section to finance the improvements in Tribes. That is the most valuable acreage you have. You could live off what that farmer pays to lease it."

"Yes, but…"

David waved a hand to cut me off. "I have a vested interest in that land."

"Yeah," Lane added. "David and I risked our six to get that land for you girls."

"That means their butt," Lexy explained. "I heard them talking about it."

"Thank you for clarifying," I said.

"God is out of the land-making business," David continued. "He hasn't created any lately. When you own land, you should hang onto it. For posterity. Fortunately for you, the Dale family believes that. You don't sell land. It's sacred." He winked.

"Yes, but…"

Lane laughed. "You're starting to repeat yourself."

"Yes, but…"

"Look," David interrupted again. "I've talked to Jackson and my dad. Jackson is holding off on calling a realtor. He's having that land appraised. My dad has agreed to invest in Tribes an amount equal to the appraisal. Jackson thinks it will bring around $4,000 an acre."

"What?"

David chuckled. "I think it's my inheritance."

"But why?"

"I've told Dad about it. He'll want to come see it for himself."

"I don't know what to say," I said. Truer words were never spoken.

"David is really interested in Aunt Mattie's house and school," Lexy said. "If you want to add a replica of her house and the Indian

School to Tribes, I could help you with that. In fact, we could work together on the authenticity of the Kiowa camp."

"Really?" I stammered. "I better sit down."

"Yeah, you better. We have more news," Lexy paused for effect. "David and I are getting married." The words summersaulted, tumbling over each other in their effort to escape.

Well, I'm no longer confused about David's good mood.

Chapter Sixty-Seven

What?" I looked at David. "A woman who doesn't exist in this century can't suddenly show up and get married. Can she?"

David laughed. "There's a vacancy in Dallas since Alison Taft left. Lexy is just the gal to fill it. I think we can pull this off."

"So, she'll just become Alison Taft? When? I need to sit down."

"I told you," Lexy said.

"Yeah," David winked. "I do learn. In answer to your question, soon."

The way she was looking at David must be how I look at Lane.

"Soon? You can't put a big wedding together overnight."

"Yeah, Mom will have a heart attack." David rubbed a hand over his face.

"She will be thrilled, though," I said. "And if anyone can do it, it's Daydreon."

"I've left home," Lexy said. "I'm not going back. We're on our way to Dallas."

"Where will you stay?" I asked.

"Your apartment," David said. "I haven't cancelled the lease."

"I'm shocked, but it makes sense. You two are perfect together. I'm thrilled for you both." I hugged Lexy. Then I hugged David. It was true. Lexy and David, who had been born over a hundred years apart, were meant to be together. I stared at her. "Whoa. That's why there's no grave for you in the cemetery."

I went into my bedroom and pulled an envelope from a drawer. When I looked up Lexy's face was reflected in the mirror beside mine. A worried frown puckered her brow.

I've seen that look on my face, but never hers.

"Are you all right with this?" she asked. "My heart would be broken if you aren't."

"Absolutely." I pulled her into a hug. "I shouldn't have been surprised. From the day you two met, you've dealt with David better than I. You've changed him. He's softer."

She smiled and perched on the side of the bed.

"You've changed me, too," I said.

Lexy leaned in, listening in that intent way she has.

"You were right about wealth and poverty both being a test. Because I grew up in a slum, I thought I wasn't worth knowing. But the feeling didn't go away when I got out of it. Lexy, your life has been more difficult than mine, yet you are so joyous. In the well I remembered you saying, 'None of us are getting out of this alive, so while we are here, we should get the most out of every moment.' I feared it was too late."

Lexy smiled and tilted her head, waiting for me to go on.

"I had rather enjoyed blaming God for my circumstances because He didn't protect me from Margaret," I shook my head. "I've been such a fool. We may not like our role in life but complaining is wasting valuable time."

"But see, it all came together," Lexy pointed out. "Enduring Margaret developed the strength of character you would need to face what you've been through. Not only surviving the well but rescuing Lane and Stormy."

I thought about it. "That's what God said." I laughed. "Remember how scared I was to go to Blue Sage?"

She laughed with me. "But you went because I wanted to go. You are the best friend I've ever had," Lexy said. "Because you came through that tunnel, I can leave home knowing my family will be fine. You not only improved life for them, you changed it for generations of Dales. James White Eagle got that right."

"It sounds like David did that," I said.

"We all had a part in making this work."

I handed her the key to my Dallas apartment and an envelope. "This is for you."

"What is it?" She looked up at me, her brows raised in question.

"Open it," I said.

She pulled out my Dallas driver's license, complete with picture ID which looked exactly like her, and the Alison Taft birth certificate.

"I have no idea how Margaret obtained it," I said. "The birth date is the day she pulled me from the wreck. You're going to need these. My real birth certificate is here in a safety deposit box and I have an Oklahoma driver's license. So, there you go, Alison."

Lexy threw her arms around me. "Daydreon is suspicious. She saw the fear in my eyes when she mentioned getting me back in the show ring. I didn't know what to say."

"Yeah, she'll be tough. She trained me. We've been together at horse shows. She saw something in me before I saw it in myself. I will miss her. She loves me. She will love you, too. But you have an excuse. You've had a head injury. Your memory is spotty. You can call me if you get in a tight spot."

"We told her I found a twin in Oklahoma," Lexy said. "Will you be the maid of honor at my wedding? David is going to ask Lane to be his best man. David said we will have to have a big wedding because his father wears contacts. I think he doesn't see too well."

"What? Oh. His father has contacts. He knows lots of people," I said.

"I guess his father is a big important brain surgeon." Lexy frowned.

"He is," I said. "Both of his parents know a lot of people. Then there's all the people in David's law firm. Your wedding will be a big deal. And yes, of course I'll be there."

A burst of laughter erupted from the kitchen. I'd heard David and Lane laughing together at the hospital. I shouldn't be surprised they're friends. They're a lot alike in good ways. Lexy and I rejoined them. I don't deserve to be this happy.

"How did the Branch Barlow trial go?" I asked David.

"We got an acquittal, but I wasn't there."

"You missed it? No way. That was your career-making trial. You've prepared for it for months. It's all you've talked about."

"Something more important came up." He grinned. "Had to find a ditzy blond."

I opened my mouth, but nothing came out. I should say something. "I have to pee," I said and rushed to the bathroom.

I really just needed time to think but decided I might as well use it while I was in there. I looked down at my cutoffs and paint splattered t-shirt. I don't remember if I combed my hair this morning. I wasn't expecting company. I planned to paint all day while Lane worked on the reports he had to get out.

I should look like someone worthy of the gift I had been given. David had not only saved my life, he'd given up his dream trial to do it. A trial that would have added his name to the Alan Dershowitz, Jose Baez, Robert Shapiro, or Johnny Cochran list. A trial equal to a star-making movie role. David had given me extravagant gifts in the past, but nothing compared to this.

As I washed my hands, I noticed how badly they were shaking. I stared into the mirror over the sink. Lexy might have words to convey my gratitude. My reflection didn't.

The door opened and Lexy slipped in beside me. She took one look at my face and began dabbing at my tears with toilet paper.

"Your eyes are leaking," she said. "What is going on?"

"I'm overwhelmed. I can't believe the sacrifice David made for me."

"Ali, why are you surprised? You said he didn't know you. I think he did. But you never knew him."

She was right. "But to give up the trial of a lifetime for a girl who loves someone else—when *he* loves someone else... I don't get it."

"Well, to start with, he didn't just do it for you," Lexy said. "He did it for both of us. He knew I wouldn't survive losing you. I was a soppy worthless mess. Lane too. David didn't just save our land for me, he did it for both of us. The land you have now. But when you think about it, it's hard to know where one of us ends and the other begins."

"Hey, do we need to call 911?" David yelled through the door. We could hear them talking on the other side.

"Women's emotional stuff scares the hell out of me," Lane said.

"Only an idiot wouldn't be scared," David agreed. "You never know what you did. You just know it was wrong."

"And whatever you say is going to make it worse."

"Yeah. That's the only thing you know for sure," David laughed.

"We'll be out in a minute," Lexy said. She grinned at me. "Okay?"

I nodded. She opened the door and we stepped out.

David and Lane looked at each other both waiting for the other to say something.

I stepped forward and hugged David. "Thank you," I gasped. "I would have died in that well. Nobody but you would have come up with the idea of the Lexy impersonation.

"Actually, that idea was Lane's." David said.

"We tried everything else. Nothing worked. Fred knew we would never find you. He wasn't talking. It was my idea, but I didn't know how to find Lexy," Lane said. "If David hadn't been here to go get her, we wouldn't have found you. He wrapped an arm around my waist and pulled me in close. "Thanks again, David," he said. "No words, Man."

"As it turns out," David told me, "Lane and I make quite a team."

"Before the hearing I went to your room," Lexy picked up the story. "I told the office girl I was locked out of my room and she let me in. Your keys were still in there. I wore your clothes to the hearing. I'd watched you put on makeup and style your hair. I used your curling iron. If we hadn't gone to Blue Sage that night, I wouldn't have known how."

"Thanks for saving the Dale family's land, too," I said to David.

"That was selfishly motivated," David said. He grinned again. In fact, the grin hasn't left his face since he walked through the door. "No altruism there. Lexy wouldn't come with me until she knew her family was okay."

Before they left David pulled out Lexy's new cell phone. We put her number in my contacts and my number in hers. He snapped a picture of us together.

"You will always be my BFF," Lexy said, proud she knew the term.

"Well, lawsy me." I said. "If that don't beat all."

And then they were gone.

Chapter Sixty-Eight

After Lexy and David left for Dallas, Lane and I had the afternoon to ourselves. We drove out to the spot we'd selected to build our house. Austin ran with Cricket; my black cocker spaniel David had brought from Dallas. I made sketches and notes of colors to finish my painting.

We had parked the Jeep and started up the stairs to the apartment when I heard the hawk. I stopped and looked around until I found It watching me from the top of a pole across the street.

"I think I'm okay, now," I said.

"You talk to hawks?" Lane asked.

"That one. And if the Kiowas are right about spirits of ancestors inhabiting animals and watching over us, I've figured out who is guiding that hawk."

"I'm guessing you think it's your aunt."

"Fred killed his mother. She of all people would know what he was capable of. Lexy asked if a relative had died recently. I said no. I didn't know about Sharon at the time."

"That's all pretty far-fetched."

"I know," I said. "But that hawk has stayed close to me ever since I got here. Starting with a hawk perched on a billboard when I drove into town. She led me to the tunnel when I lost Mariah. She was with me in the cemetery the night I helped you get back to town. A hawk saved me from a rattlesnake. She led me to you and Stormy and then to the root cellar."

"It is pretty weird," Lane agreed. "A hawk attacked Fred when he dumped you into the well. Tore his face all to heck. Between the hawk and what Austin did to him, Fred needed stitches."

"The hawk made him miss when he shot at me in the canyon."

"Yeah, Jackson couldn't believe Fred shot at you because he wouldn't have missed. He was a sniper in the Army."

"He missed twice," I said.

"I'm sure glad," Lane said. He slipped an arm around me and pulled me close.

As we talked the hawk flew to the top of the giant maple in my parents' back yard. The tree stood halfway between their house and my apartment. I grabbed Lane's arm. "Look, she's building a nest."

"They don't usually nest this close to people," Lane said.

I grinned up at him. "I already have a neighbor that I know."

As we climbed the rest of the stairs to my apartment, my cell rang. I dug it out of my jeans pocket, expecting the call to be Lexy on her new phone. I didn't recognize the number.

"Hello."

"Ali? Darling? Is it really you?" a woman asked breathlessly. It was the voice I'd longed to hear since the day I found the newspaper clipping. I said what I'd waited my whole life to say.

"Hi, Mom, I'm home."

Chapter Sixty-Nine

His eyes focused straight ahead, he stood tall and handsome. He didn't look tense, but the jingle of loose change in his pocket said otherwise. He felt my eyes on him, took his hand from his pocket and winked. My father's face softened as his eyes met mine. April was right. He reminded me of Lane. He reminded me more of the guy in *Gone With the Wind*. But a little like Lane, too. When I first saw him I knew where I got my cleft chin.

"You look stunning," he whispered. "My beautiful daughter."

A make-shift aisle lined with baskets of sunflowers and daisies stretched before us. Lane stood at the end of it wearing a huge grin and a white suit. His best friend, Judge Lyle Wade, waited at the altar to marry us. Stormy's brother, Larry, Lane's other best friend, served as best man. Behind Larry, stood Tony and David. They all wore white Stetsons. On the other side of the aisle were my attendants, April, Stormy, and Lexy, who had recently returned from a trip to Greece with David's family.

With Lexy's deep tan and long black wig designed to disguise our similarity, she resembled Moon Flower more than she did me. When anyone mentioned that she reminded them of someone we gave them a blank stare. I'd introduced her to everyone as Alison Phipps. David calls her Sunny. Jackson, however, kept calling her Gladys.

As soon as my mom arrived, she was knee deep in wedding plans. April and Penny helped. The four of us worked tirelessly. It had been a labor of love which transformed Jackson and Penny's back yard, already a showplace. We chose to have the wedding here to show off my flair for landscaping. I modestly admit Jackson and Penny's yard is simply stunning. Penny loves it and I'm proud of it. I learned to do things I want to copy at Tribes. With the evening sun painting the lake, and hundreds of tiki torches and solar lights sprinkled through the sunflowers, hollyhocks, and early fall flowers, the setting was breathtaking.

April is still grumbling about wanting hollyhocks. Lexy and I look at each other and laugh. April had brought her stylist from Weatherford to do everyone's hair. My up-do was a combination of tendrils and curls with daisies tucked into strategic places. It took hours to achieve and looks like I'd had a motorcycle wreck with a flower cart. But it covers the area of my head that had been shaved for corrective surgery after my rescue.

Janet, who does beautiful calligraphy, scripted the invitations. I had asked her to be a bridesmaid, but she thought she would be more useful shepherding the kids. She was right. The twins, who were candle lighters, and Janet's and April's kids, who were older, would be cutting the cake and pouring punch. Jackson and I agreed Janet would be an integral part of Tribes permanent staff.

Six months have passed since that phone call from Naples. I had been too excited to wait patiently for my parents to fly into Oklahoma City. Lane and I met them at LaGuardia in a joyfully tearful reunion which turned the heads of anyone within a three-block area. My mother and I recognized each other as soon as my parents exited customs.

The four of us spent five days in New York City doing touristy stuff and getting acquainted. Then Lane had to go to D.C. and get back to work while my mom, dad, and I flew back to Cheyenne Falls.

I'm getting over the separation anxiety I experience when Lane leaves for Washington. He's working on a transfer to Oklahoma City, but in the meantime, I get to see him every couple of weeks.

With him gone, I've spent most waking hours working on plans for Tribes with Jackson and spending time with my parents. They've moved back into their big stucco house. And, as I knew we would, a path has been worn through their back yard to my apartment. Adjustments are still being made to the blueprints of the house Lane and I will be building up on the ridge. But I am in no hurry. I'm enjoying being this close to my mother.

Abby knows I spent my childhood in a Dallas slum. She hasn't pried. I think it's best she doesn't know everything. The details would upset her. Maybe because of my past, the present shines brightly. It's all I dreamed it would be. It's rather ironic that the day I found my mother, Lexy chose to leave hers behind—we're both happy.

When asked, "Who gives this woman to this man," my parents will say, in unison, "We do." Last night at the rehearsal dinner Mom joked now that she had me back, she would not be giving me away. But with me in her back yard, she realized she isn't. Looking incredibly young and beautiful in a filmy aqua dress, she stands next to Lyle waiting for my father to walk me down that aisle.

The keyboardist glanced up, saw that we were in place, and switched from *Lara's Theme* to the opening strains of *The Wedding March*. My father and I began our walk. My mother, who swore she wouldn't cry, dabbed at her tears and smiled through them. Watching her reminded me of the words of James White Eagle. When asked if I would find my mother, he'd said, "A smiling woman waits for you."

The End
(Actually, the beginning)

Afterward

Alone Indian walked along a ridge, his silvery hair glistening in the light of the full moon. He looked up and measured the angle of the moon with his hands. He bent to scoop dust and let it sift through his fingers testing the current and direction of the wind. He gathered leaves, rocks, and twigs and built a small fire. He fanned the flame, protecting it until it blazed steadily.

Satisfied, he lowered himself to sit cross-legged on the ground. He reached into a buckskin pouch and withdrew a white eagle feather. He held the feather into the flame. He collected the ashes and mixed them with a potion in a small earthen bowl and began to chant. He lifted the bowl high and poured the contents, in a slow steady stream into the fire. Nearby a hawk watched from the top of a giant cottonwood.

A rumble began deep in the bowels of the earth. As it rose toward the surface the sound grew to a muffled roar. The ground began to shake. Below him rocks and boulders began to fall. Dust rose as the door between centuries closed. The cottonwood would no longer need to guard it.

He rose in one fluid motion, turned and bowed to the four directions.

The wind grew stronger. Dust swirled around him. James White Eagle was gone.

Two hawks flew away.

If you enjoyed this story, please share the love and leave a review at https://www.amazon.com/dp/B0CCXX4FWZ.

AUNT MATTIE'S

FAVORITE 'RECEIPTS'

Sweet Breads and Wild Mushrooms

Plunge sweet breads in cold water and swish. Place them in a pot of salt water with one stalk of celery and slice of onion and simmer until tender. Remove from pot, pat dry, and set aside.

- 1 cup wild mushrooms, cut into smallish pieces. Leave a Couple of small ones whole for garnish.
- 1 tsp salt
- Butter size of walnut
- 2 Tbsp. flour
- 1 cup cream or little more
- 1 cup good beef or chicken stock
- Butter size of walnut

Swish wild mushrooms in cold water. Dirt collects in pockets.

Let soak in cold water until ready to use. Then remove, drain on clean kitchen towel and pat dry.

Cook mushrooms in. butter. Don't salt until after cooking, salt makes them cry. Set mushrooms aside.

In same pan, add the other butter, melt and stir in flour.

Stir until flour is cooked, then add stock a little at a time, stirring constantly. Stir in cream and allow to cook down. If cream gets too thick, add more beef stock a little at a time. Add mushrooms and simmer until tender. Break up sweetbreads and add to mixture. Serve warm on best China. Garnish with small mushrooms and parsley or celery leaves.

This is a fine dish to impress company.

Find wild mushrooms in woods by the falls the last part of March through April. They are brown and look like cone-shaped sponges. Good luck finding them as deer, squirrels, and wild hogs love them, too. If you can't find morels, you can use other mushrooms as morels have a short growing season.

Suet pudding

- 1 cup molasses
- 1 cup sweet milk
- 1 cup suet, chopped fine
- 1 cup raisins
- ½ cup currents
- 2 ½ cups flour
- ½ tsp. soda

Mix together, add any spices you might have and steam 2 hours. Nutmeg and cinnamon are best but are hard to find in stores.

Prune whip receipt

- ¾ lb. prunes
- Whites of 4 eggs

Sweeten to taste and stew prunes.

If you have spices, add them. Not too much nutmeg. Drain and cool. When cool, fold in egg whites, beaten to stiff froth.

Pour into a baking dish.

Bake 20 mins. Serve with sweetened whipped cream.

Excerpt from

April's Song

Coming out Fall, 2023

Where is Grant? He'd asked what time I'd be speaking, so I assumed he'd slip in unnoticed—like that ever happens—to catch my presentation. He always tries to act modest and swears he doesn't want to 'steal my thunder.' He can't help it, it's who he is. He enjoys the stir he causes when he's recognized. Grant is charismatic and impossible to miss. When a politician's head emerges from the birth canal, he's already surveying the room for votes. Working the crowd. Don't let anyone tell you different.

Although he's fifty-two, he looks forty and is still turning heads. He's deeply tanned year-round and stays fit because he's addicted to tennis. His decision to go into politics interrupted a successful pro tennis career. Between him and our son Ridge, who inherited his father's talent, our den is full of trophies. Our daughter, Riley Grace, has begun to add her own.

Grant's been a United States Senator for two years now and we've settled into a comfortable routine. It helps that Southwest Airlines has a direct flight from Oklahoma City to Baltimore. The kids and I visit DC often and he's home when the Senate isn't in session.

Several people complimented me as I left the stage. I smiled and thanked them. I snagged my purse, fished out my phone, and scrolled through messages and missed calls. Nothing from Grant. Strange. The uneasy feeling I'd ignored all morning burrowed its way back into my stomach.

Three texts from Riley Grace explained, in great detail, her dire need for new tennis shorts and a straightening iron. It appears her bottom is practically bare in her old shorts and her straightening iron is a "piece of crap, embarrassing beyond belief".

Her straightening iron is 'embarrassing beyond belief', but her bottom being practically bare isn't? The drama is so Riley Grace. I chuckled.

This morning she tried to call eleven times during my half-hour presentation, which is rather unusual. When I'm on the speaking circuit, she doesn't call me at all and doesn't bother to answer when I call home. But if she wants something, she never just calls once and might call 20 times. Having eleven missed calls from her would be alarming, except she's Riley Grace. If she had been seriously injured, someone else would be calling. If she was in jail, she wouldn't get eleven calls.

I looked up from my phone. A man leaned against the cement block wall next to a red fire extinguisher. His stance appeared casual, but he was zoned in on me. A press pass hung from his neck.

"April Frazier?" he asked as I approached.

"Yes." I plastered on the polite smile I've perfected with just the right amount of benign interest and regret over not being able to respond to a yet unspoken request. "I'm sorry, I don't have time for an interview right now. Please make an appointment." I handed him my card.

He stepped into my path. "I'm Fred Knight with the Washington Post."

A reporter, an enterprising stringer who hoped he'd lucked into a byline in the Post.

I tried to move around him to the stairs. With a step to the side, he blocked me again.

I finally looked at him. He was balding, wearing a black knit shirt dusted with dandruff. His baggy pants looked as though they belonged to someone else. His shoes were scuffed. He needed a shave.

"What do you want?" I demanded.

"Sorry to bother you at a time like this." He peered at me over his glasses.

"Well, then, don't," I snapped, trying to step around him again.

"I wanted your reaction to what happened to your husband last night."

"What? Something happened to my husband?" Suddenly, Grant not being here became a bigger deal. I focused on the tape holding Knight's glasses together and tried to look like my heart hadn't just leaped into my throat.

"You are April Frazier, right?" He thumbed up his glasses. They promptly slipped back down. "Mrs. Grant Frazier—the Senator's wife?"

"Yes." I backed away.

"What can you tell me about Sable Amhurst?" He followed me.

"Who?"

"Sable Amhurst." He referred to his notes. "The woman in your husband's car."

"Woman in Grant's car? What...?"

"Have you not heard?" Confusion flickered in his eyes.

"No." I shook my head and backed away. "No." Did this idiot seriously think I'd be on a stage speaking to 4,000 women if I knew something happened to Grant last night?

Whatever it is that I don't know, I do not want to hear from Fred Knight.

I looked down at my phone. The unanswered calls from my daughter took on a whole new meaning. I turned and bolted.

The crowd making their way from the Leesburg Convention Center surged around me like sheep unable to find a gate. I frantically plowed through them searching for a place where Fred Knight couldn't follow. I ducked into the women's restroom, darted into the nearest empty stall and locked the door.

Riley Grace's best friend, Alise, says never go into the first bathroom stall because it gets the most use and therefore accumulates more germs. It's also more likely to be out of toilet paper. Alise thinks if people are too lazy to go farther down the line to find a cleaner toilet, they often don't flush. She's not wrong. The toilet hadn't been flushed. Gagging, I backed as far away as possible, flushed the toilet with my foot, and hit send on Riley Grace's number. Above the sound of water swirling around the bowl, I heard women shrieking.

Knight had followed me into the restroom.

"Mrs. Frazier?" Knight said. "Are you in here?"

Riley Grace answered, crying too hard to talk.

There are phone calls that bring you to your knees. Instantly. You get news that rips through your heart. News that leaves gashes so deep that your yesterdays are forever separated from your tomorrows. Everything surrounding that time is seared into your memory. You can recite in detail what you smelled, tasted, and experienced. That call came in a bathroom stall. Beside an unflushed toilet.

"Riley Grace, what are you trying to say?" I asked, terrified. "Talk to me."

"Mommy," she sobbed, sounding like she had when she was little and, still needed her mama. "Daddy is dead."

Acknowledgements

A boat load of thanks goes to former Kingfisher, Oklahoma Police Chief, Dennis John Baker. My grandmother, (God rest her soul) would be happy that I included his middle name. Dennis always tolerates my law enforcement questions with patience. A girl needs to know what law she's breaking. I'd also like to thank Oklahoma City Fire Chief, Richard A. Kelley, who is incredibly busy overseeing 37 fire stations, but took time to answer my myriad of questions about removing someone from a well. He might have been a bit concerned, but he knows me. Although I've often been tempted, I won't be stuffing bodies into a well. Probably. Except in a book.

I owe a debt of gratitude to my Oklahoma City friends and fellow writers at Writers Corner, in no particular order: Trina Lee, Becky Knight, Linda Lee McDonald, Mike Fry, Robert Williams, Woody Gimbel, Hugh Talley, Don Garrison, Virginia Patterson, and Joe Moore. They are all amazing writers, still they let me join them. Their suggestions, laughter, and groans were all duly noted. They were there from the beginning and waded through every chapter.

To those of you who badgered me without mercy (you know who you are), to finish writing *Ghost Horse*...Thank you! I am overwhelmed with appreciation to my beta readers. You guys are my circle and have my heart. Donella Strawn, Marilyn Baker, Robert Williams, Woody Gimbel, LouAnn Meyers, Joann Rogers, Liz Kelley, Linda Kodad, and Mick Benderoth. They fine-tuned these pages and made valuable suggestions. If there are any errors in the printed copy in your hands, they're mine and occurred after their edits.

I'm very impressed with the talent and professionalism of Krystine at krystinekercher.com. Krysti has been a dream to work with.

My angst caused by the cover of *Ghost Horse* has driven people crazy. Seriously. I'm quite sure many of them are alcoholics or have been committed by now. I have pulled my hair out, lost sleep, and searched for more than a year for a cover. Nothing looked right. In fact, some of them gave me nightmares. Enter Krysti who said, "Let me play around with it." What she could do was nothing short of a miracle. I love this cover! She didn't just find a beautiful horse, she found Mariah. She's also an excellent formatter. I'm grateful to God (and Woody) who through a strange chain of events, discovered Krystine. I am so happy with this book.

There are not nearly enough letters in the alphabet to properly convey my appreciation to my husband and best friend, Woody Gimbel. His dogged determination to get things done and done right no matter what, has often been a pain in the posterior to a girl who flies by the seat of her pants. You are holding *Ghost Horse* in your hands because Woody held my feet to the fire. Without him, Ghost Horse would still be in that afore-mentioned shoe box. When we were married, I had no idea how badly I needed a writing coach. And from the beginning, he loved this story. He has invested hours of his valuable time going over my rewrites. He's also a very good poet and writer in his own right. He's pretty darn decent at other at other things, too. Woody, SDB, you have turned my world upside down and filled it with rainbows and light. I will love you to my last breath and beyond.

About the Author

Carol Gimbel grew up in a small Oklahoma town, exploring the surrounding area on her bay mare, Penny. It's only natural that her books are often set in small towns. She's extended her love of exploration to Ecuador, Guatemala, and Panama where she and her husband lived for a year.

Her weekly cooking column appeared in an Oklahoma City newspaper for eight years. She's been a frequent contributor to *Guideposts Magazine*. During her ten-year radio career, she interviewed celebrities, county music artists, and people with interesting lives. It was during an interview with a DEA agent on her talk show, *This That and the Other*, that ideas for two books were born, *Ghost Horse* and *Then He Was Gone*.

She currently resides in the Pocono mountains in Pennsylvania with her husband, Woody, and schnauzer, Sage. When she isn't writing, she's reading, cooking, painting, or riding. She's still crazy about horses.